Dear Reader,

It's the holiday s[...]me of year when car[...] playing, cider is mulling, perfect pine trees are for sale on every corner, and shoppers are crowding the store aisles, searching for just the right gift. And once again we have something special to offer you; our latest collection of Christmas love stories, written by four of your favorite authors.

Start off with Lisa Jackson's *The Man from Pine Mountain,* the story of a mountain man who discovers that not every gift comes conventionally wrapped when he rescues his former fiancée from an icy river. Move on to *Naughty or Nice* by Emilie Richards and learn along with heroine Chloe Palmer that Christmas wishes have a wonderful habit of coming true just when you least expect—and that Santa Claus can sometimes be a very handsome fellow! Experience a *Holiday Homecoming* in Joan Hohl's tale of a family torn apart by Diana and her stepbrother Matt's one night of passion, then magically mended when Matt comes home for Christmas—and finds the gift of love waiting under the tree. Finally, join Lucy Gordon in *A Kiss for Mr. Scrooge,* the story of a heartbreaking Christmas past and a miraculous Christmas present— along with dreams of celebrating a joyous Christmas future every year to come.

So here's to a holiday season filled with love and good wishes that will last throughout the year.

All the best,

The Editors
Silhouette Books

1993 SILHOUETTE Christmas STORIES

**LISA JACKSON
EMILIE RICHARDS
JOAN HOHL
LUCY GORDON**

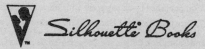

Silhouette Books

Published by Silhouette Books
America's Publisher of Contemporary Romance

SILHOUETTE BOOKS

Silhouette Christmas Stories 1993

Copyright © 1993 Harlequin Enterprises B. V.

ISBN 0-373-48264-7

The publisher acknowledges the copyright holders of the individual works as follows:

THE MAN FROM PINE MOUNTAIN
Copyright © 1993 by Lisa Jackson

NAUGHTY OR NICE
Copyright © 1993 by Emilie Richards McGee

HOLIDAY HOMECOMING
Copyright © 1993 by Joan Hohl

A KISS FOR MR. SCROOGE
Copyright © 1993 by Lucy Gordon

CONTENTS

THE MAN FROM PINE MOUNTAIN

Lisa Jackson

GRANDMA'S OREGON WILD BLACKBERRY CAKE

1 cup sugar
¼ cup butter
3 eggs, well beaten
3 tbsp sour milk*
1½ cups all-purpose flour
1 tsp cinnamon
1 tsp nutmeg
speck of cloves
1 teaspoon baking soda
1 cup wild Oregon blackberries, cooked**

Cream sugar and butter, add eggs and sour milk. Mix flour and spices, add to sugar mixture. Dissolve baking soda in a little boiling water and add berries. Mash with a fork and add to flour/butter mixture. The batter should turn blue before you put it in the oven. Bake at 350°F for 30 to 35 minutes or until inserted toothpick comes out clean.

*To prepare sour milk, take 8 teaspoons of milk and add 1 teaspoon of vinegar. This will make 3 tablespoons of sour milk.

**These berries grow wild in Oregon but may be substituted with any small commercial blackberries.

Chapter One

The feeling that something wasn't right crept up his back with footsteps as cold as death.

"Just your old demons again," Brett told himself as he lifted his field glasses to his eyes. The snow was coming down hard, as it had been for the past thirty-six hours. Eight or ten inches had accumulated at the base of Pine Mountain. There was probably twice that much at the summit, and the drifts near the bottom of the ranger tower had piled over two feet deep. The wind was up, too, blowing and whistling through the mountains with the eerie voice of winter.

"Nothin' out there," he said, still squinting through his binoculars. From the eagle's nest of the tower, he had a wide-angle view of the hill and valleys of this part of Oregon, the place he'd called home for a good part of his life. "Just your imagination..."

He stopped short, the hairs at the back of his neck lifting one by one as he strained to listen. In the distance, the whine of what sounded like a truck's engine echoed through the canyons. He swung his glasses to the south, though no one in his right mind would be traveling on the old camp road.

He'd lived most of the past twelve years at the tower, and he'd learned to gauge the sounds in the distance. He could pinpoint the soft hoot of an owl, the lonely call of a coyote, or the shouts of hunters stalking game through the heavy pine forests.

That noisy rig, whatever it was, was way off course. The fool behind the wheel should know better; these old logging roads weren't graded or secured by guardrails, as the county roads were. Dangerous enough in the summer, those gravel-and-mud ruts turned treacherous and deadly with the coming of the first winter storms.

His jaw tightened, and he adjusted the focus on his field glasses. The engine's roar was definitely coming from the south... from the direction of the old church camp. But it couldn't be. The camp had been closed for five years, and now that the man who'd owned the property, Preacher Bevans, had passed on, the old gate was chained and padlocked. Anyway, no one ever used the twisting road that crossed White Elk Creek in the winter. Canoers and fishermen in the summer, hunters in the fall, but no one in the dead of winter.

Until now. Less than two weeks before Christmas. He only hoped the idiot had enough brains not to try and cross the ancient bridge that spanned the creek. Constructed a hundred years ago of timbers that had slowly rotted, the bridge was meant for horse or cart travel, and was without rails of any kind. The rotting boards weren't safe, and now, piled with a blanket of snow, the bridge would appear deceptively secure. The driver wouldn't see the sagging pilings and broken boards until it was too late.

But surely the gate and padlock would keep the trespassers out.

Nonetheless, he climbed quickly down the ladder and strode through the piled snow to his Bronco. He reached for the door handle, but then he stopped, his mind clicking ahead. By road it would take him forty-five minutes to get to the camp, but on horseback, down the deer trail, he could arrive at the bridge in a third of the time. He slammed the door of the Bronco shut and headed to his small barn, which was really little more than a lean-to attached to the cabin.

Inside, the barn was dark and smelled of horses, musty hay, leather and dung. Several of the horses pawed the straw in their stalls. Flintlock, his big sorrel gelding, greeted Brett with a soft nicker and a flick of his pointed ears. He was a huge animal, part Belgian draft horse. Brett had bought him from a logger who'd used him to drag old-growth timber down trails too steep for trucks. The gelding snorted impatiently, his breath clouding in the dark barn.

"Believe me, pal, you're not gonna like this," Brett said as he strapped a bridle to the gelding's head and cinched the saddle tight. "Let's go."

With his rifle in the saddle holster and his walkie-talkie in his pack, Brett led the gelding out of the barn, kicked the door shut and climbed into the saddle. Hoping that the stupid driver of the truck hadn't brought a bolt-cutter that could clip through the chain of the gate, he spurred the eager horse forward, down the steep, snow-covered trail.

Snow and ice pelted his head, and with gloved fingers he drew the hood of his down jacket closer around his freezing face.

Bloody fool!

For the next ten minutes, the horse plowed through the drifts. He stumbled twice, but moved steadily through the snowbanks and fir trees. Brett scanned the horizon. The sound of the engine had grown louder, but had changed slightly, to an idle. The driver had reached the gate and had to stop. Good. Brett felt a moment of relief before the engine started again and he knew that whoever was in that rig was through the gate.

"Come on, blast you!" he growled to the already sweating horse. They broke through the trees, and he looked down upon the camp. It was a smattering of boarded-up buildings, now covered with snow, on the far side of what, during the hot summer months, was a lazy stream. Now White Elk Creek was a racing torrent of icy water that slashed through the canyon at the base of Pine Mountain.

A battered Jeep was slowly creeping across the bridge.

"Son of a bitch!"

Easing Flintlock down the steep trail, Brett watched in horror, wondering if the Jeep would make it. "Come on, come on..." he ground out, not knowing if he was talking to the horse or the driver.

The old bridge shuddered. Brett's heart stood still. "No!"

Timbers cracked. One of the Jeep's rear wheels punched through the soft wood, and it landed hard on its back axle. Still the driver pushed on the throttle.

"Idiot," Brett muttered, kicking his horse to speed him over the slippery terrain and down the hillside to the creek.

The driver, apparently finally realizing the danger, climbed out of the Jeep, and Brett's heart stopped. His mouth turned dry at the sight of her—so much the same, as beautiful as he remembered, her head bare, her hair sleek and black, her features unmarred by lines after five years. She walked around the Jeep, looking for the problem, and his lungs constricted. Didn't she know to get off the damned bridge, to leave well enough alone? He saw the sagging bridge shimmy again. Hundred-year-old cables, rusty with age, moaned in protest and began to unravel.

"Libby! Freeze!"

She started to turn. Her hair fanned away from her face just as the cables gave way.

"Oh, God, no!" He was so close. Only feet from the bank when she slipped and pitched, screaming, through the ice-crisp air, toward the surging water.

"No!" Brett thundered, watching her hit the water. Viciously he kicked his horse down the slope. Snow sprayed up and hit him in the face. His old gelding was working hard, plowing through the drifts. "Come on, come on!" Brett ground out, watching, horror-stricken, as Libby—his Libby—tumbled with the swollen stream. Icy water crashed over her, dragging her downstream with the furious current.

Only fifty more feet . . .

Sweating and grunting, Flintlock plunged through the knee-high powder and skidded down the steep embankment. "Come on, you devil! Move!" The usually game horse balked at the creek, and Brett swung out of the saddle, running through the raging water, yanking off his gloves with his teeth, his eyes focused on Libby.

Overhead, the bridge creaked loudly, threatening to collapse with the weight of the Jeep.

Brett swam with the current, gulping too much water, breathing frigid, lung-burning air, oblivious to the freezing water and the fire in his lungs. Where was she? Oh, God! He saw her body, trapped against a fallen log, facedown. "Hang on, darlin'," he yelled, plunging forward again, swimming with the icy current to surface at her side. His hands were frozen by the time he reached her still-submerged body.

The bridge groaned and swayed sickeningly.

Brett threw an arm around Libby's shoulders and let the swift current carry them farther downstream, away from the impending disaster.

With an eerie groan followed by an ear-splitting shriek, the old boards gave way and collapsed into the creek. Thick cables snapped in the air. Snow and splintered wood crashed downward, throwing up a wall of water. The Jeep smashed on top of the debris.

Brett dragged Libby to the shore before any of the boards and logs could be ripped along with the current. He carried her up the slippery bank, swearing under his breath, the cold air chilling his soaked body. At the top of the embankment, he laid her on the ground, and watched in horror as her skin, usually tanned, turned an ugly blue.

He forced her mouth open and lowered his lips to hers. "Breathe, damn you," he murmured before forcing air into her lungs. His chilled lips lingered a second too long on hers. Then he lifted his head, pressed firmly on her chest and blew into her mouth again.

"Come on, Libby, fight!" he urged, pushing hard against her chest and trying to stem the panic that seeped through him.

She couldn't die! She couldn't! Not like this! He blew into her unmoving lips again. "Come on, come on..."

He pushed on her chest, forcing the air out.

Still she didn't move. Her eyelids didn't flutter open to reveal eyes as blue as the sky in June.

Angrily he placed his mouth on hers and drove air into her water-logged lungs once more. How many times had he kissed her, covered her lips with his, all those years ago? Now, as he blew into her mouth, he felt an incredible ache that he might never see her alive again, never hear her laughter, never twine his fingers in the soft blue-black strands of her hair.

With a roar, he fought his own violent grief. He couldn't lose her! Not this way! Not now! Though he was a man who had long ago given up his religion, he whispered, "Don't let her die. Dear God, don't let her die!"

Chapter Two

She had to be dreaming.

Blinking rapidly, her body aching from retching, Libby stared up at Brett's worried face. Water dripped off his hair and his face, and his eyes, usually a warm brown, were dark with concern.

She was cold. So bitterly cold. She closed her eyes again, and she was giving herself up to the warmth of unconsciousness when she was shaken so hard she had to gasp.

"Libby! Wake up! Don't let go!"

With a heave, her stomach revolted. She twisted quickly and lost water from her lungs and stomach. Her teeth chattered. Strong arms were holding her tight.

"Are you all right? Libby, can you hear me?"

She tried to speak, but her throat wouldn't work, and she could only nod. She ached everywhere, and for the first time she remembered where she was, recognized the snow-draped mountains where she'd grown up, realized that she'd come back home . . . She remembered driving the narrow switchbacks, listening to Christmas carols over the static on the radio, wondering if she'd ever see Brett again.

"Come on. You're freezing." He lifted her as easily as he would have a child, carrying her through the slippery snow, his wet, waterlogged boots squishing as he headed toward the camp. Her father's camp. She knew she should try to make it on her own, to force her own numb feet to carry her, that depending upon Brett for anything was a mistake, but she couldn't find the strength or the desire to try to stand. Though he was as cold as she, she felt some inner warmth from his body where it pressed against hers, and her fingers clung to the collar of his wet parka. He smelled of the creek, but she didn't mind, and she closed her eyes again, drifting off.

"Libby...stay awake.... Libby..." His voice filtered through her subconscious, but she couldn't force her eyes open, and she gave herself up to the dream that he was with her, caring for her, worried about her. It was a nice feeling, really, it was just that she was so cold, cold to the bone.

Brett trudged onward through the snow, to the main camp, where a cluster of the cabins, including the chapel and the dining hall, were still standing. All the buildings were locked, but, still holding Libby, he kicked at the door of the dining hall enough times for the rusty lock to give way. Inside, the room smelled of dust and disuse, but he didn't care. There was still an old couch and some chairs, and if the rats hadn't eaten out the stuffing of the cushions, the meager furniture would suffice. This was the one cabin with a fireplace. He laid Libby on the lumpy couch, drew it close to the river-rock hearth and walked quickly outside.

His memory of the camp hadn't dimmed in the five years since he'd last been here, and he found the old woodpile, now a home for squirrels and chipmunks, no doubt. Dusting off the snow with numb fingers, he wrestled with a few logs and some kindling and hurried back to the main hall. His plan was simple: Warm Libby, check her for injuries and, if need be, ride back to his ranger station and call for help.

First things first. She was just where he'd left her, lying on the couch, shivering in her sleep, her skin still tinged a worrisome shade of blue. He reached into the pocket of his parka, prayed for the watertight properties that the salesman had assured him of when he bought the damned thing, and withdrew a sodden box of matches. "Great." He searched through the hall and into the kitchen that angled off the eating area. In the pantry, beneath a layer of cobwebs and mouse dung, he found a box of matches, kerosene lanterns and, wrapped in plastic, several old quilts. "A bonanza," he told himself as he hurried back to the hearth.

His fingers found the old damper. He yanked hard, and in a cloud of dust and feathers from some long ago inhabitant, the flue was open. The tinder-dry kindling ignited quickly, and soon yellow flames crackled against the dry wood. Libby stirred, her face golden in the light of the fire. He wasted no time stripping her of her clothes—boots, jeans, sweater, bra and panties. He forced himself to be distant and not to stare at the curves he'd known so well five years earlier. Her breasts, blue-veined and covered with goose bumps, her legs, long and slim and— Oh, damn it all! Gritting his teeth, as much to force aside his wayward thoughts as in response to the cold, he quickly wrapped one of the quilts around her, fitting it as close as a shroud, to hold in whatever body heat she retained. He dried her hair with the other blanket, until the damp ringlets were no longer dripping. Through the quilt, he rubbed her arms and legs, hoping the friction would keep her blood warm and flowing. "You're going to be all right," he said, to convince himself as much as her. "You're going to be all right."

When he was satisfied that she had stabilized and her breathing was strong and regular, he warmed his hands, then headed outside again.

The force of the storm hit him with an icy blast that tore through his wet clothes and swept the breath from his lungs. Any heat he'd collected in the cabin was stripped away.

He trudged through the driving snow to the bridge and saw that the Jeep hadn't moved. Still balanced on a pile of debris beneath the broken bridge, it seemed wedged in. Flintlock was on the far bank, and Brett braved the creek again, wading through chest-deep water until, on the opposite shore, he grabbed the horse's reins and led him back through the water. Flintlock objected, rearing a little, and Brett, who'd lost all feeling in his hands and feet, jerked roughly on the reins.

"This isn't a picnic for me either, you know," he growled at the animal as he tossed his rifle onto the bank. "Let's go." Clucking his tongue, he led the wild-eyed Flintlock into the stream. They followed the course of the current to the Jeep, and Brett yanked open the door. Some of the supplies and luggage seemed only slightly damaged, so he carried what he could and threw the soft luggage over the saddle.

Once he'd packed what he could, he tugged hard on the reins and forced the horse to the opposite bank, then recrossed for his rifle. By the time he'd made it back to the camp, he was frozen to the bone. He stabled Flintlock in an old barn, rubbed the horse down with the saddle blanket and tossed him an old bale of hay. With a final pat to Flintlock's withers, he promised, "I'll check on you soon," and grabbed a pail off a peg in the wall.

Outside, the snow had become a blizzard. He shielded his eyes with his arm, and his legs moved without feeling as he trudged back to the main lodge.

His teeth were chattering, and he'd never been so cold in his life, but he scooped snow into the bucket and shouldered open the door. The fire was blazing, casting red-gold shadows over the old wooden walls and filling the room with the scent of burning wood. Shutting the door firmly behind him, he made his way to the fireplace and found Libby breathing easily, still sleeping or unconscious.

His shoulders sagged with relief. Setting the bucket near the fire, he then peeled off his wet clothes, hung them over the screen and stood buck-naked in front of the flames. He found a little grain of cynical humor in the fact that he was totally nude in the dining hall with the preacher's daughter, but he didn't laugh. Instead, he wrapped himself in the blanket he'd used to dry Libby's hair, hung his clothes over one side of the fireplace screen and lay on the floor, rubbing his extremities, blowing on his fingers, hoping to avoid frostbite.

He wondered if he'd ever be warm again—and if Libby would survive. His gut twisted, and he glanced at her. She was breathing easily, her dark lashes curved against her cheek, her chest moving with each breath. She'd make it, and sure as he was sitting here, she'd be furious with him when she discovered she was naked as the day she was born.

Smiling a little, he stretched closer to the fire. His mind wandered back in time to the summer when he'd first met Libby Bevans, daughter of the minister of the single church in Cascade, Oregon. She'd been living in Portland, going to college, and she'd come home to care for her dying mother.

Brett had seen her in town a couple of times, which was no surprise, because Cascade was so small it was hard not to notice a new face. And what a face it was. High cheekbones, easy smile, blue eyes that sparkled when she talked. Her hair had been longer then, nearly to her waist, thick and black and wavy. She'd been like no other woman he'd ever met.

He'd always prided himself on being a loner, a man who needed no one, a person who enjoyed his solitary life in the mountains, and, though attracted to the opposite sex, he'd avoided any kind of emotional entanglement. His father was long dead, and his mother had remarried and was living her life in Seattle, loving the hustle and craziness of the city. Brett saw her only a couple of times a year, and that suited them both just fine.

He'd seen no reason to change his uncomplicated lifestyle. Until he'd met Libby. Then his entire world had turned upside down.

Leaning up on one elbow, he looked at her. So peaceful. So beautiful. Gently he touched a finger to her cheek and felt the warmth of her skin. She'd be okay. She was going to make it. Thank God. His throat closed in on itself when he thought of just how close he'd come to losing her. This time forever. His eyes burned, and his hand was suddenly unsteady.

Just nerves, he told himself. *A normal reaction.* Or was it? Just because she still haunted his dreams, that didn't mean that he wasn't over her. The fact that he'd thought of her nearly every day since she'd left him didn't mean that he still loved her. Sure, he cared about her, but when they'd broken up, it had been for good.

He'd been her first love; she'd been his last.

Scowling at the turn his thoughts had taken, he settled back on the floor again and wondered what would happen once she awoke. And why the devil was she back here? When she'd left, she'd vowed never to return, and she hadn't given a damn about breaking her old man's heart—or his own.

A little finger of guilt pierced his mind. He knew, deep inside, that he'd driven her away. But it was easier to blame Libby, to convince himself that she was a conniving, malicious woman who had used him, a woman who had no depth of conviction.

But he'd lied to himself. As he thought of the past, remembered how much they'd meant to each other, he realized that he was the reason she'd run away from everything she ever loved.

He squeezed his eyes shut tight, hoping to sleep, but rest was elusive. Thoughts of Libby and that fateful summer kept him awake long into the night....

Chapter Three

It was hot, late July, and Brett had driven into town for the Saturday breakfast special at the Derringer Café: a short stack of pancakes, a side of bacon, two fried eggs, and all the coffee he could drink.

He'd left a healthy tip for Velma, the redheaded waitress who always flirted with him, then sauntered outside and into the morning sunshine. Heat was already rising from the pavement, causing the asphalt to shimmer as he opened the door of his pickup. He spied her in the rearview mirror; a small, authoritative woman herding a group of kids onto the local church camp's joy bus.

One of the kids wasn't too keen on climbing aboard.

Brett turned and, shifting a toothpick to one corner of his mouth, watched the showdown.

"I hate camp!" the kid yelled belligerently, his chubby arms crossed in front of his chest. A freckle-faced boy of about ten, he smirked up at the woman. "I'm not going!"

Brett glanced at the parking lot, but no set of parents stepped forward to set the little brat straight. In fact, it seemed that the lithe young woman was solely in charge of about twenty kids ranging in age from seven to fifteen.

Amused, Brett lounged against the side of the café and openly watched the young woman square off with her wayward charge.

"Get on the bus, Sean," she said with a sweet but determined smile.

"No way."

Her blue eyes snapped suddenly, and she looked up to see an older boy with short blond hair and a slight case of sunburn. "Kevin, will you help Sean onto the bus? You can be his big brother. He's a little nervous this morning."

"Sure, Miss Libby, I—"

Libby? As in the preacher's daughter? Brett had never met Libby Bevans, but he knew from his acquaintance with her father that as the only daughter of Edwin and Marla Bevans, Libby was adored by both her parents.

"I don't want no sissy for a big brother!" Sean insisted, his eyes, behind round glasses, dancing with glee.

Miss Libby's smile was suddenly strained. "Then get on the bus by yourself."

"Make me."

"Sean, I don't want to have to embarrass you. Just get on the bus by the time I count to three."

By this time, the whole lot of children, those already boarded and hanging out the windows, a few climbing up the steps of the brightly painted bus, and another couple of stragglers who were gathering their packs and bags from the sidewalk, were staring at the confrontation. Miss Libby was either going to make her point, or she was going to lose the respect of the whole group of kids.

"One," she said.

Grinning, Sean didn't budge, just looked from side to side, hoping the rest of the kids were seeing how tough he was.

"Two," she said, a little louder. "Better start moving."

Sean stuck out his tongue.

It was all Brett could take. He moved as swiftly as a hungry cougar into the midst of the group. "I don't think you heard the lady," he growled, hoping he looked as fierce as a mountain lion.

"Wh—who are you?" Sean stammered. His eyes, behind his thick lenses, had gone round with fear.

"Yeah, who do you think you are?" Libby demanded, concern evident on her face.

Brett slid her a glance before turning his eyes on Sean. "Think of me as a messenger of God."

"A *what?*" she said on a gasp.

Brett's gaze never left Sean's surprised face. "That's right, and he says you'd better haul your backside into the joy bus before you come across serious trouble."

"You can't do nothin' to me, mister," Sean said, still full of bravado, though his voice was beginning to tremble.

"You're right. It's not me you have to worry about." He cast a meaningful look at the sky, then watched with amusement as Sean hightailed it onto the bus.

Libby whirled on him. "You had no right!" she whispered.

"I know. But it worked."

"I was doing fine—"

"The kid was working you. And you painted yourself into a corner with that counting routine."

"It's a good way—"

"To make a fool of yourself." He saw the fire snap in her eyes, and he gave her a totally uncivilized smile. Didn't she understand that he'd done her a favor? The preacher's daughter was beautiful, all right, but an impertinent snip. "You can't treat a ten-year-old like he's three. It won't work."

"What makes you such an authority? Do you have a dozen kids, or something?"

"Or something." He shook his head. "I was ten once."

"So was I!"

"But I was a wiseass. Any woman tried to cow me into crawling onto the bus by counting would have seriously regretted it."

It seemed as if she suddenly believed him. Agreement registered in her eyes, and she blew her dark bangs off her forehead in a rush of exasperation. She bit down on the corner of her lower lip, which was nearly thrust outward in a pout, and Brett had the unlikely urge to kiss her—to take that soft lower lip and press his own to it. He wondered how she would react to such he-man tactics, and decided he would probably be rewarded with a swift kick.

She sighed and shook her head, her black hair shimmering blue in the morning light. "Okay, so your heavy-handed approach worked better than my cajoling. I guess I should thank you, Mr.—?"

"Brett Matson," he supplied. "And you're Miss Libby."

"Ms. Bevans."

"Edwin's daughter."

Her back stiffened a bit. "That's right, and you can only call me Miss Libby if you sign up at the church and spend a week at the camp."

A smile stretched across his chin. "That could be arranged," he heard himself say. He wondered why he felt obliged to banter with this small woman. As it was, he would probably see more of her this summer than he should.

"Good. Take it up with God, since you're on such a buddy-buddy basis with him. And in the future, Mr. Matson, please, keep your nose in your own business."

"Even if the good Lord sends me a message?" he said, unable to stop baiting her. The woman rankled him, pure and simple.

"Especially then!" She whirled on her heel and headed back to the bus. He was left standing on the sidewalk, sweat collecting on the back of his neck as he watched her climb into the bus and take the driver's seat. In a cloud of diesel smoke, the old vehicle rumbled away from the curb and out of town, toward Pine Mountain, and the church camp that sprawled along the shore of White Elk Creek.

"I'll be damned," he said, sliding a glance to the heavens and figuring his remark wouldn't go unnoticed. He'd known that Ed had a grown daughter who was living in Portland and going to school. He'd heard through the trusty town grapevine that she was coming back to Cascade to help her ailing mother, but what he hadn't counted on—not in a million years—was that she would be the most interesting woman west of the Rockies. "I'll be damned," he repeated, knowing he already was.

Libby couldn't believe the gall of the man. To act as if he had some sort of personal communication with God! It was blasphemy, and if her father ever heard the tale, there was sure to be a sermon filled with fire and brimstone on Sunday. She couldn't help but grin, however, because as angry as she was with Matson, she had to admit that his scare tactics seemed to have worked where her own calmer methods of handling a wayward child had failed. Sean Duvall had settled in to become a model camper.

"Live and learn," she told herself as the bus rumbled across the old bridge and rolled into the campground. The kids were already singing songs, lead by Irene Brennan and her daughter, Sandy, a fun-loving tomboy who had graduated from high school with Libby. Mrs. Brennan was the organist at the church in town, and both she and Sandy had agreed to help with the camp, as Libby's mother, who was usually the cook, maid and general mom-to-all-campers, was ill. Seriously ill.

A sudden and bitter cold settled in Libby's heart. As an only child, she'd grown up close to both her mother and father, and she couldn't believe that God, her father's loving God, would see fit to take Marla away from them. A shadow covered her soul, and her throat grew tight as she thought of her mother battling melanoma. The prognosis wasn't good, but Libby hoped that with the right medical care, a lot of love, and her father's constant prayers, her mother would pull through. She had to.

Easing up on the throttle, Libby slowed the bus near the stables. The kids were shouting and laughing, antsy to start camp. She cranked open the doors, and they streamed out, carrying packs, bags, bedrolls and pillows as they scrambled to the six different cabins nestled in the trees and checked the rosters for their names.

The day would be hectic, she knew. She would help her father settle the campers into their respective bunks, deal with any problems, double-check the supplies, as well as the livestock, make sure she wasn't needed in the kitchen, then drive her car back to town to spend the night with her mother before rising at dawn and returning.

She didn't really mind. In the few years she'd been away since graduating from high school, she'd missed her summers here in the forest, where she'd been a camp counselor from the time she was fifteen.

It was nearly dinnertime when she saw him again. Through the open window of the craft cabin, she looked across the creek and watched as an unfamiliar pickup pulling a horse trailer parked in the clearing on the far side of the bridge.

Libby's breath stopped for a second as Matson stretched out of the cab. He was a handsome man, she knew, though she was loath to admit as much. With long legs, broad shoulders and a whip-lean body, he looked mountain-tough. Wearing faded jeans, a matching jacket and a flannel shirt, he fitted the image of an outdoorsman. His hair, brown streaked with blond, was a little longer than was fashionable, and curled over the edge of his denim collar. His face was all sharp angles, and tanned from hours in the sun. Thin lips cut across a square jaw. He looked as if he could be laughing one instant and hostile the next—a powder keg with whiskey-brown eyes.

He opened the back of the horse trailer, and Libby forgot she was supposed to be showing the children how to mix paint as the Native Americans had a century before. Burnt umber dripped from her handmade brush as she watched Matson lead a huge gelding and a stocky mare into camp.

Trailing after the mare on a separate lead was a spindly-legged foal with huge brown eyes, a fluff of a tail and a crooked blaze running down its sorrel face.

"Look!" Tammy Lewis cried, her nose crinkling in delight. "A baby horse!"

"That's a colt, stupid!" Sean told her, leading the stampede outside. However, once he caught a glimpse of

Brett, Sean hung back, while other, more anxious campers reached out to touch a velvet-soft nose.

"I wouldn't touch the filly," Brett advised the kids, "unless you want her mama to show you who's boss."

"A filly?" Tammy said, sending Sean a meaningful glance. "I thought it was a colt."

Brett laughed and cast a wicked look Libby's way. "I'd be careful if I were you," he said to the group. "Some females take their womanhood to heart, and they can be downright nasty if they are mistaken for a man. You sure don't want to get them riled, or insult them, or—"

"Or usurp their authority." Libby felt her cheeks burning as she took control of the conversation. Who did this guy think he was to come waltzing into the camp and start making fun of her?

"Brett!" Her father's voice boomed through the trees. Libby turned to find Edwin running down the few steps of the chapel, a smile on his face and his hand extended. "Thanks for lending us the stock."

"My pleasure." The two men shook hands warmly, and Libby's mouth nearly dropped open.

Her father adjusted his clerical collar and told the campers that, due to Mr. Matson's generosity, they were able to have trail rides. Mr. Matson not only was a forest ranger, but also owned several head of livestock—draft horses—that were gentle enough to ride. Matson himself would give some lessons. Libby's heart sank when she realized that she would probably be bumping into him more often than not.

Truth to tell, she didn't like him. He was entirely too cynical. Too good-looking. Too cocky and too sexy for his own good.

As if reading her thoughts, he flashed a devilish smile in her direction, and her heart did a peculiar little flip. "Great," she muttered to herself as she herded a few of the campers back to the craft shed and tried to keep her attention away from the window and her view of the paddock. On the other side of the split-rail fence, Brett was showing some of the children how to mount a horse and hold on to the reins. Libby's concentration continually strayed away from the five rudimentary paintings of Native American scenes and to the roguish man whose amber eyes seemed to see straight through to her soul.

Brett stayed for dinner, and sat directly across the table from Libby. She had trouble swallowing Mrs. Brennan's chicken and dumplings with his gaze flicking from her to her father more often than she would have liked.

He was disturbing and sensual and seemed to be laughing at her. His eyes glinted with amusement more often than not, and though he was a perfect gentleman while passing around the plates of creamed chicken, fluffy dumplings, corn on the cob and green beans, she felt his civility was all an act.

She hadn't learned much about him, just that he was some sort of mountain man, a forest ranger who lived at the "station" at the timberline on Pine Mountain and raised horses—incredibly big horses—as a hobby. He seemed a part of this wilderness. He had come from another station, in southern Oregon, about the same time she'd left Cascade for Portland. Her father intimated that Brett was a loner, but "a good, decent enough man, though I would like to see him in church on Sundays." The two men had met because of the livestock, held a distant respect for each other, and, though worlds apart, saw each other either because of the horses or because

Cascade was a town of less than a thousand citizens. Everybody knew everybody.

"I'll pack a plate for your ma," Mrs. Brennan was saying as she and a designated group of helpers started clearing the table.

"She'd like that." Libby was grateful for the conversation, because it meant she wouldn't have to dwell on Brett and his uncomfortable scrutiny.

"And I'll send along a berry pie—she can share it with some of the people who visit her during the day when we're all up here."

"That would be great."

"Isn't Sean on KP duty tonight?" Brett asked her.

"Mmm..."

"Looks like he's trying to ditch."

Sure enough, Sean had slipped off his bench and was trying to sneak out the dining-hall door. Brett leaned back in his chair and motioned toward the head table. "Why don't you start over here?" he asked the boy. "I'm finished, and it looks like Miss Libby is, too."

Sean's chin thrust forward mutinously, and he seemed about to refuse when Brett climbed out of his chair. Muttering something under his breath about "women's work," Sean did the chores grudgingly, quickly picking up plates, scraping the scraps into one bucket and dropping the silverware and plates into another bucket of soapy water, all the while casting Brett dark looks over his shoulder.

Irene wrapped up a plate of food large enough to feed five hungry loggers, along with the promised berry pie. A shame, Libby thought, knowing that her mother's appetite had waned to almost nothing.

Night was approaching. The first stars winked in a dusky mountain sky and frogs began their soft chorus.

An owl hooted quietly, and overhead a hawk swooped into the darkening branches of a pine tree.

Libby's father was busy overseeing the nightly ritual of the building of the campfire, where each night before bedtime the campers would sing songs, create skits and pray. "You go on home and take care of your ma," he told her. "But leave the car— Brett, would you mind giving her a lift into town?"

"No—" Libby said instinctively and her father looked up sharply. "There's no reason he should have to drive clear into Cascade, when he only lives a few miles from here."

"It's no trouble," Brett assured her, his eyes darkening with the night.

Libby's heart began to pound erratically. She couldn't imagine anything more difficult than spending the next half hour or so cooped up with him in the small cab of his truck. But she was stuck. Unless she wanted to be incredibly rude and ungrateful, she had no choice but to follow him down the road and over the bridge to the far side of the creek, where his truck was parked. He'd already unhitched the trailer, as he was planning to leave it at the camp until he picked up his horses after the last session.

Libby climbed into the pickup and placed Irene's basket of food on the seat next to her.

"Scared?" Brett asked as he backed around and started driving slowly down the switchbacks of the mountainside.

"Scared of what?" she repeated, knowing full well what he meant.

"Of me."

"Hardly. Unlike Sean, I don't believe you have the wrath of God at your command."

"I didn't think a preacher's kid would lie."

"I'm not—"

"You're scared."

"I can't imagine why I would be," she said, crossing her arms over her chest and wondering how it was that this man could reduce her to feeling like a girl in junior high school. She was usually levelheaded, she was considered bright by her professors, and she was well on her way to a career in nursing. She'd dated a lot of different boys and men—none of whom had interested her, particularly—and she was *not* scared of some hermit who spent his life in a ranger station in the wilderness.

"I scare you because you don't know what to do with me," he said, with predictably brutal honesty. "I stepped on your toes with that kid, and you want to step a little harder on mine."

"That's ridiculous."

"Mmm..." As he rounded a curve and the headlights threw twin beams onto the road, a doe and two fawns froze directly in the pickup's path. "Oh, hell!" He downshifted, swerving to avoid hitting the animals as he slammed on the brakes. The basket pitched off the seat and crashed to the floor. Seat belts grabbed and locked. Libby's head banged against the passenger door window. The truck bounced as the wheels skidded, throwing up gravel, screeching angrily. Libby's stomach lurched.

Bounding across the road, the deer disappeared into the forest as the truck jolted to a stop.

"You okay?" Brett asked as the truck idled on the shoulder.

"I think so." Heart pounding, she touched her head and winced.

Brett's expression was grim as he opened the glove compartment and extracted a flashlight. Muttering under his breath, he clicked on the beam and shone the light upon her forehead. Gingerly he examined the knot that was growing beneath her skin. His fingers were gentle as they probed, but they didn't alleviate the headache steadily growing behind her eyes.

He touched a tender spot, and she sucked in her breath and grimaced, shoving aside the flashlight. "I said I'd be okay."

"I'm sorry." The words, so solemn, seemed to reverberate through the cab.

"It—it's all right. Not your fault. An accident." She managed a small grin when she saw the doubts in his eyes. "Don't worry. Really. I'm tougher than I look. And I've got a thick skull. If you don't believe me, just ask my dad. He'll tell you."

Brett didn't so much as crack a smile. "I'd better get you home."

Picking up the basket and replacing it on the seat between them, he cast Libby one more worried glance. "Maybe I should take you into Bend to see a doctor."

"All that way? It's just a little bump on the head."

"You don't know—"

"I do know. I'm a nurse, remember?"

"Not yet."

"But soon. And I'll be okay. I don't need a doctor," she said, thinking of the long trip to Bend for medical attention. Cascade needed its own clinic, had needed one for years, but no doctor wanted to spend his time with the few patients the town had to offer, when he could make more money in the city. Even attempts at sharing one general practitioner with a couple of other small towns hadn't worked, and the GP who had tried to run a three-town practice—Dr. Sherman—had left central Oregon years before and moved to Eugene.

Brett shoved the truck into the gear and guided it back onto the narrow road. The silence was deafening. Only the growl of the pickup's oversized engine and the whine of tires against pavement as the truck turned onto the county highway broke the noiselessness. Libby leaned her head against the window and closed her eyes against the dull ache inside her skull. What a day. She sighed, and didn't open her eyes again until she felt Brett downshift and the pickup slowed in the gravel drive of the parsonage.

Lights glowed in the windows of the small frame house located on the lot adjacent to the century-old church. She tried to argue that Brett didn't need to help her inside, but he wouldn't hear her arguments. He didn't admit it, but Libby was certain he wanted to keep his eye on her a little while longer and assure himself that she wouldn't collapse as a result of the bump on her head.

Her frail mother was glad to see them. From her position on the couch, she clicked off the television with the remote control, smiled warmly at Brett and insisted, as Libby was reheating Irene's chicken and dumplings and trying to cut wedges from the mangled berry pie, on hearing all about the first day at camp.

Her mother's eyes, though sunken, sparkled at Libby's stories, and Libby's heart went out to the woman who had raised her. Once robust, with thick black hair and a more-than-ample waistline, Marla Bevans was a mere shell of her former self.

She ate more heartily than she had in the few days Libby had been back in town, and when she was through with a sliver of pie and had heard all of Libby's and Brett's stories about the camp, she was worn out.

Libby helped her into bed while Brett lingered in the living room. "He's handsome, isn't he?" her mother asked as she eased her thin body between the sheets.

"Who? Mr. Matson?"

"I distinctly remember he told you to call him Brett," Marla said softly.

Libby lifted a shoulder and poured water from the bedside pitcher into a glass. "I suppose. Some people might think he's handsome."

"Some? Oh, come on, Libby. Every female under fifty in this town does—and some of them older than that do, too." She chuckled, coughed, and took a sip from the glass that Libby held ready.

"Do they?"

"Mmm... But he hasn't shown much interest. Even when Sara Pritchert practically threw herself at him— and she's one of the most sought-after girls in town—he wasn't interested."

"His loss."

"I don't think so." Her mother's eyes gleamed in the light from the single lamp on the night table.

"Mom..."

"I saw the way he looked at you, Libby. I'm not too far gone to recognize when a man is smitten with—"

"Smitten? Mom, listen to yourself!"

"Well, I'll make no excuses." Her frail fingers pulled the bed covers close under her chin. "You know that I'd like to see you married before I leave this earth. Truth to tell, I want nothing more than to hold my grandchild one time, but I know that might not be possible." Libby started to protest, but her mother twined her fingers through her daughter's. "More than anything, I just want to see you happy."

"Marriage doesn't necessarily guarantee happiness," Libby said sagely, and her mother offered her a knowing smile. Libby couldn't believe they were having this conversation about Brett Matson, a man she'd only met this very day—a man who seemed intent on baiting her! She wondered if the disease had affected her mother's usually clear mind.

"Brett's a good man. Hardworking. Decent. Handsome. Sexy—"

"Mom! Listen to what you're saying!"

"Well, I'm not a dead woman yet, and just because I've been married to a preacher doesn't mean that I can't enjoy the body that God gave me. Your father and I love each other very much, and nothing is more precious than the times we've been together."

Libby flushed scarlet. "This is crazy talk...."

"No, it's not. I just don't have time to beat around the bush." With a wink, her mother said, "Just humor me. Don't rule Brett out."

"Oh, for crying out loud—"

"Now let's pray." Her mother closed her eyes and murmured a soft prayer. Silently Libby added a request for her mother to return to health, and she ignored the mention of Brett Matson in Marla Bevans's litany.

Did her mother honestly think that she would even consider a date with Brett—much less marriage?

Yet, as she turned down the lamp and closed the bedroom door quietly behind her, she felt her heartbeat quicken. Just the knowledge that Brett was in the house caused her pulse to increase in tempo.

Telling herself she was, in her own way, as silly as her mother, she walked down the short hallway to the living room and wondered how she was going to get Brett Matson out of the house—and out of her life for good.

Chapter Four

The object of Libby's mother's prayers was waiting in the living room. Drumming restless fingers silently on the windowsill as he stared into the night, Brett glanced up at the sound of her footsteps.

Libby felt a little stutter in her heartbeat. Silently she told herself that she was being foolish, that she was under the influence of her mother's silly notions, and yet, when she caught him looking at her with his magnetic amber eyes, she found her lungs suddenly straining for air.

"She all right?"

"I think so."

She walked with him to the front porch of the little house. Only an infrequent car crawled along the night-shaded streets, and the streetlights were few and far between.

"Your mother's a brave woman," he said.

"Always has been."

"Like you?"

The question hung in the air between them. "I'm afraid of some things," she admitted.

"But not me."

"Definitely not you."

She saw his smile stretch white in the darkness, and she knew an instant of fear before his arms surrounded her and he gathered her close. His lips were unerring as they found hers. She let out a startled sound, but it was cut off by the warm pressure of his mouth. Though at first she struggled, he didn't stop kissing her, and slowly she relaxed, giving in to the magic of the night and the strength of his arms. He smelled of leather and horses, pine needles and coffee. A piece of her melted inside, and she opened her mouth ever so slightly. With a groan, he pulled her closer still, until the thin wall of their clothes caused friction between their bodies.

Her skin suddenly warm, Libby felt light-headed, and was only vaguely aware of the impression of his hand against the small of her back. Her knees were unsteady, and she nearly fell over when he broke off the embrace as suddenly as he'd swept her into his arms.

"Damn!" Running the back of his hand over his mouth as if wiping away the kiss he'd stolen from her, he took a step away from her. It was as if he needed to put distance between his body and hers. His breathing was hard and ragged, and nearly as shallow.

"D-don't ever do that again," she stammered, though her voice held little conviction.

"Never?"

"That's right."

His eyes sparked at the challenge. "I don't think that's possible with you."

"Try," she said, and he grinned, a wicked curve to his lips.

"You try, Miss Libby." With that, he kissed her again, and before she could reach back to strike him, he stepped agilely away and headed for his pickup. "Well, one thing's for certain. That bump on your head sure didn't affect your lips."

"You miserable—"

The truck started with a roar, and she was left standing in the middle of the porch. She was ready to spout a stream of invectives when she heard a quiet chuckle from the open window of her mother's bedroom.

Great. Just great! she thought, taking solace in the fact that things couldn't get much worse.

Or could they?

Brett became a regular fixture at the camp. When he wasn't putting in long hours at the ranger station, he found time to ride his horse down to the camp, much to the delight of the children. He showed them how to whittle a whistle, how to track a deer, and how to ride a horse through the shallows of White Elk Creek. Though he never stayed for the campfire sing-along or for prayers, he spent more than his share of hours at the camp, and Libby found herself less antagonistic toward him.

True, he unnerved her, caused her pulse to jump and her temper to flare at unexpected moments, but for the most part he was pleasant enough, helping her father chop wood and repair some of the buildings, and complimenting Irene Brennan on her meals. He ate dinner at the camp every night, and were it not for the hours he spent helping out, Libby would have thought that he was using her father for a free meal. But those dinners were given gratefully, for Brett was the hardest worker in camp.

From the craft cabin, Libby had often watched him splitting kindling, his tanned muscles fluid and gleaming with sweat, his hair dark and damp as it fell over his forehead. She noticed the way black hair flared across his chest and angled mysteriously down past his navel. His jeans were always low-slung, riding somewhat precariously on his slim hips. More often than she liked to admit, she'd forgotten the project on which she was working while she watched him. Then a camper's voice would bring her out of her daydream, and she'd once again pay attention to the baskets being woven or the sketches being drawn by inexperienced hands.

Brett was firm with the horses, gentle, but in complete control. He lead the smallest children around the paddock on the back of a giant horse named Hercules, and the wide-eyed rider would cling to the saddle horn and grin widely. He showed the children how to brush the animal's hide and cinch a saddle tightly. He even took the time to let the kids watch him remove a pebble that was lodged in Hercules's hoof. Once he took part in a water fight that several of the kids had started, and ended up squirting Libby with the hose.

She squealed and wanted to be angry with him, but the dancing mischief in his eyes was so boyishly charming that she forgave him instantly, and she had to force her eyes away from his naked, dripping chest and his flushed face. He was dangerous, no doubt about it, and her response to him was ludicrous. She'd heard of women who'd fallen for the wrong man, and she told herself firmly that she wouldn't be one of them.

Two weeks passed, and she let down her guard a bit. Then, one night, he came upon her alone. She'd thought he'd already left, having watched him climb astride Hercules and head up the trail to the ranger station.

She was in the stables, watching the little foal nurse, his fluff of a tail wriggling, when the door creaked open and she turned to find Brett, stripped to his jeans, standing silhouetted in the doorway. The light from the campfire was to his back, the star-studded sky a canopy above him.

Her heart trip-hammered at the sight of him. "You— you startled me," she said, rubbing her arms as if chilled, though the temperature in the barn still hovered near seventy.

He swallowed, as if his throat had gone suddenly dry. "Forgot something," he said, his eyes never leaving hers as he crossed the dusty floor and reached into a saddlebag hanging from a nail driven into one of the support posts. Lantern light caught on the silver band of his watch as he slipped it over his wrist. "Aren't you going into town?"

She shook her head. "Dad . . . he's going to stay with Mom for a few days. Irene and I can handle the camp. Things are settling down. He'll . . . he'll be back Monday morning, after services on Sunday."

In the darkness, Brett's gaze landed full on hers. Her heart missed a beat, and she licked her lips nervously.

Electricity seemed to sizzle in the barn. Libby couldn't force her gaze from his. She felt him drawing nearer to her, knew she had to turn and run, or at the very least put up a hand to ward him off.

Instead, she quivered inside, and when Brett took her into his arms, she lifted her face of her own accord, her mouth waiting, her lips accepting as he kissed her, long and hard, drawing the breath from her lungs, touching the depths of her soul.

This is insane, a part of her cried in silent rebellion as the rest of her surrendered utterly to the primal assault on her senses. She clung to him, and her anxious lips opened willingly to the eager ministrations of his tongue. Liquid and warm, her body seemed to dissolve as a tide of emotion tore through her body and soul.

When he lifted his head, she could barely breathe. "I didn't want this," he admitted.

"I *don't* want this."

"Liar." His mouth curved into a knowing smile, and he kissed her again, his hungry lips molding over hers. Her mouth clung to his, and she shivered when his hands spanned her waist. This time his weight drew them downward to a bed of straw, and her knees willingly gave way.

She gasped when his callused fingers found the bare skin at the gap between her T-shirt and the waistband of her jeans, but her own fingers dug into the sinewy strength of his shoulders as she kissed him with utter abandon.

"Libby," he murmured. "Sweet, sweet Libby." His knee wedged between her legs, and she felt the length of him pressed intimately against her body. A fever burned inside her veins, and her breasts ached with the want of his touch. Never before had she lost her head, never had she wanted, *needed,* to be caressed.

His fingers inched up her ribs. Her diaphragm slammed against her lungs as he cupped a breast, tracing the scalloped lace of her bra. From deep in her throat, she moaned, and he stroked her with his thumb, causing her nipple to pucker with want. His mouth moved easily over hers, sliding and molding to hers as he lowered himself, his greedy lips pressing wet hot kisses against her chin, her throat, her collarbone.

Deep inside she felt a moistness, an aching void that grew to a chasm of dark lust. Her fingers twisted in his hair as he lifted her T-shirt and touched the tip of his tongue to her breast. She jerked as if a jolt of electricity had rocked her, and he gathered her close, burying his face in the soft mound of her breast, kissing and laving her nipple through the lace of her bra. Her spine arched, and she tried to press more of herself into him, to give him what he needed, to offer comfort and solace and satisfaction.

With a groan, he lifted his head, leaving her nipple cold and wet and desolate as he stared deep into her eyes. His own were glazed, and she watched him try to drag in one calming breath after another. "This...this won't work...." he said, his gaze drifting downward to her breasts, still hindered by her scrap of a bra. With shaking hands, he tugged her T-shirt back over her skin. "Damn it, Libby, we both know it."

"I don't care."

"Of course you do." But he glanced to her face again, and he must have seen the decision in her eyes. "Come on. Get up." With a tender smile, he pulled a few pieces of straw from her hair. "You're the minister's daughter, for crying out loud!"

"I'm a woman."

His gaze flicked down her body. "No argument about that."

"I make up my own mind."

"Not this time." He pulled her to her feet and placed both hands on her shoulders, keeping her at arms' length. "Don't get me wrong. I want you, Libby. More than I've ever wanted a woman. And if you weren't the daughter of the reverend, who happens to be a friend of mine, and if your mother wasn't sick and hoping to see you marry a good man before she has to leave this earth, and if I thought you could live with yourself after we made love, then I'd bed you right here and now. God knows I want to."

Shame washed up her face in a hot wave. "I didn't ask you to bed me."

"Call it what you will. But we *can't* make love."

She recognized the wisdom in his way of thinking; she knew he was right, darn it, but still she felt disappointed and bereft. Pulling out of his grasp, she tossed her hair off her shoulders and said, "Don't label me, Brett. And don't think of me as the preacher's daughter, okay? As a matter of fact, don't bother thinking about me at all!" Turning on her heel, she left him standing in the barn and told herself that she would never, *never,* allow herself to get into a compromising position with him again! Hell would freeze over before she did.

Her vow lasted all of two days.

Brett didn't come the next night for dinner and when he arrived the following day, he looked right through her, as if she didn't exist. Rankled, she forced him into conversation. His answers were polite but crisp. The air between them fairly crackled with unspoken emotion. She caught him looking at her several times, from a distance, the heat still simmering in his eyes.

So he wasn't as immune to her as he pretended to be. She felt a little vindication at that thought, but still, he never touched her, and when he left that night, without so much as saying goodbye, she watched him go with a heavy heart.

Unable to stand the strain any longer, she made excuses to Irene about being unable to sleep, saddled a quick little mare and took off after Hercules's trail. With the silver glow of the moon as her illumination, and her memory of the paths surrounding the camp as her compass, she pressed her knees into the mare's sides and urged the eager horse forward, over the bridge and up the steep incline leading to the ranger station.

The rush of creek water dulled to a soft murmur, but the drone of insects and the thunder of bats' wings kept the night alive. The mare shied at a bend in the trail as an unseen creature scurried through the undergrowth. Libby's heart pounded with fear. Her nerves were strung tight. She was on a fool's journey. She could get lost in this rugged wilderness; the horse could make a misstep and tumble over the sheer cliffs that were less than a quarter of a mile away now, or the mare might step into a hole in the path and break her leg.

"Fool," she muttered. Glancing over her shoulder and gazing down the dark canyon, she saw the dying campfire still blazing through the branches of the pine trees and small beacons of lantern light shining from the windows of the cabins.

Suddenly the mare snorted, her ears flicking anxiously, as she sidestepped.

Libby's heart slammed to the dusty ground. "What—?"

The mare started to rear as a hand reached out of the darkness and held firmly to the reins. "Following me?" Brett asked, his eyes mirrors of moonlight as he stared up at her.

Libby felt suddenly foolish. Her heart was still triphammering with fear and apprehension. "Yes."

"Why?"

"We need to talk."

He raised a critical eyebrow. "Talk?" he repeated as she climbed off the mare and stood face-to-face with him. In the dark he seemed larger, his size intimidating.

She squared her shoulders. "We can't go on like this."

"Like what?"

"Seeing each other, not talking, avoiding contact."

"Contact?" he repeated. "That's what you want?"

Her teeth ground together in silent fury, but she would not be baited. She would *not!* "What I want is for us to be friends."

He snorted and glanced at the starry sky. "I already told you what a lousy liar you are. Don't stretch my patience."

"What do you want from me?"

Sighing, he looked again at the star-dappled heavens. "What I want... Oh, Libby, it would scare the living daylights right out of you."

"I don't think so."

His lips flattened over his teeth, and he let out a stream of invective that would have absolutely turned her father's hair snow-white. "What I want is for you to get back on that horse, ride *carefully* back down this damned mountain, and leave me the hell alone."

Her throat closed and tears flooded her eyes as he turned his back to her. "You're a lousy liar, too," she said, her voice catching.

At the sound of her trembling words, his shoulders slumped. "Libby, don't—"

"Don't what? Don't love you? Don't hate you? Don't touch you? Don't talk to you? What?"

"Oh, hell—don't fall for me."

A lump filled her throat. "It's too late for that."

He bit his lower lip, and with a curse leveled at himself he turned and looked into her eyes again. "I should never have started this," he said.

"But you did. Why?"

"Because..." He struggled for the right words, struggled to find a lie. But as he gazed into her eyes, he gave up all pretense, and his emotions were stripped bare. "Because I couldn't stop myself. With you. I couldn't...can't..." He stepped closer, tilted her chin upward with one finger, then wiped away a solitary tear that trickled from the corner of her eye. "You make me crazy."

She smiled. "I know."

"You asked me what I want from you. The answer is that I want everything." Cupping the back of her head with his hand, he drew her lips to his and kissed her with a tenderness that caused her soul to shatter. "Everything," he repeated against her open mouth.

She wound her arms around his neck, and they tumbled to the soft carpet of pine needles at the bend in the trail. His hands found the buttons of her blouse, and she held on to him as if to life itself.

This time, he didn't stop. This time, he made love to her. Under the wide expanse of star-studded sky, with the mountains rising above them, he claimed her for his own.

Their affair grew over the summer, and as Marla Bevans's health declined, Libby clung tighter to her love for Brett. She gave herself to him willingly and often, and the secret they shared, the tenderness they felt for each other, helped ease the pain of watching Marla slowly die.

"It's not fair!" she cried, storming into the small chapel at the camp, where her father was praying. She'd spent the afternoon with her mother, her heart slowly shredding. Tears streamed from her eyes, and a deep rage flowed in her veins. "Mom's so young, so good, so— Oh, damn it, we need her. *I* need her!"

Her father placed a comforting arm around her shoulders. "I know you do, honey. So do I. But we have to understand that God works in mysterious ways."

"Well, God made a mistake this time!" Libby threw back at him.

"Shh... Be patient, Libby."

"I can't, and I won't! This is wrong! Wrong, wrong, wrong!"

Her father's face turned chalk-white. With stricken eyes, he said, "Don't ever doubt the word of our Lord. His wisdom is all-seeing."

"Oh, Dad, how can you be so blind?" she cried, running out of the small chapel. She waited restlessly all day for Brett. He arrived at camp that evening, and Libby threw herself into his arms, unafraid of her father, who, from his position near the flagpole, could hardly miss seeing that his daughter was in love with Brett Matson.

He didn't seem to mind. Nor did her mother. In the last few days of Marla's life, she was at peace, telling Libby that she could go happily to her reward, knowing that her daughter had found happiness with a good man.

All in all, Libby spent the waning days of summer either ecstatically happy with Brett or miserably wretched as she prepared for her mother's death.

During the last session of camp, Libby realized she was pregnant. She'd guessed that something was wrong when she skipped her first period, but she'd chalked up the change in her cycle to her ragged state of emotions. Falling in love with Brett while tending to her sick mother had placed her in an emotional mine field. However, by the time she missed her second period, morning sickness had set in, and she had to confide in Brett.

"I think we're going to have a baby."

It was night. The stars were shining through the window of the barn, and Brett was repairing a bridle. He looked up sharply from his stool, and the corners of his mouth tightened. "You're sure?"

"No. But I'm a nurse... Well, I will be soon. I know the symptoms. So, yeah, I'm pretty sure."

He didn't smile, but he reached forward, drew her close to him and held her tight, his head pressed intimately to her abdomen. "Then we'll get married," he said, without a trace of emotion. "As soon as possible."

He didn't say he loved her, didn't even mention his joy at the prospect of becoming a father, but Libby knew he must feel the same state of elation that had brought her so much happiness already. Her only regrets were that her mother wouldn't live to see the birth of her first grandchild, and that Libby would have to put her own career on hold for a while. But it would be worth it. She was to become a mother. She placed her hand over her flat abdomen and smiled at the thought that she was carrying Brett's child.

The baby was their secret—hers and Brett's. After the wedding ceremony, she would break the happy news that she was pregnant to her family.

Her parents, predictably, were thrilled at the news of her upcoming marriage and her mother blinked against hot tears as she held her daughter's hand and smiled up at her. "Didn't I tell you?" she asked Libby. "I knew from the first time I saw the two of you together."

During the next few days, while she was home with her mother, Libby planned a small wedding. Her father would officiate in their home, where her mother could be a part of the ceremony. Marla seemed to improve for a while. Just the thought of her daughter's marriage lifted her spirits. However, on the last day of summer camp, Marla took a turn for the worse. She was rushed to the hospital in Bend, and there, with her family waiting anxiously beside her, she passed away.

Despite the prayers.

Despite the hospital and the doctors.

Despite the fact that Libby still needed her.

Libby had told herself she was prepared, that she could handle her mother's passing. But she'd been wrong. The hole in her heart was deep and painful. Her grief encompassed her, and she felt lost in the little house she'd called home for so many years. Involuntarily she listened for the sound of her mother's footsteps, her quiet cough, the tunes she hummed as she worked, but the house was empty. The ticking of the clock and humming of the refrigerator were no replacement for the warm sound of dishes rattling or beans snapping or the whisper of a broom as it brushed the floor.

Think about the baby. About Brett. About the happiness in your future, she silently counseled herself as she tried and failed to help her father through his grief. He spent long hours in the church, praying and talking with God, but in the end he seemed as lost as Libby.

The congregation sympathized. "She's gone to her final reward.... She's with God now.... At least she isn't suffering any longer.... She's found her peace...." The platitudes swirled around her, sounding suspiciously empty.

Libby held on to Brett through the funeral and in a fog of agony, watched as her father, with his unwavering faith, eulogized his wife of twenty-eight years.

"I know it's hard, but you have to get over it," Brett said on the day after the funeral. Libby's eyes still felt hot and burned with tears. Her father's final prayer for his dead wife played over and over in her mind, and the depth of her sorrow seemed bottomless. She barely ate, and found it difficult to smile.

"I thought I was prepared. But I guess you never can be," she said.

"Try." Brett took both her hands in his. "For me." His arms surrounded her, and she leaned against him, letting the tears flow and holding on to his strength. She would get over this darkness in her soul. With Brett and the baby, she had reasons to live, reasons to find joy in life.

Slowly, day by day, her grief subsided. With the promise of the future, she found her smile again, and though she thought of her mother often, she concentrated on the future and helping her father, who, despite his faith in God, was utterly lonely and griefstricken. Libby taught him how to use the microwave, showed him how to wash and iron his own clothes, and found a woman who could come into the parsonage once a week to clean the place.

Life was settling down, the wedding was less than a week away, and Libby had thrown herself into her wedding plans. The invitations had been sent, the flowers and cake ordered and a dress purchased, and nearly everything was set. A small traditional wedding, nothing fancy. Everything was going as smoothly as possible.

Two days before the ceremony, Libby planned to surprise Brett with a wedding present—a spirited gray Percheron colt Brett had been eyeing for most of the summer. The colt, owned by a farmer in the valley, was expensive, but Libby bought the two-year-old with funds she'd planned to use for school and had the gray delivered to Brett's home on Pine Mountain.

Once the farmer left, she waited expectantly for Brett. Astride the stocky horse, her heart nearly bursting with anticipation, she rode around the small paddock, patting the colt's sleek neck and visualizing the smile that would curve Brett's mouth at the sight of the animal. "This is gonna be good," she confided in the horse when she heard the whine of Brett's truck climbing the steep hill. The colt's dark ears pricked forward, and he pawed at the ground.

"It's all right," Libby assured him, but the animal's shoulders quivered. "Wait till he sees you."

The engine grew louder.

The colt snorted and minced, as if he, too, were anxious.

"Hold on, boy."

The truck rounded a curve, emerged from the trees and slid to a stop near the barn.

Libby, grinning widely, waved a hand in the air as Brett climbed out of the cab.

"What the devil—?"

From another paddock, a horse whinnied, and the colt, nervous, reared and twisted.

"Libby!" Brett yelled as Libby scrabbled for the reins. Her knees tightened around the horse's sides, but her weight carried her downward. She tried to catch hold of his mane when she realized she was falling, but she couldn't. Out of the corner of her eye, she saw Brett vault the fence.

"Hang on! Libby!"

His warning was useless. The sun-baked ground rushed up at her, and she hit the dirt with a sickening thud that jarred her from her shoulders to her toes.

Brett yelled at the beast, and the gray backed away as Libby's body smacked into the ground. "Oh, God," he whispered as he raced across the packed dirt and fell to his knees at her side. "Are you all right? Libby?" Fear pricked his heart, and he felt a sense of relief when her eyes fluttered open. She'd be all right. She had to be.

She moaned as he pulled her into his arms. Kissing her dusty forehead, he held her tight, and didn't notice the dark stain spreading across her jeans until it was much too late.

Chapter Five

Libby was cold. So very cold. A dirty, retching taste filled her mouth, and her nose felt rough, like sandpaper. She'd dreamed ... horrible dreams ... and yet Brett had been in those dreams, holding her close, carrying her, saving her from some hideous watery beast.

With a groan, she opened her eyes, blinking against the shifting light of a crackling fire. The room was familiar, yet strange, and her mind swam, like the torrents of an icy creek that even now threatened to pull her under.

Fear caused her to shiver.

She was lying down ... on a couch ... and her entire body ached. She heard the creaking of floorboards from the darkness behind her.

"Libby? Thank God!"

Brett?

He loomed in front of her, and she thought she was still dreaming. Wrapped in an old quilt, he bent on one knee to be at eye level with her. She blinked, but his image remained, and in her soggy mind she knew that she was safe, that somehow he'd brought her to safety. They were in a cabin ... no, in the main hall of the camp. She was wrapped in blankets, and her hair was damp.

"Are you all right?" Gently he touched her face, his eyes dark with worry.

For a second she didn't move. Mesmerized by his gaze, by the feel of his fingers brushing her skin, she licked her lips. Then, as her memory jolted, she remembered the bridge giving way, felt the torrent of water rushing up at her, filling her lungs, drowning her scream. She jerked away from him. "Oh, God," she whispered, shivering as she realized that Brett had somehow found her and pulled her from the deadly current.

"Libby," he said again, his voice a caress, his fingers once again warm and gentle against her skin. She smiled slightly before all the old painful memories pierced through her semiconscious state and she remembered that she no longer loved him.

"Get your hands off me!" she tried to yell, but only managed to whisper hoarsely as she jerked her face away from the traitorous magic of his fingers. He bent closer, and she glared up at him. "I mean it, Brett."

He rocked back on his heels and had the audacity to grin. "Back to your old sweet self, I see."

"I'm not old, and I've never been sweet."

One of his dark eyebrows arched. "Weren't you?"

"Just leave me alone." Her head, suddenly pounding, dropped back onto the arm of the couch, and she closed her eyes.

"Don't you even want to thank me?"

She bit down on her tongue. She should feel gratitude; no doubt he had saved her life, but she couldn't quell the rush of anger that burned through her veins. All the old rage exploded and she could only manage a sarcastic "Thanks" without even opening her eyes.

"You should be more careful."

Please, Lord, give me patience. "I'll remember that," she replied, her words harsh.

"Libby." His voice was soft again, its low timbre creeping into the crevices of her heart. "When I saw you on the bridge, I couldn't believe it. I thought... I was afraid that you... Oh, hell, look—we'd better get you to a doctor."

"I don't need a doctor."

"You took in a lot of water, and—"

"I'm fine." To prove her point, she pushed herself up to a sitting position, and the blankets cocooned around her threatened to slip off her shoulders. That was when she noticed that she was naked beneath the blanket. Brett had obviously taken off her clothes, as well as his own, and her cheeks burned hot at the thought that he'd seen her naked again. It was silly, of course. He'd *had* to strip her of her wet clothes and it wasn't like he'd never seen her naked before.

Involuntarily her fingers clenched in the folds of the blanket. "Look, Brett, I'm a nurse," she said, forcing her vocal cords to work. "A nurse practitioner. I know what I'm doing. I don't need a doctor. Really. Thanks for all you've done, but I'm fine."

She glanced up at him, and her breath caught in her throat. His face was more angular than she remembered, his whiskey-hued eyes as erotic as ever, and the gaze that touched hers seemed to slice into her very soul.

"You're welcome," he said slowly.

She clutched the blanket tighter, telling herself not to notice the flare of lines at the corners of his eyes, or the dusting of hair on the backs of his hands. But her senses were working overtime, and she couldn't look at him without her heartbeat quickening.

"Is... is it still snowing?"

"A damned blizzard."

"So we're stuck here."

"The only reason to risk braving the storm again is if you need to go to a hospital. The nearest one is in Bend."

"I remember," she whispered, thinking of the time she had been rushed to the emergency room and had woken up to learn that she'd lost the baby. Her throat grew suddenly hot, and Brett, as if realizing the painful turn of the conversation, stood and rubbed his lower back.

"If you need a doctor..."

"I told you—"

"I know, I know. You're fine."

"I will be."

Eyeing her skeptically, he said, "You want to tell me why you're out in the middle of a storm, driving across a bridge that should've been condemned years ago?"

"I wanted to come back."

His spine stiffened slightly. "That's a surprise."

"This is—was—my home, Brett." She wanted to tell him more, to share some of the pain she'd suffered. But she couldn't. Not when he'd been the source of that agony. Pride clamped her jaws together, and she forced her gaze away from the relief in his eyes and back to the fire. Red-and-gold flames crackled, filling the cabin with the sweet scent of burning wood. His wet clothes had been hung over the screen, which was so warm now that his jeans were beginning to steam.

He'd obviously dived in after her. She shivered at the thought that she could have drowned in the cold depths of the creek. "I...I guess I owe you one," she said.

"You owe me nothing."

Damn it, he wasn't making this any easier. He shoved the screen out of the way, tossed another log onto the fire, causing sparks to explode, then prodded the pieces of fir into place with an old, bent poker. "This isn't easy, but I'm trying to say thanks," she said.

He didn't respond, and, exhausted, Libby closed her eyes again. She knew that she should be careful around him, that being with him was emotionally dangerous, but there didn't seem any way to avoid him at present, and she let herself drift back to sleep, feeling a peace and security just in knowing that he was nearby.

Brett stared at her a long while, surprised that he could gaze so long at her face. Her breathing was even, and he believed that moving her to a hospital would serve no purpose while the blizzard raged.

His clothes were still damp, but as soon as they were warm enough, he dragged on his jeans, shirt and jacket and braved the lashing wind and snow to carry water to Flintlock. It took several trips, hauling wood back and forth, before he was satisfied that there were enough chunks of oak, fir and pine to keep the fire blazing for twenty-four hours. Back in the dining hall, he melted another bucket of snow and replaced his clothes over the screen. Wrapping himself in the blanket once again, he propped his head with an old cushion from a rocking chair and closed his eyes. He and Libby had no choice but to wait out the storm.

Libby woke once in the middle of the night. The storm was howling, rattling the panes in the old windows and ripping at the shingles of the roof as it whistled through White Elk Canyon. Libby shivered, held the old blanket tighter to her and leaned over the edge of the couch to see Brett, sleeping as if he hadn't a care in the world.

Still as handsome as ever.

Still as sexy.

Firelight played upon the angles of his face, making him appear harsh and cold, but she knew better. She remembered well enough that his hands upon her could conjure up magic, that his words could warm even the coldest heart. She remembered his laughter, and the feel of his body pressed intimately to hers.

If only things had been different. If only she hadn't lost the baby and, for a while, her will to go on. Dealing with her grief over her mother's death hadn't prepared her for the depth of depression that assailed her when she woke up in the hospital room, certain she would be fine.

When she'd asked about the baby, the doctor had avoided her eyes and said, "I'm sorry, Miss Bevans. There was nothing we could do. But you'll be able to bear more children."

The world had seemed to go dark, and she had felt as if she were being pitched into a bottomless well of desolation. She had heard Brett trying to console her, but she had been destroyed. To make matters worse her father, her loving father had turned on her, as well.

"You were pregnant!" he'd raged, his eyes filled with anguish and humiliation. "You slept with Brett without being married to him!"

She'd tried to tell him that the baby had been loved and wanted, and that she hadn't sinned, but the condemnation in his eyes had been all too visible. "I'm a man of God," he'd reminded her. "What will the parish think?"

"To hell with the parish," Brett had spat out, and all respect between the two men had died.

Brett had nearly come to blows with her father, and yet he hadn't loved her, had never taken her into his arms and told her everything would be all right, had never breathed words of love into her anxious ears. Their reason for getting married, the baby, was gone, and so, when she'd been released from the hospital, she'd turned her back on this place and returned to Portland.

Brett hadn't come looking for her.

Now tears rolled silently down her cheeks as she thought about the baby. She and Brett would have married, lived here, and maybe even had another child by this time. Their first child would have been four years old, and Christmas would have been filled with secrets, teddy bears and Santa Claus. Childish laughter and the scent of cookies baking would have filled the cozy interior of their house.

Closing her eyes on what might have been, she silently told herself that she was happy. After losing the baby and Brett, she'd gone back to school and become not only a nurse, but a nurse practitioner. Fully independent, she was now able to open her own practice.

Still, there were nights, nights like this one, when she was incredibly lonely. She'd never again been close to her father after the miscarriage, even though they'd both tried to patch things up. He'd never again thought of her as innocent. And his own health had declined. She'd had to move him to Portland, where, after a series of strokes, he'd finally joined his wife in heaven.

So here she was, back at the church camp, back with Brett. Her life had come full circle.

She stared at him in the darkness and wondered what it would feel like to stretch out beside him, to wrap her arms around his chest as it slowly rose and fell, to hold on to him and press her face into the curve of his neck.

Oh, foolish, foolish, girl. Give it up. He saved your life—just as he would have saved anyone's. He's alone with you because of the storm, because he's worried about you and because he's trapped here himself. Don't make any more of it than there is.

Sighing sadly to herself, she closed her eyes and prayed that she'd find sleep.

Hours later, she awoke to the smell of hot coffee. Her stomach rumbled, and when she opened her eyes it took her a few seconds to remember where she was and with whom. Brett. She was alone with him in the mountains—alone and *naked* with him.

Propping herself up on an elbow, she looked around at the old hall. It was dusty, filled with cobwebs, probably infested with mice and bats, from the looks of things. She sat upright and, after a few dizzy seconds, felt fine. But the hall seemed empty. Tentatively she stood, and found that her legs supported her. She listened for Brett, but heard nothing.

"Brett?"

No answer. His jeans and jacket were no longer hanging over the screen, but the fire was blazing, and her own enamel coffeepot was resting on coals in the hearth. She saw her suitcase, open and resting on an old table. There were other supplies, as well: food, cleaning products, and some of the bedding she'd brought with her.

She didn't waste any time. Near the fire's warmth she found clean underwear, a pair of jeans and a turtleneck sweater. Some of her clothing was water-damaged, but all in all, she'd been lucky. She poured a cup of coffee into a mug she'd brought with her and walked to the window.

Outside, it was still snowing. She noticed the footprints leading to the dining hall, the woodpile and the barn, and she was certain Brett would be back. She remembered the worry etched upon his features, and the concern deep in his eyes. He wouldn't leave her until he was certain she could take care of herself.

Sipping the bitter coffee, she gazed at the land her father had often referred to as "God's country." She'd come back because she'd felt compelled to return.

Her friends at the clinic where she worked in Portland had tried to talk her out of returning to Pine Mountain Camp. Trudie, another nurse practitioner, had been the most vocal. "Going back there will only bring back all the old heartache," she'd said. "Mark my words, Libby. This is *not* how you want to spend your Christmas vacation."

But Libby hadn't listened. In her heart she'd known that she had to come back to Cascade, to face her past, before she could make a start on her future.

And now her past had come crashing back to her, in the guise of a six-foot mountain man.

She'd known she'd see him again, of course, but she hadn't planned on it being as an accident victim or, worse yet, as a fool. She'd planned to meet him as a woman with a mind of her own and a heart made of stone. Unfortunately that stone heart seemed to have developed some cracks.

"Idiot," she muttered. Angrily she wiped the dust away from the windowpane and stared past the icicles hanging off the porch roof. Snow covered the ground and coated the tree branches, causing them to droop. Squinting, she could see the bridge, or what was left of it. Even though it was blanketed with white powder, she noticed the gaping hole over the creek and recognized her Jeep, axle-deep in debris, but still, it seemed, in one piece and, for the most part, above the water. No wonder her clothes had remained dry.

She scanned the camp and the surrounding hills, looking for Brett. Rather than wait in the hall, she decided to don her jacket and boots and brave the elements. The icy air hit her like a blast from the North Pole, but she trudged through the knee-deep snow, pausing at the barn. Snow was still falling, and her breath fogged in the frigid air, but she couldn't help smiling at the thought of a white Christmas—a Christmas at home.

She'd grown up in these hills, had spent every summer with her parents at the camp, and a small tug on her heart told her she hadn't completely shaken the small-town dust from her heels when she moved to Portland so long ago.

Nor had she completely forgotten Brett Matson. She set her shoulder to the door, and it opened with a creak. The long-familiar smells of warm horses, hay and dung greeted her.

Brett was forking hay into a manger in the first stall, where a tall sorrel gelding stood on a layer of straw. He glanced up when the door opened, and scowled at her before shaking more old hay into the feed trough. "What do you think you're doing?"

She closed the door behind her. "Looking for you."

"You shouldn't get cold again, you should—"

"I'm fine," Libby said, tossing her hair out of her eyes and approaching the huge animal. The horse's ears pricked forward, and he snorted. "Who're you?"

"Flintlock. The reason you're alive."

"I thought I owed *you* my life."

His brows twitched slightly. "It was a joint effort."

"Then I guess I should thank you both." She patted the gelding's sleek shoulder, and was reminded of another time, in this very barn, where she'd been alone with Brett.... Her throat tightened in on itself. "How did you find me?"

Brett hung the pitchfork on a rusting nail. "I heard the Jeep from up in the tower, knew that whoever was driving might get himself into trouble." His eyes held hers for a heartbeat. "Looks like I was right."

Libby's heart squeezed. *More trouble than you know. More trouble than I bargained for.* "So what do we do now?"

"Wait."

"Here?"

"Until the storm blows over. It won't be long. Maybe another day. Then we'll ride up to the station."

"Won't you be missed?"

He snorted. "Could be. My guess is that a storm like this probably knocked out all the power in town. People are probably in pretty much the same state as we are. Of course, I'll be called on the radio, but no one will really worry for a while. Everyone's got his own hands full."

Apparently satisfied that the horse was warm and fed, he took hold of Libby's arm and propelled her outside. The wind whistled through the pine boughs, and clumps of snow dropped from the uppermost branches.

Brett cast a worried look at the gray sky. "It's not over yet."

"You think it'll get worse?"

"Before it gets better." He paused at the woodpile and grabbed several heavy chunks of wood. When Libby tried to pick up a piece of dry maple, he argued with her, but she didn't listen to him, and carried in an armload of firewood.

"Always were a stubborn thing," he remarked once they were in the warm dining hall.

"Some things never change," she replied before she saw the clouds in his eyes.

"And some things do."

"Yes. Well..." The silence stretched between them, and his gaze shifted from her eyes to her lips. She couldn't move, didn't dare breathe.

Clearing his throat, he turned back to the fire. "I'll cook us some—"

"I'll cook," she said quickly, glad for something to do. She walked to the table where her meager supplies were set and found some instant oatmeal and powdered milk; not exactly gourmet fare, but hearty enough.

While Brett toured all the old buildings, looking for supplies, she made breakfast. He returned with a couple of old kerosene lanterns that still had wicks and oil, a few tools, and an appetite for soggy oatmeal and toast.

They spent the rest of the day trapped in the same room, avoiding each other, trying to make small talk when they had to. Libby felt as if she were walking an emotional tightrope. Yes, she'd planned to see Brett again, but she hadn't intended to spend hours, maybe days, trapped alone with him.

Brett acted like a caged animal, restlessly pacing from one window to the next, his gaze trained on the cloudy sky. He tried to keep his mind off Libby, off the beautiful, independent woman she'd become, but he found it difficult not to stare at her. She'd changed a little. Her hair was cut shorter, falling just below her chin, and her features were more womanly—no hint of the girl in her cheeks or chin. She was also much more self-confident, though she carried a load of sadness with her that seemed far too great a burden for her. He knew he'd been a part of her private hell.

They'd eaten lunch—tuna sandwiches—and were stuck staring at the fire, waiting for the storm to break, when he could stand the tension between them no longer.

"I'm sorry about your dad," he said finally as he lit one of the lanterns.

"Me too." She looked away from him, obviously uncomfortable with the conversation.

"I tried to talk to him once."

Her head whipped around, and she pierced him with those blue, blue eyes. Her throat worked. "You did? When?"

"After you left. I thought I should explain ... about us...about the baby..." He shrugged his shoulders and shook his head. "I don't know that it did much good."

"He never said anything."

"Figures."

Libby's throat felt hot. "Doesn't matter."

"It did, damn it." He crossed the few feet separating them and grabbed her by both arms. His gaze drilled deep into hers. "I'm tired of both of us acting as if what happened between us was just a...a...an inconvenience."

A small sound of protest fell from her lips. She suddenly felt weak. "Is that what you thought?"

The fingers around her arms tightened, and his lips turned white. "I didn't know what to think. I couldn't get through to you, couldn't shake you out of your grief. I've never felt so damned helpless in my life!"

She held back a sob, because she knew in her heart that he was speaking the truth. The loss of the child had devastated her. "I tried to talk to you...."

"You threw me out of your hospital room, Libby," he said, the words scraping her soul. "As if what had happened was all my fault."

Tears streamed from her eyes, and she trembled from the violent emotions that had ripped through her then, and were ripping through her now. At the time, he'd seemed cold and distant, and she'd felt that she'd failed him in losing the baby. Later, her father, trying to console her while balming his wounded pride, had given her platitudes, telling her that God, in his divine wisdom, had done what was best. "I didn't blame you," she whispered to Brett. "I blamed myself."

"It was no one's fault." He wiped a tear from her eye with one finger. Then, slowly, as if he regretted the very movement, he lowered his lips to hers and kissed her with a tenderness that nearly broke her heart. She couldn't stop the sob that started in the back of her throat.

"Shh... It's all right."

"It's not! It will never be!" she said, blinking back fresh tears and stepping away from him. Sniffing loudly, she swiped at her eyes and glared up at him. "I'll never forget what happened."

"Unfortunately, Libby, neither will I."

Chapter Six

The storm broke in the early afternoon. Brett eyed the horizon through the window, rubbing at the stubble that covered his chin. "I'm going up to the station," he said, shoving his hands into the back pockets of his jeans.

"What about me?"

Turning, he surveyed her. "I think you should come with me. If you're up to it."

"Of course I'm up to it."

"That fall was no picnic."

"Brett, I'm fine. Let's just go, okay?" She was already stuffing her arms into the sleeves of her jacket, glad for a reason to escape the close confines of the cozy room.

Brett didn't seem convinced that she would be able to survive the elements, but he, too, dressed in his jacket and pulled up the hood. He placed a few supplies in his pockets, grabbed his rifle and, after ordering her to wait, plowed through the snow to the barn. A few minutes later, he arrived with Flintlock and insisted that Libby ride.

She wanted to argue, but the determination in his eyes persuaded her to swing into the saddle.

Though the snow had stopped falling, the wind was fierce as it blew through the canyon, and before they reached the creek, Libby was chilled to the bone. Flintlock balked at crossing, but Brett yanked insistently on the reins and forded the rushing water at a wide section where the water never climbed past his thighs.

For the first time, Libby had a close look at her Jeep and the gaping hole in the bridge. Icicles hung from the rotted boards, and the broken cables were frozen solid and dangling above the water.

"Not a pretty sight, is it?" Brett asked when he saw her staring at the frigid debris. "The whole thing will have to be replaced if you want access to the camp. 'Course, there's not much need, unless you're planning to reopen the campground or sell the place."

"I don't know what I'm going to do," she replied honestly.

Brett clucked to Flintlock as they began climbing steeply. The trail was covered with unbroken snow, and both man and beast labored as they trudged steadily upward.

"Look, I can walk for a while," Libby offered, feeling stupidly like a damsel in distress.

"Stay put."

"But—"

"Just stay on the damned horse. It's easier for him to carry you than me, and I'm taller, so the snow doesn't hit me any higher on the leg. Besides, I'm stronger."

"Is that supposed to put me in my place?" she threw back, and to her surprise, he smiled. It was a slash of white against his dark jaw.

"Yeah. I suppose it is."

"Well, it doesn't."

"Nothin' much would, Libby. Nothin' much would." He laughed, and the sound echoed through the ravines and crevices of the mountains.

Libby knew she should be angry, but she wasn't. She smothered a smile and eyed the countryside. Branches of pine, fir and mountain hemlock drooped under the weight of heavy loads of snow, and the cathedrallike spires of the Cascade Mountains sliced upward to a winter-blue sky. Her heart ached for a silly moment when she realized how much she had missed this place. Her fingers tightened on the reins, causing Flintlock to toss his great head and snort in twin streams of steam.

Her legs were beginning to ache by the time they finally reached their destination—the lookout tower and ranger station. It hadn't changed much in the past five years, she thought as she studied the small cabin and lean-to barn at the base of the tower.

"Come on, let's get you inside, and I'll take care of Flintlock and the rest of the herd." He helped her down from the saddle. When she slid to the ground, her legs threatened to give out for a second, but Brett was quick, as if he had anticipated her weakness. He grabbed hold of her arm and held her upright, supporting her. Rather than fling off his arm and risk falling, she let him guide her into the cabin.

Inside, he flicked the light switch, but nothing happened. "No surprise. Usually happens during a big storm. The good news is that I've got a backup generator for the water pump, and these—" He opened a closet and pulled out two kerosene lanterns and a large flashlight. "While I'm working with the stock, why don't you take a shower? There's probably a little hot water left in the tank. No reason to let it go cold."

"No, I—"

"I insist."

Before she could discuss it any further, he was out the door again. Through the icy window, Libby saw him leading Flintlock to the barn. She glanced around the cabin—an austere man's abode, with only a foldout couch, a recliner, a television and a coffee table. A wood stove provided heat for the small building, though the fire had long since died.

Knowing he would probably be angry with her all over again, she tested her legs, then followed him out to the barn.

Brett was already rubbing Flintlock's sleek coat as the gelding greedily swept all trace of oats from his manger. There were three other horses in the barn—a sorrel stallion, Hercules, and a burly gray Percheron.

Libby's throat closed at the sight of the horse that was to have been her wedding present to Brett. She'd never asked him what he'd done with the animal, hadn't cared, for, even though she'd known it to be foolish, she'd found some consolation in blaming the gray for the loss of the baby. "Oh, God."

"Recognize him?" Brett asked.

"I . . . I . . ." She blinked back hot, painful tears. "I thought you got rid of him."

"I wanted to. In fact, I even thought about pulling a Rhett Butler and having him shot on the spot, but that seemed a little cruel. Besides . . . I couldn't let him go." With a tender smile, he sauntered over to the huge horse and was rewarded by a massive head being thrust into his chest. Brett scratched the gelding's ears. "There ya go, boy."

Libby leaned against a post for support, and the kerosene lantern hanging by a hook over her head swayed, causing the light in the barn to move and dance upon the rough wooden walls. The horses snorted and stomped before settling back to their grain. Soon the only sound that could be heard was the loud grinding of teeth.

"You gave him to me, Libby. That, in and of itself, made him special. He didn't mean to do anything—he just reacted. I kept him because I wanted to remember."

Her world seemed to spin, and her fingers dug into the rough wood of the post behind her back. As Brett rubbed the gray's winter coat, Libby squared her shoulders and fought back the demons of her past. Tentatively she reached out to touch the deep charcoal face. Warm brown eyes blinked at her as she stretched out her fingers, and a heavy, velvet-soft nose moved across her palm. Snorting in disgust at the lack of a treat, he turned his head back to the manger.

"Did . . . did you name him?"

"Sure did." He patted the gelding's rump. "I wanted to call him Satan. Somehow I thought that fit. Or Devil. Or Demon. Or Hell-raiser. Any of the above."

"But you didn't," Libby guessed, her stomach turning over.

"He came with a name. Remember?"

She shook her head. For so many years she'd tried to erase everything about that horrid day from her mind.

"Slingshot."

The horse's ears flicked.

"Yeah, you're okay, aren't you?" Brett asked the horse. Then his gaze met Libby's again. "And what about you?" he asked, taking a step in her direction and reaching out to hold her gloved hand in his. "Are you all right?"

"I . . . I will be. It was just a shock. . . ."

"I know." He looked suddenly old. His eyes held a great sadness, and Libby's heart nearly broke. Without a word, he drew her into his arms and whispered against her hair. "It was hard . . . for me, too, Lib. I . . . I wake up some nights and wonder what might have been."

Her heart squeezed painfully, and she sniffed back tears. He smelled of leather and horses and a familiar male scent that filled her with sensual memories. "So do I." To keep the sobs that were burning in her lungs from exploding, she stepped away from him, and swiftly brushed her tears away. "I don't want to think about it. Not now. Not ever. It's over."

His mouth turned into a sad smile. "I don't think it will ever be over, Libby. Much as I'd like to believe it."

She shuddered, and he mistook the pain in her heart for a chill. "Go on in and warm up. I'll be along soon."

Without a backward glance she hurried out of the barn and followed the short path through the snow to the cabin. When she was inside, she told herself she would *not* dwell in the past. Not tonight. Not when her emotions were as raw as the bitter north wind that ripped through these canyons.

To keep herself and her mind busy, she cleaned up, giving herself a sponge bath at the sink and washing her hair, and steadfastly shoving all thoughts of the past aside.

By the time Brett returned to the cabin, she felt reasonably refreshed and had started a fire in the stove. "I saved you some hot water," she said, forcing a smile. For a second he stared at her, and she thought he would draw her into his arms again and all the old scars would reopen.

He started to say something, but thought better of it and headed to the bathroom. Soon she heard the sound of running water.

She felt a little awkward, but told herself to get over it. They were stuck together for a while, and they both had to make the best of an uncomfortable situation. She found the ingredients to make pan corn bread and vegetable soup and was soon humming in the kitchen, glad for something useful to do. But then she realized that the water pipes were suddenly silent, and she experienced the uncanny sensation that she wasn't alone.

She turned and saw him, one shoulder propped against the frame of the door leading to the living room, his gaze on her. He'd shaved and showered, his hair was still wet, and he was dressed in clean Levi's, socks, and a long-sleeved flannel shirt that he hadn't bothered to button. His chest, covered with a sprinkling of dark hair, was visible where the shirt gaped, and Libby had trouble keeping her gaze level with his eyes.

"Turning domestic on me?" he asked, cocking his head toward the mixing bowl.

"Hardly," she replied dryly. "In fact, you can help me carry this to the stove."

While she finished cooking on the blackened stove in the living room, he threw on his jacket and gloves and went out to climb the lookout tower. After surveying the surrounding area, he called several other stations by radio and learned about the damage the storm had caused.

"Nothing serious," he reported later as she cut thick slabs of corn bread and put them on separate plates on the coffee table. They were seated next to each other on the floor, backs propped against the couch, legs stretched over the braided rug. "Power outages throughout the mountains, lack of phone service, that sort of thing, but no one's reported hurt or missing. A few elderly people in town were taken in by neighbors who have wood stoves, but by this time tomorrow, power should be restored and we can get into town."

She was lifting a bite to her mouth, but stopped midway. "Tomorrow? Not today?"

He shook his head. "It's too late. It'll be dark soon, and I need to stay by the radio in case there are any more problems." She wanted to argue with him, couldn't imagine spending another night alone with him, but a part of her found the prospect of being with him again romantic. She dropped the corn bread and shoved the uneaten portion of her soup aside. Alone with Brett. Another night. Oh, Lord. It wasn't romantic, it was just plain stupid.

"Will being here be so bad?" he asked, his voice deep, his gaze penetrating.

She rubbed her arms, as if suddenly chilled. "I just don't think it's wise."

He lifted his eyebrows in silent agreement. "Look, it's not my choice, either."

"I don't want to be a burden."

He snorted, and his lips compressed into a thin, angry line. "You're not a burden, Libby," he said, shoving his empty plate and bowl away. "I'm just doing what I think is best."

"What about what I think?"

"Your judgment is a little off."

"Is it?"

He stared at her long and hard. He didn't mention her trying to cross the rotten bridge, but she knew it was on his mind. Her gaze lowered to his lips, and she felt the slightest change in the atmosphere. His fingers were suddenly in her hair, and he drew her face close to his. "Believe me, Libby, if there was a way to get you out of here safely, I would do it. Being around you...this close to you . . . is hell." His lips settled over hers in a kiss that tore the breath from her lungs.

She knew she should stop this madness, but her rational mind couldn't control her impulses, and she returned the fever of his kiss with a passion that had burned bright in her veins for five long years.

He shifted, leaning against her, pushing her down on the floor until he was half lying over her, his body forcing hers against the rug.

"You still drive me crazy," he admitted, lifting his head to gaze into her eyes.

She was having difficulty breathing. Her breasts rose and fell, pressing up against his chest, and through the clothes that separated them she felt the heat of his body. "This... this isn't a good idea," she said.

"You're right. It's insanity." With a groan, he kissed her again. His tongue pressed against her teeth, and her mouth opened easily, accepting him. Her blood was beginning to pound at her temples. With gentle flicks, his tongue met hers, dancing and weaving, causing desire to race through her bloodstream.

His hands slid downward to her shoulders and arms, surrounding her, moving against her, rubbing her sweater until the friction caused a fire deep in her loins. Dully she knew she should stop him while she still could, but his hand captured her breast, squeezing slightly, and she arched up, inviting more, her reservations fleeing.

He found the hem of her sweater, and his fingers scaled her ribs and cupped her breast. Within her bra, her nipple responded, and her clothes suddenly seemed too tight.

"Libby:.. Oh, Libby..." he whispered against her ear, while his fingers delved past the filmy barrier of lace and skimmed her nipple. She let out a cry, and he deftly pulled her sweater over her head. Her blue-black hair settled back against her shoulders, and he gently prodded the strap of her bra off her shoulder, releasing her breast.

"Oh, God!" she cried as he drew her nipple into his mouth. Her spine curved inward, pressing her abdomen and hips tight against his. With one hand he gently pushed more of her breast into his mouth, and she shivered in ecstasy.

His other hand cupped her buttocks, drawing her against the hardness buried in his jeans. "Oh, Libby, I want you," he whispered, lifting his head and staring at her wet nipple, before forcing his glazed gaze up to hers. "I want you more than I've ever wanted anything in my life."

She closed her eyes, hearing the reluctance in his voice, trying and failing to regain her equilibrium. "Why do I feel like you're leading up to something?"

With a sigh, he said, "I don't want to make another mistake."

"You mean like you did the first time?" she asked, her heart shattering into a thousand pieces.

"I mean, we're older now. We should be more responsible. More in control." Slowly he released her, putting distance between his body and hers. "We're not kids anymore."

"You don't have to explain," she said, blushing as she covered her breasts and reached for her sweater. "If you don't want to—"

His hand snaked out and clamped over her wrist so quickly that she gasped. "I *want*. I want very much. I just said so. But I'm trying to be smarter than I was before."

"And more noble."

"Believe me, nobility doesn't enter into it," he said, and the blaze of desire in his eyes convinced her. "Before we make a mistake we'll both regret for the rest of our lives, and hurt each other all over again, I think we should use our heads. I'm not sure that's possible, because I seem to lose my common sense when I'm around you, but I'm going to try. I'd appreciate it if you did the same."

Jerking her hand away, she rubbed her wrist. "No problem, Brett. You keep your distance, and I'll keep mine."

"Just like that?"

"Just like that."

He stared at her for a long moment, as if he didn't believe her, then strode to a closet. He took out a bedroll and tossed it on the couch. "I'll sleep out here. You take the bedroom.

"Oh, no, I couldn't—"

"You damn well better, lady. And maybe you should lock the door. Just in case I change my mind." He tossed her an old key, and she caught it and promptly threw it back at him.

"You keep it. Just in case I change *my* mind."

Chapter Seven

Brett snapped a pair of sunglasses onto the bridge of his nose. Sunlight glinted off the new-fallen snow, and the Bronco's wheels spun in some of the drifts. He hazarded a glance at Libby, who was staring through the windshield. They hadn't said much this morning, and he felt as if he hadn't slept in a week. Two nights of tossing and turning with Libby only a few feet away had kept his eyes open and his mind straying into dangerous territory. She'd changed, all right. If anything, she was stronger than she had been five years ago, more sure of what she wanted. And even more desirable. If that was possible.

He wondered about the men she'd dated in the past five years. How close had she become to any of them? Why hadn't she married?

Disgusted with the turn his thoughts had taken, he switched on the radio and listened to the weather reports. His jaw was clamped tight, his muscles ached with tension, and he wondered how he'd gotten involved with Libby again. Because, damn it, like it or not, he had to face the fact that he *was* involved.

He shifted down and muttered under his breath at his bad luck. He'd sworn never to let a woman under his skin again—especially the one woman who had the power to turn him inside out. Just one glance into her June-blue eyes had him thinking twice about all the convictions that he'd held for five years. Until now, he'd been able to convince himself that he was a loner by nature, that he didn't need a woman to nag at him, that he'd go through life by himself.

Now he wasn't so sure. From the corner of his eye, he sneaked a glance at her, and his diaphragm clenched. God, she was beautiful—but that wasn't the worst of it. He'd met a lot of beautiful women in his life, some more gorgeous than Libby. But none of those women had even come close to her in genuine intelligence or wit or spark. When he was with Libby, he felt more alive than usual; he saw a different, brighter side to a world he'd long ago decided was dark.

Hell, his thoughts sounded like they came from some lovesick fool. Grinding the gears, he turned onto the main highway. The road was plowed and sanded. Traffic was moving cautiously but steadily past the sawmill, where men and women were already working the early shift. Pickups and cars, still covered in snow, were parked in the lot, and machinery was moving logs into the cluster of sheds on the other side of the tall chain-link fence that separated the work area from the office.

Libby eyed the sawmill, but didn't see the men in hard hats, or the cranes, or the trucks. Long-ago memories filtered through her mind. Memories of happier times, when she'd been in love with Brett.

The church and the parsonage were on the outskirts of town. Libby's heart constricted at the sight of the Nativity scene nestled between two pine trees, located in the same spot it had been each Christmas season for as long as she could remember. Cedar boughs and red ribbons adorned the rail of the steps leading into the church, and, as always, lights had been strung along the gables of the roof.

She could almost imagine her father on a ladder, a string of lights in one of his hands as he balanced near the top rung and barked down orders to her and her mother. Tears burned the backs of her eyes, and she looked away from the church and concentrated on the road leading into the town.

They passed the post office, grange and general store before Brett found a parking space in front of the Derringer Café. "I'll buy you breakfast," he offered, pocketing his keys.

"I owe you one."

"Don't worry about it. I run a tab."

He held the door to the café open for her and she walked inside. Nothing had changed much. The orange-colored plastic covering on the booths was just a little shabbier, and the menu had been expanded slightly, but the faces behind the counter didn't seem to have changed in all these years.

Velma, the big, red-haired waitress, was wearing a Santa cap today. She sauntered over to the table to take their orders and flirt outrageously with Brett. Libby found a way to stay calm, though she felt an unlikely spurt of jealousy tear through her blood when Velma placed a familiar hand on Brett's shoulder.

Velma joked with Brett for a few minutes before she disappeared into the kitchen, and Libby silently prayed that her clenched jaw wasn't visible.

Service was fast at the Derringer. Libby and Brett ate heartily from platters of ham, hash browns, eggs and toast, and washed the works down with hot coffee. Velma made a point of stopping by the table and refilling Brett's cup more often than necessary. Libby felt like a fool, with a smile as plastic as the Naugahyde she was seated upon pasted on her face.

They were nearly finished when a woman's voice commanded Libby's attention.

"Libby? Libby Bevans?" Everyone seated in the surrounding tables turned to stare. "It *is* you!" Sandy Brennan, obviously pregnant, hurried over to the table and plopped down on the seat next to Libby. "How are you?"

Libby relaxed, and as Brett paid the bill, she caught up with Sandy, who had been married to her hometown sweetheart, Leo Van Pelt, for just over a year, and was expecting her first child in March. "Can you believe it? Me—a mother?"

Libby smiled as she remembered Sandy as a girl—one who could outrun most of the boys on the track team and chew tobacco with the best of them. "You'll be a great mom," she said, experiencing a pang of envy.

"I hope so. But even if I'm not, my mom will make a terrific grandmother! She can't wait, you know. Been sewing layette clothes for nearly four months now." Sandy wound her long blond hair into a bun and tucked it under a stocking cap as they walked out of the restaurant together. Sandy cast a knowing look at Brett. "So what are you two doing together?"

Brett's lips twitched, and Libby felt embarrassment wash up her neck. "I came back for a Christmas vacation, and Brett saved me from drowning in White Elk Creek."

"No!"

Libby explained about the collapsing bridge while they stood in the cool air. Sandy's eyes were round. She had always been a gossip, and it wouldn't be long before the entire county had heard Libby's story. They talked a little while longer, with Sandy complaining about the trip into Bend to see her doctor and suggesting that Cascade could use Libby's medical expertise. "I just hope this baby doesn't come in the middle of an ice storm," she said, rubbing her stomach. "I don't know how we'll get to the hospital in Bend in this old rattletrap of a pickup." She rapped her gloved knuckles on the dented fender of a beige Ford.

"I'm sure Leo will find a way," Libby said.

"Well, I'm counting on him. I guess I'll see you around. Probably at the Christmas pageant?"

"Maybe," Libby said, not sure she could face Christmas services in the little church where her father had led the congregation for years. Some wounds hadn't yet healed.

"I'll be lookin' for you, and you, too," she said, waving to Brett before climbing into the truck.

As the pickup slid down Main Street, Brett and Libby walked the two blocks to Yeltson's Towing and Auto Body, where Brett and the owner talked about finding a way to winch Libby's Jeep out of the creek.

Hours later, after stops at the hardware store, the post office and the grocery, Brett drove her back to the ranger station over her loud and furious protests. She'd expected him to take her back to the camp, where she would ford the creek and get on with her plans, but he hadn't turned off at the church camp. He'd kept the nose of the Bronco heading up the winding road leading to the Pine Mountain Ranger Station.

So he expected her to stay with him again. That would be dangerous, no doubt about it. How could she maintain her distance, physically and emotionally? Besides, she'd told herself—promised herself—that she'd spend Christmas at the camp where her father had put all his love and most of his dreams.

She had no other options, as the Blue Ridge Motel had no vacancies, and the old parsonage where she'd grown up was occupied by the new minister and his small family. The choice was either spend the night alone with Brett or go back to the camp.

Despite the cold, despite the dilapidated state of the buildings, despite the need to ford the creek, the camp was definitely safer for her heart.

"I can't stay here," she ground out once he'd parked near the barn. It was late afternoon, and shadows stretched across the snowy landscape.

"Then I should have left you in town, at the motel." Brett stuffed his keys in his pocket and slid out of the Bronco. The Blue Ridge, with its flickering blue neon sign, was the only motel in town. Cheap and clean, with color TV, it provided rooms for out-of-town relatives and secret midnight trysts. The owners, Pat and Sid Kramer, were as tight-lipped now as they had been years ago.

Libby had no choice but to follow him onto the porch, where they both stomped snow from their boots. "I have a place of my own," she reminded him. "Down there." She pointed in the general direction of the camp.

"And no way to get there." He opened the door, and they stepped into the warmth of the cabin.

"I figured I'd go back the way I got out."

"That's crazy!"

She stopped at the door, the toes of her boots touching his. "I'm going home, Brett."

"How?"

"I'll walk. Or, God forbid, you could be a gentleman and drive me there."

"The Bronco didn't come with sails and a rudder. It wouldn't make it across the creek."

"I'll wade."

"Like hell!" He strode into the house.

Her temper, which she had tried religiously to keep under control, snapped, and she followed him inside. "You can't tell me what to do!"

He turned to her. "I can damn well keep you from making a mistake that could cost you your life." He moved closer and caught her wrist.

"So what are you going to do? Lock me up and throw away the key?"

His amber eyes darkened. His fingers tightened.

"Let me go!"

"That's where I made my mistake the first time." From his pocket he withdrew a single sprig of mistletoe, a piece he must have picked up while they were in town. "Merry Christmas, Libby," he whispered gruffly.

"Brett, please—" Her words were cut off as his mouth covered her own and the tension that had been building between them exploded. He kicked the door closed as anger turned to passion and Libby, knowing she was a fool, kissed him back, her eager tongue mating with his, her willing body fitting perfectly against the hard contours of his. "Don't—" she whispered as he drew back his head.

"Don't what?"

"Don't . . . stop." She closed her mind to the doubts and let the weight of his body pull her to the floor. His kisses were hungry and hot, his tongue and lips touching her eyes, her cheeks, her throat. His hands worked quickly to remove her clothes, stripping her bare as she, too, fumbled with the buttons and zippers that held his clothes to his body. Still kissing him, she felt muscles, hard and sinewy, beneath her fingers, and soon, when they were naked, he was lying beside her, his body hard with want, hers warm and anxious.

"I never stopped thinking about you," he admitted, and in the half-light his eyes were dark with sincerity. "I tried. God knows I tried. But it was impossible."

"For me, too," she said, her throat closing, as he gathered her into his arms and carried her to his bedroom. She clung to him, her arms around his neck and her head resting against the hard wall of his chest. She listened to his heartbeat—it was as strong and wild as her own—as he laid her gently on the sturdy bed, parting her knees.

"I've waited for this for five years," he vowed.

"Me too."

His lips found hers again, and he came to her, as man to woman, lover to lover, fusing their bodies with long, sure strokes that caused her to whimper and beg, pant and cry out. "Brett... Oh, Brett... Please..."

His own release came suddenly. With the power of an avalanche, he fell against her, flattening her breasts and throwing back his head in ecstasy. "Libby..." he whispered, once he could speak again. His fingers twined in the sweat-soaked strands of her hair. "Sweet, sweet Libby..." His breathing was loud and rapid, as was her own. He twined his fingers in her hair and sighed loudly. "So, what're we going to do now?"

Chapter Eight

For five long years Brett had all but convinced himself that he was over Libby, that he was lucky they hadn't married, that though the loss of their child caused a pain that seared him to his very soul, things had worked out for the best.

Now he knew he'd been lying to himself.

The past three days he'd spent nearly every waking hour with Libby, and he felt a new electricity in the air, an awakening of his soul. He'd never been a romantic man and he'd always prided himself on his lone-wolf tendencies, but Libby had turned his thinking inside out, and for the first time in a long time he was second-guessing himself.

He liked having her around. He'd never felt lonely, but he knew that when she left there would be a vast emptiness that he'd never be able to fill. And it was coming soon.

Her Jeep had been winched out of the creek and towed to the auto body shop so that the damage it had sustained during the collapse of the old bridge could be repaired. Fixing the bridge would be more difficult, however. The weather was against the crew he'd rounded up—men who would work on the weekends, lumberjacks and sawmill employees and a lot of people in town who knew Libby and remembered her folks.

In the meantime, Libby insisted on moving back to the camp. "I just can't stay here indefinitely," she'd pointed out one night as they finished the dishes in his cabin.

"Why not?"

Her eyes had been shadowed with a deep sadness. "You have your work to do, Brett. I interfere."

"Have I complained?"

"And I did come here with a purpose, you know. I want to stay at the camp."

They'd argued, but he'd given in. The last thing he wanted was a woman who didn't want him. The trouble was, she sent him mixed signals. True, she acted independent and determined and able to take care of herself, and yet, whenever he kissed her, or held her in his arms, he *knew* that she'd come to care for him again. No matter what she said.

They carried supplies back to the camp, on horseback fording the creek, as the bridge was only partially rebuilt. Christmas was only a few days away, and Libby seemed bound and determined to spend the holidays in the rustic cluster of cabins her father had owned for so many years.

"You're sure you want to stay here?" Brett said, eyeing the old buildings.

"Absolutely," she replied, though a part of her longed to go with him, to stay in the cozy little ranger cabin for as long as he wanted her to. But what then? Could she live here and be content with an affair, without the prospect of marriage and children? She'd learned five years before, after losing the baby, that Brett wasn't interested in settling down. Yes, he would have done his duty, married her and given his child a name, but without the baby, their relationship had quickly unraveled. Her father's fury and humiliation that his daughter had been pregnant and unwed hadn't helped an already rocky situation. Some of the blame had been hers, as well. She'd been inconsolable.

Now she stood firm. "I need to stay here and sort things out," she told him. "That's why I came back."

He rubbed a hand over the back of his neck and stared at the craggy peak of Pine Mountain. "Whatever you want, Libby, but I'd feel better if you were with me. It wouldn't have to be forever."

Her heart cracked. *That's the problem,* she thought, realizing that she'd never stopped loving him. "I think we need some time to think things through."

His lips tightened. "It is hard to think when you're around." To add emphasis to his point, he picked her up, carried her over the threshold of the dining hall and deposited her on the old couch, where he made love to her as if he'd never stop. Libby's soul seemed to shake in the earth-shattering climax, and the thought that she loved him echoed over and over in her mind. They slept together wrapped in old blankets in front of the fire. He came to her again in the night, and she eagerly responded, kissing and holding him with a desperation borne of the knowledge that with the morning sun he'd be gone and their affair would surely cool.

In the morning, he lingered as long as he could, then left Flintlock in the barn, insisting that she needed some sort of transportation. In the end, she reluctantly relented.

She spent the next two days cleaning the dining hall and decorating the room with a few strings of lights she'd brought from home and a small tree she'd cut herself. She planned on spending Christmas Eve alone and attending church on Christmas morning. As for the pageant . . . she wasn't quite sure she could watch the festivities.

And what about Brett?

She shoved that thought aside. Dealing with her complex emotions concerning Brett was too difficult. Instead, she concentrated on the everyday facets of her life.

The new bridge—a temporary structure at best—was finished the weekend before Christmas. Three huge beams, milled at the Cascade sawmill, were used as supports, and heavy planks were nailed carefully over the beams. Though wide enough for only one vehicle, the bridge was sturdy, and Libby could shore it up at a later date if she planned to open the camp again.

"Looks like you're back in business," Brett said after crossing the bridge in his Bronco and parking near the dining hall.

Libby's heart beat faster at the sight of him. She wondered if she'd made the right decision, living without him, but she was determined not to second-guess herself. "All I need is my Jeep."

"Bill Yeltson called this morning. It's finished. I thought I could give you a lift into town."

When they drove into Cascade, the little community felt as familiar as a favorite old slipper and was bustling with activity. The Christmas tree situated at city hall was blazing, and a holiday bazaar, complete with baked goods, quilts, dollhouses and ceramics, was in full swing at the grange hall.

She sampled cranberry cake and bought a dozen cookies along with a couple of handcrafted ornaments for her little tree. Familiar Christmas carols wafted through the grange's warm interior, and the merchants chatted freely with their customers.

Libby remembered attending the bazaar each year. Her mother had always helped with the quilting of several patchworks during the year, and had baked rum cakes and banberry tarts the entire week before the festivity. As the melody of "Silver Bells" swept through the hall, memories flooded Libby's mind. She missed her parents, and the security she'd felt in this small town.

Though she loved the excitement of the city, a part of her still belonged here, with these people who had lived in Cascade for generations.

"Hey, Libby, how about a cup of hot cranberry-apple cider?" Sandy Van Pelt stood on the other side of the counter separating the kitchen from the main hall, where the dry goods were displayed. "It's on the house if you buy a piece of my mom's gooseberry pie."

"How can I resist?"

Libby picked up a paper plate with a thick slice of pie, and while Brett talked with one of the nearby ranchers about a bay mare, Sandy, wearing a red-and-green apron over her protruding belly, joined Libby. "I shouldn't, you know. My doctor's telling me I'm gaining weight too quickly, but I figure, who cares? This might be my only chance to gorge myself and get away with it. You know, a slice of pie for me and a cookie for the baby."

They chatted while they ate. Sandy was obviously very much in love with her husband and was content to live the rest of her life as a wife and mother in Cascade. "I'm even going to quit my job at the sawmill after the baby gets here.... Well, I'm going to try. At least for a year or two, if we can afford it. I'd like to have another baby right away, and then I figure I could baby-sit, take in other people's kids for a little extra spending money." She sighed happily as she swallowed a bite of her lemon meringue pie. "So, enough about me. What about you and Brett?"

Libby shifted uncomfortably in her folding chair. "What about us?"

"Well? Are you dating, or what? I remember you two were gonna get married once, and from the way he looks at you I figured I'd be hearing the sweet sound of wedding bells sometime soon."

Avoiding Sandy's probing gaze, Libby said, "I don't think so."

"Why not?"

A million reasons, starting with he doesn't love me and doesn't ever want to settle down! "I've got a life in Portland. I've just finished my training to be a nurse practitioner, and I've got some offers to consider before I open my practice. That's part of the reason I came back here—to sort things out."

"We can always use medical help around these parts," Sandy pointed out.

From the corner of her eye, Libby saw Brett, and she wondered if he'd overheard any of their conversation. She shook her head and cradled her cup of cider in her palms. "I don't think so. I'm used to city life now."

"But you're a small-town girl at heart."

"Sandy! We could use a little help in here," Irene Brennan said over the heads that were clustered at the counter.

"Oh-oh, duty calls."

"Let me help!" Over Irene and Sandy's protests, Libby donned an apron and washed her hands. "You certainly pinch-hit for me when mom was sick," she explained, smiling as she started cutting thick wedges of carrot cake.

Brett had to return to the ranger station, but he was back in Cascade by the time the bazaar ended. During the afternoon Libby had broken down and bought a quilt and an antique dollhouse, though she really didn't need either one. But the quilt reminded her of the happy years she'd spent as a child at her mother's knee while Marla had pieced together tiny squares of calico, and the dollhouse was something she'd always wanted but had never been able to afford. Someday, she thought as she packed the Victorian replica in the back of her Jeep, she might have a daughter.

Someday.

Her little tree looked pathetic. And Libby was lonely. Without Brett, the dining hall seemed empty and cold. She'd placed the dollhouse on a table near the window and thrown the new quilt over the back of the sagging couch, but still she felt empty inside.

She thought of her apartment in the city—a studio in southeast Portland. It wasn't particularly charming, but it was cheap, and it had been her home ever since she moved to the city. The single room with its kitchen alcove and bad plumbing held no fascination for her either.

I'm in no-man's-land, she thought as she walked onto the porch and looked up at the sheer face of Pine Mountain. She knew approximately where the ranger station was and she wondered what Brett was doing. The ache in her heart seemed to go on forever and she suddenly realized that she'd never stop loving him—not entirely.

Surely someday she would marry and she'd love the man she wed, but she doubted that she'd ever feel the same raw passion, the deep emotional whirlpool, that she experienced whenever she was with Brett. Even now she could see, in her mind's critical eye, the slash of white of his smile, the warm whiskey color of his eyes, the way he looked when he blinked his eyes open upon first awakening in the morning.

First love, last love, she thought, and had to squint her eyes in disbelief when he appeared before her, astride Slingshot. Her lungs constricted and her heart squeezed at the sight of him, sitting tall in the saddle.

"I was just thinking of you," she said as he dropped to the ground and icy snow crunched beneath his boots.

"Only good thoughts, I hope."

"About you? Never," she said teasingly, unable to keep from flirting with him.

His lips curved upward, and his voice lowered, "Now, Miss Libby, don't tell me you were thinking of anything wicked or wild or wanton?"

"Me?" she responded as the first few flakes of snow fell from the sky. "Not on your life."

He took her into his arms and kissed her lightly on the forehead. "What would I have to do to get you to stay?"

Just say you love me, she silently cried, her eyes beginning to burn as she stared up at him. "You . . . you couldn't."

"Not even if I was extremely persuasive?" he asked, kissing her so slowly her heart began to pound. He found the zipper of her jacket and tugged on it. With a slow hiss, it opened.

"Not even then—" When his hand surrounded her breast, she gasped. Suddenly he was kissing her, anxiously, hungrily, his body hard and straining.

"I'm warning you, woman," he said, lifting his head to stare into her eyes. "I can be *very* persuasive."

"Prove it," she said, and before she realized what was happening, he'd carried her back into the cabin and they were making love on the new quilt, firelight crackling around them, the tiny Christmas tree glowing in the corner of the hall.

I could be happy here, she thought as she gave herself to him body and soul, though deep in her heart she knew it would never work. Much as he wanted her, Brett still didn't love her. She'd spend the night with him, but she would leave in the morning—Christmas Eve morning. Staying any longer would tear her up inside. She'd pack up her tiny tree and her supplies and take her new dollhouse, her quilt and her memories back to Portland.

Her future was somewhere else, without Brett, without the heartaches of the past. Though she'd intended to spend Christmas here, she'd go back to the city, where she belonged, and start her new life, knowing that she'd put the past to rest.

The day before Christmas dawned clear, but the air between Brett and Libby was thick and murky with unspoken emotions. He didn't try to talk her out of leaving, just kissed her gently on the lips and said, "Do what you have to do."

Methodically she packed her Jeep while Brett snapped a lead rope on Flintlock and saddled Slingshot. "So what will you do with this place?" he asked as she put a new padlock on the door.

"I don't know. Sell it, I guess."

He rubbed his jaw, not meeting her eyes. "Makes sense, I guess."

"I might donate it to the church. Even though Dad bought it with his own money, most of the years it was open it was run for the congregation."

"I'm sure the congregation would appreciate it." He stared at her for an endless moment, and the sounds of the mountains, the rush of water spilling over the stones of the creek, the hum of tires on the highway in the distance, the flutter of the wings of winter birds, seemed to echo in her heart. "I'll miss you, Libby," he said quietly.

Her throat felt suddenly clogged. "And I'll miss you."

Without so much as a wave, he climbed into Slingshot's saddle and, with a clucking sound, began the trek back to his cabin, leading Flintlock behind him. Libby wanted to run to him, to tell him that she loved him, to say all the silly romantic things that were lodged deep in her heart, but she didn't.

She needed marriage and children and a future of growing old with one person. He needed no one but himself.

Ignoring the tears that were damp against her lashes, she climbed into the Jeep, started the engine and drove across the new bridge. Through the branches of the trees, she saw Brett and his horses climbing the steep terrain, and she wondered if she'd ever see him again.

"Forget him," she told herself, and snapped on the radio. The strains of "White Christmas" boomed over the speakers, and tears continued to drizzle down her cheeks. Why she was so miserable she didn't really understand, but as she drove into Cascade she felt as if she were on the road to her doom.

Chapter Nine

He couldn't let her go. Not without a fight. Whether she knew it or not, she belonged with him. Here. In Cascade. By the time Brett had returned to the ranger station, he knew that he had to stop Libby, that he had to convince her to stay with him, that he wanted her to be his wife.

At the barn, he whisked the saddle and bridle off Slingshot, rubbed the gelding down quickly and tethered both animals before climbing into his Bronco and tearing down the hillside. Packed snow and ice made driving treacherous, but he didn't care.

The phone in the truck rang, and he picked up the receiver, half expecting the caller to be Libby. Instead, he heard the dispatcher for the volunteer fire department.

"Fire broke out at the mill. All men on duty," she commanded. Brett gritted his teeth. His showdown with Libby would have to wait. He glanced toward the horizon and noticed the cloud of black smoke billowing to the sky. "Son of a bitch," he ground out as he stepped on the throttle and the Bronco's wheels spun crazily.

Libby was driving out of town when she passed the church and parsonage where she grew up. Without understanding her reasons, she slowed the Jeep to a stop at the curb and let the engine idle as she watched nine or ten children playing in the snow. Bundled in scarfs, hats and mittens, they laughed and screamed as one group tried to build a snow family while another, more rambunctious group engaged in a serious snowball fight.

Her heart squeezed. How often had she, as a child, waited for school to be let out for the holidays so that she and the neighborhood kids could build snow forts? She watched as an older boy was chased by three younger girls who were hurling packed snow balls at him. He ducked behind a huge sign that announced the potluck dinner and pageant slated for Christmas Eve.

Tonight.

Should she stay?

No way.

But why not?

Because if you stay, Brett Matson will break your heart.

Maybe he wouldn't. Maybe she should stay and take a chance on Brett. They could have a child... another baby. Her jaw tightened as she realized that she still had unfinished business with Brett. She'd come back to Cascade to face her past, and yet she hadn't owned up to the fact that she loved Brett, that she wanted to marry him and bear his children. He might laugh in her face, or try to let her down gently, and if he did, well, then she'd have to realize that he wasn't the man she thought he was. But there was a chance... a slim chance... that if he knew how she felt, he might tell her he loved her.

She sent up a silent prayer as she wheeled the Jeep back toward town. Her heart was beating as quickly as the wings of a frightened bird, and her hands were sweating on the wheel, but finally she was going to set her life back on the right track.

Gritting her teeth, she started planning her speech, but then she heard the first horrifying wail of a siren. She pulled the Jeep over by instinct, her heart thudding, and a fire truck and a rescue vehicle, lights flashing, roared past. More screaming sirens filled the air as police and fire trucks all headed out of town.

Her heart in her throat, Libby cranked the steering wheel one more time and followed the emergency vehicles. A cloud of smoke, black as obsidian, roiled toward the sky. With a sinking heart, she realized that the sawmill, where many of the townspeople worked, was in flames.

"Oh, God," she whispered, tromping on the accelerator and beginning to pray.

The sawmill was bedlam. People, healthy and injured, were streaming out of the open gates, running away from the roaring flames that were shooting skyward.

Firemen were dragging heavy hoses and hooking them up to pumps to attack the blaze that was consuming one of the sheds. Heat, in crackling waves, scorched the air. The fire chief barked orders, people coughed and screamed, and those who were uninjured stared through the mesh of the fence to the work yard, where the fire burned out of control, melting snow and threatening other buildings.

"Hey, lady, where do you think you're going?" the chief yelled as Libby tried to brush by.

"I can help. You're going to have wounded, and I'm a nurse."

"I don't need anyone fouling up—"

"You need volunteers," she countered, and he seemed to relent a bit.

"We've alerted the hospital in Bend. Ambulances are on their way."

"Good. Then I can help sort out the most severe injuries."

The chief didn't argue any further, and he quickly introduced her to the paramedics. They worked side by side as people walked or were carried to them. Libby examined each person, determined the extent of the injuries and ranked them, worst to least. Smoke clogged the air, burning her eyes and throat, and huge jets of water streamed toward the blaze pumped through gigantic hoses.

"Must've been a 'lectrical spark," one of the wounded said. "In shed C, near the saw. I never seen nothin' like it before."

"Shh . . . Looks like they're getting it under control," she said, examining the man. And the flames, burdened by the water, did indeed seem to be dying.

Firemen ran throughout the yard, and she recognized Brett as one of the volunteers, but she didn't have time to talk to him. While he tried to save buildings, she was busy saving lives. Many of the victims were only slightly injured—a few burns and cuts that would be painful but would heal. However, one man had been blinded, and another's back was burned severely. They were loaded in the first ambulance.

The firemen had contained the blaze and the worst of the burn victims were on their way when she heard Brett shout. "Libby. Over here!" His face was streaked with soot, and his expression was grim. Beside him, on a stretcher, was a woman who was writhing in pain.

"Oh, my God," she whispered when she recognized Sandy.

"She fell. Thinks she might be losing the baby."

Libby felt her face drain of color as Sandy moaned low in her throat.

"Please, no... Please... no!"

Libby knelt beside her friend. "Hang in there. You're going to be fine. So is the baby," she said firmly, though at that point nothing was certain.

"But the baby—"

"Is tougher than you might think," Libby said, forcing a smile, though her insides were frozen. She remembered all too vividly lying in the hospital bed, feeling a vast emptiness and the paralyzing fear that she'd miscarried. "Now, calm down. Show me where you hurt."

"I ran out of the shed and twisted my ankle," Sandy said, tears streaming from her eyes. "I landed on the concrete, right on my stomach, and I felt— Oh, God, I felt like I crushed the baby."

"Okay, let's take a look..." As discreetly as possible, Libby examined Sandy, saw the streaks of blood on her legs, and bit her lip.

"Is it—"

"I think you're okay. You're bleeding, but not much..." She looked for the fire chief. "Any free ambulances?"

"Just one."

"Put her on it."

"Oh, Libby..." Sandy cried.

"I'll come with you," Libby promised. "You just stay calm."

Within seconds, they were on their way to Bend. Despite the wailing siren and the breakneck speed, the miles seem to go by at a snail's pace. Libby held Sandy's hand all the way, and they prayed together. "Brett was going to call Leo. He'll meet us at the hospital."

"I can't lose this baby... I just can't..." Sandy whispered, her face as white as the sheet tucked around her neck. The fingers tightening over Libby's were nearly bone-crushing.

Finally the ambulance ground to a stop at the hospital, and Sandy was rushed into the emergency room. Leo and Brett arrived shortly thereafter, and Libby nearly collapsed in Brett's arms. They held each other while Leo filled out the admission forms. Then, over cups of lukewarm coffee, they waited in a room clogged with the relatives and friends of the victims of the fire.

"If only we had a clinic or somethin' in Cascade," Leo said as he stubbed out his third cigarette. "Lord, what's takin' so long?"

"They're busy," Libby said.

"All the more reason we should have a clinic of our own."

Brett caught Libby's gaze, and her throat constricted.

Nearly an hour passed before a thin doctor with a worried expression caught Leo's attention. "Mr. Van Pelt?"

Libby's heart stuck in her throat as the doctor took Leo aside. She braced herself against the wall, her heart nearly stopping. Then she saw a huge smile cross Leo's lips and tears fill his eyes. "Sandy and the baby are fine," he said as he returned. "Aside from a sprained ankle, that is. Sandy will have to rest in bed, but the baby—my boy—is okay!" Eyes gleaming, he shook Libby's hand. "Thanks," he whispered.

"I didn't do anything—"

"You did everything, Libby. You probably saved my son's life. I'll never forget it." He took off down the hall after the doctor, and Libby felt a warmth spread through her insides.

"He's right, you know," Brett said as he tucked his hand around her elbow and guided her outside. Dusk was turning the sky a soft shade of lavender, and the first few stars were visible.

When they were alone, Brett wound his arms around her and kissed her sooty forehead. "I was coming after you when I got the call about the fire," he said. "Watching you drive away, I knew that I couldn't let you go. Not until I told you that I love you and I want you to marry me and live with me the rest of my life."

Time seemed to stand still.

Tears burned behind Libby's eyes, and she hardly dared breathe. Had she heard him correctly? "But I was coming back to you. I'd seen some kids in the churchyard and knew that I'd never be happy without you ... without children of our own."

"I need you, Libby," he said, his eyes suspiciously bright. "And the town needs you. You could set up your own clinic."

"And what about our children?"

"Didn't Sandy say she was thinking of babysitting? Couldn't she start a day-care center? I bet we could find a building in town big enough to house a preschool and a clinic."

"You think so, do you?" she asked, smiling.

"I do if you'll marry me."

Blinking back tears, she grinned up at him. "I've been waiting for five years for you to ask."

With a hoot, he swung her off her feet. "You think the preacher could squeeze in a Christmas wedding?"

"For tomorrow?"

"Or tonight."

"Oh, Brett, I don't know. He's busy."

"No harm in asking. Come on—"

"Now?" she asked, laughing, as he led her to his Bronco.

"No time like the present. We'll go home and change, then show up at the pageant. I'll corner the preacher and see what he can do for us." Once they were inside the cab, he turned on the ignition and drove back to Cascade. They passed the church, where people were preparing for the night's festivities, then stopped at the sawmill's parking lot to grab Libby's suitcase from her car. There were still fire fighters and millwrights cleaning up the mess, but Brett didn't linger. He drove up the narrow road to his cabin at Pine Mountain.

He helped her from the cab and held her tight, as if he were afraid she might disappear. The night, Christmas Eve, seemed to close around them. A thousand stars glittered above the snow-crusted forest, and Brett's warm body hugged hers as if his very life depended upon her. "I'm going to make sure that you'll never walk away from me again," he vowed.

"I won't."

His lips found hers in a kiss that promised to last a lifetime. Far in the distance, church bells chimed, their melodic peals resounding through the mountains.

It's Christmas, Libby realized, *and I'm home. I'm finally home. With Brett. Forever.*

* * * * *

A Note from Lisa Jackson

You may have heard that it rains a lot in the Willamette Valley of Oregon. That's not a lie. It usually rains on Christmas. But not always. We've had snow and ice and even pale winter sunlight. But the weather doesn't matter. Not even the Oregon rain can dampen the spirit of Christmas.

When I was a child, growing up in the small logging community of Molalla, Oregon, Christmas was my favorite time of year. The family gathered together, much as it had for generations, at Grandma's house. Dinner was always sizzling turkey, potatoes, gravy, cranberries and an array of pies, from berry to mince. A fire roared in the fireplace, and there was always a large boot print in the ashes where Santa had inadvertently left his tracks. We played games, shared stories and laughter, and all gathered around a table that extended from the dining room into the living room. Perched on chairs, the piano bench or a sewing stool, we sat together before opening the presents piled beneath the Christmas tree. Many of the gifts were homemade, and those were the best of all.

These traditions didn't change until I married a man whose parents had been born in Europe and had moved to Portland, Oregon's largest city. I was introduced to the Christmas traditions of Austria and Holland. Christmas carols in a foreign language filled the rooms of a house that held memorabilia from a faraway land. The smells and sounds of Christmas were different. A goose replaced the turkey, and strudel or tortes became favorite desserts. Candles burned low as Christmas Eve lasted well into the morning.

My husband and I have tried to incorporate the best of both worlds into our holiday traditions for our children. The result has been rewarding, and Christmas is still my favorite time of year.

Lisa Jackson

NAUGHTY OR NICE

Emilie Richards

CRANBERRY NUT LOAF

2 cups all-purpose flour, sifted
1 cup sugar
1½ tsp double-acting baking powder
½ tsp baking soda
½ tsp salt
¼ cup shortening
¾ cup orange juice
1 tbsp grated orange rind
1 egg, well beaten
½ cup nuts, chopped
1 cup fresh cranberries, coarsely chopped

Sift together flour, sugar, baking powder, baking soda and salt; cut in shortening until mixture resembles coarse corn-meal. Combine orange juice and rind with egg. Pour all at once into dry ingredients, mixing just enough to dampen. Carefully fold in nuts and cranberries. Spoon into greased 9″ × 5″ × 3″ loaf pan; spread corners and sides slightly higher than center. Bake in a 350°F oven for about 1 hour or until crust is golden brown and toothpick inserted in center comes out clean. Remove from pan. Cool and store overnight for easy slicing.

Variation: If you can't find fresh cranberries, substitute 10 ounce container of frozen cranberry-orange sauce for ¼ cup of the sugar, all the cranberries and orange rind.

Chapter One

When Chloe Palmer, director of the Last Resort, left the house to run an errand, an unadorned artificial tree—old and tired a decade ago, when it had been rescued from someone's trash—tilted sadly toward the front bay window.

When Chloe returned, a lush blue spruce filled the same space so perfectly that a passerby paused to ask where the Resort had purchased such an extraordinary tree.

Chloe didn't know—but she knew exactly whom to ask.

She took the recently shoveled front steps two at a time, slipping on a patch of ice in her haste. The heavy door of the old Victorian mansion slammed behind her, newly hung sleigh bells sounding a yuletide greeting. "Egan!"

Music was her answer, a mixture of downstairs Bing Crosby and upstairs Michael Jackson. "Egan, where are you?"

A man materialized in the living room doorway. *Materialized* was not an exaggeration. Someone had lighted candles in the living room—dozens of them, if Chloe's eyes weren't playing tricks on her. Candles, in a house where at least one of the residents had been tossed out of her last foster home for setting a mattress on fire. As Chloe's eyes adjusted, Egan seemed to appear, one magnificent body part at a time, in rhythm with the flickering flames.

"Did you buy the kids a tree?" she demanded.

"Not me."

She slipped off her boots, even though that meant a shorter Chloe would have to confront Egan. Boots off was a house rule. No one, not even someone as exalted as the director, was allowed to track snow or mud through the house.

Chloe didn't take her eyes off Egan's face, or what she could see of it. Her gloves came next, then her scarf and hat. As she shook back her long black hair, he moved to help her with her coat, but she waved him away.

"Okay, you didn't buy it," she said. "Did you twist someone's arm for a donation?" She watched the corners of his mouth turn up. Granted, he had a wonderful mouth, wide, expressive and usually smiling. Her eyes were drawn to it now, as always, and some outlaw portion of her mind wondered what wonderful things that mouth could do.

"Did you steal it? Rent it? Cut it down yourself?" She saw a flicker in his green eyes, eyes the exact color of the brand-new pine-and-holly wreath hanging at the bottom of the stairs.

"Exactly where did you cut it?" she demanded. "And where did that wreath come from?"

"Which one?"

"Egan!"

"Come see what we're doing." He turned, and she padded helplessly after him in her thick wool socks.

The living room was a Christmas-card scene: Santa and his elves spreading Christmas cheer. Only Santa wasn't fat, and he didn't have a beard. He was tall, broad shouldered and lithe, and his head was covered with a close-cropped thatch of golden curls instead of a Santa Claus hat. His elves were even less traditional.

Elf Mona was singing "White Christmas," right along with Bing. Mona's singing was reason to run for cover, but tonight no one seemed to notice. Nor had anyone noticed that her precociously lush eleven-year-old body was clothed in shorts and a tank top, although it was only ten degrees outside.

Elf Jenny was standing on tiptoe trying to hang a paper crane from a branch high above her. Everything was always too high for Jenny. Chloe and a flock of medical specialists still had hopes that Jenny would grow to a normal height, but there had been eight years of malnutrition before she was placed under the care of the state of Pennsylvania.

Then there was Elf Roxanne, who was sitting crosslegged on the floor, staring at the tree's twinkling lights as if she were hypnotized. And Elf Bunny, who had already placed the same cookie-dough ornament on four different branches in the few seconds Chloe had been in the room. Bunny, whose search for perfection was, as always, exhausting to observe.

The elves were four of the twelve girls who lived in the Alma Benjamin Home. Four of a long line of children who had rechristened the facility the Last Resort, because by the time some of them arrived, there really was no other place left for them to go, except a detention center with bars on the windows—which was certainly no resort at all.

The Last Resort was both a place to turn lives around and a haven. And the girls who lived there were as full of problems and possibilities as the average Christmas morning.

"Chloe!" Bunny ran to Chloe's side as soon as she spotted her. "I can't figure out where to put this!" She held the ornament in front of her, her hands trembling.

Chloe took it and turned it over, smoothing her fingers over the brightly colored Santa Claus. "Wherever you put it will be fine."

Bunny didn't seem convinced. Chloe held it out to her. "Try and you'll see," she encouraged. "Whatever you do will be right. I promise."

Bunny returned to the tree. Chloe lifted her eyes and saw that Egan had been watching the exchange. His gaze was warm. Something peculiar ran through her. "Are you ever going to tell me where you got this tree, Egan O'Brien?"

"He cut it down at his parents' house!" Mona jumped off a small stepladder without taking the necessary time to descend the steps. The old oak floor absorbed the blow, as it had absorbed thousands of others. "His parents have a farm, Chloe. With animals. Real animals!"

"Dogs," Egan said. "They stopped raising anything bigger than a German shepherd years ago."

"No horses?" Mona's disgust was as comical as her rendition of "White Christmas" had been.

"Mona wants to learn to ride," Chloe explained. "Don't you, Mona?"

"I know how to ride. Only I never get to. Not anymore. I *always* got to ride when I lived with my family!"

Mona's parents had been criminally neglectful, and their house had been a hovel by most people's standards. Mona had survived the first ten years of her life by retreating into fantasy. But in Chloe's opinion, the time to retreat had come and gone. "No, you didn't," she said.

"How do you know? Do you know everything about me?" Mona asked.

"I know I like you. And I don't care if you had horses or fancy cars or a big house before you came here."

"You're always saying stuff like that!"

"Yeah, you always are," Egan said. His smile bathed Chloe in warmth. "Good stuff."

Mona's shoulders drooped. Egan had assumed heroic proportions for the girls since the day three months before when he had sauntered into the Resort and announced that he and his brothers would be taking over the renovations on the old house.

There were men in the girls' lives—male counselors, male teachers, the occasional family member who came for a visit. But none of them was quite like Egan. No one had his careless masculine grace, his easygoing, cockeyed smile, his talent for defusing arguments and giving compliments. When Egan spoke, even the most recalcitrant resident stopped to listen.

Only sometimes they pretended they didn't like it.

"I don't have to listen to this! I'm going to get some cocoa," Mona said.

Chloe stroked her shoulder. Mona's expression was still defiant. "Mona, would you take Roxanne with you?" she asked softly.

"No!"

"Please?"

"You're always making me do things!"

"That's because I know you *can* do them."

"Come on, Roxanne!" Mona went to the girl, who was still staring at the lights, and put her hand under her elbow. "Let's get some cocoa."

"Cocoa?"

"Yeah."

Roxanne rose obediently and followed Mona out of the room. Bunny hung three more ornaments, then wandered off, too exhausted from her internal struggle to hang any more. Jenny, who had decorated all the lowest branches, followed her a minute later, and Egan and Chloe were alone.

"Tell me you're glad I chopped down the tree and brought it here," Egan said.

"You've got to stop giving these kids gifts, Egan. They'll start to expect it. And none of them is in a position to expect anything."

He walked toward her, and she tried hard not to appreciate his masculine swagger. His hands came to rest on her shoulders. A light touch; a sure touch. But nothing about that touch was comforting.

"And what about the woman who lives here?" he asked. "Am I allowed to give her anything?"

"She doesn't expect anything, either. She doesn't want anything."

Egan studied her. He saw more behind Chloe's defiance than he knew she wanted him to. She was as intriguing as an exquisitely wrapped Christmas present, as haunting as "O Holy Night" sung at a candlelight church service, as vulnerable as a child who has just been told that Santa couldn't fit a pony down an urban chimney.

"Chloe..." He said her name like a caress. "Don't you believe in Christmas?"

She tried to harden her heart. "Sure. I believe Christmas is the one day of the year when people of a certain religious persuasion try to put aside their disagreements and love each other. When all the other days of the year take on that kind of meaning, I'll be a fan of Christmas, too."

"Then you don't believe in Santa Claus? In miracles?"

She just stared at him. Finally he dropped his hands.

"Well, Merry Christmas anyway," he said, warming her with another smile.

"Christmas is almost four weeks away."

"All the better. Four more weeks to savor the suspense."

Unaccountably flustered by the warmth in his eyes, she turned, and the candles caught her eye. "Don't tell me you cut the candles from a grove at your parents' farm, too. And the wreath. And the bells on the front door."

"Don't the girls deserve Christmas, Chloe, no matter what you think?"

"Sure. They deserve everything every other kid takes for granted. But these girls aren't going to be handed Christmas when they leave here, any more than they're going to be handed a college education or a cushy job. They've got to learn that they can only have what they want if they work hard to achieve it."

"No Santa Claus?" He stroked her shoulder with the sides of his fingers.

She tried to ignore his touch. "Nobody's ever going to give these kids anything, Egan. I'm trying to teach them that doesn't matter. They can make good things happen. On their own."

"Just like you did."

She stiffened, but if he realized he had breached the unbreachable by mentioning the past she never discussed, he didn't seem to care. He continued his stroking. Up and down. Soothing. Reassuring.

"Something like that," she said at last.

"You're talking to a man who owns a Santa Claus suit."

"Leave it in mothballs when you come here."

Gently he gripped her shoulder and turned her to face him again. "You know every girl in this house is making a list."

"If there *was* a Santa Claus, this crew would get nothing but coal in their stockings."

"They're good kids."

She melted a little, but she couldn't let him know. The Resort girls *were* good kids; they were her passion, her reason for existing. She was glad he saw their potential, but she wasn't going to tell him. "Of course you'd think so," she said. "If one of them held a gun to your head you'd tell her how well it went with her eyes."

"They're just kids making lists."

"You don't have to worry. They're on a point system, so the ones who've earned it will be getting extra spending money to buy something special. And whether they're naughty or nice, the staff will be sure they all get Christmas presents."

"Christmas presents? What? Socks? Underwear? Sweatshirts?"

"This isn't *Oliver Twist*. We care about these kids. Everybody on my staff cares. The board cares."

"New tennis shoes?"

"Heck, no. Have you priced tennis shoes lately?"

He couldn't help but smile. Golden brown eyes stared back at him, as defiant as Mona's—and the defiance was just as counterfeit. "These girls want cassette players, electric guitars and skis," he said. "Mona wants riding lessons. Bunny wants her ears pierced, and birthstone earrings."

"Bunny? Bunny's already decided what she wants for Christmas?"

He watched her faked defiance melt into excitement. "She's one-hundred-percent sure."

"That's wonderful!"

He knew when to keep a good thing going. "Roxanne wants a blue angora sweater, ice skates and a Barbie doll with lots of clothes. She said her sister had one."

"Roxanne talked to you? About her sister?"

"Only that much."

"Her sister died. Roxanne still has nightmares."

He didn't ask what else had happened to the blondhaired wraith with the perpetually vacant stare. He wasn't on staff, and he knew there were rules about confidentiality. But there was another reason, too. He didn't really want to know the details of the girls' pasts. Sometimes he could see those details in their eyes, read them in their yearning, aching hearts. He had fallen in love with all of the Last Resort's residents, and he was perilously close to falling in love with their director. Their pain was his now, too tender and new to explore fully.

He preferred to take their pain away.

"I can give them what they want," he said. "It's not so much, Chloe. My brothers and I always have money set aside for this sort of thing. It would mean so much to me, to all of us, if you'd let us play Santa Claus. Joe could—"

"You haven't heard a word I've said."

"I heard. I just don't agree."

"You're a big, oozing puddle of sentiment. You know that, don't you?"

"I'm a big strong man without a heart."

"You're all heart."

She didn't sound as if she thought that was *all* bad, but Egan knew when to change the subject. "Come to dinner at my parents' house on Sunday."

For a moment, Chloe didn't know what to say. She and Egan had always waltzed around the idea of going out on a real date. In his months underfoot, he had casually maneuvered her to Dutch-treat movies at the end of his workday, shooed her into restaurants so that they could discuss the renovations without interruption, given her complimentary tickets to the symphony—and gone along when she'd pointed out that it was too late to find anyone else to accompany her.

But he had never asked her out ahead of time, never, never asked her to do anything as intimate as spend time with his family.

She floundered. "There's so much paperwork to do, and I—"

"Chloe." He gave in to temptation and touched her hair, wrapping an impossibly long strand around his fingers. "Please?"

Finely tuned warning devices went off inside her. "Egan, I—"

"I won't bite. They won't bite."

"I don't know what I'll talk to your parents about."

"You have something in common."

"What?"

"You think I'm wonderful." He didn't give her time to respond. He just smiled his breathtaking, cockeyed smile and leaned toward her. Her treacherous feet were rooted to the ground; her eyes closed involuntarily. She felt the brush of lips against the tip of her nose. And by the time her eyes were open, Egan O'Brien was gone.

She might actually think he was wonderful. Hours later, Chloe sat at her dressing table on the third floor of the Resort and brushed her hair until it was a satin cape hiding a utilitarian flannel nightgown. The woman in the mirror stared back at her, confused, suspicious and much too vulnerable.

What was it about Egan that set him apart from the other men who had tried and failed to impress her? He was impossibly gorgeous, but she had known other men nearly as attractive in her twenty-seven years. He could be funny and kind, bullheaded or sensitive. He was intelligent enough to challenge her, and humble enough not to be impressed with himself. But he was more than the sum of all his wonderful qualities. He was Egan. Simply that. And somewhere in these past months, as she'd kicked and squirmed and fought against it—

She left the thought incomplete and cut off the yearning feelings inside her as efficiently as she had cut off Egan's talk of Santa Claus.

Her arms began to ache, and she gathered her hair behind her to braid it. When she finally stood, it swung in a tidy rope to her waist. She hadn't cut her hair since the day she turned eighteen and moved out of the last foster home the state of Pennsylvania had found for her.

Her hair had been her mother's pride. As a child she had worn it long, and her mother had braided ribbons into it or fastened it back from her face with colorful barrettes. Then, when she was seven, her mother and father had died in a house fire, and there had been no one left to fuss over her. The woman at her first foster home had taken one horrified look at her new charge and marched her to a chair in the kitchen where she had skillfully bobbed a dazed Chloe's hair to her chin.

She had been persuaded to keep it short at the other four homes where she had been placed, too. Long hair had been considered a waste of time, hot water and shampoo. No one had ever meant to be cruel. All her foster parents had been overworked and underpaid, and quiet Chloe had never been able to communicate how much she yearned to reestablish that link with the mother she hardly remembered. So she had dutifully lined up for haircuts, just as she had lined up for showers and meals. But once she'd faced the world on her own, no one had ever come near her with scissors again.

She knew she had been marked in other ways by the experiences of her childhood. Her feelings about Christmas came from eleven of them spent with families that had celebrated the holiday with severely limited budgets and used-up energy. One family had been rigid in their religious beliefs. There had been no gifts or decorations during that stay. Another home had been so crowded that individuality was a dream, and the best Chloe could hope for was that the jeans she received year after year were actually going to fit.

But Chloe had made it through those Christmases and those homes. Along the way she had made friends. She and her second foster mother still exchanged Christmas letters. A foster sister had visited her recently while passing through Pittsburgh. Her last foster family had turned out en masse for her college graduation so that she wouldn't have to celebrate alone.

She had learned the things she needed to know to survive, and the discipline and pressure applied by the best of her foster parents had taught her the value of hard work and goal-setting. But she had come out of the child welfare system with the determination never to place herself at anyone's mercy again. And that determination had carried her straight to her position as director of the Last Resort.

Now she was in charge of twelve girls who were at *her* mercy. Somewhere on the road to adulthood she had taken a good look at what she had to offer and realized that her own experiences would be invaluable in dealing with girls like the one she used to be.

Not that the girls at the Last Resort were exactly like the well-behaved preteen Chloe Palmer. These girls had flunked out of foster home care. They were too troubled and too *much* trouble to make it in a home environment.

Their crimes and sorrows were legion, and they needed strict supervision and intensive counseling to get back on track. They had nightmares and tantrums and hair-pulling cat fights. They zinged between As and Fs on report cards and refused to attend Girl Scout meetings or Sunday school.

But they also giggled endlessly about the boys in their classes and wept over *Old Yeller* on video. They watched out for each other when no one was looking and asked for Barbie dolls or riding lessons on their Christmas lists.

Christmas lists. Chloe got up to wander her apartment, an attractive space that Egan had carved out of the narrow, low-ceilinged rooms that had once comprised the servants' quarters in the days when the Alma Benjamin Home had still been the fashionable Shadyside residence of Alma Benjamin.

Christmas lists. Egan didn't have to tell Chloe that all the girls at the Resort had lists. She'd had one herself, although she hadn't thought about it for a long time. The list had stayed the same for many Christmases. Ever practical, she had started with the possible. A kitten had been at the top, a helpless little kitten, warm and cuddly and entirely her own. She had wanted a dollhouse, too, a wooden one with electric lights that really worked.

Farther down—because even as a child she had known it was impossible—she had asked the Santa Claus she was too old to believe in to give her a real mother, someone to bake Christmas cookies with, to shop with and dream with. Plus a father who thought she was the most beautiful girl in the world. And sisters or brothers who didn't change from year to year.

Last of all—and also impossible—she had wanted someone—Santa Claus or the state of Pennsylvania—to find her father's family in Greece, the family that her mother had told her about before she died, the family that her father had refused to acknowledge because of a fight. The family that would welcome her because she was one of them. Really and truly one of them.

Quite a list.

She couldn't smile at that memory now. The list had remained a dream. There had been no kittens or doll-houses, no adoptive parents or long-lost relatives. There had been disappointment, then the realization that she would have to make her own dreams come true.

She wanted the girls at the Resort to learn that lesson, too. Only she wanted them to learn it gently and with love. She wanted them to know that they could do anything they wanted, that they didn't have to depend on other people. She wanted them to know they could earn what they most desired. She wanted them to face the world filled with courage and hope and confidence.

And that meant that Egan couldn't fill their lists. Because when Egan was gone, who would take his place?

Santa Claus?

Back in her bedroom, Chloe opened the drawer of her nightstand and took out a savings-account passbook. Someday she would tell the girls about the money she had been saving for three years. There wasn't as much as there should be. Social workers weren't paid well, and she still had student loans to pay off. Still, there was money in her account, money that grew slowly every month because she was going to give herself something important from her childhood Christmas list. She had already spoken to a private investigator. When she had enough money, she was going to hire him to find her father's family.

She would do this for herself. And if she stood firm, the girls would learn that they could do things for themselves, too. There would be more than jeans under Egan's blue spruce on Christmas morning. But there would not be a lavish display.

There would be evidence that the girls were loved and wanted here. There would be gifts tailored carefully for everyone, gifts that showed they were individuals. But when Christmas was over, Chloe would be sure that they had been given the greatest gifts of all. Courage. Initiative. Determination.

She slid the passbook back into the drawer and climbed into bed after snapping off the light. She knew she was right. She knew what was best for the girls. No matter what Egan thought, she had to follow her own instincts.

She squeezed her eyes shut and saw a golden-haired Santa Claus with gentle hands and a heart as expansive as the North Pole. She turned to one side and felt warm lips against the tip of her nose, turned to the other and heard a melodious, resonant baritone pleading to give a houseful of bratty, damaged children the Christmas gifts they had always wanted.

She didn't fall asleep quickly.

But when she did, she dreamed of kittens.

Chapter Two

"Bunny gets two more checks on her chart, Heidi four, Mona..." Chloe looked up at Martha, the head counselor, and made a wry face. "None."

Martha sniffed. "Just so you know. Mona says if we try to move her out of her room, she'll make us sorry."

"We're bigger than she is." Chloe looked down assessingly at her own slender five-foot-four-inch body. "Almost," she amended.

"Well, whatever. But if this keeps up, she's going to lose the privilege of living in the east wing."

"I know." Rooms at the Resort were assigned on the basis of seniority and points. The privilege of living in the larger one-girl rooms in the east wing had to be earned by doing jobs around the house and working hard in school. Since the extra space and privacy were coveted by all, there was plenty of incentive for everyone to do her best.

The girls could also earn extra spending money and special privileges, such as trips to the movies and the ice-skating rink, by good behavior and hard work. It hadn't always been so.

Before Chloe had taken over as the Resort's director two years ago, there had been few rules and fewer incentives. The Resort had been on the verge of being closed by the state. The house itself had been a shambles, the staff disenchanted, the residents terrifying. Then Chloe had arrived, and under the suspicious eyes of the staff, residents and board of directors, she had scoured and reorganized and pleaded for funds until four hours of sleep a night had seemed like a hopeless luxury.

Since then she'd been told often enough that she had worked a miracle. But she knew about miracles. They didn't exist.

"Will you talk to Mona, or shall I?" Martha asked. Martha was an older woman who had raised four children of her own before she went back to college. She claimed there was nothing any child could say to her that one of her own hadn't said first. The residents had long ago stopped trying to shock her.

"I'll talk to her." Chloe stood, stretching her aching limbs. An afternoon of building snow forts with Egan and six residents yesterday had reminded her about muscles she'd forgotten. "When I come back tonight."

"You're going out?"

She looked down at her desk. "I told Egan I'd go with him to visit his parents."

"Uh-oh. Sounds serious."

"Martha..." Chloe looked up long enough to aim a haughty stare.

Martha redistributed the sixty pounds that her diet program had never been able to budge and stared right back. "He's nuts about you."

"It's just dinner."

"And you're nuts about him."

"How do you know that?"

"You go all soft when you look at him. Like melting taffy."

"Ridiculous!"

"Better watch out before he gives you a ring for Christmas."

Chloe thought about Martha's warning while she waited outside for Egan to arrive. She was waiting outside because she knew if he came inside they would be late. There wasn't a girl in the house who would miss the opportunity to show off for Egan. He was the father they'd never had, the man they would someday hold up as a model when they searched for husbands.

He might even be a man like the man she would search for herself, someday. When she had grown too old to hope for a new father, her mind had turned to something possible. A man who would love her best. A man who would believe she was the most beautiful woman in the world. A man with a ready smile and a warm heart. A man like...Egan.

But that thought terrified her. *Egan* terrified her. When her guard was down, he reached inside her and touched all the sentiment, all the yearning that she had locked away years ago.

She wasn't ready for that; she didn't want it. Someday she might want a calm, rational relationship with someone, but she was afraid that the depth of commitment Egan would expect in return for *his* love would be stunning, scandalous. He would want so much that if he ever abandoned her—and that certainly happened, didn't it?—she wasn't sure what would be left of her.

So she would keep what she could from Egan. They had never really kissed, certainly never made love. She just knew, she was absolutely sure, that if they did make love, she would never be able to say no to him about anything again.

She made vows to herself as Egan's Blazer pulled into a parking space at the curb. But she forgot her fears temporarily when he leaned over the gear shift and opened her door.

"You look gorgeous," he said.

"Your mother will probably think this sweater is too flashy."

He shot her a grin. "My mother wears red, too."

The same foster home that hadn't celebrated Christmas had left Chloe with a fear of expressing herself with color. It had taken twenty-three years and twice as much courage to make herself buy two skirts and a blouse in primary colors. She had a complete wardrobe of bright, pretty clothes now, but she still felt vaguely guilty about it.

"Is the jewelry too much?" she asked, touching the hoops in her ears. "I don't look like a gypsy?"

"I'm extremely attracted to gypsies."

"Then that explains my allure."

"Your intelligence, sense of humor, stalwart character and upstanding moral code explain your allure." He pulled into traffic. "Not to mention your great body."

She laughed, but the compliment left her feeling as warm as a summer afternoon.

Egan's parents, Dick and Dottie O'Brien, lived almost an hour north of the city, near Slippery Rock. The hills had leveled a bit by the time Chloe and Egan pulled into a snow-covered driveway winding through a grove of sycamores and poplars.

On the way Egan had explained that he hadn't been raised here, that this land and the two-story house just ahead of them had been a summer place that his parents had only moved into permanently when his father reduced his hours at the family construction company.

But Egan had summered here. He had run over these charming fields with his three brothers, fished in the now-frozen creek fifty feet from the drive. Chloe could imagine him here, growing up surrounded by family and love and the experiences that would make his childhood memories good ones. She was fiercely glad that places like this existed, and that some children, at least, grew up in them.

"There's nothing fancy about the way my parents live," Egan said. "But this is us, Chloe. This is where I come from, who I am."

"Well, you didn't turn out so bad. If it's helped make you the man you are, it's a pretty good place."

He turned off the engine and faced her, surprised. "Thus speaks the city girl?"

"Not a city girl by choice, Egan. By default. Every time Child Welfare had to find a new foster placement for me, I'd beg them to send me to a farm."

He surprised her with a touch on the cheek, pleased she had opened a tiny little door to her past. "Were there so many placements? Were you so hard to handle?"

"Not me. It was just bad luck. Foster parents got sick or moved away. One woman only wanted young children, and she wasn't comfortable once I got interested in boys."

Silently he cursed the woman who had rejected Chloe at such a critical time in her development. But he didn't show his anger. She would think it was pity.

Instead, he casually took her hand. "My parents tried to be foster parents. They wanted a daughter, but the agency thought they already had too many sons." His smile was warm enough to melt the snowbank in front of their car. "Just think, you could have been my sister."

For some reason, she didn't like that thought at all. She smiled to let him know she wasn't completely unhappy with him for digging deeper into her life. Then she opened her door to let him know the subject was closed.

He was beside her, reaching for her hand again before she could start up the walkway. She felt his reassurance and knew that he realized she didn't want to be here. She doubted he understood the whole reason why. The truth was that she didn't want to meet his parents or put herself in a situation where she might show how little she knew of regular families and the way they really lived. Everything she knew came from books and distant observation. And too many of the families she'd observed in her work were nothing like Egan's.

"Watch out for the dogs," he warned when they neared the front door. "They'll bowl you over if you let them."

She appreciated the warning. It gave her just enough time to brace herself. The door opened a second later, and three German shepherds and a collie launched themselves in her direction. Or rather, Egan's direction. One moment the man was on his feet, pretending to protect her, the next he was kneeling in the snow with four slobbering dogs jumping all over him.

"Well, if Egan can't see fit to introduce us, I'll introduce myself." A small woman with pale blond hair and Egan's lively green eyes stepped down off the porch and extended her hand to Chloe. "I'm Dottie O'Brien, and nobody calls me Mrs."

Chloe stripped off her glove and shook hands with Dottie, surprised by the strength of the woman's grip.

"And you're Chloe," Dottie continued, before Chloe could say a word. "I can't tell you how happy I am you're here. There isn't going to be another female in the house today. Just you and me, and that's one more than usual. Think you can stand the pressure?"

Chloe laughed, the tension inside her easing. "We won't be outnumbered, will we?"

"You don't know, do you? Egan didn't tell you."

"Tell me what?"

"He's invited all his brothers to come, too. And not a one of them is married yet, the oafs!"

They weren't oafs. They and Dick, their father, were exuberant, handsome men who treated both Chloe and Dottie exactly as they treated each other.

Chloe had already met all of Egan's brothers except Rich, who didn't work in the family business. Months ago they had tramped through the Resort to give their estimates on repairs, and she had seen them on and off ever since. They had given the Resort a huge price break for doing the renovations between their other jobs. So they came and went at odd times, each overseeing his own specialty. She hadn't failed to notice any of their assets. Nor their boundless energy.

An hour into the afternoon, Chloe was exhausted. Two hours into it, Dottie packed her up and drove her into town for a break.

"Do you see what I've been living with all these years?" Dottie asked, not a trace of self-pity in her voice.

"They are . . . spirited."

"Good thing we left before they went after the Christmas tree. They'll fight about which one to chop down, you know. They'll fight even if they all want the same one. Then they'll argue about who chops, even if not a one of them really wants to do it."

Dottie pulled into a parking space in front of a row of gaily adorned stores. "Then they'll come back home and get out the decorations. Joe will do the lights. That's tradition. Then Gary will unpack the boxes and lay everything out for the others. Egan and Rich will see who can put up decorations the fastest. Dick will make egg-nog strong enough to kill a rattlesnake, and it will all be gone by the time we get back. Finally, they'll turn on the television or team up to play Ping-Pong, and I'll come back home and change everything around to suit me."

"I'm pale just thinking about it." Chloe followed Dottie into a small supermarket and down the first aisle.

"They need to get married. All of them. Need to settle down and start families and leave Dick and me alone. Here, see which of these is the best deal, would you?"

Chloe dutifully compared prices on packages of chocolate chips. She handed Dottie a pack to put in her cart. "That one."

"Think we should get chopped walnuts, or buy halves and chop them ourselves?"

An hour later, they were home, after a tour of town and four bags of groceries. An hour after that, Dottie had taught Chloe how to make the family's favorite fruitcake, a creation generously studded with chocolate chips, dates, and candied cherries. An hour after that, the two women were sitting at the kitchen table with their feet up, sipping wine and exchanging confidences.

"I wanted a daughter," Dottie said. "So I kept getting pregnant and kept having boys. I got to like them after a while."

Chloe laughed. Dottie's eyes twinkled when she talked about the sons she obviously adored. "What do you suppose your boys are doing now?"

What they were doing was unforgivable. Rich had decided that a train set that had been packed away in the attic would be the perfect addition under the proudly installed Christmas tree. But somehow they hadn't been able to stop at a few yards of track. By the time Dottie discovered their plan, her living room had been converted into a small, dusty city.

Only after a wonderful dinner, when she was in the car with Egan, driving back toward Pittsburgh, did Chloe have time to consider everything that had happened that day.

"You liked them, didn't you?" Egan asked.

"How could I help it?"

"I told you you would."

"I know."

Egan watched Chloe out of the corner of his eye. She looked awestruck, like someone who had just narrowly missed being hit by an eighteen-wheeler. Sometime during the afternoon, she had taken down her impressive, perfect twist of hair and tied it back in a simple ponytail. He wondered if that had happened before or after his mother had gotten her out of her heels and into a bottle of Dottie's own mulberry wine.

"They like you, too."

"Do you think so?"

"All of them. My father pulled me aside and told me that if I didn't get with it, he was going to marry you himself."

She kept her voice light and pretended—hoped to heaven, actually—that Egan had just been trying to provoke a reaction. "I like your father," she said. "He probably says that about every woman you bring home."

"Just every beautiful woman."

"Your mother taught me to make fruitcake, and she gave me a stack of recipes for cookies."

"Next time she'll have you shopping and wrapping presents. Maybe even sewing slipcovers."

"Slipcovers?"

"For her dollhouses."

Chloe frowned. "What?"

"She makes dollhouses, reproductions of old Pennsylvania homes. Dad does some of the carpentry, but she does everything else. She furnishes them, too. There's an exclusive little shop in the city that will take anything she makes, and the demand's high this time of year. It's extra income, but mostly it's something she loves to do."

"You're kidding."

"No. I'm just surprised she didn't show you. She will next time, I'm sure."

Chloe stared straight ahead. Dollhouses. Wasn't that a coincidence? Once there had been a little girl who had hoped and prayed... She hadn't thought about those hopes and prayers for a long, long time, not until she and Egan had argued about the girls' Christmas lists.

"I have one at my apartment."

Chloe brought her attention back to the conversation. "A dollhouse? You?"

"Not exactly a dollhouse. Come and see."

She tried for lightness again, but a fifty-pound weight seemed to have attached itself to her vocal cords. "Is this the O'Brien twist on inviting me up to see your etchings?"

"Any excuse that works."

She recited excuses. "Sorry, but I can't get back too late. I have to have a talk with Mona, and tomorrow's a school day, so she'll be going to bed early."

"Trust me. I'll get you home in time."

Chloe had never been to Egan's apartment. He had invited her to see it many times, but she had always avoided that intimacy. Egan at the movies or in the middle of a snowball fight was one thing, but Egan in his own apartment scared her to death.

Now she was still afraid, but she had run out of excuses. Of course she was sure he had known all along why she always refused. But he was a patient man, a confident man. She imagined that he had just been biding his time, waiting for a chink in her armor.

Half an hour later, they crossed Murray Hill Avenue and parked at the top of a steep rise. Egan lived near Shadyside, in Squirrel Hill, a picturesque section of the city filled with interesting shops and kosher delis. Warily Chloe followed him up the steps of a small apartment building. His apartment took up the whole top floor, and she saw immediately why he had chosen it.

Wariness was momentarily forgotten. "This is beautiful. You can see forever from here." She walked to a bare window and looked out on a sea of lights.

"Not forever. Mount Washington is forever. This is half of forever."

"Enough of it." She counted lighted Christmas displays and stopped at nine. Egan came to stand behind her. Without thought, she leaned back against him, and his arms encircled her.

His voice buzzed against her ear. "I'm glad you came."

"I think I'm glad, too."

He laughed, and the sound rumbled through her. "Chloe, I asked you up here to see my apartment, not to make passionate love to you."

She felt a strange stab of disappointment. "Well, good."

"I don't even want to make love to you…until you're ready."

At his first words, disappointment overwhelmed her, then her spirits rebounded—until she realized he was waiting for an answer. And what could she say?

"I'm sorry. I don't know what to think about this. I don't even *want* to think about this. You're different . . . I mean I'm different when I'm with—"

"This is special, important," he translated. "And you don't want anything to ruin it."

He was moving too fast for her, even though he made the tortoise in Aesop's fable look like an Olympic sprinter. "You're special, Egan. You're a very special person. The way you treat the girls is spe—"

"Even though making love won't ruin what we have—" he went on, ignoring her interruption. He turned her slowly to face him. "It will bring us closer, until you can't hide the truth from yourself anymore. And when you can't hide, you'll find that I'm right here waiting."

She couldn't blither or blather any longer. He was looking at her with eyes that saw everything, eyes that promised she had no reason for fear. With a sigh, she abandoned caution and leaned into the kiss that had been inevitable from the day they met. He smelled like pine and spruce forests, tasted like the candy canes hanging on a Christmas tree.

And he felt like a Christmas miracle.

Egan knew he was holding a miracle in his arms. His hands settled at her hips to draw her closer. His lips moved over hers, seductive, sure—and capable, he hoped, of convincing her he was right.

And he knew he was right. He had dreamed of holding Chloe like this until the dreams had become torture. He had told himself to go slow, told himself to be cautious, but only a small portion of his brain had accepted the need for patience. He had told himself that falling in love with a woman so obviously afraid of commitment was dangerous. But *no* part of his brain had accepted that. Because the woman was Chloe, and somehow he had always known that holding her like this would be worth any price he had to pay.

She sighed and leaned further into his kiss. Her body was pliant against his, and the fragrance of her hair and skin seemed to penetrate his skin and sing in his bloodstream. His hands tightened, and even through her clothes her flesh seemed to warm against his fingertips.

After a long interval, he told himself to let her go. He knew better than to prolong this intimacy. Her guard would go up. The warm, pliant woman in his arms would turn to stone.

But he wanted to prolong it. He wanted to thread his fingers through the black silk of her hair, wanted to press his lips against the dark rose of her cheeks, the warm ivory of her neck. Wanted to feel the soft give of her generous breasts against his sweater.

He knew now that he had wanted Chloe Palmer since the first moment he'd seen her. And the more he had of her, the more he wanted. That was never going to change.

Chloe framed his cheeks with her hands and lifted her face to his. But when her good sense had disappeared and fear had been smothered by desire, she felt Egan set her away from him.

"I haven't shown you my dollhouse."

She stared at him as she tried to reorient herself. "No," she said breathlessly. "You haven't."

He brushed his thumb across her bottom lip. "That's why I brought you here."

"Yes."

He managed a smile as the bewilderment slowly faded from her eyes. Then, because he couldn't stand there any longer looking at her reddened lips and her sparkling eyes, he took her hand and led her into his bedroom.

Chloe tried to ignore the huge bed with the elaborately carved headboard, the bathrobe draped lazily over a chair, the attractive clutter that shouted that a man slept and woke and yearned for a woman in this room. She tried hard to focus on the tree trunk sprouting from a small table in the corner.

In a moment she was at rapt attention, and Egan's kiss had been reduced to a dull roar that still played tricks with her hearing. "Egan, it's wonderful!"

"My mother says she thought for weeks about what to build for me. Joe already had a log cabin with a pioneer family. Rich had a stable with horses and cows and real straw. Mom knew she was going to have to make Gary a fire station when he got old enough, because from the age of two on, he never went anywhere without his fireman's hat."

"And that left the tree house for you." Chloe reached inside and drew out the fuzziest, tiniest squirrel she had ever seen. "This is wonderful."

"That's Chatters." He held out another. "And this is Merlin."

There were four other squirrels inside the hollowed-out log. They lived in four wonderful rooms, with squirrel-size furniture and utensils. They had a family history as elaborate as any Chloe had ever heard, and personalities that set them apart from each other. They ate at a table with a checkered cloth, bathed in a squirrel-size basin and slept in cozy little bunk beds.

As Chloe held Chatters in the palm of her hand, she could almost hear the squeals of a five-year-old Egan as he lectured and cajoled and moved his furry playmates from room to room. She looked up into the eyes of the twenty-nine-year-old Egan and almost drowned in them.

"No one sees my tree house, unless I'm very sure about them," Egan said solemnly.

She smiled, because there was nothing else she could do. The smile felt as if it stretched into infinity.

The kiss that followed—a kiss they were both helpless to control—almost did.

Driving back to the Resort, Chloe felt a peculiar sort of emptiness settle over her. Egan had shared so much with her today. His family, his Christmas traditions, his childhood, his patience, some portion of his heart. And what had she shared?

Nothing. She had never shared anything with him but caution and fear. She had blocked his attempts to get close to her until he had to be bruised from trying. She kept her secrets locked tightly inside her, guarding them from the laughter of others. But what had she ever gained by doing so?

What had she gained from keeping Egan at a distance?

And what joy had she already received today from letting him into her life?

She searched for something to tell him, something to share that wouldn't make him sad. Then she knew.

"Egan?"

"If you're going to tell me you want me to turn around and take you back to my place, I can make a U-turn up ahead."

She put her hand on his knee and felt his muscles contract in response. "Have I ever told you that I have family somewhere?"

He heard her trying to be casual. Had she ever told him? She'd never even told him her middle name. "No," he said, trying to be casual, too. He covered her hand. "You haven't." He waited.

"In Greece."

"That's a pretty far somewhere."

She was quiet for a while. He thought she might be finished. Frustration filled him, but he knew better than to communicate it to her.

He was surprised when she continued. "My father was from Greece, one of the smaller islands, only I don't know which one. My mother told me once when I asked why I didn't have grandparents like my friends did. She said I had lots of family in Greece, but that my father was angry at them. He left home and came to the U.S. without even telling them where he was going."

"And that's all you know?"

"That's all."

"Palmer isn't a Greek name."

"I don't think his name was really John Palmer. I think he changed it."

"Did anyone try to find your relatives after your parents died?"

"My caseworker tried, but I don't think he tried very hard. I was one of dozens of kids on his caseload, and it was just easier to keep me in foster care. Having family somewhere made it tricky to have me released for adoption. So I stayed a ward of the state."

"Have you tried to find your family?"

She was silent for so long that he thought he had frightened her away. More frustration filled him at having to continue this cat-and-mouse game with her. Kissing Chloe had been everything he had known it would be, and suddenly his patience was hanging by a thread.

"I'm saving my money," she said at last. "To hire a detective. I'll have enough in a few more months to start the search. But it won't be easy. Everything my parents owned was destroyed in the fire that killed them. I don't have a name or a place to go on. Nothing, except that Daddy was from Greece.''

''And your mother?''

''Had no family. That part was easy for the state to determine.''

He was surprised she had shared so much. And oh so pleased. ''You'll find them,'' he said.

''Do you really think so?''

''Somewhere you have relatives. And they'll want to know you as much as you want to know them.''

She released a deep breath. Telling him hadn't been so hard. She had kept that secret since childhood, afraid, terribly afraid, that someone might discourage her or tell her she was foolish to care. Now it was no longer a secret. It was a fact. Egan understood. Egan believed she would be successful.

''Egan? Thank you.''

He released a deep breath, too. He wanted to say he had done nothing at all. He wanted to confront the people who had so carelessly dismissed the child Chloe's need to have a family of her own. He wanted to stop the car and hold her and tell her that she had a family now. Him. His family. Forever and ever. Instead, he just kept driving.

''You're welcome.'' She shut her eyes and relaxed against the seat.

Chapter Three

"Fifteen dollars, three chocolate bars and a fast-food gift certificate in every girl's stocking. Two paperbacks apiece. New coats for the ones who need 'em. Sweaters and what? Jeans for the ones who don't?"

"Absolutely not jeans!" Chloe looked up and saw the surprised expression on Martha's face. "I'm sorry. I didn't mean to sound so vehement."

"Something wrong with jeans?"

There was nothing wrong with jeans, just something wrong with Chloe's Christmas memories. She grimaced. "Let's go for something a little more frivolous."

Martha went back to her list, pen poised. "Like?"

The debate had been going on all morning. Chloe imagined that if she ever had children of her own, choosing *their* presents would be a breeze. Few decisions were made at the Resort without staff consensus. That was part of what made the program work so well, but sometimes it made even the smallest choices exhausting.

"Jewelry, maybe?" she suggested. "ID bracelets? Chains or lockets? Simple earrings for the girls with pierced ears?"

"Bunny wants to get her ears pierced. And she wants ruby earrings."

"Too much money," Chloe said. "Way too much."

"Everything is too much money."

"We'll get a good deal on the coats. Two retailers have promised discounts."

"Probably last year's coats."

"Well, the styles aren't so different from this year's. The girls won't know."

"Ha!"

There was a knock on the office door and a giggle on the other side. "Come in," Chloe called.

Mona opened the door just wide enough to poke her head through. "I get a check mark on my chart for this. I'm running an errand."

Chloe tried not to smile. "Run it first, Mona, then ask for credit."

"There's somebody downstairs to see you." Mona directed her message to Chloe. "A lady named Mrs. O'Brien. She says she's Egan's mother. Isn't Egan too old to have a mother?"

"*I* have a mother," Martha said.

Mona's eyes widened, but, surprisingly, somewhere she had learned the self-control not to comment. Chloe silently decided to give her two check marks. "Would you tell her I'll be right down?"

"Sure. Besides, she's giving out Christmas cookies, and I don't want to miss mine."

Chloe guessed that Mona had already taken twice her share, anyway. "Be sure Jenny gets some."

Mona rolled her eyes. "I already did."

Chloe couldn't help herself. She rose and gave Mona a spontaneous hug. "I really do like you," she said.

"You're always saying that!"

"She likes *you,* too," Martha said when Mona was gone. "She's been trying a lot harder since you spoke to her on Sunday."

"I told her I'd personally move her into the smallest room in the house if she didn't get her act together."

"Yeah, yeah . . ."

"Well, I did! Sort of."

"Go see your guest. I'll finish up here and start making calls to get some prices."

Chloe was stopped three times before she could get all the way down the wide staircase. Dottie had just finished giving out the last bag of cookies when Chloe found her in the kitchen. She was watering a plant on the windowsill as if she had always lived in the house.

"What a nice surprise," Chloe said, and meant it.

Dottie answered with a hug. Chloe hugged her back before she could even think about it.

"I came to see if you had time to go Christmas shopping with me," Dottie said.

"Right now?"

"I know you're probably busy."

Officially, Wednesday afternoon was time off for Chloe, only she rarely bothered to take it. Suddenly taking it seemed like the best idea in the world. "I'd love to go," she said. "I haven't even thought about shopping."

"Great. I'm glad I stopped by. And I'm glad I had a chance to see this house. It's spectacular."

Chloe smiled proudly. "Let me give you a tour."

She showed Dottie every nook and cranny. Months before she would have had to apologize for all the problems, the faulty heating system, the plaster flaking off the walls and ceiling, the loose floorboards, the antique bathrooms. Now she could point with pride to those repairs and to the lovingly refinished paneling, the new paint and wallpaper, the rooms that had been cleverly divided or enlarged so not to compromise the integrity of the architecture. The house was far from finished, but even so, it was already a source of pride.

"O'Brien Construction did it all," Chloe said on the stairs leading to the third floor. "And if we hadn't found your sons, I don't know what we would have done."

"Do you mind climbing these stairs every day?" Dottie paused to rest a moment.

"Not at all. I'll show you why." She unlocked her door and ushered Dottie in.

"This is wonderful." Dottie admired the suite of rooms.

"Egan's idea and hard work. The board didn't want to spend anything on a director's suite. They thought it would be cheaper to raise my salary so I could just find an apartment nearby. But when I told Egan, he figured out how to do it so cheaply that the board couldn't say no. He worked two weekends to finish it for me. The girls helped me paint it."

"Why was it important to be right here? I'd almost think you'd need to get away every night."

"The girls need someone consistent in their lives. Someone they can count on. Someone who doesn't change with the shifts."

"Someone like a mother?"

"I wish."

Dottie touched her arm, as if she understood. "Let's go. We'll eat first. Lunch is my treat."

Lunch *was* a treat. They chatted about everything, clothes they both liked and their tastes in music and movies. Chloe told Dottie silly stories from her college days, and Dottie told tales about Egan's exploits as a toddler. Three hours after lunch, arms laden with Dottie's Christmas presents, they found another restaurant where they ordered coffee and French silk pie.

"I have never seen anybody shop with both hands the way you do," Chloe said. "Never!"

"I'm just getting started." Dottie sat back and slipped off her shoes. "And *you* didn't get started at all."

Perry Como was asking a musical "Do you see what I see?" over the restaurant loudspeakers, while outside the window a thin but cheerful Santa Claus jingled a bell over an iron kettle that wasn't filling up with donations fast enough. "I guess I'm in shock," Chloe said. "Christmas always throws me for a loop."

"Don't you like Christmas?"

"Well, I did... when I was very little."

"What are some of the things you liked?"

Chloe tried to remember. After her parents died she hadn't wanted to think about the holidays with them. It had been too painful. But she was an adult now, and, strangely, she found that the memories were still there, hazy perhaps, but still somewhere inside her. And they weren't painful anymore.

She smiled a little. "I always got to hang the star at the top of our tree. My father would lift me up high over his head, and I would put it on the highest branch. And my mother would bake baklava. Of course, I didn't know what it was then, but someone served it to me again when I was in college, and I remembered."

"Have you ever made it yourself?"

Chloe shook her head.

"I'll teach you how."

"Don't tell me it's part of your family Christmas tradition."

"No. It's too good just for Christmas."

Chloe sipped her coffee, and when Dottie didn't say anything else, she continued. "We always had a real tree. We would go out to a lot and choose the prettiest one we could find. And when the star was hung, we would sing carols. My father would sing in a language I didn't understand. Once my mother told me it was Greek, and that he had learned the songs from his father.''

"I would say those are very good memories.''

"Very good. My parents...well, they were wonderful.''

"And you miss them, still.''

"Yes.'' Chloe found that very easy to admit to Dottie. It was almost as if Dottie expected her to be honest about her feelings, as if her feelings were important and completely understandable.

Just like Egan.

"Dottie...'' Chloe looked up. "Egan tells me you make dollhouses.''

The dollhouses were all masterpieces. As soon as Dottie realized she had a fellow enthusiast sitting across the table from her, she cheered Chloe on until the pie was a memory and they were out on the busy sidewalks again.

The store where Dottie sold her houses was only six blocks from where she had parked her car. A bell tinkled merrily as they made their way inside. A village of miniature houses flanked the doors, each decorated with twinkling lights and tiny Christmas trees.

The proprietor made a fuss over Dottie, then over Chloe, before she was called away to help a customer.

"I'll show you mine first,'' Dottie said. "They're the best.''

They were the best, the most incredible dollhouses Chloe had ever seen. As a child she had wanted a simple little house with lights that turned on and off and sturdy furniture she could move from room to room. These houses were museum-quality, with hardwood floors that had been lovingly laid, piece by tiny piece, and stairs with carved wood trim. The fireplaces were real stone veneer; the tubs and sinks were genuine porcelain.

Chloe picked up the crib in an old-fashioned nursery complete with a nanny in uniform. There were beads hardly larger than poppy seeds decorating the side of the crib, just like those on full-size ones Chloe had seen.

"I've never imagined anything so wonderful," she said. "Never. But could a child play with this?"

"The houses are built for children. I'm always careful to be sure of that, even if I have to sacrifice a little detail. Some of the furniture isn't appropriate for young children, but we always suggest parents buy sturdier, less expensive things for them until they're old enough to start collecting."

Chloe came to attention. "Collecting?"

"Lots of adults buy these houses for themselves. You didn't realize that, did you?"

"Not really. I never thought about it."

"Collecting's just an excuse. There's a little girl inside each one of us."

Chloe was surprised. "Do you think so?"

"Absolutely. Why else would I spend my time doing this when I could make twice as much money doing almost anything else?"

Later that afternoon, back at the Resort, Chloe thought about the little girl inside her when Egan came to finish what his mother had started.

"Not more Christmas shopping!" She shook her head, but the little girl inside her, who had been enchanted with the hustle and bustle of shoppers, the piped-in carols, the insidious magic of Christmas, was screaming "yes."

And "yes" at spending time with Egan, too.

"Chloe." Egan smiled his cockeyed smile. "My mother told me you shopped all afternoon. But this'll be different. I've just got a few things left to buy." He reached for a lock of her hair and watched in fascination as it slithered over her shoulder.

She felt the tug in odd places inside her. "Christmas is three weeks away. There's plenty of time to shop."

"Please?" He reeled her in closer. "I don't want to go without you."

She wondered where her defenses had disappeared to. Apparently the stone she had built them from was only for show, like the stone on Dottie's miniature fireplaces. She tried to be stern. "One store. Just one store."

From the expression on his face, she knew he saw right through her.

He chose the largest department store in the largest mall in the city. As they slowly made their way through the aisles, she relished being pushed against him again and again by the crowd, searching for his golden hair and masculine profile when they were accidentally separated, watching his large, strong hands stroke the smooth satin of a conspicuously displayed nightshirt, the plush pile of a mohair scarf.

She relished all those things, plus the sheer exhilaration of being the object of his cockeyed grin, but she couldn't imagine why he'd demanded company or moral support just to buy Rich a silly sports video. Four men's departments—and no sales—later, she began to understand.

"Look, aren't these pretty?" he asked. Egan pointed out a display of birthstone earrings on the top shelf of a glass case in the jewelry department. "Reasonable, too."

She looked at the price and whistled. "Forty-five dollars isn't reasonable. It's extravagant."

"They pierce ears here for free, though. Can't have them done somewhere cheap, or you have to worry about infection."

"I think you'd look cute," Chloe said. "Your stone is a diamond, right?" She peeked at him and saw his cheeks turn pink. "Which ear, is the question?" she continued. "I always forget which is traditional for men. Maybe you should pierce both of them. And if you get tired of diamonds, I probably have an extra hoop. I'm terribly attracted to pirates."

She felt a hand under her elbow, and she was summarily dragged away from the display case. "No hoop?" she asked innocently.

"Let's look at toys."

"Whoever for?" she asked, knowing the answer full well.

They looked at trucks first, then footballs and handheld video games. Slowly, so slowly, Chloe felt Egan edge her toward the dolls.

"Dolls and earrings and angora sweaters," she said. "You certainly have eclectic taste."

"Look at this. These things are so lifelike I could swear that baby doll in the corner has colic." They stopped in front of a shelf of fashion dolls.

She faced him, arms folded. "I'm on to you, you know."

"On to me?"

She leaned against a pegboard shelf holding enough clothes to outfit Princess Di. "You."

"I might have kids someday. I just like to check things out. You want to have kids someday, don't you?"

"You are shopping for *my* girls! You are trying to soften me up so I'll let you. You're trying to fill me with Christmas spirit."

"Is it working?"

"What am I going to do with you?"

He stopped pretending. "Let me play Santa Claus."

She shook her head, although it took more effort than she'd expected. "We've been through this before."

"But you've had time to think about it now."

"I haven't changed my mind."

There was a subtle change in his expression. She saw that he wasn't angry that she was thwarting him again— still. Instead, he was sad, as if the girls' holiday wishes had somehow become his own.

"It's not that—" she began.

He waved away her explanation. "You still don't understand, do you? Christmas isn't about hard work and earning gifts. Christmas is about dreams and miracles. It's about things that can happen when you least expect them."

Chloe clamped her lips shut and searched his face. Egan stood there, profoundly saddened because he could not play Santa Claus. Saddened because the world was the kind of place it was, and he wasn't going to be allowed to change it.

As she stared at him, he made one last attempt to change her mind. He touched her cheek. "Chloe, Christmas is about trusting, about believing that for no reason at all something wonderful can appear out of nowhere, just for you."

She was afraid something wonderful had appeared just for her, and it—*he*—was standing in, of all the ridiculous places, a brightly lighted department store in front of a shelf filled with doll clothes. Everything inside her melted into a sentimental puddle. There wasn't another man in the world like this one. There couldn't be. She was sure of it.

For one brief moment, caution dissolved, and she leaned forward and kissed him. She didn't care if the other shoppers noticed; she didn't care if she threw Egan completely off-balance. She didn't care what the kiss told him.

Except for one thing.

"I can't let you do it," she said regretfully when she finally realized that two preschoolers were watching from three yards away, their baby chins scraping their velvet coat collars.

"You can't?" Egan's voice was unusually husky.

"I can't. Everything I told you before still goes. It's my responsibility to make sure the girls at the Resort learn that they don't need the attentions of some mythical fat philanthropist who may or may not slide down their chimneys from year to year. Who's going to make Christmas for them when you're not there to do it, Egan? I can't let them get used to something that might be snatched away next Christmas, or the next."

"And what if it isn't?"

"Don't you realize how precarious their lives are? I fight for them, but when it comes right down to it, I can't keep them at the Resort if the state says they have to go somewhere else. And when they're back home with minimally competent parents, or in a detention center, or a foster home like some of the ones I lived in, who's going to be Santa Claus for them? You? You won't even know where they've gone."

"At least they'd have the memory of one perfect Christmas. One perfect Christmas, when all their dreams came true."

She stared at him for a long time. It was a great temptation. She was sure Egan had no idea how tempting it was. But then she remembered Christmas after Christmas when she had been like the girls. Waiting. Hoping. Until she had learned her lesson.

She shook her head regretfully. "It wouldn't be enough. They need to learn that they have to make their own dreams come true. Now. When it won't hurt so much."

He sighed. A tired, defeated sigh. "Okay."

Her heart—and her resolve—twisted a little. "Okay?"

"I don't have the right to keep hacking away at you on this. I trust you. And I don't want to make you unhappy. I care too much about you."

She couldn't help herself. "You do?"

"What do you think?"

She thought she was probably the luckiest woman in the world. Strange to realize it here, with "Jingle Bell Rock" buzzing overhead and two tiny, dumbstruck strangers standing at her feet. Strange to realize it when she had just told Egan he could not have something he really wanted.

"I think you're...something else," she said in a husky voice.

"That'll have to do, I guess. For now." He held out his arm. "Come on, let's go. It's time to get you home."

Somehow she wanted to say more, but there was nothing left to say, was there? She linked her arm through his, and they stepped around the toddlers and walked through the store and back into the mall.

Chapter Four

One week before Christmas, Egan found the kitten. He had entered an alleyway to get a side view of an apartment building he planned to renovate. Busy peering three stories above him, he almost didn't see the tiny stray. From the corner of his eye, the scrap of black fur looked like a child's bedraggled earmuff, thrown out with the week's garbage. Then the earmuff trembled and mewed pitifully, and without another thought Egan whisked the kitten under his jacket and nestled it against his chest.

He spent another ten minutes looking for the remainder of the litter, or perhaps a mother cat who had been too frightened by his appearance to rescue her baby. But the alley turned up no new creatures. Wherever the kitten had come from, it—she, he ascertained quickly enough—was alone, and nearly frozen.

Back inside the building, he examined his find. She was already warmer and more active, and he judged from the activity that he had probably rescued her in time. She was tiny and thin, but there was enough meat on her bones to have helped her withstand the cold. Her long fur was completely black, except for microscopic white paws and a heart-shaped spot just under her chin. Clean, with her fur fluffed out, she might have been cute. As it was, she looked exactly like the alley kitten she was.

Immediately he thought of Chloe.

Then he lectured himself. Chloe had never shown the slightest interest in having a pet. During their one abortive Christmas-shopping expedition, he had steered her through the mall on the way back to his car, and they had passed a pet shop. He had stopped—because he was biologically incapable of *not* stopping to croon over animals—and Chloe had been forced to stop, too. There had been three Siamese kittens playing together, and he had laughed at their antics. Chloe had been quiet—bored, perhaps—beside him.

"They'll be gone before the end of the day," he'd said. "Do you want to go in and see if they'll let us hold one?"

She'd looked at her watch. "Maybe another time."

"A woman who doesn't like kittens?"

She'd given him a peculiar look, her Chloe-closed-off look. "I really can't stay. We're having a staff meeting at nine tonight."

And they had left the kittens playing in the window.

This kitten was nothing like the pet shop's picture-perfect specimens. It wasn't purebred or well nourished. It was dirty, sad and cold.

And still he thought of Chloe.

Maybe it was because Chloe had been orphaned, too. Certainly she had never been thrown out into the cold. Her basic needs had been met. But she had been left to shiver on the inside, to long for the warmth and love of a real home, and a family that wouldn't change with the seasons.

The kitten mewed and cuddled into his palm. His hand vibrated with her baby purrs. He held her up to his cheek, and her tiny eyes opened. It was like looking into Chloe's eyes when she was most vulnerable.

"Do you want a home?" he asked softly. "Because I think I might know just the place."

The kitten shut her eyes and fell asleep.

Gary O'Brien had stopped by last week to measure the windows for replacements, and to ask Chloe's opinion about perfume for a woman he had dated several times. Joe had taken Chloe aside in the middle of renovating a basement office to tell her what Dick was giving Dottie for Christmas. And Rich, who didn't even work with his brothers in the company, had made it a point to call one evening and offer her six tickets to a Greek dinner the following month at a local Orthodox church.

"How did you come by that many tickets?" she had asked.

"I helped a member of the church get citizenship last year," he explained. "I thought you and some of your girls might enjoy attending."

They *would* enjoy it, of course. She had already posted a notice on the incentive bulletin board, and she planned to chaperon. She wondered if Egan had told Rich about her mysterious heritage, and if that was why he had thought of her.

She really wondered why any of them did. And not just Egan's brothers. His father had dropped by several days ago to inspect the renovations and invite her out for coffee. And Dottie. Dottie, who three times in the past few weeks had whisked her along snow-covered roads back to her country house, where they had baked and laughed and, yes, sewn slipcovers for a rush order on a perfectly wonderful dollhouse.

If there had ever been even the slightest trace of compassion in the way Egan's family treated her, she would have been mortified. But there were no hints, none whatsoever, that any of them wanted to spend time with her because she had no family of her own. Despite the small voice inside her that still asked why, she was beginning to think that the answer might be simple. The O'Briens liked her. She filled a hole in their family that had always been there. She was the sister Egan's brothers had never had, the daughter Dottie—and, she suspected Dick, too—had always longed for. She was available to participate in all their corny Christmas secrets and traditions, and they were grateful.

Grateful to her. It was almost funny.

But not quite. No, it wasn't quite funny, because all the attention, all the enveloping warmth of being part of the O'Brien family, was beginning to mean so much to her that it couldn't be funny. Wonderful, maybe. An experience to be cherished. But not funny.

Then, of course, there was Egan. Egan of the holly green eyes and the shoulders wide enough to take on anything and everything. Egan, who hadn't been able to spend last Saturday afternoon with her because he was playing Santa Claus on the children's ward of a local hospital. Egan, who, she had ascertained from a careful audit of the renovation bills, wasn't going to make one thin dime on his work at the Resort.

Sitting at the top of the Resort's front steps, hands poised to catch the long paper chain that Roxanne had fashioned to decorate the banister, Chloe tried to banish Egan from her thoughts. But, as always, it was next to impossible.

Roxanne tossed the chain toward her. The fact that she had noticed Chloe was there was nearly as surprising as the chain itself. Chloe was encouraged that the girl knew it was Christmas, and more encouraged that Roxanne had felt compelled to do something about the holiday. The task had been perfect for her at this stage of her emotional development. Repetitive, soothing, simple.

"My sister and I made a chain like this once," Roxanne said. "We wrapped it around a tree outside our apartment. Around the tree. Around the tree." She slowly twirled one finger in the air.

Chloe almost forgot to breathe. She forced a neutral, carefully unemotional comment. "You miss your sister."

"At Christmas, especially." Roxanne smiled a wistful little smile.

It was the first smile, the first expression of emotion Chloe had ever seen on the child's face. She wanted to hug her. She wanted to shout in jubilation.

She wanted to cry.

"It's very hard to lose someone you love," Chloe said, in the same restrained voice.

"How do you know?" Roxanne sounded as if she were really interested. A connection was being established. A very slight, very tentative connection.

Chloe said a small, silent prayer. "I lost both my parents, when I was seven," she said.

"You did?"

"For a very long time, I didn't want to feel anything."

"My parents are still alive."

"I know."

"They hurt me. And Mary Jane."

"I know."

"Why?"

Chloe searched for an answer. "Because no one ever taught them how to be good parents, Roxanne. Someone must have hurt them when they were children, too."

"I hate them."

"Yes, I know."

"That's bad, isn't it?"

"No. I don't think so. Feelings are never bad."

"*I* don't hurt people, even when I hate them."

"Then you're already more grown-up than they were."

"I don't ever want to see them again."

"You don't have to. Not ever."

"You're sure?"

"Absolutely."

Roxanne looked down and fingered the chain. "Really?"

"Really. You can ask me every single day, if you like, and I'll tell you the same thing."

"Mary Jane's favorite color was red. I used a lot of red in this chain."

"You could make a chain every Christmas for Mary Jane. To remember her by."

"Do you still remember your parents?"

"Oh, yes."

That seemed to satisfy Roxanne. Carefully, as Chloe held her end, Roxanne wound the chain in and out the balusters, until it was a bright banner of color on the mahogany staircase. When she was nearly finished, she removed the last loop from the chain, a red one, and placed it in her pocket. "To keep with me," she explained.

Then she disappeared down the hall.

Egan found Chloe sitting on the steps. He couldn't recall ever having seen her quite this still, quite this pale and visibly shaken.

He sat beside her and put his arm around her shoulders. She leaned against him and turned her face into his neck.

"Can I help?" he asked.

He felt her shake her head.

"Do you want to call off the caroling tonight?"

She shook her head again.

"You might want to after you hear me sing. You've never heard me sing, you know."

"Just keep your arms right where they are for a minute." The words were smothered against his collar.

"Hey, we can sit this way forever."

"Not quite that long."

He waved at Bunny and Jennifer, who were passing by in the hallway below.

"I grew an inch," Jennifer called up to him. "A whole inch! The doctor says I'm on a growth spurt."

He wanted to cheer. "Terrific, Stretch! Now go eat a couple of hamburgers and grow another one."

"What's wrong with Chloe?"

"I think she's tired." He felt Chloe nod. "She says yes."

"She can't be tired. We're going caroling, aren't we?" Bunny asked.

"I'll carry her piggyback," Egan said.

Giggles trailed behind the girls as they disappeared.

Egan thought his neck was suspiciously moist. "An inch?" he asked softly. "That's a good sign, isn't it? Chloe, I'd do anything in the world for you, sweetheart, but if you shake or nod once more, my neck is going to be permanently dislocated."

Her laugh sounded as if she were strangling. She raised her tear-streaked face to his. "Are we alone?"

"Momentarily."

"Good." She found his lips with hers. He tasted salt and sentiment and liked the combination immensely. Warmth filled him, turning rapidly to desire. Desire was lightning quick these days. Her voice on the telephone, the subtle drift of her special fragrance, a glimpse of satin black hair, and immediately he ached for her touch.

"Piggyback?" she asked at last, with a sad little hiccup.

"That was just for effect. You walk."

"Darn."

"You're sure you're up to this?"

"I'd be lynched if I said no. Nine girls signed up to go with us. That's a record. I've never had nine girls agree to do anything."

"I'm amazed three of them could resist my charm."

"Shandra has a sore throat, and Vicky and Lianne are going to a concert at school."

"Acceptable excuses." He stood up, because he was too tempted to kiss her again. Temptation doubled when he watched her bare her midriff as she lifted the hem of her turtleneck to wipe her eyes. He turned away. "Let's round them up."

The night was crisp and cold, and snow from a recent fall crunched under two dozen booted feet. The Shadyside neighborhood surrounding the street where the Alma Benjamin Home had been built one hundred years ago was one of graceful older homes adhering to an architectural style dubbed "Gilded Age high-ceilinged." The exploits of the girls at the home had not always been looked on favorably by their neighbors, but forgiveness had generally been the watchword. Tonight Chloe hoped they could make up just a little for past indiscretions.

The first house had tasteful wreaths tied with red ribbons at every window, illuminated by soft golden floodlights. A single elegant taper burned on every sill.

"This is a 'Silent Night' kind of house," Egan said.

"That's a dumb song. I don't understand it. Who's John Virgin, anyway?" one of the girls asked. "And why is he round?"

"Because he ate too many Christmas cookies," Egan answered. He hummed a note. "Everybody ready?"

"Well, he's a pig! I hope he gave some to his mother and child."

"Just sing." Egan began the hymn in a clear, mellow baritone. Chloe joined in, and little by little the girls took it up until they were carrying it by themselves.

"Little angels," Egan whispered in Chloe's ear.

"Too many Christmas cookies?" she whispered back.

"Did you want me to get into the entire story of the Nativity?"

"Never lie to these kids, Egan. They'll catch you every time."

"You explain the virgin birth to her, then."

Lights came on in the hallway of the house and the front door opened. The girls sang on gamely. When they'd finished they went on to "O Little Town of Bethlehem" with Egan's help.

The residents of the house insisted on giving Martha a donation. The girls had decided ahead of time that if that happened they would send the money to UNICEF. By the look on Martha's face after they had caroled at the next three houses, Chloe guessed that a hungry child in Africa or Asia was going to have several months of meals courtesy of the Last Resort.

By prior arrangement, the last house they visited belonged to the chairman of the Resort's board of direc-

tors, who just happened to have prepared a dozen cups
of cocoa with marshmallows and plate after plate of
Christmas goodies. Chloe kept her eye on the Persian
carpets, and Martha kept hers on the fragile bone china.
Egan charmed the chairman into a medley of carols at
the full-size Steinway grand that took up only a small
portion of the living room. The girls stood around the
piano and sang, and by the time they were ready to leave,
the chairman had agreed to give three interested girls piano lessons.

"It's too bad she didn't have a horse on the prem-
ises," Chloe said, trailing the girls back to the Resort,
Egan at her side. "You could have wheedled riding lessons for Mona, too."

"Not necessary. My parents are willing to keep a horse
or two for that purpose."

She stopped. "You're kidding."

He took her hand and pulled her along beside him.
"Nope."

"I thought you said they didn't want to fuss with large
animals?"

"They don't, necessarily. But they'd do it if it meant
having some of the girls come out to the house regu-
larly. We're not talking Thoroughbreds, just a couple of
sturdy, gentle nags."

"You're incorrigible."

"Think about it. I'll await your command."

"What am I going to do with you?"

He wondered about that himself, particularly considering what was waiting for her back at the house. They
finished the remainder of the walk without speaking,
listening as the girls made up silly verses to "Jingle
Bells," until they were inside the Resort once more.

"Can you stay a while?" Chloe asked.

"A little while," he said.

She started up the stairs. The evening had made her daring. "Let's go up to my suite and get away from the crowd."

"Good idea." He collared some of the crowd to drag along with him.

"Hey, what're you doing?" Mona asked, trying to escape Egan's strong arm around her neck.

"Yeah, what?" Heidi, a dark-haired, dark-skinned beauty, demanded.

"I just haven't had a chance to talk to you two in a while. Come on up and fill me in on school."

Chloe turned around and shot him a questioning look.

"That's okay, isn't it?" he asked.

"Well . . ."

He dragged Mona to the next step. "Tell me about the play you're in."

"I told you about it yesterday!"

"But you didn't tell me what you did today, did you? I mean, the play's tomorrow, isn't it? You must have had your dress rehearsal." He chatted nonstop without giving either girl a chance to say another word. One glance at Chloe's stiff back told him her reaction to the unwelcome guests.

But he wasn't going to face her by himself when she opened her apartment door. No, he was not.

Chloe kept her door locked to discourage snooping. Now she fiddled with her key while Egan kept up the chatter. She couldn't imagine what had possessed him to bring Mona and Heidi along. She and Egan had never had much time alone together. Now that she was offering some—offering it against her own best instincts—he was acting as if he would prefer a crowd. Hurt sneaked over her lowered defenses and reminded her why she should continue to be cautious.

Just inside the doorway, she snapped on a lamp. The soft pastels of her rooms soothed her a little. She had furnished the front room with sturdy old furniture that she had re-covered in soft floral prints. There was a sofa plumped high with blue-and-green cushions, a rocking chair with a needlepoint insert and a curled-up black kitten, a wing chair with a crocheted—

"Kitten?"

"Where?" Egan looked around nonchalantly. He tightened his grips on Heidi and Mona's necks. No way were they going anywhere now.

Chloe slowly crossed the room. The tiniest, fluffiest kitten she had ever seen was sleeping smack-dab in the middle of a needlepoint flower arrangement. The kitten was decked out in a red velvet bow, and someone had obviously spent time brushing and combing its downy black fur.

"Where did this kitten come from?" Chloe asked.

"I don't see a kitten. Do you girls see a kitten?"

"Egan, I'm asking you a question."

Heidi and Mona wiggled free to see what the fuss was all about. The kitten took that moment to yawn and stretch. Its little eyes opened and stared directly into Chloe's.

Egan couldn't decide whether to hightail it or confess and take his punishment. He did neither. He just stared at the ceiling and busied himself trying to decide if it needed a second coat of paint.

"Look, it's got a little teeny white spot just under its chin. Like a heart." Mona knelt so that she was kitten-level and examined it. "You could call it Valentine."

"I could, if it was my kitten," Chloe said.

Without looking down, Egan weighed and reweighed the traces of emotion in her voice. Still unsure of her reaction, he progressed to estimating the cost of a new light fixture.

"It has tiny white feet, too," Heidi said. "You could call it Boots. Or Mittens."

"Pick it up," Mona said. "It wants you to."

Chloe reached for the kitten, because the girls told her to. She was in shock. She would have done anything they said. The kitten was as soft as a feather, and as light as one, too. It mewed softly when she pressed it against her sweater and it snuggled into the folds.

"See, it likes being held," Mona said wisely.

"Did you ever have a kitten before?" Heidi asked Chloe.

"No."

"I did," Mona said. "Lots of them."

Chloe looked up from the kitten to search Mona's eyes.

"No, I didn't," Mona admitted. "But I wanted one."

Chloe tried to speak. She wanted to tell Mona that she had wanted one, too. It was the right thing to do, the director thing to do, the social-worker thing to do. But she couldn't get the words past the lump in her throat. She tried, and they sounded strangely like a sob.

She collapsed in the chair and held the kitten tighter. Tears streamed down her face.

"Chloe's crying," Mona said. "Egan, for God's sake, Chloe's crying!"

He was at Chloe's side in a heartbeat, kneeling at her feet. He felt like a heel, a complete and total slob. He had done this. How on earth had he done this?

"My Christmas list," she sobbed when the words would come. "This was at the top.... I wanted... I couldn't buy myself one later... It didn't mean the same... How on earth did you—"

He put his arms around her and held her, wanting to cry, too. He peeked at the girls and saw their distress. "She's happy," he assured them. "Very, very happy."

He wished somebody would reassure him.

"She doesn't look happy," Mona said doubtfully.

"Can the kitten breathe?" Heidi asked.

"Absolutely. I can hear it breathing," Egan said. "Go to bed."

"Bed," Mona said. "Right. Bed." She turned and grabbed Heidi. "Bed."

"Right." Heidi went willingly. "Good night. We're going to bed."

"They went to bed," Egan said, when the girls had closed the door softly behind them.

"My Christmas list," Chloe said, with a fresh flood of tears.

"Chloe...sweetheart...I'm sorry. I don't know what I've done, but I'm so, so sorry. It's just that I found the kitten in an alley, and I couldn't leave her there. She was a mess. A real mess. So I took her to the vet—" He didn't know why he was babbling this way. He just had to say something.

"The vet?"

"He says she's about six weeks old. Just old enough to make it away from her mother. He checked her over and gave her a shot. He thinks she'll be fine. Really. Of course, she had a shock when I gave her a bath, but then I rubbed her fur dry—"

"You gave her a bath?"

"Well, I had to. You wouldn't have wanted her the way I found her."

She clutched the kitten harder. "Not wanted her?"

"You're repeating everything I say." He stroked her cheek, brushing tears away. "Try this. I'm going to love you forever, Egan. And to show you, I'm going to go home with you tonight and we're going to make soul-shattering love until dawn." He waited expectantly.

"You're a psycho, you know that?"

"That's not quite what I said." He smiled tenderly and turned her face to his. "Do you want her, Chloe? I'll find another home if you really don't. I just thought...well, I just thought maybe you'd like to have her."

She swallowed. "Yes."

"What were you saying about a Christmas list?" He brushed away more tears—the final tears, he hoped.

"Christmas list?"

"Yeah."

"You probably didn't hear me right."

"Didn't I?"

She put her arms around him and pulled him close, fiercely, never-gonna-let-you-go close.

Purring contentedly as Chloe kissed Egan, the kitten settled into a furry ball in a corner of her lap and fell sound asleep again.

Chapter Five

On the Sunday before Christmas, Chloe woke up with Angel curled under her chin. Her bedroom was quiet, except for the chiming of church bells somewhere in the distance. She stretched, and Angel opened her eyes to pounce on a long strand of hair snaking across her pillow.

"Silly little Christmas present." Chloe lifted the kitten and kissed her nose. "And how did you get up here, anyway?"

Angel pounced again as soon as Chloe set her back on the pillow. Chloe untangled the kitten from her hair and got out of bed.

Winter sunshine flooded the room. From her third-story vantage point, she could see snow-dusted slate roofs and the twisted, leafless branches of century-old trees. The spire of the church chiming the gift of Christmas music was just visible to the west.

Christmas was nearly here, and she still hadn't gotten Egan a present. She didn't lack for ideas; she only lacked the right one. What did a woman get the man she was falling in love with? Nothing as plebeian as a tie or after-shave. Surely nothing as intimate as the silk boxer shorts she had seen in a lingerie boutique or the gilt-edged volume of erotic art from a downtown museum store.

What, then? She turned and watched Angel wiggle down the comforter to drop to the floor.

"So that's how you find your way up and down." She scooped Angel up in her palm and carried her into the kitchen, where the kitten gamely attacked her breakfast.

Nothing she could give Egan could possibly mean as much as Angel had meant to her. How had he known? She shook her head. Of course he hadn't known. Finding Angel had been an accident. Egan wasn't the kind of man who could leave an animal to suffer. And she had been the obvious choice to give the kitten a home. A pushover, really, although he hadn't known how much of one.

Accident or not, the gift hadn't meant any less than it would have when she was a child. Apparently there was still a little girl inside her who longed for the things she had never had.

And, increasingly, there was a woman inside her who longed for the man who had brought love and laughter into her heart—not to mention a tiny black angel.

She made herself breakfast and dressed. She had the day to do Christmas shopping, just this one last day, since tomorrow she and Martha had to finish shopping for the girls. She needed every minute. She would have to search every store in Pittsburgh to find Egan the perfect gift.

Hours later, searching through a dusty import shop in a section of town where she had never ventured, she found what she was looking for. The chess set sat amid the surrounding clutter, treasure amid trash. The board was crafted of alternating blocks of highly polished black and white stone. The chess pieces were hand-carved and individual, each with grace and character.

One queen, carved of a sleek black stone, had long hair that flowed to her waist in such a realistic manner that Chloe was sure that if she touched it it would cling to her fingers.

The queen looked like her.

The shopkeeper lifted his head and smiled as if he scented a sale.

Chloe clutched her purse a little tighter. "I don't know," she said, pretending doubt. "This set's a little stark for my tastes. But I have a friend who likes chess. I might think about it for him, if it's not too expensive."

Egan's apartment windows were dark when she arrived there half an hour after the bargaining had ended. The chess set was heavy and clumsy to carry, although now it was beautifully wrapped in marbleized paper and tied with real silk bows. She supposed the exceptional gift wrapping was the shopkeeper's way of apologizing for getting the best of the bargain.

At Egan's door, she reconsidered. She had accepted an invitation to his parents' home for Christmas Eve. Egan swore that Christmas Eve was the family's traditional time to open gifts, although she strongly suspected that the tradition was brand-new this year, because she wouldn't be able to be with them on Christmas morning.

But whether it was true or not, she *would* be with them on Christmas Eve, and Christmas Eve was the right time for Egan to open this present. So why was she standing at his door, knocking loud enough to wake everyone in Squirrel Hill?

"Chloe?" A water-beaded, shirtless Egan opened the door, towel in hand.

"I know you weren't expecting me."

He hadn't been expecting her; in fact, he had carefully schooled himself not to expect anything from her.

She was not a woman a man could tackle and carry off into the sunset. She had to be wooed. She had to be won. She had to be . . . swept into his arms.

Chloe leaned into Egan's kiss and willed it never to end. He smelled like soap and warm, wonderful male. Unerringly his supple fingers found the exact points of tension along her spine and eased them away. Just when she thought she might get her wish and kiss him forever, he tugged her into the apartment and closed the door behind them.

"Is that for me?"

She had almost forgotten the gift, although her arms were growing tired from holding it. She thrust it toward him. "Yes."

"It's a work of art."

"I know."

"Tell me there's nothing living inside."

"No puppies or kittens."

He took the gift and thought he might drown in the emotion in her eyes. He asked the right question. "Do you want me to open this now?"

"You don't have to. You probably should wait until Christmas Eve."

"Have-tos and probably-shoulds don't make an answer."

"Okay. I want you to open it right this minute."

"I thought so." He smiled his cockeyed smile. "Let me put a shirt on."

She wanted to protest. Egan without a shirt was better than her wildest fantasies. The hair on his chest was light and, without a doubt, as silky as it looked. He was tanned and muscular, a man who enjoyed using his body.

And that thought brought color to her cheeks.

"Unless you'd rather I didn't," he said.

Her gaze drifted to his hips, shrouded in low-slung jeans that had seen better days. She guessed there was nothing under those jeans except more water-dewed flesh.

"Maybe I'll just open the present first," he said.

She focused on something safer than Egan's bare skin—the gift in his hand. "I don't know if you're going to like it. It's probably silly. I don't even know if you..."

"If I what?"

"Open it, and then I'll tell you."

He motioned her to the sofa and sat close beside her. The soft wool of her blazer brushed against his side, and the spicy scent that was so much a part of her filled his senses. He put his arm around her and felt the sensuous silk of her hair glide along his nerve endings. Whatever she had gotten for him was not what he wanted most. Increasingly he realized that what he wanted for Christmas was Chloe. The woman. The whole woman.

"You untie it," he said. His tongue felt strangely thick.

"Okay. I know how you feel. This is too pretty to destroy."

The truth was that he was afraid if he tried to untie the ribbon, she would see that his hands were shaking. Her fingers were graceful, and far too slow. He watched her pick at the ribbon with her nails, and imagined her nails raking his back.

He told himself what he'd told himself many times before. He needed more patience and less imagination.

The same answer shuddered through his body. He needed Chloe.

When the ribbon dangled to the floor, he separated the paper and removed the top of the box. Black and white stone glistened in the soft light of his apartment. One by one he unwrapped and fingered the beautifully wrought chess pieces, then, finally, he uncovered the board itself.

"It's beautiful," he said, his voice sounding strained even to his own ears. "A wonderful, wonderful present."

She sat forward and put the chessboard on the coffee table. "Look, we can set it up here."

He watched her place the pieces, one by one. She was obviously pleased with her choice, almost childlike in her excitement. He had never desired her more.

"Look. She looks like me, don't you think?" She handed him the black queen.

The queen did resemble Chloe. She was slender hipped and full breasted, without doubt a woman. The hair, the proud posture, the grace, the poignant, yearning expression, were all Chloe.

"And the white king reminds me a little of you." She held the king up for him to see. "Although, of course, he's not as perfectly made."

She took the queen from his fingers and placed her beside the black king. "But there's a problem here," she said, not quite looking at him. "This queen wants to be with that king. Only they're separated, and they can't reach each other."

"What's keeping them apart?"

"Maybe they're afraid."

"They?"

"No. You're right. It's only the queen."

His heart sped faster. "What is she afraid of?"

"I think she might care too much about him. She's never felt this way about anyone before. She doesn't know what's going to happen." Chloe couldn't look at Egan. She couldn't bear to see if he understood.

Egan reached beyond her with one hand. The other rested at her waist. "Then he has to show her there's nothing to be afraid of," he said. He lifted the queen. "This is a magic carpet," he said. "Let's see what happens."

She leaned against him, and her eyelids drifted shut. He was warm, and his skin was as firm and smooth as the chess pieces. "Egan . . ." she said softly.

Something akin to a shudder ran through him at the promise in her voice. "The white king fights the black one for his woman. He's attacked by knights, by scheming bishops and foot soldiers who try but fail to capture him."

"Then they're doomed?"

"No. When all hope seems lost, the queen realizes she's had a choice all along. She jumps on the white king's carpet, and they fly far away to a place where no one and nothing can ever touch or hurt them. Where the white king will spend his life telling his beautiful queen that he loves her and that she has nothing to be afraid of." He set the two pieces side by side at the edge of the board.

"Does the queen tell the king that she loves him?"

"Every day."

"Does he really love her?"

"With all his heart."

"Then she's the luckiest woman in the world," Chloe said. "The very luckiest."

Fiercely he gathered her close. Her eyes opened and told him that he had understood her correctly. She wanted him; she would have him. Her lips settled against his. They were soft and generous and promising. She gave more than she had ever given him before, as if the invisible barriers that had separated them were gone and the castle walls that had kept his queen a prisoner had crumbled away.

Her hands rose to the top button of her blouse. "I have another gift for you," she whispered, as his lips traced the curve of her jaw.

"Tell me I'm not dreaming."

"Dream about me."

"I do. More than you know."

She unbuttoned the top two buttons, and his lips followed the path of her hands. He paused at the base of her throat to savor the pounding of her pulse while his own ran wild. Two more buttons and his lips grazed the white lace covering her full breasts. Two more and he rose and lifted her in his arms to carry her to his bedroom.

He didn't leave her while he undressed—undressing was only a zipper away. He laid her on his bed and settled against her, caressing her hip with one denim-clad knee. "This is more than making love," he whispered. "Much, much more."

"How much more?"

He told himself he still had to go slow. "As much as you want it to be," he said cautiously.

"It couldn't be enough. Not nearly enough."

He wondered if he would dissolve with joy. The words were abstract, but the promise in her voice was infinite. The white lace parted in his hands, and he knew the reality of his dreams. Her clothes fell away, and he found that passion had been her dream, too.

She was the black queen, and more. Her supple, perfect limbs demanded that he give her everything, and yielded everything to him. She had reservoirs of passion and intensity that he, in his most promising dreams, had never suspected. Hesitancy melted away, incinerated by the fire of their joining. He tasted and touched and forgot to be cautious.

She was everything his besotted brain had promised, warmth and secrets revealed, and an infinite capacity to love. She serenaded and surrounded him with her soft flesh, enticed him with the glorious length of her hair. She was as giving as he had known she would be, as abandoned and, somehow, just as innocent. She was woman and lover and heartmate. And when the explorations were over and desire could not be denied, she was part of him, the best part, the half he had longed for forever.

"You never told me if you play chess," Chloe said. The words surprised her. Except for their breathing, the room had been silent for a long time. She was amazed she could still speak, that the voice that came from her throat still sounded the same.

"And you never told me if you'd jump on my magic carpet and fly away with me."

"You never really asked."

He cuddled her closer. "Will you listen if I ask?"

"You don't play chess, do you?"

He kissed her earlobe, knowing she was evading his question. "I do, I love the game, and I'm very good. Almost as good at chess as I am at . . ." His voice trailed off, and for moment after moment there was silence again.

"If you're that good, you should compete," Chloe said at last.

"Do you know how long I've wanted you?"

"As long as I've wanted you?"

"I want you to marry me."

She almost turned away. But she couldn't hurt him that way. Instead, without looking at him, she covered him with her hair, wrapping him in it until they were cocooned together and the rest of the world was far away. "I'm dazzled, Egan," she said softly.

"Chloe, I think I've known I wanted to marry you since the first day we met. You were the most beautiful woman I'd ever seen. Inside, outside, everywhere it mattered. I saw you first with one of the girls. You were listening so intently to her that I realized nothing in the world would tear you away until she was finished. Everything you are was right there in your eyes. I walked out of that room and asked one of the counselors if you were married."

She was so touched she could hardly speak. Her voice emerged as a whisper, but she met his eyes. "And if I had been?"

"I couldn't have stayed around. You would have had to find another contractor."

"One who would have charged something for his trouble?"

He was silent.

"I know you aren't making anything at the Resort, Egan. I figured it out."

"It wasn't just my decision to bid low. My family agreed."

"Did you do it because you...love me?"

He realized he had never said the words. She needed to hear them. He tried them out. "I love you." The words felt like the release of all fears, the shining moment when darkness is replaced by light. "I love you."

"What can I bring you, when you've brought me so much?"

He rested his hand on her cheek so she wouldn't look away. "What can you possibly mean by that?"

"Sometimes I feel like you're looking inside me, figuring out all the things I've always wanted and giving them to me, one by one." She saw he didn't understand, but she still couldn't bring herself to talk about her childhood Christmas list.

He laughed a little. "I'm spoiling you rotten."

"Yes."

"But it's mutual."

"Is it?"

"I watched my parents together when I was growing up, and I knew I wanted someone I could love the way my father loved my mother. I'm twenty-nine now, and there hasn't been anyone like that for me. Not until now. And sometimes I was afraid there never would be."

She had seen the way women looked at Egan, enough to know that any number of females would have liked to try out for a place in his dreams. But he had waited. And now he had chosen her.

"You haven't said yes," he said gently.

There was so much to think about, so many feelings to sort out. She realized that understanding feelings— her own, anyway—was something she was not very good at.

"You don't have to say yes right now," he said. "But you could tell me you love me, too."

She thought of the man she had secretly longed for, the man who would love her best and think she was the most beautiful and special woman in the world. In that instant she knew that the man she had longed for was the man lying in her arms.

"I love you," she said. "I do love you, Egan."

He pulled her closer, although closer hadn't seemed possible.

She shut her eyes as he pulled her closer still. For no apparent reason, she thought of the girls at the Resort. Christmas lists and unexpected gifts. Determination and hard work and . . . unexpected gifts.

"What did I ever do to deserve you?" she whispered.

"You deserve everything. But love isn't about deserving." He kissed her fiercely. "Love is about love. Don't you understand, sweetheart? Love is nothing more or less than a miracle."

Chapter Six

On Christmas Eve, moonlight sparkled on snowdrifts, a million infant stars fallen to earth to light Chloe and Egan's trip to the O'Briens' house. Carols floated from the car radio and filled the comfortable gaps in the conversation. Chloe thought a more perfect night had never existed.

"What do you think the girls are doing right now?" Egan asked.

As director, Chloe had decided that the home needed unshakable Christmas traditions, traditions the girls could count on every holiday, no matter what else was topsy-turvy in their lives. Because of that, she knew exactly what the girls would be doing.

"Sitting down to the dinner they voted on." Chloe had counted the votes herself. Ham and roast beef had tied, and there had been unanimous agreement that nothing even vaguely green was to be served along with them. "And they'll be doing their level best to act like ladies for one night."

"No cursing or pinching?"

"Not tonight. They were choosing what to wear when we left. After dinner they're going to exchange presents. It has to be something they've made for each other, or a promise, like helping with homework or taking over that person's week of dishwashing."

"Good idea."

"Then they're putting on a little show."

"I heard Saint Nicholas—Mona wanted to come down the chimney, and you wouldn't let her."

"She does get to hide behind the fireplace screen and jump out. They're doing "Twas the Night before Christmas.' Jenny's going to play Rudolph."

"Show me Rudolph's name in the poem."

"This is their own personal version. Something like "Twas the night before Christmas, and at the Resort, Heidi got a zit, and Bunny a wart.'"

He gave a low whistle. "I'm sorry I'll miss it."

"They made me promise you'd come see them tomorrow."

"Of course I'll be there."

"Hands full of presents?"

"Just a few little things."

"Really?"

"Unless you change your mind before the stores close in about—" he glanced at his watch "—fifteen minutes."

"Think you could buy everything you want to give them in fifteen minutes?"

"I have salesclerks all over town just waiting for the go-ahead."

"I'll bet."

"There's a car phone in the trunk."

"Sure there is."

"With automatic dialing."

"I hate to tell you, Toto, but we're not in Pittsburgh anymore."

"There goes that idea." He turned onto the road leading to his parents' house. "You've made a good Christmas for the kids, Chloe. They seem happy."

"As happy as kids can be who aren't spending the holidays with their families."

"None of them are going home?"

"A few are leaving late tomorrow morning for an overnight. A few more might have visitors. Too few."

"That makes what you're doing even more important."

She smiled her warmest smile. "Tomorrow will be a good day for them. As good as I can make it."

"Are you going to make it a good day for me, too?"

For a moment she was afraid he was demanding an answer to his proposal. The past week had been wonderful, intimate and warm and undemanding. But she knew that Egan wasn't endlessly patient. He had asked her to marry him, and soon she had to give him an answer.

His eyebrows lifted suggestively, and with relief she understood his question. "I can't imagine what you mean," she said innocently.

"Santa Claus, all I want for Christmas is a little time alone with my woman."

She laughed. "Have you been naughty or nice, young man?"

He smiled, but it was an effort. He wondered if she would think he'd been naughty or nice when the evening was over. He was afraid their relationship might hinge on the surprise he had arranged for her.

"Santa will just have to see," she said.

The O'Briens' house was a blaze of red and green lights that blinked on and off so fast that Chloe had to close her eyes against dizziness. "It's very...Christmasy," she said when Egan came around to open her door.

Before she could get out of the car, he bent to kiss her. The kiss was unexpectedly passionate, considering that his entire family was looking on.

"Just look down at the path, and I'll guide you," he said when he had finally let her go. "We'll be inside before you know it."

The dogs came to greet them, followed closely by the O'Briens. Apparently no one wanted to risk being left out.

On the porch, Dick pressed a cup of hot spiked cider into Chloe's hand, while Dottie insisted loudly that somebody find the switch to adjust the lights. When Dottie was satisfied the house no longer looked like a roadside tavern, they went inside.

There was a fire in the fireplace and chestnuts roasting in the ashes. The house smelled like gingerbread and butter-basted turkey. When they were alone in the kitchen, Dottie dropped her arm around Chloe's shoulders. "We're not very formal, I'm afraid. I always had a rule that on Christmas Eve the boys had to sit at the table for the whole meal and wear their shoes, but that was the best I could do."

"I'd hate it if you were all stiff and formal. This—" Chloe paused.

"What, dear?"

"Well, this is a home, and you're a family."

"You're part of it, you know. We all love you."

Chloe didn't know where the tears came from. One moment she was taking part in a casual conversation, the next her eyes were blurred and her throat felt as if something were caught in it. She turned into Dottie's arms for a hug. "Thank you. I . . . love you, too."

"It's the funniest thing. I used to wish for a daughter. Oh, I was never unhappy I had the boys. I was crazy about every one of them from the minute I saw him. But I always felt like something was missing in my life. I used to tell Dick that's what I wanted for Christmas. A daughter. He'd laugh and say he'd do what he could, but that darned man couldn't find a female chromosome to save his life. And now it doesn't matter anymore. Looks like Egan gave me my daughter for Christmas this year."

Chloe couldn't answer. She made a noise that sounded as if she were strangling.

"Whoops, I bet I said too much." A worried Dottie patted her shoulder. "I don't mean to put any pressure on you, honey. You and Egan take your time. I'm not trying to marry you off tomorrow. I mean, even if you don't want to marry him, I hope we'll still be—"

Chloe lifted her face. "Did you really wish for a daughter at Christmastime?"

"Silly, wasn't it? I knew all about the birds and the bees and I was too old to believe in Santa Claus."

"I wished for a family."

Dottie wiped away a tear from her cheek, then one from Chloe's. "Well, you've got one now."

Egan came through the door. "What's going on in here?"

Dottie smiled at Chloe. "Oh, girl talk. Sentimental girl talk."

"About what?"

Chloe turned around and launched herself into Egan's arms. "Christmas secrets."

He held her close and debated keeping her in that position all evening. "Well, I don't know what I did to deserve this, but I'm not above taking advantage."

"How about taking the turkey into the dining room, too?" Dottie said. "When you're through with the mushy stuff."

The meal was scrumptious, Thanksgiving replayed with a few Christmas touches, like chocolate peppermint pie and a plate of baklava in honor of Chloe. Afterward everyone took a walk together, crunching through snow-drifted paths around a frozen pond at the back of the property. Egan pointed out a clearing just the perfect size for a riding ring, and Dick described two quarter horses a neighbor planned to sell. Chloe hugged them both and told them a firm "maybe."

They left corn and seed for the birds, and pelted each other with volleys of snowballs before they tramped back to the house.

Finally, it was time to open presents.

Chloe had never felt more complete, more wonderfully mellow. The fire had thawed her toes and fingers to a pleasant tingle. Egan's arms around her were a stronger tingle. She leaned against him and thought about the years ahead, and the Christmases like this one that they could spend together. Someday their children could be part of this happy family, joined by aunts and cousins, as Egan's brothers found their own mates.

If she said yes, she could have the man she loved, the man who loved her best. She could have a real family who loved her, too. She already had Angel. It was almost enough to make her think that Santa Claus had been saving her Christmas list all these years to fill in his own good time.

The next gift made her a believer. Most of the presents had been given out by the time Dottie and Dick placed one of the largest boxes in the room in front of her. Gary, Rich and Joe, inveterate sweet tooths, had already opened Chloe's offerings of homemade pralines and chocolate-almond truffles. They'd had to tear Dick away from his copy of a brand-new adventure novel by his favorite author, and Dottie had crowed over the hand-embroidered sweater she had admired on one of their shopping trips together.

Chloe couldn't imagine anything better than the laboriously chosen gifts of perfume and scarves she had received from Egan's brothers. She knew she would smile for months every time she imagined one of them trying to choose something so relentlessly feminine.

As she untied the ribbon, everyone stopped to watch. The gift was from Dick and Dottie, and from its unwieldy size Chloe suspected it was a scratching post for Angel.

She unfolded the top flaps of the carton to reveal a dollhouse—a perfect model of the Last Resort.

"It's not nearly finished yet," Dottie apologized. "Dick and I have been working on it every chance we got. He made the design and did most of the carpentry. But we just didn't have time to do all the interior or the finishing touches yet. Some of the fireplace mantels—"

"A dollhouse." Chloe stared. Not just any dollhouse. One she could treasure for the rest of her life. One that represented her past as a foster child, her present as director of the home, and probably a big chunk of her future, too. The dollhouse she had always wanted, and was still not too old—she could never be that old—to appreciate. "A dollhouse." Dazed, she shook her head.

"Let me get it out of the box for you," Egan said.

She watched as Egan and Dick lifted it out and set it on the floor in front of her. "It has lights," she said.

"Well, sure," Dottie said. "I did research. Alma Benjamin herself had electricity installed in that house just as soon as it was available. She was a forward-thinking woman. As near as I can tell, this is what the house must have looked like about the turn of the century. Before these lunkheads here, and others like them, got hold of it and started making their so-called improvements."

"That's what Mom calls bringing the house up to code," Egan said.

"Do you like it?" Dottie asked.

Chloe looked at all of them. They were waiting for a simple yes or no. But she had so much more to say. And she could say it. She knew that now. She could tell them about the little girl inside her, because they loved the big girl, and the little girl was just a part of her.

"When I was little," she said softly, "I had a Christmas list. Every year I wished for the same things, but I never got them. I wasn't really unhappy. I was taken care of, and I made good friends along the way. I'm proud of the person I turned out to be."

She looked at Egan, to draw strength from him. He took her hand and held it tightly in is. "But somewhere along the way I stopped believing in Christmas and Santa Claus and what it was like to get something for no reason at all except that I wanted it. Then I met all of you."

She turned away from Egan so that she could see all their faces. She saw understanding and caring. She saw tears in Dottie's eyes.

"I've never told anyone before, but I want to tell you about my list. I wanted a kitten. I wanted a dollhouse with lights that worked. I wanted a family that would be my own, a mother who would bake Christmas cookies with me and shop for presents, a father who would think I was special. Brothers or sisters who stayed in my life and didn't move away."

She felt Egan squeeze her hand. She squeezed his back. "And when I was old enough to understand about love, I wanted a man in my life who loved me best. One I could love as much as he would love me." She smiled.

Radiantly. The tears she had cried in the kitchen were gone.

The tears a little girl had never been able to cry were gone forever.

"Thank you for filling my list," she said. "Every one of you. So very, very much. But especially you, Egan." She turned slowly back to him. Her heart shone in her eyes. She knew in that moment that she had never really doubted him, or the perfection of their union. She had let fear paralyze her, the fear of a child who had never been given what she most desired.

But that child was an adult now, an adult who suddenly believed in miracles. An adult who believed in love.

"Chloe." He framed her face in his hands. His eyes shone suspiciously.

"I'll never say I don't believe in Santa Claus again," she said softly.

When Egan finally let her go, the family tried to set a world's record in hugs per minute. She laughed and hugged them all back, wallowing shamelessly in their affection. And when everyone else had backed away, she nestled safely in Egan's arms again. The best place in the whole world. The place she wanted to stay forever...and she would be sure to find a way to tell him so when they were alone.

The room grew silent again, as if there was more to come.

"I've got a present for Chloe, too," Egan said quietly. "Actually, it's from Rich and me."

Surprised, she squirmed around to face him. "But you already gave me Angel, remember? And Rich gave me earrings."

"This is something a little different."

She heard the strain in his voice, and sobered a little, from inexpressible joy to just plain happiness. She read apprehension on his face, and thought she understood it. He was going to propose again. Here. In front of his family, and the poor man didn't know that she would joyously accept. She just couldn't imagine what Rich could have to do with it.

He reached inside his jacket, but no carefully wrapped jeweler's box emerged. Instead, he pulled out an envelope and passed it to her without a word. She frowned as she read his name on the thin stationery with the odd, foreign stamps. "This is addressed to you," she pointed out.

"Open it."

She stared at the envelope. The words blurred, and for a moment she couldn't make sense of them. "It's from Greece," she said at last.

"Open it."

Strangely, her hands seemed to have comprehended more than her brain. They trembled a little as she took two pages from the envelope. Photographs fell into her lap, but she ignored them, carefully reading each word of the letter. It wasn't until the second paragraph that the words began to make sense.

She looked up. "My aunt?"

Egan nodded. "Helena Palavos. Palavos is your family name, the name your father changed when he came to this country with your mother."

"My name is Chloe Palavos?"

"If you go to court to have it changed back."

"Does she say why my father changed his name?"

Egan recognized shock when he saw it. He knew that later Chloe would read the letter, probably memorize it.

But now she needed time to assimilate the news. And she needed quick answers.

"He met and fell in love with your mother when she went to Greece for a vacation. His family didn't want him to marry an American. They were afraid he would forget who he was. But he couldn't be persuaded to give your mother up. When his father—your grandfather— told him that he would never speak your father's name again if he married your mother, your father took him at his word. He just vanished one day. He came back to the States with your mother and never contacted his family again. His father wouldn't speak of him for years, but his brothers wanted to find him—"

"Brothers?"

"You have a lot of relatives," Egan said.

"Where?"

"Most of them live on the island of Zante, near a town called Zákinthos. They're farmers. Olive groves, your aunt says. Maybe if they'd lived somewhere more populated, they would have been easier for the state to find after your parents died. But without your father's last name..."

"How did you...?" Her voice trailed off.

"Figure it out? That took Rich. He works for the Immigration and Naturalization Service—"

"I didn't realize that. Not exactly."

Rich explained. "I knew how to search the records. It only took a few hours to find your father listed under his new name, find his old name, and trace him back to Zante."

"A few hours?"

Egan knew what she must be feeling. A few hours of work, a few questions asked of the right people, and she would have grown up in Greece, surrounded by family.

Her family. "They want to know you," he said. "They were easy to trace once we had a name and your father's birthplace. I was able to reach your aunt by telephone."

Chloe didn't respond. She tried to imagine what her aunt had felt.

"She was...sad," he continued after a moment, "when I told her about your father and mother. She had always suspected that something had happened to them. She believed your father would have patched up the quarrel eventually if he had lived. When he didn't come back home, she guessed."

"Did anyone ever try to find him?"

"Yes. Your grandfather relented at last and let your uncles search, but the family was as unsuccessful at finding your father as the state of Pennsylvania had been in finding them. They just didn't have the resources they needed."

"My grandfather?"

"Died ten years ago," Egan said. He touched her cheek. "Your grandmother is eighty, and she says she refuses to think about dying until she sees you. They want you to fly over as soon as possible."

She thought of the money she had saved for so long, money that was to have been spent on a private investigator.

Money that was no longer in her account.

"All the way to Greece," she said.

"They sent photographs. This one will interest you most of all." Egan lifted one from her lap.

She looked down and saw the faces of her parents staring back at her, faces she hadn't seen in twenty years. There had been no photographs salvaged after the fire.

Her parents' likenesses, like everything else, had disappeared from her life.

Egan watched the way she avidly drank in every detail. "That picture was taken right before they left Greece. Your aunt hid it and kept it all these years."

She didn't, couldn't, look up. She went through the other photos, seeing for the first time the family she had never known. When she had finished, she sighed. "What can I say?"

"You can say you aren't angry."

She met Egan's eyes and saw that he was serious. "Angry?"

"I know you've saved money for years to find them. And I know how you feel about doing things for yourself."

"It would have been many more years before I could have found them."

"Years?"

She nodded, but didn't explain. "My grandmother would probably have been dead. Now I'll have the chance to know her."

"You really aren't angry, are you?"

"I love you." She rose and kissed him. "I love all of you!"

Everyone else in the room collectively released a deep breath. Then there were more hugs and good wishes, and the normal O'Brien pandemonium broke out again. Chloe put her aunt's letter in her blazer pocket to savor at length when she was alone. There would be plenty of time in the months ahead to figure out what it meant to be part of the Palavos family. Time to write letters herself. Time to realize that she wasn't an orphan after all, that people who shared her bloodline were waiting for her on an island named Zante, far, far away.

Now she shared herself with her other family, the one with whom she had no blood ties. The one that loved her just because they loved her. The one, she suspected, who would always be closest to her heart.

The trip home was nearly silent. There were few other travelers on the road, and the carols on the radio had grown even more mellow. Chloe shut her eyes and thought about all the wonderful things she had been given since Egan walked into her life. Egan peeked at her from time to time and saw the contentment on her face.

"I wish you could just come home with me," he said when he parked in front of the Resort.

She gave him a sleepy, adoring smile. "Wouldn't that be perfect? But I promised Martha I'd double-check to make sure everything's been put out under the tree and stuffed in stockings. And if I know the girls, it won't be much after midnight before they'll be up, insisting it's Christmas morning."

"I know. I just can't help wishing."

"Oh, I wish, too. You don't know how much. But we'll be together tomorrow night."

They shared a promising kiss at the front door. Chloe didn't want to go inside. The night was perfectly still except for the gently falling snow. The man in her arms was more than enough to keep her warm, to keep her happy forever. She held on to him, willing the moment to go on forever. But forever ended with the midnight chiming of a church bell.

"Merry Christmas," Egan said.

She kissed him once more, her tongue tangling with his in her rush to let him know that this was the merriest Christmas of her life. Then, reluctantly, she unlocked the door.

He followed her inside. The hallway was dark, only the thin glow of a stairwell chandelier lighting their way. "What were you thinking about on the ride home?" Egan asked.

She had been thinking about how to tell him she would marry him, but she hadn't been able to find the words. She still couldn't. "Christmas wishes and unexpected gifts. Finding my father's family was the last wish on my list."

"And the only one you ever told me about."

She caressed his unbearded chin. "I can keep a secret. Are you really Santa Claus?"

"I'd like to spend my life making you happy. Does that make me your Santa?"

"It would make you the most wonderful man in the world, if you weren't already."

"Chloe." He cupped her face with his hands.

She leaned toward him and gathered her courage. "I have a gift for you. I wanted to give it to you in private."

"You already gave me a gift."

"But I don't think it was what you wanted most."

He frowned. "No?"

"I think you said that you wanted me."

"Seems to me we made a good start on that Sunday."

Her smile was dangerously seductive. "Well, if that's all you meant . . ."

"You know it wasn't."

Suddenly she was no longer afraid. She didn't think she would ever be afraid again. She looked him straight in the eye. "Do you still want to marry me?"

"More than anything."

"Then let's do it."

He stared at her. "Just like that?"

"We already did the hard part. Falling in love. The rest will be easy, don't you think?"

He struggled to keep his voice as low as hers. "Simple as pie."

"Soon?"

"Tomorrow soon enough?"

"Not a chance. Your mother would have a fit. We have to make plans. I have to arrange some time off so we can go away for a honeymoon afterward."

He dropped his hands to reach inside his jacket pocket and pull out an envelope. "I was saving this for Christmas morning. But this is close enough. Open it."

"Don't tell me you already bought the license."

"Just open it."

She did. In the dim light, it took her a moment to make out the print. Inside were two round-trip airline tickets to Greece.

"I thought you'd want to introduce me to your family," he said.

"We're going to Greece?"

"For our honeymoon, if you'd like."

"I thought..."

"Thought what?"

"Well, I thought it would be years before..."

"I didn't want you to use all the money you'd saved for the detective on airfare."

"The detective?"

"The one you've been saving for." She still looked dazed. He frowned. "The one you were going to hire to find your relatives."

"That one." She shut her eyes. "Oh, Egan..."

"Of course, if you want to go alone, I'll understand. We can go somewhere else for our honeymoon."

"Alone? Of course not! It will be the best honeymoon in the world!"

"I'm glad you said that." He put his arms around her, and for a long, long time, the hall was silent again.

"Come on," he said at last. "I'll help you check the presents."

She changed from wanton to wary in his arms. "No. I mean, that's okay. I'll bet you're tired from all that driving. I'll just take care of it."

He steered her toward the living room and the big blue spruce. "Don't be silly. This will be good practice for when we have our own kids."

She tried to stall him. "We don't need to practice yet, do we? It's a little early. We haven't even set a wedding date."

"I just want to see—" Egan flipped a switch that flooded the room with soft golden light. He fell silent.

Chloe looked everywhere except at him.

"I've never seen anything like it," he said.

"Like what?"

He stared. The room was cluttered with gifts. Most were wrapped, but some had been impossible to cover. Skis stood against one wall, tied together with a huge red bow. A stereo system like the one Heidi had been hoping for was set up in a corner. Everywhere he looked, there were presents and more presents. He guessed that the girls at the Resort had received every single item on their Christmas lists.

"I didn't do it," he said at last. "Believe me, Chloe, I didn't do it." He faced her, resting his hands on her shoulders. "A promise is a promise. I wouldn't have gone against your wishes this way."

"My wishes," she repeated.

"Really. I don't know where these presents came from. I have no idea. But they're not from me or my family."

She cocked her head and pretended to assess him. "I trust you."

"But who did it?"

"I guess it was Santa Claus."

He hardly listened. "The board? Somebody on staff?"

She thrust her hands in her pockets. *Empty, empty pockets. Pockets nearly as empty as the savings account she had closed on Monday. Pockets nearly as empty as her checking account would be after she paid all her charge-card bills in January.*

"A neighbor? A silent benefactor?" he asked.

"Santa Claus," she repeated.

As she kissed away his questions, she thought about Christmas wishes and unexpected gifts, about conquering fear and finding love. About the simple, perfect beauty of giving.

She decided there would be plenty of time in the future to tell Egan everything she'd learned about Santa Claus. Plenty of time.

A lifetime.

* * * * *

A Note from Emilie Richards

My best memories of Christmas are tied with the arrivals of my four children. I use the word *arrivals* because not all of them came into our family in quite the same way. My three sons came by way of hospital delivery rooms with their proud daddy standing right there to help them greet the world. My daughter, Jessie, came on a plane from India when she was a frightened six-year-old. Jessie arrived just three days after Christmas, and the two boys then in residence were convinced that we had thoughtfully arranged it that way so that the family could have a second Christmas celebration.

There is a special memory connected with each of my sons, too. I think of Shane's first Christmas as the one when I was hugely pregnant for the first time, living far from all my family while my husband, Michael, attended seminary in California. Like all graduate students, we were poised on the brink of poverty, and after careful consideration, Michael and I decided that we could only spend ten dollars on each other for presents. Neither of us will ever forget those small gifts, selected with such love and care, or the joy of waiting to greet the first child we had conceived together.

Galen was born four years later, a considerate tax deduction who waited until the Christmas wrapping paper had been cleared away and most of the Christmas cookies eaten before he made his appearence on the twenty-seventh. To protest the disruption of his holiday, Shane locked the young couple who were baby-sitting him in the basement. To this day, those generous people have never had children of their own.

My most poignant memory of Brendan's first Christmas is of weeks spent wondering how our family could possibly celebrate the holiday when I had been ordered to remain flat on my back for a month or risk losing my unborn child. The children were trying to be helpful. Michael *was* helpful. But there I was, unable to shop or decorate or prepare our traditional Christmas dinner.

Enter the Christmas spirit in the guise of members of Michael's congregation. On Christmas Eve, our house was invaded by half a dozen elves carrying the most wonderful Christmas dinner I have ever eaten. Someone had baked a ham, someone else a sweet-potato casserole. There were pies and rolls and vegetables. And most surprising of all, without knowing that it was a long-standing Christmas tradition for our family, a friend had baked a loaf of cranberry bread for us to eat on Christmas morning. It's the same recipe that I've shared with you.

If I'd ever had doubts about what kind of world I was bringing my children into, they were put to rest that night. Now, whenever I think about Christmas, I think about those wonderful people, about *all* the wonderful people who care for each other, who share, not just at Christmastime, but whenever and wherever they are needed. And I think of my children, your children and all the children of this world, who are the ultimate proof of Christmas miracles.

This year I wish each of you a holiday season filled with wonderful memories and miracles of your own.

Emilie Richards

HOLIDAY
HOMECOMING

Joan Hohl

CREAMY CHEESE CAKE
A delicious (and easy) holiday dessert

1 lb softened cream cheese
⅔ cup of sugar
3 eggs
prepackaged graham-cracker-crust-lined pie pan

Preheat oven to 350° F. Combine ingredients and beat until light, fluffy and lemony in color. Pour mixture into prepackaged graham-cracker-crust-lined pie pan. Bake for approximately 30 minutes. Set out to cool for 25 minutes.

Topping

1 cup sour cream
3 tbsp sugar
1 tsp vanilla

Combine ingredients and spread over top of cake. Bake 10 minutes. Chill before serving.

Don't count calories. Enjoy!

Chapter One

Snow!

Diana Blair stood entranced outside the narrow four-story office building, by the sign that read Blair & Daughter, Architects, Specializing in Historic Preservation and Interior Design.

When had it begun snowing? she mused, staring in wonder at the swirling white flakes glittering in the soft glow of the turn-of-the-century-style street lamps.

How beautiful, she thought, how like a scene from a Victorian Christmas card. Her mind filled with a sense of wonder as she ran a glance up and down the narrow street, taking in the tall, stately buildings that lined it. Her father, Henry, and then Diana in company with him, had restored most of the buildings to their original splendor, as they had many of the other businesses—and many of the private homes—in the small city of Riverview. And yet, for all the familiarity of the scene, at the first snowfall of the season, Di always experienced the same sense of surprised wonder.

Di had reached the conclusion years ago that her ever-renewed delight in the wintry scene could be attributed more to the city than to the snow itself.

Situated along the Schuylkill River, less than an hour's drive from the modern and bustling city of Philadelphia, Riverview had been named a national historic site. The entire city had a special ambience, the look and feel of a time gone by. The dedicated citizens of Riverview worked hard at maintaining the quaint and unique appearance of the city.

Diana loved her hometown at all times, particularly during the holiday season, and most especially when it snowed.

The last time Di had glanced through one of the office windows, around noon, watery, cloud-filtered sunlight had illuminated the mid-December day. Now, nearing seven-thirty in the evening, large snowflakes pirouetted before capricious gusts of stinging wind.

Perfect, Di thought, quickly surveying the area for witnesses before sticking out her tongue to capture a delicate flake. She laughed to herself as the snow melted on her tongue. A perfect ending to an exciting day.

An exciting day, but a long day, she reflected, judging the depth of the accumulated snow with a measuring stare. About an inch, she decided as she stepped gingerly in her three-inch heels from beneath the awning above the entranceway.

Di's toes were wet before she had traversed half the short distance to the tiny company parking lot situated next to the century-old building.

Once inside her car, Di immediately fired the engine, then flicked on the heater. Warmth began curling around her ankles as she pulled the car off the lot to join the procession crawling along the street.

Simply keeping the car moving in a straight line required all of Di's concentration, but when she inched to a stop at a red light, her thoughts flew back to the phone call she'd received earlier that morning. A smile curved her lips as she recalled the bubbly sound of her stepmother's voice on the other end of the line.

"Oh, Di, it's so wonderful!" Miriam Blair had exclaimed in a gushing rush.

"That's nice," Di had answered, smiling for whatever had infused Miriam with such enthusiasm. "But exactly what is so wonderful?"

"Oh!" Miriam's burst of laughter had held the tinkling sound of a young girl's giggle. "How silly of me. I just had a phone call from your brother—that's what's so wonderful. Now Terry's coming home for Christmas, too."

Terry. Her baby brother. Di's smile grew into a grin. Terry always claimed to hate it when she referred to him as her baby brother. His claim was a pretense; she knew it, and he knew she knew it.

The light turned to green, and Di slowly moved forward, careful to keep a comfortable distance between her car and the vehicle in front of her.

Of course, Miriam's news was wonderful and exciting—the icing on their Christmas cake, so to speak, coming as it had so soon after hearing that the others would be home for the holidays, as well.

For the first time in years, all the assorted yours, mine and ours—all the members of the Blair and Turner families—would be together for the holidays.

Well, no, not *all* of them, Di reminded herself, reflexively tightening her grip on the steering wheel.

Matt would be noticeably among the missing.

A chill unrelated to the plunging temperature feathered the length of Di's stiffened spine.

Matt.

Thinking of her stepbrother, the eldest child of the combined families—an indulgence Di rarely allowed herself—brought his image to mind, an image undimmed by the nine years since she had last seen him.

Unfortunately for Diana, the love she kept secreted in her heart and soul for him was equally undimmed.

Diana could see Matt, sense him, as if he were seated in the bucket seat beside her. His image was as clear as a sun-spangled summer day, and more biting than the December storm raging outside.

At age twenty-five, Matthew Turner had stood six foot one and a half and had been reed-slim. Matt's shock of jet-black hair—so similar to Di's own as to convince strangers of a blood connection that in fact did not exist—shimmered with a healthy gleam and vitality. His strong, sharply defined facial features were a perfect setting for his cool, remote, incisive-looking gray eyes. Even at such a comparatively early age, Matt had possessed a mature and formidable appearance. And yet, in contrast, offsetting the stern look of him, his white teeth had frequently flashed in a thoroughly engaging smile that gave insight into the devilish facets of his character.

Matt had been a force to be reckoned with for any female. For Diana, the reckoning had come at the impressionable age of four, on the day her father had first brought Matt, along with his mother and younger sister, Bethany, to meet Di and her younger sister, Melissa.

Even at the gangly, cracked-voiced age of twelve, Matt had been a charmer. Giving Diana a secret wink, he had grinned conspiratorially at her and bestowed upon her the nickname Di. She had promptly fallen headlong into a state of absolute adoration for him.

Against her will, Diana recalled those early years after her father and Miriam had joined forces in marriage. Their love for each other had always been obvious, deep, abiding, and wide enough to encompass their respective offspring, knitting the separate units into a whole, creating a loving family. Henry had gained a beloved and trusted son; Miriam had gained two more daughters to fuss over and spoil with caring mothering.

Diana's growing up years had been filled to overflowing. The house had rung with the sounds of laughter, offset only rarely by the discordant sound of tears. And through it all she had remained in a state of adoration for her "big brother," Matt.

It was a state from which Diana knew she would never escape; it had merely shifted and changed from childhood adoration to unqualified love. A forbidden love, a love that had driven Matt away from home and family.

A heartfelt sigh escaped Di's usually rigid guard. Hearing it, the longing sound of it, shook her into full awareness of where she was, what she was supposed to be doing.

Not now! Di ordered her errant consciousness. *Pay attention to the traffic, the weather conditions, your driving.*

The images dissolved, and Di sighed again, this time in sheer relief. It hurt too much to think about him, to stir up memories, to recall that night of sheer madness.

With ruthless determination, Di applied every ounce of mental capacity and every bit of driving skill she possessed to getting the car, and herself, home in one piece.

Miriam was waiting for Diana in the festively decorated foyer of the big old Victorian house. Like nearly every other household in Riverview, the Blair family commenced decking the halls, and every room, the day after Thanksgiving. It had become a tradition in the city, in part because everyone seemed to enjoy getting an early start on the holidays, and in part because of the influx of tourist traffic, which increased yearly.

"I was beginning to worry," Miriam fussed, helping Di out of her coat, then hanging it in the wrap closet off the foyer. "Your father has been home for over two hours. What kept you?"

"I had some work I wanted to finish," Di explained, flexing fingers cramped and stiff from gripping the wheel. "And traffic's moving at a snail's pace."

"Well, at least you're home now, safe and sound," Miriam said on a relieved sigh. "And the snow is so pretty."

"Yes, it is," Di agreed, dry-voiced. "Wet, too."

"So I see." Miriam frowned as she eyed Di's soaked shoes. "You'd better go have a shower and get changed," she ordered. "Are you hungry?"

"Starved," Di admitted, obediently heading for the curving staircase. "Anything left?"

"Really, Diana," Miriam said, in a scolding tone. "We haven't eaten. We were waiting for you."

"That wasn't necessary." Di protested over her shoulder. "But I'm glad you did. Where's Dad?"

"He's on the phone with Terry." Miriam's expression softened, as it always did at the mention of her youngest child's name. "You know your father," she went on, smiling at Diana. "He wanted to know exactly when Terry would be arriving."

"Didn't Terry tell you all that when he called earlier?" Di asked, pausing at the foot of the stairs.

"No, he—" Miriam broke off, making an impatient face. "Diana, you're going to be chilled to the bone if you don't get out of those wet things. Now get moving. We can talk over dinner."

"I'm going, I'm going," she said, laughing, as she started up the stairs. "Give me twenty minutes."

Seventeen minutes later, warm from a stinging-hot shower, comfortable in soft wool slacks, an oversize sweater and velvet house slippers, Di, with her hair pulled back in a ponytail that made her look more a teenager than a young woman of twenty-six, strolled into the dining room.

"Oh, my great-aunt Matilda," she said, deeply inhaling the aromatic steam rising from the soup tureen set on the long, intricately carved mahogany table. "Whatever that is, it smells absolutely wonderful."

Henry Blair chuckled indulgently and strode over to Di to plant a kiss on her cheek. "Yes, doesn't it?"

"That, my dears, is the latest concoction from our priceless cook," Miriam informed them. "Janet felt creative today, and the soup is the result of her inspiration." She sniffed delicately. "And it does smell delicious."

"So, let's dig in," Di said, circling to her accustomed place at the table. "I'm famished."

The soup lived up to its fragrant promise, and the entrée and the assorted side dishes were equally successful. Conversation was kept to a minimum until coffee and a lemon sponge cake were served.

Declining the cake, Di sighed and relaxed against the needlepoint-flowered material covering the padding on the back of the roomy, curved-armed chair. "That was delicious." She smiled pointedly at her father. "And now that I feel like I'll probably survive, are you going to tell me about Terry?"

"That's not all I'm going to tell you." His lips tilted in a secretive smile, his bright eyes reflecting some inner excitement, Henry shifted an expectant glance between his wife and daughter, both of whom were clearly puzzled.

"Henry, what are you up to?" Miriam asked, her own eyes beginning to glow. Miriam always loved a surprise.

"Yes, Dad, what informational bomb are you about to toss at us?" Di demanded, not immune herself to an occasional sneak attack of good news.

"In a moment," Henry said, deliberately drawing out the suspense. "But first, Terry's plans. He's booked on a flight into Philly on the twenty-third."

"Oh, how wonderful!" Miriam exclaimed. "How long can he stay? When must he be back to work?"

"The third of January," Henry answered. "His return flight to Taos is scheduled for late in the afternoon on the second."

"That is wonderful news," Di concurred with her stepmother. "With Beth and Lissa and Terry all here, it will be like a real family holiday homecoming."

"More than you know." Henry had a positively enigmatic expression and a smug smile.

"Dad!" Di protested, laughing. "What have you got cooking in that mysterious mind of yours?"

"Enough teasing, Henry," Miriam said in a gently scolding tone. "Tell us."

Still he hesitated, drawing out the moment of tense anticipation. "It's a very special surprise for all of us," Henry finally relented. "But most especially for you, Miriam," he said, smiling at his wife. "It's going to be a real, complete family gathering this year."

Leaning forward in their chairs, Miriam and Diana hung on the expectation of his next words. He drew a deep breath and smiled on the exhalation.

"Matt's coming home for Christmas."

Henry's informational bomb had contained the power of a forty-megaton explosive device. Hours after the blast, Diana was still shivering from reverberating reaction.

The house was quiet. The century-old grandfather clock in the foyer declared the hour of three. Diana lay rigid on her bed, her eyes wide, listening to the deep-throated tolling. Sleep eluded her, banished by shock-activated memories, good and bad.

Matt was coming home for Christmas.

With her mind's eye, Di reviewed the scene in the dining room following her father's announcement.

After an instant's disbelieving silence, Miriam had sprung from her chair. Laughing and weeping, she had rushed to her husband, at the end of the long table. His expression tender with love and understanding, Henry had risen and enfolded her in a gentle embrace.

"Henry, is it true?" she cried on a broken sob. "Matt's really coming home?"

Shell-shocked, feeling the bite of emotional shrapnel, Di remained in her chair, clinging to the stability of the solid wooden armrests, staring at the happy tableau being played out by her father and stepmother.

"Yes, dear, I promise you it is true," Henry assured his wife of twenty-two years. "Matt is coming home."

"But—how?" Miriam sputtered, unmindful of the tears of joy spilling onto her cheeks.

And why now? After all these years spent living outside the country, as far away as he could get from home. Di didn't voice her questions, but continued to sit quietly, certain she'd eventually hear the answers.

"How?" Henry repeated, chuckling. "By plane, of course."

"Henry, really, that's not what I meant, and you know it." Regaining control, Miriam stepped back, out of his arms. Accepting the neatly folded white handkerchief he offered, she dabbed at her eyes before going on. "I spoke to Matt just two days ago, and he didn't say a word, didn't as much as hint that he was thinking of coming home for the holidays." She frowned. "When did he decide to do so?"

Henry's smile held a wealth of self-mockery. "When I called him this afternoon to extend a verbal olive branch."

Miriam stared at him in astonishment. "You called Matt?"

Diana shared her stepmother's amazement; her father had not spoken to his stepson since the night Matt stormed away from his house. Staring at her father, Di waited with bated breath for his response.

"Yes," he answered. "I called him right after you rang me to tell me that Terry was coming." His smile was rueful, and his eyes were gentle on his wife's glowing face. "I decided that since you, my dear, were the one suffering the most for our masculine show of stiff-necked pride, it was time—long past time—to end this dissension between us. Fortunately, Matt agreed." He shrugged. "It's as simple as that."

Now, hours later, wakeful and restless, Diana decided that there was absolutely nothing simple about it. In fact, she was very much afraid that Matt's return would prove to be very difficult—at least for her, if not for the other assorted members of the family.

Maybe she should arrange to be among the missing this holiday, Di thought, clenching her fingers against the conflicting feelings of anticipation and trepidation waging a battle inside her. Since she was the only family member who had never been away from home during the holidays, she had every right to skip this particular homecoming—didn't she?

Wishful thinking. Diana rolled onto her side and curled into a self-protective ball. She knew full well that her wishful thinking would come to nothing. She wouldn't find, or even look for, somewhere else to spend the holidays. She didn't have it in her to disappoint her father and Miriam in that way. They were so obviously looking forward to having every one of their children with them this year.

The clock standing sentinel in the foyer struck the half hour, telling the silent house that it was 2:30 in the morning of December the sixteenth. And Henry had said that Matt would try to arrange his schedule to make it home in time for Christmas Eve.

One week and two days, Diana thought, panic uncoiling in her stomach.

You can get through it, she told herself, grateful for the sudden weighty tug on her eyelids. You're an adult now, no longer an uncertain teenager. They were all grown-ups—she and Lissa and Beth and Terry and—

He had turned thirty-four last summer.

Had he changed?

Well, of course he had changed.

So had she.

She was a woman, mature, confident.

Diana's rapid-fire thoughts came to an abrupt halt when a vision of a tall, slender, formidable young man with a wicked smile rose to torment her mind and her senses.

Oh, Matt . . .

"This is rather sudden, isn't it?"

"Yes." Matt smiled at the woman seated opposite him at the intimate table in the fashionable restaurant. "I decided to fly to the States for the holidays yesterday afternoon, when I spoke to my stepfather."

The woman, who was really quite beautiful, worked her lips into a strained smile. "But I had thought, hoped, that you would accept my invitation to spend the Christmas holidays with me and my family in London."

He very likely would have accepted, Matt silently acknowledged, if not for that astounding call from Henry. Fortunately, Henry's call had come before he accepted Allyson Carruthers's invitation.

"Sorry," he murmured, meaning it, even though he was still feeling euphoric from the unexpected call. "But I couldn't refuse my stepfather's invitation. It has been nine years since I spent the holidays with my family."

Besides that, he added silently, Henry said it was snowing at home.

Home. Matt suppressed a sigh. Where was home? During his self-imposed exile, he had moved around Europe, staying here, then there, calling no one place home, while establishing himself as a management consultant.

Allyson sighed; the sound held a faint but unmistakable tinge of sadness. "When will you return?" Her soft voice, her intonation, indicated her acceptance of the inevitable.

Matt absorbed a flashing sensation of regret; he had never wanted to hurt her, or any of the women he had shared time and intimacy with over the years. His relationships with Allyson and the others had all been open-ended. From the very beginning, by mutual agreement, the parameters had been set for the affairs—first and foremost of which was that there would be no strings attached.

Matt genuinely liked Allyson. She was wealthy, sophisticated, intelligent and amusing; she was also good in bed. But then, Matt reflected, if the endorsements of his partners could be taken into account, so was he.

Come to that, Matt could lay claim to all of Allyson's other attractions, except one—he wasn't quite as wealthy as she, at least not yet. But he was working on it, not only with his consultancy business and various other interests, but also with the flair he had discovered he had for successfully playing the stock market, and he was gaining on her with each new client, each new acquisition, each new market coup.

Not that any of it mattered to Matt. He had arrived at a comfortable position—financially, at any rate. But emotionally? Well...

"Matt?" The gentle nudge in Allyson's voice snagged his distracted attention. "I asked when you would be back."

"Sorry...again. My thoughts were wandering." Matt's smile was self-mocking. "I'm not sure, so I requested an open return flight."

"I see." Her tone now revealed resignation and acceptance. "It's over for us, isn't it?"

Matt could only match her bluntness. "Yes, Allyson, it's over. I'm—"

"Please, don't," she said, interrupting him. "Don't say you're sorry again."

"But I am," he insisted, feeling very much the cad, and hating the feeling. "I never meant to hurt you."

"I know." She shrugged; it didn't quite come off as careless. "If I'm hurt, it's my own fault. I knew your emotions were never engaged." She put a bright smile on her sad face. "But we did have some good times together, didn't we?"

"No." Matt shook his head. "We had some wonderful times together."

"Thank you for that." Allyson's voice betrayed the emotion gathering in her throat. "You were—are—a gentleman, Matt." She smiled. "A gentleman and, as they say in your country, a straight shooter."

Matt laughed through the stab of remorse he was experiencing. He didn't feel like a straight shooter; he felt like a jerk. Damn, he thought, she deserved better. Why hadn't he been able to fall in love with her? he asked himself. Or any of the others, for that matter?

Matt knew the answer, had always known the answer. He just always refused to acknowledge it. And he wasn't about to do so now, either.

Mentally avoiding a confrontation with his inner conflict, Matt raised his wineglass to Allyson. "Merry Christmas, and health, happiness and love in the New Year."

"The same to you," she murmured, raising her glass and sipping from it. "Will you tell me something, Matt?" she asked hesitantly.

"Of course."

Allyson wet her lips, then quickly asked, "Is there another woman? Someone I might know?"

Matt shook his head. "No."

It wasn't until hours later, when he was alone, that Matt reconsidered Allyson's questions. His answer had been truthful, as far as it went. But in actual fact, there was another woman, had always been another woman. A woman who haunted him, lived inside his mind wherever he happened to be. A woman he had not set eyes on for nine long years. A woman who had then been no more than a child. A child he had adored. A child who had grown into a beautiful teenager, with a woman's mature body and long, silky, enticing legs.

A teenager Matt had not been able to resist. A teenager he had, through his weakness, cruelly betrayed.

Matt shuddered and paced the confines of his bedroom, the Spartan furnishings of which reflected the barrenness of his existence.

But Matt could not outpace the feelings generated inside him by the startling call he had received from his stepfather. The man he had loved as much as a natural father. The man Matt had also betrayed.

Muttering a curse of self-condemnation, Matt stalked to the window to stare sightlessly into the diamond-studded, black-velvet night sky.

By the means of a transatlantic telephone line, Henry had in effect extended an offer of peace and forgiveness, tacitly inviting Matt, not only home for the holidays, but also back into the family fold.

The stars Matt was staring at grew fuzzy around the edges. He blinked against the moist film blurring his vision.

He was going home.

Anticipation and excitement simmered inside him. This time, *this* holiday, he had to make it right, because if he didn't, his future didn't bear thinking about.

Memory crouched, waiting to pounce on Matt the instant he lowered his guard. The stinging memory of another holiday season, and a bitter New Year's Eve.

Cursing aloud, Matt held the memory at bay by allowing himself to speculate on the intervening years.

What kind of person had that child-woman grown into? Matt wondered, swinging away from the window to resume his restless pacing. From the sparse bits of information he had gleaned from his mother and sister over the years, via telephone calls and the meetings he'd had with them in New York and Washington during his few brief visits to the States, he'd learned that she had matured into a lovely and intelligent young woman.

Matt felt the tingle of excitement and anticipation intensify, dance along his spine, at the realization that he would see for himself, judge for himself, in a little over a week.

Tired and keyed-up from the building inner tension, Matt felt his guard sag, just a bit. Her name rushed into the breach, filling his mind, his senses, his desolate soul.

Diana.

Chapter Two

Six days and counting.

The recurring thought ran through Diana's mind as she searched the faces of the deplaning passengers streaming along the concourse. If the flight from Chicago had arrived on schedule, Di's sister, Melissa, should be among the horde of humanity surging toward her.

Six days had passed—passed with excruciating slowness—since the night Diana had learned of Matt's intention to return home for the holidays. Six days, during which she had experienced mood swings from eager anticipation of his arrival to flat-out fear of facing him again.

Now, with only a few days remaining until Christmas Eve, Diana was more than a mite edgy. Her nerves were twanging like a guitar being thrummed by a musician caught up in a frenzy. Appearing calm required every ounce of control she possessed. Yet, so far, she had somehow managed it.

Two down and two to go, Di reflected, grinning and waving as she spied her sister's smiling face. Bethany had pulled in late yesterday afternoon, having driven through a fitful snowfall from New York City. Terry was booked on the red-eye flight from New Mexico, scheduled to arrive early in the morning of the twenty-fourth. That left Matt, who had said he would try to get home for Christmas Eve—just three days away.

"Okay, Di, what's up?" Melissa asked, after the greetings and hugs were exchanged.

"Up?" Diana repeated, smiling despite the clenching of the muscles in her midsection. Linking her arm with Lissa's, she matched her sister's stride as they joined the throng heading for the baggage claim area. "What do you mean?"

"The surprise Miriam said we're getting." Melissa arched her delicate dark eyebrows. "What sort of surprise has she got in store for us?"

"Assuming I knew, it wouldn't be much of a surprise if I told you," Diana replied. "Now would it?"

Melissa snatched her large suitcase from the carousel, grunted, and shot Diana a sour look. "I am assuming you know what it is, and unlike you and Miriam, I can live without surprises, thank you." Lugging the case, she trailed after Diana through the automatic swing doors. "Especially if that surprise concerns the announcement of your engagement," she went on, panting from the exertion.

"My engagement!" Diana stopped dead in her tracks; Lissa crashed into her, nearly sending both of them tumbling. "What engagement? I mean, to whom?"

"That dorky CPA you've been seeing." Lissa set down the case and drew a deep breath. "Who else?"

"Melissa, Mike Styer is not a dork," Diana said, even though she secretly agreed with her sister's assessment. "Besides, we are merely friends. Our relationship is not and never has been a romantic one."

"I should hope not." Lissa made a face. "I also hope the car's not too far away." She stumbled after Di when she stalked away. "This thing weighs a ton."

"Loaded with Christmas presents, is it?" Diana inquired, deliberately changing the subject.

"Yeah," Melissa admitted. "Scads of things."

"Hmm…" Diana murmured, slanting a taunting look at her. "But I thought you didn't like surprises."

"Get bent," Lissa retorted, grinning.

"Tsk, tsk." Diana made a clicking noise with her tongue. "I'm afraid that living in Chicago is corrupting you." Reaching out, she curled her fingers around the suitcase handle, relieving Lissa of her burden. "Wow!" she exclaimed when she felt the sudden dragging weight on her arm. "Did you buy everyone gifts made of cast iron?"

Lissa flexed her fingers and smiled disdainfully. "I do have a few things of my own in there, you know."

"Like what?" Di shot back, sighing with relief as they approached her car. "The kitchen sink?"

Lissa laughed, and enfolded Diana in another quick hug after she set the bag down at the rear of the car. "I have my blow-dryer, my curling iron, my garment steamer, my—"

"Lissa!" Diana exploded. "You didn't need to lug all that stuff. You could have used mine."

Lissa shrugged and helped Di heft the large case into the trunk. "Well, I remembered how you always used to yell at me to keep my hands off of your things when we were kids, and—"

"I absolutely do not believe you," Diana again interrupted her younger sister. "We *were* kids at the time," she reminded her, slamming the trunk shut. "And, as I recall, you had a positive talent for ruining every single thing of mine you got your sticky little hands on."

"Yeah." Lissa's eyes and smile were softened by remembrance. "We've both grown some since then."

"Yes." Her own eyes misty, Diana unlocked the door and slid behind the wheel. She turned to give her sister a more thorough examination after Lissa settled into the passenger seat. "You look terrific. I love that new hairstyle on you." Lissa's sable-brown tresses were now cut in a sleek, swingy bob.

"Thanks." Lissa shook her head. Her gleaming hair swirled, then settled neatly back into place. "You're not exactly looking like dog meat yourself. Your hair's really getting long. I like it."

"Thank you." Grinning, Diana raised her hand to smooth her shoulder-length mane of shiny black spiral curls. "Do you suppose we should adjourn this mutual-admiration-society meeting and head for home?"

"Home," Lissa repeated, her eyes growing bright. "Lord, it seems like forever since I was home last summer." She heaved a contented-sounding sigh as Diana set the car in motion. "I'm as excited as a kid. I can't wait. It's going to be like old times, with Terry and Beth coming."

"Beth got in yesterday."

"Great." Lissa laughed. "It's going to be fun—I mean, all of us home for the holidays this year." She grew quiet, then sighed again. "Well, almost all of us," she murmured.

Like it or not, little sister, you're in for a big surprise, Diana silently informed Lissa, who had also adored her big, forever teasing older stepbrother.

"Oh, it's snowing!" Lissa cried as Diana drove the car from beneath the protective covering of the parking deck.

"Again," Diana said, tensing behind the wheel. "The last couple of years, we've had hardly any snow at all. And now winter has barely begun, and this is the third snowfall." She sighed. "I'll be glad when we're home."

"Oh, doesn't everything look pretty!" Lissa cried as they drove through the streets of Riverview. "I can't wait to see the house."

The house, their home, glowed from within, the candlelight flickering in the windows glittered on the snow blanketing the front lawn, and cast halos around the deep green holly draping the windows and the front door.

Lissa flung the car door open and leaped out the instant Diana brought the vehicle to a stop in the driveway. An understanding smile curving her lips, Diana followed a short distance behind her sister.

As she had been the week before, Miriam was waiting in the foyer. But she was not alone in her vigil.

Diana's smile widened when she heard Lissa let out a whoop of delight. But her smile faded when she saw the reason for her sister's exclamation of joy. While Di's father, Miriam and Bethany stood watching with obvious pleasure, Lissa was being swung off her feet, caught up in the embrace of her grinning stepbrother.

Matt.

"Oh, Matt! Oh, Matt!" Lissa kept repeating, as if unable to believe he was real, and there.

"Oh, Lissa, oh, Lissa," Matt echoed teasingly. "As gorgeous and spontaneous as ever."

Frozen with shock, her breath shallow and constricted, Diana stood just inside the door, staring hungrily at this tall, handsome man she had not seen in nearly nine years—the only man she had ever loved.

Matt looked the same, and yet he appeared different, more handsome, more imposing, more forbidding, even with his face alight with laughter and love for Lissa. Maturity stamped his sharply delineated features; lines radiated from the corners of his deep-set dark brown eyes and bracketed his sensuous mouth. Silver streaked the short black hair at his temples, and the shock of hair that had tumbled onto his forehead.

Diana's gaze drifted to his body. A shiver of awareness, blatantly sexual, skittered up her spine. His slender hips, flat belly and long straight legs were encased in tight black jeans. His broad shoulders and flatly muscled chest were displayed to advantage in a white cableknit sweater. The slimness of youth was gone. At thirty-four, Matt had the lean, long-muscled look of a man at his physical peak.

Diana experienced an immediate response to the magnetic allure of his body. Her senses reeled, her skin grew warm, her insides quivered. Shaken by her reaction, physical and emotional, she dragged her gaze back to his smiling face.

"Are you the surprise Miriam promised me?" Lissa demanded when he set her back on her feet.

"Yes," Matt replied, his smile gentle, as he raised a hand to smooth a tear away from her cheek. "I'm the designated Christmas surprise for you and Terry and Beth." He turned his head to glance at his grinning sister, and went still when he caught sight of Diana.

There was a momentary hush. Or was the hush only inside her? Diana wondered, unable to breathe or move, ensnared by the intensity of his dark-eyed stare. The hush obviously wasn't felt by the rest of the group, for the laughing Lissa spun out of Matt's arms to rush forward to bestow hugs and kisses on Henry, Miriam and Beth.

"Hello." Matt's low-voiced greeting shattered the inner hush—and every one of Diana's nerves.

"Hel—hello, Matt." Diana hated, but couldn't control, the tremor in her voice. She couldn't tear her riveted gaze from his beloved face, either.

Matt's eyes flickered, and in that instant Diana knew memories were flooding his mind, the same memories that were flooding through hers, washing away the present, her chattering family members, sweeping her back in time to that New Year's Eve, nine long years before.

The house was ablaze with lights, from chandeliers, lamps, candles, and the sparkling twelve-foot Christmas tree rising majestically from the floor to the ceiling in front of one window. Laughter and animated conversation rang through the living room, foyer and dining room from the throats of the thirty-odd guests gathered to celebrate the arrival of the New Year at the traditional Blair family party.

Dressed in a long black velvet skirt and a chic, clingy gold silk blouse, Diana felt like Cinderella attending her first ball. Her short, shiny black curls bounced with her every light step, her dark eyes glowed from within with happiness. Matt had told her she looked beautiful—and sexy.

A shiver trembled through her. No one had ever before said that she either looked or was sexy. Had Matt meant it? Or had he been indulging in his usual pastime of wicked teasing?

A new sensation, strange yet exciting, held Diana in thrall. Matt had appeared serious, his eyes dark and intense, the light of deviltry smothered. If he had meant what he said...

Sexy. She shivered again. The possibilities implied by his comment sent her heartbeat into overdrive and con-

stricted her breathing. How could she find out? Diana
mused, smiling absently at a guest as she glided by a
laughing group of celebrants.

Did she dare to test the sensuous waters of Matt's
murmured remark? The shiver intensified along Diana's spine. But what manner of test could she apply?
she asked herself. Other than a few moist, fumbling
kisses from boys her own age, Diana's experience of the
opposite sex was nil.

Perhaps if she were to employ the wiles displayed by
the actress playing a seductress in a movie she had recently seen, Diana mused.

But where was Matt? Diana wondered, smiling as she
sailed by another animated group of guests on her way
to the kitchen to replenish an empty canapé tray. She
could hardly experiment, run a test, without the presence of the object of her foray into experimentation.

Come to think of it, she hadn't seen Matt for over an
hour, ever since he had gently but firmly disentangled his
arm from the clinging grip of his current lady friend.

Diana grimaced. In her estimation, Sondra Taylor—
not Sandra, but *Sondra*—was a real piece of work.
Snooty, condescending, supercilious. And grasping.
Sondra wanted Matt in the worst way, as was evidenced
by her cloying possessiveness.

What did Matt see in the woman? Diana had been
puzzling over that question since the first time Matt had
brought the rarefied Sondra to the house to meet his
mother, his stepfather, and his assorted siblings.

It wasn't that she was jealous or anything, Diana had
repeatedly assured herself, all the while knowing full well
that she was positively green from that demeaning emotion. But, darn it, Matt could do so much better than the
nose-in-the-air Sondra—Diana herself, for example.

And, over the past month, Sondra had given clear indications that she intended to have Matt—to own him. She had even confided to Diana her belief that an engagement ring might be coming for Christmas.

To the other woman's obvious chagrin, and Diana's intense relief, the expected ring hadn't materialized. Still, the relationship between Matt and Sondra appeared to be as solid as before.

So why did Matt seem to be hiding out now, when the party, and his lady, were in full swing?

Her curiosity aroused, Diana went searching for Matt after refilling the canapé tray, as well as the nut, potato chip and pretzel bowls. She found him ensconced in the roomy wingback chair in her father's dimly lit office.

"Got a headache?" Diana asked, quietly closing the door, shutting out the sounds of revelry.

"No." Matt drew his gaze from the flames leaping in the fireplace and settled a brooding look on her. "What are you doing in here?"

Startled by the underlying harshness in his soft voice, Diana forced a faint laugh, and an even fainter shrug. "Looking for you. Why did you cut out of the party?" she asked ingenuously, hoping to hear him admit that he was fed up with Lady Sondra's clutching hands and devouring glances.

"To get away from you," he muttered, pushing out of the chair to stand taut and rigid, his face set into harsh lines, his eyes dark and unfathomable.

Diana stared at him in bewilderment, devastated, not only by his cruel words, but also by his cutting tone of voice. What had she done to warrant this kind of treatment from him? Diana asked herself, racking her brain for some infraction, real or imagined. The only answer that came to her shocked mind was in connection to his earlier comment on her appearance.

Looking more closely at him, Diana felt amazement sweep through her; unless she was greatly misreading his expression, Matt gave every indication of being afraid of her!

Diana thrilled at a never-before-experienced feeling of feminine power. Trying on a copy of the seductive actress's method, she walked slowly toward him. The tingling thrill expanded inside her at the wary, uncertain expression that flashed across Matt's face.

Matt was never uncertain!

Watching him, watching his eyes, she took another slow step. His eyes flickered, lowered to her breasts, then quickly lifted to stare, stark and fierce, into hers.

Diana was young, and she was innocent, but she was by no means stupid or dense. She could feel the silky gold material of her blouse gliding over her breasts, could imagine how sensuous it might appear to Matt, to any man.

She moved her shoulders, just a bit. The silk caressed her flesh, igniting a spark of budding passion deep inside her. She took another step.

Matt raised a hand, palm out, as if to halt her progress. "Diana, don't—" The tight strain in his low voice struck her like a blow to the heart.

Diana's bravado deserted her. She couldn't go through with it. She simply didn't have whatever it took to play the role of the temptress. Not with Matt. She loved him, and for her, loving precluded role-playing.

Raising her own hand, Diana pressed her palm to his. "Oh, Matt, I'm sorry... I... I..."

"You have nothing to be sorry for," he said, interrupting her, staring intently at their fused palms. "It's me. I'm the one in the wrong here." He frowned as his fingers moved between hers, as if of their own volition. A defeated-sounding sigh whispered through his lips as his fingers lowered between hers, lacing their hands together.

"But why?" Diana cried in confusion, clasping his hand in a grip of desperation. "How— What have you done wrong?"

"Thought of you." His voice was even lower, barely a whisper. "In all the ways I should not think of you."

Diana knew. Of course she knew, every living part of her being quivered with the knowing. Yet she had to ask, had to hear it from his lips. "What ways, Matt?" she asked softly, taking another hesitant step.

Suddenly loosening his fingers, Matt pulled his hand from hers. "In the ways of a man with a woman—his woman." His voice was a strangled rasp. "But you're not a woman, Di. You're still little more than a child." Inhaling a ragged breath, he stepped back, away from her.

That heady sensation of feminine power swept over Diana again, washing away all thoughts of caution, all consideration of consequences. In so many words, Matt had just confessed to wanting her—her, not Sondra, *her*. Obeying impulse, she moved toward him, hands raised imploringly.

"I am not a child, Matt. In a few months I will be eighteen, an adult under the law, old enough to vote. A woman in the eyes of the world." Her fingertips brushed the soft material of his shirt, tingled in response to the firm flesh beneath the smooth cotton. She moistened her lips with a quick glide of her tongue before finishing, "I know what I want, Matt."

A light flared to life in the depths of his eyes, almost frightening in its fierceness. "How do you know?" he demanded with unconcealed fury. "Who have you been with? Who taught you?"

"Matt, you don't under—" That was as far as she got before his raw voice cut through her attempt to clarify.

"I'll kill the—"

"Matt, no!" Diana grasped his shirt. "There has been no one. I want you. Only you."

"You don't know what you're saying." His hands shot up to clasp her upper arms. "This isn't a game, Di."

"I know," she whispered. "Games don't hurt, not like I'm hurting now."

Matt's eyes flashed a warning, and his fingers tightened on her tender flesh. Diana expected to be shaken by his hard, rough hands, and she was thoroughly confused, thrown off balance, by the gentleness of his touch, the careful way he drew her close to the warmth of his body.

"Oh, Di, help me," he pleaded on a rough groan. "Tell me to let you go, please." His fingers flexed, as if to release her, then convulsed once more around her arms. "Di, please, get the hell out of here, away from me, while I still have the strength to let you go." It was a cry from the heart.

"I can't. I won't. I don't want to." She flattened her palms against the rock-hard wall of his chest. Even through the soft material of his shirt, Matt's body heat shocked her system, aroused her senses, caused a deep inner ache for...something.

Without conscious thought, she stroked his chest.

Matt's low groan of pleasure drenched her senses. "Di, don't." He shook his head. "No, please, do," he said in a strangled, pleading tone. "Unbutton my shirt, then touch me, stroke me."

Sheer exhilaration froze Diana for a second. Then a rush of wild excitement sent her trembling fingers to the buttons on his shirt, fumbling them free. Her avid gaze fixed on his face, she slid her hands beneath the soft material, thrilling to the sensation of caressing his hot, hair-roughened skin.

Matt shuddered. An expression of near-pain flickered across his face. "Oh, dammit, Di, that feels so good." He closed his eyes, as if savoring the feeling. "Your hands are so soft, so exciting, so arousing."

Her hands, *her* touch, held the power to excite him! Elation shot through Diana, overpowering the lingering traces of trepidation, releasing her inhibitions. Obeying an urgent inner command, she leaned forward and pressed her parted lips to his now-moist flesh.

Matt drew in a sharp breath, and his body jerked, as if it had been prodded by a live electrical wire. "Diana, Diana..." As he groaned her name, he released his grasp on her arms and clasped her head with his unsteady hands. Lifting her head from his chest, he tilted her face up to his.

Diana trembled at the look of him. His face was stark. His eyes were open, and their nearly black depths were alight with a leaping flame of unbridled desire.

"Diana, I must kiss you." Matt lowered his eyes to her trembling lips. "Let me, love . . ." He moved his mouth closer, to within a breath of hers. "May I?"

He needed to kiss *her*. Diana's mind boggled at the very thought. May I? *May I?* Her mind laughed; Diana didn't. She stared into the inciting fire in his eyes and knew she could happily burn to a crisp from the merest brush of his beautiful mouth against hers.

"Diana," he whispered when she didn't respond. "Let me. I need . . . I need . . ." His voice faded into a wisp of warm, wine-scented breath that bathed her lips and intoxicated her rioting senses.

"I . . . I need, too," she whispered in a faint little cry, lifting her mouth in invitation.

Matt made a sound that was half sigh, half groan, then closed the scant space between them. The touch of his mouth on hers was feather-light, tender, sweet. Diana felt it to the soles of her feet, the depths of her soul. It made her hungry for more. Gliding her palms up his chest, she curled her arms around his taut neck, urging him closer.

Matt's reaction was swift and stunning. His strong arms enfolded her quivering form, drawing her into a fiercely possessive embrace. His mouth hardened, claiming hers. His tongue probed at the barrier of her closed lips.

Diana knew what he was silently demanding of her, and yet she hesitated, unsure of herself, of her ability to please him.

A ragged growl of frustration rumbling from his throat, Matt lifted his mouth a fraction from hers. "Part your lips for me, love," he ordered. "Let me in. Give me your sweetness."

She parted her lips . . . a bit.

"Wider." Matt's raw tone conveyed urgency. "I want to fill you with a part of me."

His words drew a picture in Diana's mind, an erotic vision that sent a bolt of sensation ricocheting from her head to the depths of her femininity and back to her lips, setting them on fire . . . for the feel of him.

Diana parted her lips.

Matt's tongue surged inside, filling her mouth, swamping her senses. His hands moved with restless intent, molding her soft curves to the hard, angular planes of his muscular body.

Passion exploded inside Diana. Guided by impulse, she arched into the taut form curved over hers. Her hips made contact with his. Diana gasped at the urgent nudging of his manhood against the mound at the apex of her weak and trembling thighs.

Matt released her mouth to kiss her cheeks, her eyelids, her temples. His tongue outlined the curve of her ear, then delicately dipped into the opening.

Diana shuddered in response to his erotic play.

"Do you like that?" His voice was low.

"Y-yes."

"So do I, but it's not enough," Matt murmured seductively. "Filling your sweet mouth, your pretty ear, only makes me hungry for more." His hands clasped her bottom, pulling her body tightly to the fullness of his. "I want to fill you completely. Feel your body throb, tight and hot around mine. I want to make you wild with desire for me, only me. I'm damn near crazy with the need to make love to you until you shatter for me, while I explode inside you."

His soft voice drew images in her imagination, images that lit a raging fire in the core of her being. The blood coursed sweet and hot in her veins, and massed in a molten flow around her aching femininity.

Still Diana teetered on the edge of decision, wanting, yet fearful of the initiation into womanhood.

"Diana..." Whispering her name, Matt covered her lips with his, ending her uncertainty with the evocative rhythm of his thrusting tongue.

Without conscious direction, Diana's body moved against his. His mouth fused to hers, Matt moved, taking her with him as he crossed the room to the long leather couch set at an angle to the fireplace. Diana moaned a soft protest when the rhythm ceased, and gasped when his deft fingers released the fastening on her skirt, sending the garment to the floor in a pool of black velvet around her ankles.

"Lord, Diana, you have the longest, sexiest legs," Matt said in a husky whisper. "Your legs have been driving me out of my mind for almost a year."

Diana blinked, both thrilled and startled by his confession. "My legs?" she said, unable to believe she had heard him correctly.

"Your legs," he assured her, reaching out to stroke one thigh encased in sheer black nylon. "I ache to feel them curled around my waist." Matt's fingers trailed up her leg to the juncture of her thighs. One long finger stroked the dark down unconcealed by the filmy panty hose. "I burn to feel your long legs contract, drawing me deeper and deeper into the moist heat of your body." His stroking finger probed, testing the nylon barrier to the portal of his desire.

His intimate caress completely swept away Diana's inhibitions. Extending her hands, she cupped the fullness straining against the material of his trousers. Matt's body jerked in reaction; she felt a responsive spasm beneath her palm.

"Let me show you, Diana." Matt's harsh voice betrayed the need driving him. "Make love with me. Here—" A movement of his head indicated the couch. "Now."

"Yes," she answered without hesitation.

Matt's eyes blazed, seeming to shoot sparks of fire to the heart of Diana's desire. She murmured a protest when he drew his hand and tormenting fingers away from her body, but sighed with satisfaction when he lowered her to the butter-soft leather cushions and settled his length between her thighs.

Recalling his earlier confession, Diana coiled her legs around his slim waist. Matt responded by arching his body, thrusting it against hers, tormenting them both with a preview of the delights in store when the barriers of their clothing were at last torn away and discarded.

Gasping at the fiery sensations his movements sent through her, Diana fullfilled his fantasy by tightening her legs and arching high into his rhythm.

"Diana..." Matt crushed her mouth with his, and then his tongue began moving in time with his body.

"Good grief! Diana!"

"Matthew! How could you?"

The shocked voices of her father and Matt's mother pierced the sensual haze clouding Diana's mind. Muttering a vicious curse into her mouth, Matt pulled his head back, and angled it to glare at the open doorway. Henry and Miriam stood in the opening, while Bethany, Melissa, Terry, and a number of their guests— Sondra included—crowded around in the hallway.

Horrified at being caught in such a blatantly humiliating position, Diana buried her face and a muffled sob in the curve of Matt's neck. She could feel the waning warmth of his passion, the growing heat of his fury.

"Shut the damn door."

Chapter Three

"Diana, did you hear me? I asked if you would you please shut the door."

The sound of her father's voice dammed the flow of memory in Diana's mind. Moving like a sleepwalker, she reached behind her to pull the door shut, Matt's angry voice of nine years before still echoing in her mind.

Shut the damn door.

Blinking, she focused on the man standing, silent and watchful, across the foyer from her.

The memories, *their* memories, were still reflected in Matt's dark eyes.

How much time had expired while she and Matt stared at each other, reliving those memories? Diana wondered, dragging her gaze away from him to skip a glance from her father to Lissa, then to Miriam and Beth. They were still in the process of exchanging hugs and greetings; Lissa was still wearing her coat, as indeed was Diana herself.

Deciding the elapsed time was a matter of mere seconds, rather than the hours it seemed to her, Diana shook her head to reorient herself, and set her fingers to work on the buttons of her own ankle-length wool coat.

Her fingers trembled as much as they had that night, when she fumbled with the buttons on Matt's shirt. The thought brought the memory, that night, close once more, too close, making her feel vulnerable and fragile.

There came a sudden touch on her shoulder, then her nape, at the collar of her coat. Even after nine years, Diana recognized that touch and shivered in response to it.

"The scars inflicted on you that night still haven't healed, have they?" Matt asked, in a hushed voice pitched to reach her ears alone.

Diana went stiff. She was cold outside, yet traitorously warm inside. Fighting an insidious melting sensation and an overwhelming impulse to turn into his arms, she shook her head quickly.

"Liar," he said in a rough whisper. "I could see, read it like print on your face. You were reliving that night, just as I was." His voice went rougher, sounding harsh, bitter. "You are still suffering the shame and humiliation of being found, seen by everyone, with me between your legs."

Diana flinched as though he had struck her. Her eyes closed against a rush of tears from the stabbing pain of the emotional wound. Barely aware of what she was doing, she slipped her arms free of the sleeves when he tugged on the coat. The heavy garment was lifted from her shoulders, but still she felt weighted down.

"I suppose I can't blame you," he murmured, heaving a tired sigh as he made a half turn toward the foyer closet. His lips twisted. "It was not a pretty scene."

Matt's flat statement flung her back in time once more....

"Shut that damn door," Matt ordered in a strangled snarl as he scooped her skirt from the floor. "Diana, I must get up," he whispered, easing away from her.

Mortified by the horrible situation, Diana could do no more than stare up at him with pleading eyes.

Ignoring the babble of voices from the doorway and the hall beyond, Matt slowly backed away from her, drawing the long velvet skirt over her exposed legs as he did so. When the lower half of her body was decently covered, he rose from the couch and turned to face the battery of condemning eyes.

"Oh, Matthew, how could you?" Miriam repeated in an anguished whisper. "Your sister!"

"She is not my sister," Matt shot back.

"No, she is my daughter." Henry's voice was choked with rage; his face was red, mottled by fury. "I treated you like a son, trusted you, loved you." Tears escaped to trickle down his flushed cheeks. "And in return you betray me, my love, my trust, by attacking my daughter."

"No!" Diana's cry of denial went unheard, overshadowed by the grating sound of Matt's voice.

"I asked you to shut that door." He stood tall, poised and taut, as if ready for a battle, or a full-scale war. "We don't need an audience."

"What difference does it make now?" Henry shot back, his usual sense of decorum and reserve destroyed by the depth of his pain and shock. "They have all witnessed the extent of your depravity." Nevertheless, he reached back to grasp the door, and slammed it shut in Sondra's face.

For one shameful yet satisfying instant, Diana's humiliation was soothed by a glimpse of Sondra's chagrined expression. Her satisfaction was short-lived.

"Henry, no! Please, no!"

Miriam's cry tore at the jagged edges of the wound inflicted on Diana's heart by the evidence of her father's visible suffering and pain.

"I am not depraved," Matt bit out through clenched teeth. "And Diana is unharmed."

"By God's grace, and our intervention," Henry retorted in tones of utter revulsion. "And not by a sense of conscience, or even caring, in you."

Diana set bolt upright, unable to bear any more. "Dad, I was as much to—"

Matt cut her off, stunning her into silence with his savage tone. "Shut up, Diana. I'll handle this."

"Handle it? Handle it?" Henry shouted, shaking with fury. "No, you will not handle it! I will!" His voice rose by degrees to a deafening roar. "I want you out of my home, now, at once, and I never want to see your face again!"

"Dad!"

"Henry!" Miriam cried, drowning Diana's cry of protest. Rushing to him, she clutched at his rigid arm. "Henry, you can't mean that!"

"Yes, I mean it!" Henry roared. "I want him gone, for good." His tear-filmed eyes pinned Matt. "What's more, if I had the guts, I'd get my shotgun and blow your filthy-minded son off the face of the earth."

"Oh, God! Oh, God, no!" Miriam sobbed in heartbroken supplication.

It's my fault. It's all my fault, Diana cried in silent anguish, thinking that none of this would have happened if she hadn't invaded Matt's privacy in the first place, or had obeyed his plea to her to leave him while he still had the presence of mind to let her go. She accepted the blame without question, knowing instinctively that, even having refused to leave him, she had held the power to stop Matt at any time.

"Blowing me to hell won't be necessary," Matt said, facing Henry unflinchingly. "I will marry Diana."

Silence screamed in the room.

Diana wished only to die to escape the excruciating pain of the insult piled atop the humiliation.

"There, you see, Henry?" poor Miriam exclaimed, clutching at a thread of hope. "Matt will set everything right."

Henry ruthlessly dashed his wife's hopes. "I'll see him dead before I see him wed to my daughter. The trust is gone, Matthew Turner," he said. "The trust, the love, all feeling. Gone. To me and mine, you are dead. I want you gone, as well. Now."

Matt didn't look at Diana. He didn't move as much as a flicker. Then he smiled—a hard, cynical smile of defeat. "As you wish," he said, walking away from the couch, and Diana. "I will call you in a few days, Mother." He paused to kiss Miriam on her tearstained cheek. Then he strode to the door and pulled it open, the cynical smile reappearing as the other family members and guests started and backed away.

"And a happy New Year to all of you, too," he drawled, sardonically, clearing a path through the ranks.

"Matt!" Sondra called after him anxiously. "Wait, I'll go with you."

"I don't think you'd like where I'm going," he tossed over his shoulder, continuing on to the front door.

"But where are you going?" she demanded.

"Straight to hell." Matt gave a short, harsh laugh and quietly shut the door.

Inside her father's office, curled into a ball of sheer misery, Diana shuddered in response to the note of agony she had heard in his laughter.

Banishment. Matt had been banished from the house he had thought of as home since his teens. She had brought him to this, Diana thought, numb to the comforting sound of her father's voice. Driven by inner urgings she couldn't comprehend, she had willfully played with the fire of temptation. And the flames of passion had seared her heart and soul.

Diana knew, intuitively, that she would carry the scars for as long as she drew breath.

"Diana, don't."

The soft, urgent sound of Matt's voice broke the thread of memory unwinding in Diana's mind. Suddenly at loose ends, and feeling vaguely as though she were twisting in the winds of desolation, Diana glanced around in search of something of substance to anchor her to reality.

Her gaze collided with the most solid-looking substance in the foyer—and he was monitoring her every move, every breath, every emotion.

Matt.

Diana felt hollow, and the emptiness inside her yawned wider with each successive moment. Had he said something about scars? Diana swallowed a bubble of hysterical laughter. Emotional scars? She could dash off a degree-worthy dissertation on the subject in minutes.

Dammit, it wasn't fair, Diana railed silently, staring at him, unaware of the pain shadowing her dark eyes. It had taken her the majority of the past nine years to knit the emotional scars—and still the stitches were none too tight.

"Please, don't, Diana." The urgency in Matt's voice was gone, replaced by a whispered plea.

"What?" Diana gave a brief shake of her head in hopes of rattling her thoughts into a semblance of coherency. "Don't...what?"

"Don't look at me like that," he murmured.

"Like what?" Of course, now she was staring at him even more intently.

"With that haunted look," he said in a harsh whisper, slanting a glance at the others to see if they were taking notice—they weren't. "That look of remembering that night, and resenting me, my being here."

"That's not true." Diana was fighting a sense of encroaching unreality again, feeling once more as though she had been standing in the foyer for hours, days, a lifetime, instead of mere minutes.

"Isn't it?" Matt raised one dark, wing-arched brow in a show of patent disbelief.

"No, I—" That was as far as she got, which was fortunate for her, since she had no idea of what to say to him.

"Supper's on the table, folks," Janet called from the dining room.

"And not a minute too soon." Laughing, Lissa crossed the foyer to Matt. "I'm starving," she announced. Her eyes bright with teasing humor, she shrugged out of her coat and offered it to him. "Are you going to stand there holding Diana's coat, or were you thinking of wearing it?"

"I see you haven't changed much, Melissa," Matt drawled, plucking the coat from her hands and turning to hang both garments in the closet. "You always were a flippant, nagging brat."

"I do my best," Lissa retorted, hooking her arm through one of his. "Nagging is my vocation."

"Yeah, well, take a vacation from your vocation." Grinning, Beth strolled over to them and captured Matt's free arm. "I hear enough nagging at work, thank you."

"Come along, children, you can fight it out over dinner." Her face and smile reflecting her contentment, Miriam clasped Henry's arm and started for the dining room. "Isn't this wonderful? Just like old times."

"Yes, dear, it's wonderful," Henry agreed indulgently, tossing a satisfied look over his shoulder at their assorted offspring. "Just like old times."

The two men's eyes met in silent, forgiving communion. Diana was the sole witness to the masculine reunion. A sigh lodged in her throat, a sigh of relief at the end of the nearly nine-year estrangement.

"Yes," Beth piped up. "Do you remember the time..." she began enthusiastically.

Diana tuned out her stepsister's bubbly voice, feeling left out as the trio trailed after her father and Miriam. It was not just like old times, she thought, slowing following the laughing, chattering group. For, while she rejoiced for the repair to the family breach, she feared things could never again be quite as they once were.

The chatter and laughter continued around the table throughout the meal. Quiet, speaking only when she was directly spoken to, Diana observed her family, concluding that her unvoiced opinion was correct.

For all his display of hearty congeniality, there were faint but definite signs of strain in Henry's tone. And, for all her show of contentment and delight, Miriam's eyes mirrored an underlying anxiety.

No, it was not just like old times, Diana mused, playing with the scant amount of food she'd served herself. Lissa and Beth were trying too hard to appear natural, and it was obvious, at least to Diana. And Matt, though friendly, seemingly relaxed, was watchful and wary, as if he anticipated an ambush.

Diana skimmed a glance over the faces of her table companions. They were all working very hard at maintaining a festive atmosphere. She released a soundless sigh, deciding that the ghost of New Year's Eve nine years past hovered over the table, undermining the holiday spirit.

A roar of laughter penetrated the murky thoughts clouding Diana's mind. The laughter contained the sound of genuine amusement. Forcing a smile, she ran another, clearer-eyed glance around the table. The others, including Matt, appeared to be thoroughly enjoying themselves.

Had she been projecting her own misgivings onto the other members of her family? Perhaps she was the only one experiencing undercurrents of unease. Startled by the consideration, Diana studied each smiling face in turn.

Miriam's still-lovely face was flushed with pleasure.

Beth's eyes were sparkling.

Lissa looked like an eager teenager.

Henry appeared smugly complacent.

And Matt—Diana's thoughts fractured.

Matt was staring intently into her startled eyes.

Feeling suddenly exposed, naked and vulnerable, Diana wrenched her startled gaze away from him. But from the corner of her eye she saw him frown.

What was Matt thinking? she wondered, automatically rising when the others slid their chairs back and stood up. The intensity of his stare unnerved her.

Certain that Matt was blaming her for all the years, all the holidays, he had missed sharing with his family, Diana gave him a wide berth as they all leisurely made their way out of the dining room and into the living room.

"Oh, the tree is magnificent!" Lissa exclaimed, rushing across the room to the majestic blue spruce.

"It certainly is," Matt agreed, sauntering over to her. "Smells good, too."

"Must I wait till Christmas Eve, or may I put my presents beneath it now?" she asked, turning a hopeful look on Henry and Miriam.

"You know we were never allowed to place gifts under the tree before Christmas Eve, Lissa," Beth said chidingly.

Lissa made a face. "That was when we were kids," she reminded Beth. "We're all grown up now."

"Coulda fooled me," Matt drawled, his dark eyes dancing with devilry, his grin wicked.

The evocative and so-familiar sight of his tormenting grin elicited responsive grins from Lissa and Beth, a girlish-sounding giggle from Miriam, and a soft chuckle from Henry. Diana didn't grin, giggle, chuckle, or even smile. She couldn't. His teasing, endearing grin stirred too many precious memories of happier times, when she had loved Matt with childish innocence, before that innocence had blossomed into sensuality, precipitating that dreadful confrontation.

They had been such a close-knit family, regardless of the fact that they had not all shared the same blood ties. And yet, Diana reflected, in one night—no, within little more than one hour—she and Matt had rent the fabric of their family by surrendering to sensuality and need.

She and Matt were both guilty as sin for the years of separation and unhappiness borne by the family. Diana accepted the burden of guilt without question, even as she acknowledged that she would do the same again to experience the thrill and excitement of Matt's embrace, his kiss, his loving.

She loved him. She had always loved him. She would always love him. She sighed. Merely surviving Matt's visit was going to be pure hell, loving and wanting him as she did, concealing her true feelings from the others—and most especially from Matt himself. But she would have to do it. The problem she had to deal with was how she could do it.

Keep busy.

The answer that sprang into Diana's mind mobilized her into determined action. Turning away from the bantering group, she headed for the foyer.

"Diana?" Henry's call halted her in the doorway. "Where are you going?"

"To the car," she replied, moving into the foyer. "I'm going to get Lissa's suitcase."

"Wait, I'll get it," Henry said.

"It's my case," Lissa called. "I'll get it."

"No, both of you stay here." Matt's tone held a note of command. "I'll get it."

Diana didn't pause to see who won the argument. Crossing the foyer, she pulled open the door and walked into the snow-tossed evening.

Dammit. Cursing to himself, Matt strode after Diana. Coming home had been a mistake. If he had had any doubts on that score, they had very effectively been demolished by the shattered expression shadowing Diana's eyes.

She didn't want him here, in her father's house. The realization caused a twisting pain inside Matt. He had waited so long to come back. It had been a deliberate decision on his part to stay away, a decision that had nothing to do with Henry's dictum.

Diana had been so young, and she had been caught up in the throes of first passion. He had forced himself to wait, giving her time and space to grow up, mature, learn something of the world, and the explosive nature of physical attraction.

Matt felt a stab of pure male jealousy. Diana was now twenty-six, and had probably long since been tutored in the act of sensuality. Resentment burned in his mind, in his gut, resentment of the man upon whom she had bestowed the honor of being her guide into the realm of erotic pleasure.

Matt had forced himself to wait, to persevere, and the emotional cost had been exceedingly high.

Throughout the intervening years, existing on the snippets of information he could garner about Diana from his mother and Beth during their brief visits together, Matt had bided his time, denying each urgent impulse to come back and demand that Diana recognize him, not as a teasing brother, not as a sensualist indulging his appetites with an untried girl, but as a man—the man who loved her, the man for her.

But was he in truth the man for her? Matt asked himself, stalking her to the back of the car. As far as his feelings went, there was no longer any question. After nine years of fruitless rationalization and self-denial, telling himself that she was too young, that he had merely been lust-driven and that, in any event, he had blown his chances by giving in to his desires, Matt had finally faced the truth.

He was in love with Diana. Matt grimaced as he crunched through the snow toward her. Hell, the truth was, he had always been in love with her, if in different ways. Coming to a stop beside her at the open trunk of the car, Matt felt the blade of pain twist deeper when

Diana flinched and stepped aside, putting a measured distance betweem them.

He loved her—and she couldn't bear to be near him. Diana had made that abundantly clear from the instant she spotted him after she followed her sister into the house. Her eyes had betrayed her, revealing the shock and the remembered pain and humiliation she was experiencing.

"I said I'd get it." Matt's voice was harsh. He couldn't help it; he was feeling his own pain.

Diana didn't respond, but just stood there, staring down at the snow-covered driveway.

Calling to mind every curse he knew, Matt grasped the handle of the suitcase and heaved it from the trunk. Damn, the thing was heavy! What in hell did Lissa have stuffed in there? he wondered, closing the trunk with a slamming *thunk*.

Diana just stood there, staring at the snow.

"You planning to spend the rest of my visit out here?" he asked, slanting a hard look at her.

Her head jerked up, and she transferred her stare to him. "No." Her voice was reedy, barely a whisper. "But I was giving serious consideration to Cancún, Hawaii, maybe Australia."

"Cute." Taking her by the hand, he hefted the case and started back toward the house, literally dragging her along with him. "But I feel I must tell you that Australia isn't far enough away."

Diana gasped and jerked her arm back, trying to free her hand from his.

Stopping in midstride, Matt tightened his hold on her hand and wheeled around to face her. His chest contracted, cutting off his breath. Words weren't needed— Diana's stark expression said it all, and then some, about her feelings. He had flat-out terrified her by telling her she couldn't run far enough for him not to follow, find her and bring her back.

Diana didn't want him to find her, not here or anywhere. Despair settled in Matt's mind. He loved her, and she didn't want him. He was thinking that he might as well return to Europe when his fighting spirit shot through him, zapping the despair. Matt was a success in business not only because he was good at what he did, but also because he relished a challenge. And the biggest challenge of his life was standing before him now, watching him warily, probably wondering why he was staring intently, silently, at her.

He'd meet the challenge Diana presented. Somehow, someway, he would make her love him.

The tension inside Diana seemed to crackle, sizzling from her to him, jolting him from his reverie. Matt imagined he could feel the seething electricity coiling around him, singeing his body hair. Smoldering, he stared at her, drinking in the sight of her.

Her dark eyes looked huge, bottomless, in the watery light flittering through the curtains on the windows. Snowflakes got tangled in her long lashes, spiking them as they melted. The stinging wind whipped flags of pink in her cheeks. Her long spiral curls glistened with beads of moisture.

She was wet! The realization drew Matt into awareness. His narrowed eyes skimmed the shivering length of her. Dammit! he railed against himself. She was cold!

"We'd better get back inside before you catch pneumonia." Pivoting abruptly, Matt gave a hard, no-nonsense tug on her hand. The weight of the suitcase yanked on his arm. "What in hell does Lissa have in this thing?" he muttered, more to himself than to her.

"Everything she owns, I think," Diana replied, in a rather wry tone.

Surprised that she had bothered to respond, Matt shot a keen glance at her as he strode into the foyer. Diana was actually smiling at him. Strained though it surely was, her smile still had the power to stop Matt in his tracks. The suitcase dropped from his hand, unnoticed.

"Everything she owns?" Matt asked, not caring about the answer, simply wanting to bask a moment longer in the warm glow of her smile. His breath caught when, amazingly, the smile leaped from her red lips to sparkle mischievously in her eyes.

"Well, maybe not everything." She raised her hand to ruffle her damp hair. "But a lot of stuff," she went on. "Including Christmas presents."

Christmas presents! Bells rang in Matt's head, celebrating the birth of an idea. He needed time with Diana, time alone, away from the rest of the family. Time to let her get to know him as a man, not a brother. And he hadn't done any Christmas shopping before leaving for the States. And he had never met a woman who didn't love to shop. A smile began inside Matt and worked its way to his lips.

"That reminds me. I still have shopping to do." Matt infused his voice with a note of chagrin. "And I haven't a clue as to what to get for everyone." He heaved a deep sigh. "Can I impose on you to go with me, help me with my selections?"

Chapter Four

"You want me to go with you?" Diana stared at Matt in sheer astonishment, certain she had misunderstood him. After telling her mere moments ago that she couldn't go far enough away to suit him, she couldn't believe he was now requesting her company on a shopping expedition.

"If you would, I'd appreciate it." Matt shrugged, drawing her eyes to the damp patches on his sweater. "I confess I haven't an inkling of what to buy."

Diana shivered, and not only because of the chill from her own wet sweater, but also from a gnawing uncertainty about the wisdom of spending an extended period of time alone with him. A burst of laughter wafted into the foyer from the living room. She sighed. Still, how could she refuse to accompany him without appearing churlish, if not downright childish? she asked herself, unconsciously revealing her ambivalence by absently tugging at the hem of her sweater with trembling fingers.

"Forget it," Matt said with harsh abruptness when the silence stretched too long between them. "Your reluctance to spend any time at all with me is obvious." His gaze homed in on her fingers, and a derisive smile crooked his lips. "I'll muddle along on my own."

"No." Diana blurted out, already feeling both churlish and childish. "I'll go with you," she said, the sound of an animated discussion inside the living room reminding her that this holiday visit was supposed to be a time of family peacemaking and healing. "When do you want to go?"

"Well, there are only a few days left until Christmas," Matt replied, his derisive smile changing subtly to one of self-satisfaction. "But, of course, I do realize that you work, and so..."

"And so?" Diana prompted when he paused, made uneasy by his self-satisfied smile, and positive he was about to make a suggestion she wouldn't like.

"How about tomorrow, after work?"

Diana took a moment to consider the idea. How long could it possibly take to buy a few gifts? she mused. If she left the office early, they could zip through the local shops, Matt could make his purchases, and they could still be home in time for dinner. Men hated to shop, anyway, didn't they?

Pleased with her conclusions, Diana smiled—and pondered the sudden taut, alert look on Matt's face. "Tomorrow will be all right," she said, puzzled by the flicker of emotion that briefly altered his watchful expression.

"Fine." Matt nodded, and it seemed to Diana that he was fighting to control a smile, or his feelings, or something. "What time do you usually leave the office?"

"The official closing time is five, but I often stay late." Shrugging off a sense of bafflement about the cause of his fleeting expression, Diana went on to outline her hastily put-together plan. "Since I'm caught up with the current project, I thought I'd leave the office at four. That way we could get an early start. Would that suit you?"

"Perfectly." Matt apparently lost the inner fight, at least against a smile. It curved his lips in a way that sent a tingle skipping up her spine to shiver along the fine hairs at her nape. "Do you ride to the office with Henry?"

"No." Diana frowned at the unexpected question. "As my hours are rather erratic, I drive myself. Why?"

Matt shrugged. "I thought it would save time if I could use your car and pick you up at the office."

Liking the idea of saving time, thus shortening the time she would have to spend with him, Diana pounced on his suggestion. "Yes, that makes sense. I'll drive into the office with Dad tmorrow."

"Good." Matt's tone of voice could only be described as a purr. The sound of it instilled apprehension in Diana. "I'll pick you up at four. We can shop for a while, then take a rest break and have dinner, then finish shopping refreshed."

Suddenly aware that she had good reason for apprehension, Diana opened her mouth to protest. "But—"

"Hey, what are you two doing out there all this time?" Lissa called from the living room doorway. "Are you cooking up Christmas surprises?"

"Yes," Matt admitted, turning to stroll toward the laughing woman. "So mind your own business—or you just might find your present pile short on Christmas morning."

Trapped. Convinced she had made a very big mistake by stupidly falling in with Matt's plans, Diana mentally kicked herself as she watched Matt and Lissa walk arm in arm into the living room to join the family.

Toting a bulging, oversize shopping bag, Matt kept his eyes pinned to Diana's enticing form. He was following in her wake as she adroitly weaved through the crowd of holiday shoppers bustling along the sidewalk.

Over an hour had passed since he had brought her car to a stop in front of the office building to find Diana waiting for him. Expecting to drive to one of the nearby malls, Matt had been surprised when, instead of getting into the car, Diana suggested he park in the office lot, since the restored shopping district was within walking distance.

Slushy snow covered the ground and lay in hard little piles along the curbs in front of the shops, lending an aura of authenticity to the quaint turn-of-the-century look of the area, which was three blocks long and closed to traffic.

Straight out of the pages of *A Christmas Carol,* Matt thought, noting the changes that had been made during his nine-year absence from the town.

Matt decided it would be easy to imagine having been flung back in time, if not for the modern dress of the shoppers, the piped Christmas music filling the crisp air from discreetly placed loudspeakers and the periodic blare of a car horn one block away from the confined area.

It was all very charming, Matt mused, dodging a group of giggling teenagers and extending his stride to catch up to Diana. Or it *would* be charming, he thought, if not for the damp cold seeping into his bones, the jostling of harried shoppers, and the breakneck pace Diana had set from the moment they reached the area.

Of course, Matt allowed, progress had been made—due to her single-minded determination. The bag he was lugging contained gifts for over half the names on his list. But, good God, the price he'd paid—not in currency, but in the wear and tear on his nerves, his patience—and his libido.

And there, four steps in front of him, strode the per-
petrator of his activated libido. A grim smile tightened
Matt's lips as he ran a slow look over Diana's curva-
ceous form.

The upper half of her body was concealed beneath a
waist-length fake fox jacket. It was the lower half of her
that was driving Matt to distraction. When she left the
house that morning, Diana had been suitably attired for
the office in a crisp white silk shirt and a knee-length
wool skirt. Along with her attaché case, she had carried
a small bag. The contents of that bag now encased her
hips and legs—tight, straight-legged, soft denim jeans.

Heat rushed to converge in a very vulnerable part of
Matt's body. No woman should look that appealing in
pants, he silently protested. It simply wasn't fair to the
male population, especially if that particular woman
possessed a compact, neatly rounded tush, and legs that
went on forever.

A nine-year-old image filled Matt's mind and senses.
An image of those same long legs, encased not in denim,
but in tantalizing sheer black nylon.

Matt smothered a groan, and murmured an apology
to the elderly gentleman he had absently clipped with his
shoulder while striding by. Damn. This was ridiculous,
Matt railed, at himself and at the situation he had
worked so hard to set up. His plan had been to get Diana away from the house, so that they could talk, one on
one. Why hadn't he realized that streets and shops
jammed with eleventh-hour holiday shoppers were not
conducive to private conversation?

A sigh of undiluted relief whooshed through his lips
when he saw Diana come to a stop in front of a brightly
decorated jewelry store. When he came to a halt beside
her, she took scant notice of him. Her lower lip caught

between her teeth, she was intently perusing the glittering contents of the display window.

"I'm parched. Can we break for dinner now?" he asked, his eyes trailing her roving gaze, but getting snared by a small blue-velvet tray of diamond engagement rings. One ring in particular caught his fancy. Nice. Very nice. He imagined how that large, pear-shaped stone would look gracing Diana's finger. Better than nice. It would be perfect.

"I just know your mother would adore that coat pin."

"What?" Shoving the consideration of the ring to the back of his mind, Matt turned to frown at her.

Diana heaved a long-suffering sigh. "I said, I believe your mother would like that coat pin." She pointed to the left side of the case. "The gold unicorn with the pearl-studded horn and tail and the ruby eyes."

"I was hoping we could stop to eat now," Matt muttered, dutifully transferring his gaze to the piece of jewelery. "I'm hungry and thirsty."

"But, Matt, we're almost finished." Diana began ticking off purchases on the fingers of her right hand. "You bought the cashmere jacket for Dad, the leather bomber jacket for Terry, and those absolutely gorgeous, wildly expensive stone-washed silk lounging pajamas and kimono for Beth. That only leaves your mother and Lissa."

And you, Matt thought, shifting his gaze back to the tray of diamond rings.

"Unless you have other names on your list besides the family..." she went on.

"No." Shaking his head, Matt dragged his gaze from the ring to her face. "But I'm still hungry."

Diana sighed again, more deeply this time. "But we could finish up here," she insisted. "As I said, I know your mother would love that pin, and I'm sure we can find the perfect gift for Lissa in the specialty shop next door.'' She gave him an overbright smile. ''We could finish up all your shopping and still get home in time to have dinner with the family.''

Matt clenched his teeth and felt a muscle twitch in his jaw. However nicely, Diana had made it clear that she didn't want to have dinner alone with him. His frustration was nearing the explosion point. But what could he do? There was no way he could force her to have dinner with him. Backing down had never been Matt's style, but, at least for now, he had little choice in the matter.

''Okay,'' he said, motioning toward the store's entrance. ''Let's get it over with.''

It was late. The house was quiet. It was so quiet Diana imagined she could hear Matt breathing in her father's office downstairs.

She couldn't sleep. In fact, she was wide awake, alternately prowling the perimeters of her room and plopping down on the side of her bed, refereeing a tug-of-war between her intellect and her emotions.

Battle had been joined after dinner, while the family was gathered together in the living room. But Diana had had hints of the brewing inner conflict for some time, ever since the evening her father had announced that he had offered the olive branch of peace in the form of an invitation to Matt, welcoming him back into his house to spend the holidays with the family.

Diana's inner conflict had begun that very evening, escalating by increments with each successive day. Intellectually she knew it was time—long past time—to resolve the anger and resentment that had separated the family for nine years. The strain had taken its toll on all of them, and most especially Diana, who had shouldered the burden of responsibility. And so, intellectually, she acknowledged that it was also time for her to make peace with Matt. And what better time to make peace than at the Christmas season?

That was when Diana's emotions came into play, causing the inner conflict. From an emotional standpoint, she felt unequal to the task of facing Matt, let alone welcoming him home like a long-lost brother.

Diana loved Matt with every cell, molecule and breath in her body. She knew she would always love him—and not as a brother, but as a man.

But, with his cutting remark about Australia not being a great enough distance between them, Matt had made his antipathetic feelings for her abundantly clear.

And yet he had almost immediately made an about-face by not only asking her to help him with his shopping, but also insisting they have dinner alone together.

Why had Matt even wanted to be alone with her? Diana's intellect repeatedly questioned. The answer that sprang to her mind was predictably logical.

Ask Matt. Talk to him. Alone.

The opportunity to have a private discussion with him had presented itself several hours ago, when Matt had asked for and received Henry's permission to use his office for a few hours later that night.

Matt was down there; Diana knew it, for she had identified the others as they passed her door on the way to their bedrooms over an hour ago.

Perched on the edge of the mattress, Diana heard the grandfather clock in the foyer strike one. The inner conflict raged on. Intellect urging her to seize the opportunity to speak with him alone, to make her peace with him. Emotions cautioning her against exposing herself to the possibility of rejection, more pain, a deeper hurt.

Matt probably wouldn't remain in the office much longer, Diana thought as the clock struck the half hour. To go or not to go, *that* was the question.

Diana absently pleated the soft folds of the full skirt she had changed into for dinner after returning to the house. When she became aware of the nervous action, she frowned at her plucking fingers.

Damn it all! she railed, impatient with herself. Was she a mature adult, or still an impetuous teenager, locked inside a woman's body?

Spurred by the chastising thought, Diana deserted her perch and strode purposefully to the door. Besides making her a nervous wreck, this situation was getting ridiculous. Pushing her emotional fears into the background, she left her room and moved quietly along the hallway and down the stairs.

The office door stood slightly ajar, the light beyond indicating that Matt was still inside. Diana hesitated a moment, drew a steadying breath, then tapped against the panel, pushed the door open and entered the room.

Matt was seated behind her father's desk, a sheaf of papers in front of him, an attaché case open and lying to one side. His expression revealed surprise at her entrance, but was quickly controlled as she came to an uncertain halt a few steps inside the room.

"Well, hello," he said softly, slicing a glance at his wristwatch. "To what do I owe this nocturnal visit?"

His ebony hair was ruffled, as if from the absent raking of his fingers. His shirt collar was open, revealing the strong column of his throat. He looked tired, but so handsome, so appealing, and so blatantly male and sexy.

"I, er...that is..." Diana's surge of courage suddenly deserted her, leaving her feeling tongue-tied, inadequate, gauche, much more the girl than the woman. Hating the feeling, she inhaled a quick breath, then blurted out, "I wanted to talk to you...privately."

"All right." Pushing the chair back, Matt stood and circled the desk. "Come sit down," he said invitingly, giving a negligent wave of his hand to indicate the long sofa set at an angle near the fireplace—the very same sofa of that awful night.

Feeling slightly sick with nerves, Diana slowly crossed the room, moving not toward the sofa, the setting of their downfall, but to one of the overstuffed chairs grouped around it.

"Afraid?" Matt softly taunted her, intersecting her to take her by the arm and redirect her to the sofa. "I give you my word that you have nothing to fear from me, Diana."

Certain he was again, however obliquely, telling her that he wasn't interested enough in her to cause her to fear him, Diana felt a hollow, desolate sensation invade her stomach. Keeping her spine ramrod-straight and her shoulders squared, she sank into one corner of the sofa and kept her eyes fixed forward.

Matt settled his long form next to her, close, too close for her peace of mind, yet carefully not touching her with any part of his body. "Comfortable?"

Comfortable? Diana nodded in response and swallowed a groan of despair. Her taut, stiff posture concealed her senses inner clamoring to touch him, cling to him, beg him to want her again. Her tightly controlled expression betraying nothing of her feelings, she slanted a wary look at him. It was nearly her undoing. Matt's expression was gentle, yet intent. His dark eyes seemed to glow from an inner fire.

"You said you wanted to talk to me," he prompted her in a low, enticing murmur.

"Yes, I..." Diana paused to swallow once more and glide her tongue over her nerve-dried lips.

"Oh, Di, don't do that," Matt muttered, raising a hand to rake his fingers through his already ruffled hair. "We'll never get around to talking if you continue to do that."

"Wh— Don't do what?" she asked in a parched and raspy sounding whisper.

"Wet your lips like that with your tongue," he murmured. "The effect is the same as it was that night, like a silent invitation to me to kiss you." He heaved a sigh, and gave her a self-deprecating smile. "And I've been waiting so long, so very long, for that invitation."

"Waiting?" Diana turned to face him, and caught her breath at the expression of near-desperate longing straining his taut features. Barely breathing, trembling, she unconsciously wet her lips again. "But I thought—"

"Don't think, feel," he muttered, turning to lean over her. Then, giving a fatalistic shrug, he bent his head and brushed his mouth over hers.

Diana's mind fractured. Part of it, a tiny, still-lucid part, insisted that he had to be playing with her, deliberately tormenting her, since he had made a point of telling her she couldn't get far enough away to suit him. But the other part, the larger part, overshadowed the lucid part, shouting a demand that she seize the moment.

The issue was decided by an inner fear that the moment might never come for her again. Surrendering to the rioting demands of her raging senses, the searing need to taste him, she raised her arms and captured his head with her hands, drawing his mouth back to her parted and eager lips.

Matt went rock-still for an instant, as if startled—or shocked, by her blatant advance. Then, with a groan rumbling deep in his throat, he crushed her mouth beneath his.

No longer the tremulous girl, Diana responded with heated fervor, initiating a sensuous play by gliding her tongue along his lower lip while arching her body, pressing her soft curves to the hard angles of his.

Matt didn't hesitate to accept her silent offering. Stroking her tongue with his, he plunged inside, deepening the kiss as he sought her breast with one hand. He stroked the full outer curve before slipping his hand between their bodies to capture the taut tip, teasing it into a tight, throbbing arousal.

Sensations splintered inside Diana, sending shards of desire streaking from her pulsating nipple to every nerve ending in her quivering body. Starved for the feel of him after her nine-year fast, she sent her tingling hands exploring his head, his neck, his shoulders, his back, every inch of him that she could reach with her searching palms and fingers.

"Diana, Diana..." he groaned, releasing her mouth to string hot, stinging kisses over her cheeks, along her jawline, then down the arched column of her throat. "I want you, I want you. Don't do this unless you want me, too."

"I do," she confessed, kissing his silky eyebrows, his eyelids, the vulnerable hollows beneath his eyes. "I want to be with you, to belong to you."

"But not here." Pulling away from her, Matt skimmed a hard look around the room. "Not here."

"No," she whispered. "Please, not here."

Matt was still for the length of a breath. Then, with a decisive nod of his head, he stood, scooped her up into his arms and strode from the room.

"Where—?" Diana's voice faded as he started up the staircase. Her room? she wondered. His?

Without hesitation, Matt strode to the end of the hallway and mounted the staircase leading to the third floor, and the bedroom that had been his from the day his mother married Diana's father. Locking the door behind him, he carried her to the side of the bed, then gently set her on her feet.

His chest heaving from his exertion, Matt stared into Diana's eyes. "You can still change your mind." His lips twisted into a smile of self-mockery. "But if you're going to, do it now, before I change mine."

Diana didn't hesitate long enough to allow common sense to overrule her emotions. Letting her actions speak for her, she slipped off her shoes, crawled onto the bed and held her arms out to him.

Matt inhaled sharply, then stretched his length next to her on the mattress. They turned as one, each reaching to embrace the other. Their kiss was deep, breathtaking. When they had to break the kiss to breathe, Matt raked his lips down her neck.

"I've waited so long, and I need you so damn much." His breathing strained, ragged, Matt glided his tongue from the wildly beating pulse at the base of her throat to the V of her silk shirt at the valley of her aching breasts. Smoothly, deftly, he undid the shirt buttons and unfastened the front clasp of her lacy bra.

After his remark about Australia not being far enough away for her to go, his claim of intense need succeeded only in confusing Diana. "I— Matt!" She gasped, shuddering, when his tongue gently lashed her nipple. "I don't understand. Just last night you told me that Australia wasn't far enough for me to be away from you. Now you say you need me. It doesn't make sense." She cried out with a quickly drawn breath when his tongue curled around her nipple.

"Then I'll make myself crystal-clear." Lifting his head from her breast, Matt stared into her passion-shadowed eyes. "What I meant last night was that Australia wasn't far enough away for you to run from me. I'll find you, wherever you go." He drew in a harsh breath, then said bluntly, "I ache for you, Diana. I have ached for you from the year you turned seventeen. And the aching has been damn near unbearable the last nine of those years." The flame deep in his dark eyes leaped into a blaze of unleashed desire. "Every woman I've been with throughout those years has been a pale substitute for you." He lowered his head to seize her surprise-widened lips with his own.

Matt's kiss, though brief in duration, was devastating in effect. It drowned her senses, and the questions still nagging at the edges of her mind. But the answers no longer mattered to Diana. Matt wanted her, needed her, if only to appease an unsatisfied hunger.

Lust. It was light-years away from love, but it was an emotion, a driving emotion that Matt felt for her. It was better than the nothing she had lived with for nine years.

Diana was vaguely aware that she would very likely regret this night, but for now, Matt was here, in her arms, needing her, eager to fulfill her own yearning.

"Stay with me. Join with me. Be one with me, Diana," he pleaded, stroking her lips with his teasing tongue, and her breast with his fingers.

"Yes," she whispered in surrender. Then, more urgently: "Oh, Matt, *yes.*"

Murmuring shocking, erotic, exciting words to her, words that described his fantasies about all the ways they could be together, Matt smoothed the clothing from her body. Then he rolled off the mattress to stand beside the bed, his glittering eyes devouring her nude form while he literally tore away his own clothing, revealing to her the extent of his arousal.

Diana trembled, not in fear, but in anticipation. She knew what to expect, and she didn't care. Like him, she had waited so long, too long to be deterred by the prospect of a moment of discomfort.

"Diana." Matt half growled, half groaned her name as he took the one step needed to bring him to the edge of the bed.

Ready, eager, desperate for him, Diana offered him the ultimate invitation by again holding out her arms, and this time parting her thighs for him.

"It will be good, it will be more than good," Matt promised, bracing his hands on either side of her as he eased his body into the cradle of her thighs. "It will be wonderful."

Lowering his head, he crushed her lips beneath his, and thrust his tongue into her mouth at the same instant he thrust his body into hers.

The tearing pain wrenched a muffled cry from Diana. Her body contracted and stiffened in reaction to the sudden invasion of her flesh by his.

Matt went absolutely still for a heartbeat. Then he pulled his head back to stare at her in blank astonishment and sheer disbelief.

"Diana..." His voice was rough, heavy with self-condemnation. "I hurt you ... But I had no idea, never dreamed that you could possibly still be a vir—"

"It's all right," she broke in, grasping his buttocks when he made as if to withdraw. "No, don't move. The pain is gone. Just give me a minute."

Matt watched her, examining her eyes, her face, for evidence of strain, his expression betraying the inner battle he was waging, between his concern for her possible discomfort and his raging desire.

Diana kept a tight grasp on him, holding him deep inside her as her body adjusted to the fullness of his. The stiffness drained from her body, to be replaced immediately by the tension of rising excitement and desire.

"Now," she whispered, digging her nails into his taut flesh and arching into his responsive thrust. *"Now."*

Set free of the constraints of his concern for her, Matt obeyed Diana's ragged command. Unleashing the power of his strong body, he drove himself, and her, mercilessly. Reveling in her uninhibited response to his every move, his body and hers gleaming slickly in the pale moonlight splashing across the bed, he drove them both over the edge, into gasping completion.

Chapter Five

"Wake up, Sleeping Beauty."

Diana emerged from the deep sleep of repletion to the feel of a sweet kiss from her own Prince Charming. Thoroughly exhausted, they had slept still coupled, and not from their first joining, but their third, his body buried deeply in hers.

"Ummm..." she murmured, stretching her cramped limbs by flexing her arms, which were circling his neck, and tightening the muscles in her legs, which were clasped around his thighs. "More," she pleaded softly, seeking the smiling lips hovering above her mouth.

"Just one more," Matt whispered, teasing her with quick stabs of his tongue into the corner of her mouth.

"Why?" Diana protested, pushing her lower lip forward in a pout of disappointment.

"Because it will soon be dawn," Matt said, gliding his tongue along her pouting lip. "And I'm cold."

"Pull up the covers."

Matt grinned. "Can't. We kicked them onto the floor sometime during the night."

Covered by his larger form, Diana felt deliciously warm, and was growing warmer by the second. She moved her hips, wriggling and arching to ease the heaviness of his weight, which was pressing her into the firm mattress. She smiled when she felt the leap of renewed life inside her.

Matt drew a sharp breath, then went still, as if savoring the sensation of his quickening arousal. "I mean, my back is cold," he said, moving his hips. "My front is warm, and heating up like crazy." Suddenly he went still, frowning down at her. "Did that hurt? Are you sore?"

"No. And yes." She did have a few twinges of soreness. "But please don't stop." She sighed in response to his gentle, tentative thrust. "It feels so good, and it makes me forget the soreness."

Matt shot a glance at the watch clasped on his naked wrist. "It will have to be a quick one, Beauty." He began moving his body as he murmured the warning. "Or we'll be risking getting caught again, this time with our pants down."

"Off," Diana told him, the sexual tension spiraling inside her negating the anguish usually associated with the memory. "Oh, Matt, hurry...hurry!"

Proving he was only too happy to comply, Matt set a rhythmic pace that hurled them, breathless and mindless, into the heights of shattering release.

Spent, Diana lay entwined with Matt as she slowly descended from the realm of unbelievable ecstasy. Feeling his heart thump in time with her own, listening as his breathing evened and regulated, she smiled and stroked her fingers through the sweat-dampened strands of his glistening black hair.

"For all your lack of experience," he whispered, his chest expanding in a sigh of contentment, "you are fantastic." He raised his hand to a long, jet-black spiral curl coiled on her shoulder and slowly wound it around his finger, as if binding her to him. "You're even more exciting as a lover than I ever dreamed you'd be."

Feeling inordinately complimented by his praise, Diana rushed to admit to her fears. "I...I was afraid you'd be disappointed ... in comparison to your other ... er—'' she hesitated, groping for another word for *lover* ''—partners.'' She blurted out the final word artlessly.

Matt raised his head from her breast to gaze at her with eyes alight with amusement. ''There haven't been all that many, Di.'' His voice, though quiet, rang with sincerity. ''And, as I told you, they were all merely sub- titutes, shadows of the one lover I always wanted.''

''Me?'' Diana asked, her tone betraying both her amazement and her aching desire to believe him.

''You.'' Matt smiled the smile of a self-satisfied con- queror. ''And to think I was the first.'' He shook his head, as if unable to believe his good fortune. ''All I can say is, being first with you is the best Christmas present I ever received.''

Diana didn't respond, couldn't respond, for while her emotional self grew flushed with his expressed pleasure, her intellectual side rejected the importance of virginity.

Matt lowered his eyes to her cheeks, noting the evi- dence of her blush, thus missing the cloud of conflict in her eyes. Then, sighing again, he buried his face in the curve of her neck. ''It must be nearly five now,'' he murmured regretfully, pressing his lips to the side of her throat. ''We've got to move.''

''I know.'' Diana agreed. ''But I'm not even sure I can move. I'm so, so...''

''Satisfied?'' Matt finished for her, pushing himself up and back to stare down into her still-flushed face.

''Yes,'' she admitted, telling herself she had moved far beyond dissimulation. ''And so sleepy.'' She yawned and turned her head to peer at his watch. ''I'd better get to bed. To my *own* bed. As it is, I'll only get about two hours' sleep.''

Grunting, Matt heaved himself up, away from her and off the bed. Then he proceeded to steal her restored breath by raising his arms and stretching luxuriously, flexing the tendons and long muscles in his fit, magnificent body. "I feel great," he declared, bending to collect their clothes. "Better than I have for—" He paused, absently stroking her shirt. "Forever," he finished, smiling, as he stepped into his briefs.

Her uncertainty, soreness and sleepiness aside, Diana felt pretty good herself. The loss of her physical innocence seemed to lend an added measure of maturity to her perceptions. Although Matt had confessed to lusting for her, not loving her, he had made love with her, not merely had sex with her, and had rejoiced in her innocence and her pleasure. And if Matt's offering was less than she desired in her heart of hearts, it still was more than she had ever hoped to have of him.

"Why don't you take the day off?" he suggested, holding her shirt for her, then raising a hand to lift her long hair from beneath the collar. "Sleep in."

"Can't." Diana fastened her skirt, then gathered up her bra, panty hose and shoes. "The office closes at noon today for the duration of the holidays." She gave him a faint smile as she slowly walked to the door. "Dad and I take the office staff to lunch after closing. I have to be there." She paused at the door to look back at him with unabashed longing. "I'll be home early, and I'll catch a nap before it's time to leave for the airport to pick up Terry."

"Wait till I pull on my pants, and I'll walk you to your room," he said when she unlocked the door and grasped the knob.

Diana gave him a chiding look. "And risk being seen together?" She arched her brows. "With you half-dressed and me carrying my underwear?"

Matt heaved an impatient sigh. "I don't care anymore, Di," he said, walking to her and pulling her into his arms. "You're a woman now, an adult. You said you wanted to belong to me, and now you do." His mouth claimed hers in a quick, hard, possessive kiss. "And I don't care who knows it."

"Matt, please, think." Diana gazed at him imploringly. "Do you really want to chance disrupting another holiday? Do you want to insult Dad after he extended an offer of peace to you?"

Matt's expression revealed his conflicting feelings. "No, of course not." He shook his head. "But, dammit..."

Diana effectively silenced him with her mouth, gently pressed to his complaining lips. "I'll be quite safe," she promised, teasing him. "There are no muggers in the hallway."

Matt favored her with a wry smile, and another satisfying kiss. "Okay, you win—this time."

"Thank you. Now I must run." She raised a hand to cover another yawn. "Have a good day, Matt."

"Oh, I intend to." Matt's expression was oddly enigmatic. "Sleep well, Beauty."

"Hey, Di, are you alive in there?" Lissa's shout followed a loud rap on the bedroom door. "Dad, Matt and Terry have gone downstairs already."

"In a minute," Diana called, grimacing at herself in the mirror as she gave one last tug of her hairbrush through her sleep-tossed riot of curls. She belted her robe securely around her waist as she headed for the door, declaring herself ready to face the traditional Blair-Turner family Christmas-morning activities.

Ever since the two separate families had combined forces to form one family unit, a Christmas-morning ritual had been observed, a ritual that had been adhered to with only slight variations to the present.

Since both the four-year-old Diana and the two-year-old Melissa naturally still believed in Santa Claus—and Miriam had doubts about the nine-year-old Bethany's professed disbelief—Miriam, Henry and Matt, then in his teens, had kept up the game of Christmas-morning wonder and surprise by trooping downstairs at the crack of dawn with the excited girls, who were too eager and impatient to wait for anyone to dress.

Then, after the gifts had all been opened and exclaimed over, and the living room looked as if it had been hit by a tornado, everyone had pitched in to clear away the wrapping paper, ribbons, bows, gift cards and other debris before trooping into the dining room for breakfast. After breakfast, everyone had then returned to their rooms to dress for church.

Of course, the game had continued after Terry's birth. By the time the youngest member of the combined families no longer believed in the largess of a jolly fat man in a red suit, a family ritual had been established.

But this was the first Christmas morning in nine years when every member of the family would be there to take part in and enjoy the gift-giving ritual.

"Di-a-na!" Lissa yelled.

"Yes, yes, I'm coming." Diana reached for the doorknob, sighed, and let her hand fall to her side.

And this was the first Christmas morning ever that she'd wanted to absent herself from the ritual.

Diana's reasons for wanting to remain in her room, hiding behind a contrived migraine, or a sore throat, or some other debilitating illness, were many—and every one of them bore the name Matt.

Matt. Diana sighed and shifted a longing gaze from the bedroom door to her bed. The soreness in her body had dissipated over the past two days. But, in direct response to Matt's baffling demeanor, the uncertainty plaguing her mind had intensified.

Not that Diana had expected Matt to betray to the rest of the family the intimacy they had shared in his bedroom, in his bed. Absolutely the last thing she wanted was a replay of that terrible scene of nearly nine years ago.

In retrospect, Diana really didn't know exactly what she had expected from him, but it certainly hadn't been the odd looks and contemplative expression Matt had worn in the course of the past two days.

What were his thoughts, his feelings? she had found herself wondering. On her return to the house the day after their night in bed together, Diana had nervously anticipated their first meeting. She'd been tired, not only from the exercise of repeated wild lovemaking, but also from a lack of sleep, the employees' luncheon, and dashing around to find the one gift she had not yet purchased—a present for Matt.

More than a little uncertain about the gift she had finally selected, she had entered the house feeling heavy with misgivings about how the gift would be construed, and not at all anxious to face the prospective recipient of her offering.

She might as well have saved herself the hours of angst. Matt hadn't even been in the house. In passing, Miriam had casually mentioned that he'd gone out to do some eleventh-hour shopping of his own. Grateful for the reprieve, and claiming exhaustion, Diana had dropped like a stone onto her bed, sleeping through dinner and straight up to a few hours before it was time to drive to the airport to collect Terry.

The day and evening before Christmas had been jam-packed with last-minute activities that allowed not a single opportunity for so much as a few private words between Diana and Matt. But she had several times caught him staring at her with that strange, reflective expression.

When the seemingly endless day came to a close with the family all bringing their gifts into the living room to arrange around the base of the tree, Diana had held back the gift she had bought for Matt, and then, against her better judgment, had thrust it to the very back of the pile.

Now, at an ungodly hour on Christmas morning, Diana hesitated, a step away from her bedroom door, wishing the small gift was safely back in her dresser drawer.

"Diana, you'd better get a move on," Beth called in a tone of voice edged with impatience. "Lissa's threatening to go downstairs without you."

What else is new? Diana thought, smiling despite her trepidation. Beside herself with excitement, Lissa had always threatened to go downstairs alone on Christmas morning. Keeping her smile firmly in place, Diana opened the door and left the room. Her smile tilting to one of apology in response to the long-suffering expressions aimed at her by Lissa, Beth and Miriam, she stifled a sigh and trailed behind the trio, down the stairs and into the living room.

"Well, at last," Terry said teasingly. "Don't tell me, let me guess. Diana held up the parade—right?"

His good-natured remark was met with affirmative nods from the women, an indulgent chuckle from her father, and an enigmatic smile from Matt.

Deciding she was getting pretty tired of his enigmatic and musing looks, Diana ignored the bunch of them as she walked to the chair farthest from the tree. Clasping her hands in her lap to keep them from trembling, she sat quietly, watching as Miriam and Lissa handed out the gifts, whittling away at the pile around the tree. Then, just as quietly, she opened the presents handed to her, softly murmuring her thanks and declaring her pleasure with each successive gift, while observing the reactions of the others, and most especially Matt.

"Hey, thanks, Matt!" Terry hooted, jumping up to try on the leather bomber jacket.

"Hmm, smells sexy," Matt said, shooting a devilish look and a grin at Lissa as he sniffed at the expensive cologne she had chosen for him. "Thank you."

"Matt, this really wasn't necessary," her father murmured, stroking the cashmere jacket. "I don't know what to say."

"Then don't say anything," Matt replied, shifting a soft gaze to his mother. "I only hope you like it as much as I like this," he went on, holding an imported Irish sweater up to his chest.

"Darling, this is absolutely fabulous!" Miriam cried, displaying the coat pin for everyone's perusal.

And so it went, Beth delighting in the silk pajamas and kimono, Lissa in transports over the small beaded evening bag Diana had spied in the specialty shop, and Matt obviously touched by the symbolism in the gift of a new front-door key from Henry.

When she opened her gift from Matt, Diana prayed she was successful in concealing the disappointment and hurt she felt about the lovely but ordinary scarf he had chosen for her. Reminding herself that her gift was every bit as ordinary, even if it did convey her deepest feelings, she waited, growing more nervous by the second for him to get to it. Hers was the last gift he opened.

Matt drew out the moment, carefully tugging the wrapping loose before lifting her gift from the paper. He held the book in his hands for long seconds, staring down at the title. When, finally, he raised his head to stare at Diana, the enigmatic, reflective expression was gone, and his eyes were soft, glowing with some strong inner emotion.

"What is the title, Matt?" Miriam asked curiously.

"Come Home to Love," Matt said quietly, reading from the book's cover.

"Oh, how clever of you, Diana!" Lissa exclaimed. "Perfect for the occasion."

"More than you know," Matt said, glancing around at everyone in turn, pausing an instant to share a secret, mysterious smile with Henry.

"Yeah, terrific, Di," Terry interjected into the brief silence that ensued. "Now, how about breakfast?" He sprang up from his sprawled position on the floor. "I'm starving."

"If all of you will be patient for a few more minutes," Matt said, bringing the rustle of movement to a halt, "I have something I want to say."

Diana had set her gifts to one side in preparation to rise, but she settled back in her chair to hear Matt out, convinced by his expression, the emotion shining from his dark eyes, that he planned to voice his appreciation to all of them for their warm and generous homecoming welcome.

"I have discussed this with Henry, and have received both his permission and his blessing."

Matt's opening statement startled and confused Diana. Her father's permission and blessing? she repeated to herself. For what possible reason... Her thoughts were scattered by a sudden leap of hope as Matt began speaking again.

"In deference to the man I had come to love, respect and regard as a father," he said, slowly glancing at the attentive faces around him, "I exiled myself from this house and frequent personal contact with the members of my family, most particularly one member." His gaze came to rest on Diana. "The one person I love, have always loved above all others."

Diana drew in a sharp breath; it blended in with the chorus of surprised gasps from the others. Her eyes wide, unconsciously pleading with him to be telling the truth, she watched him rise and slowly walk toward where she sat, riveted to the chair at the far corner of the room.

"I denied my right to that love for nine long years, paying the price for my loss of control and self-indulgence on that ill-fated New Year's Eve." He slid a hand into the pocket of his cardigan sweater as he came to a stop in front of Diana. "But, no matter how much I denied myself, I never stopped loving," he said, staring deeply into her eyes, as if attempting to see into her soul. "I knew the moment Diana walked into the house the day I arrived that I had been in love with her, am still in love with her, and will always be in love with her."

Diana's eyes were stinging from tears she couldn't hold back. She didn't notice. All she saw was Matt's beloved face as he dropped to his knees before her.

"You have given me the most precious gift a woman can give to a man," he murmured, in a heart-wrenchingly tender tone. Removing his hand from his pocket, he opened it to reveal a small black-velvet jeweler's box. "In comparison to the gift of your innocence, my offering is paltry," he whispered for her ears alone. "But I love you, and pray with all my heart that you will accept it." His hands unsteady, his fingers shaking, Matt lifted the lid of the box.

"Oh, Matt!" Diana breathed, staring in disbelief and delight at the beautiful pear-shaped diamond engagement ring winking up at her from the satin lining of the box. "It's...it's...so very beautiful."

"I know." Matt smiled with loving tenderness. "But will you accept it...and me?"

"Yes," she answered in a reedy whisper. Then, exultantly: "Yes, yes, yes!"

Matt's waist pressed against Diana's knees as he leaned forward, bringing his mouth close to hers. His lips were within a fleeting thought of touching hers. Her own lips were tingling in anticipation. Then his breath was exhaled into her mouth in a moist *whoosh* followed by a chuckle at the confused sound of his stepbrother's voice.

"What did he say to her?" Terry asked as the other members of the family discreetly headed for the doorway.

"You mean you can't figure it out for yourself?" Beth drawled, laughing, as she slipped from the room.

Lissa taunted him, following Beth. "What a brain trust."

"It's all right, Terry," Miriam said soothingly. "Your time will come, and then you'll understand."

"My time for what?" Terry demanded. "And where are you all going?"

"Your time for love, Terry," Henry answered, draping one arm around his son's shoulders to steer him in the wake of the others. "And we're all going in to breakfast."

"Love?" Terry repeated, rather as if it were an unsavory word. "Matt and Diana are in love?"

"From the way they are looking at each other now," Henry replied, his voice drifting back to the couple from the foyer, "I would say that they are."

"Are they?" Matt murmured against Diana's lips. "Are they *both* in love?"

"They are," Diana whispered, straining forward to coax his mouth into contact with hers.

Matt pulled his head back, just far enough that he could gaze into her misty dark eyes. "Then say it, Beauty. I said it. Now I want, need, am dying to hear you say it, too."

"I love you, Matt Turner." Diana's voice was strong with conviction. "I have always loved you. I will always love you." A teasing smile tilted her lips. "And don't ever even think about running away from me, because there is no place on this entire planet far enough away that I won't find you." She gave him a smug smile. "So, what do you say to that?"

Matt answered her silently first, in the form of a long, sweet, satisfying kiss. When he raised his head, his dark eyes were bright, and his verbal answer came accompanied by a wicked smile.

"Merry Christmas, Diana."

* * * * *

A Note from Joan Hohl

The Christmas holiday season has always been my most favorite time of the year. There's a special magic in the very
air, be the weather cold or balmy. Though rushed and harried, loved ones, friends, neighbors, even strangers you pass
on the street or in shopping malls, seem more inclined to
smile rather than frown at an accidental bump or jostling.

I like to believe the name of that special magic is *love,* the
love we feel year-round in our hearts for our fellow men, but
only feel free to express in celebration of the birth of our
Blessed Lord.

And so I appreciate this opportunity at this special season to express to each and every one of you my heartfelt
wishes for a joyous Christmas and Happy New Year.

A KISS FOR
MR. SCROOGE

Lucy Gordon

POLLO CON SALSA D'UOVO
(Chicken in egg-and-lemon sauce)

This is one of my husband's favorite holiday dishes, even though it's not specifically for Christmas.

4 portions of free-range chicken
salt and pepper
3 tbsp olive oil
1 oz unsalted butter
1 clove garlic, crushed
1 oz plain flour
½ pint chicken stock
1 bay leaf
½ tsp dry thyme
2 egg yolks
1 tbsp lemon juice
chopped parsley
lemon slices

Season the chicken with salt and pepper. Heat the oil, butter and garlic in a pan, add the chicken and fry gently for about 12 minutes, or until golden. Remove and set aside. Pour off all the fat except for 2 tablespoons.

Add the flour to the pan and cook, stirring for 1 minute. Add the stock and bring to a boil, stirring. Return the chicken to the pan, add the bay leaf and the thyme, cover and simmer for 30 minutes, until tender.

Transfer the chicken to a warm serving dish. Remove the herbs from the remaining sauce and discard. Blend the egg yolk and the lemon juice with 3 tablespoons of the sauce. Add to the pan, heating gently, stirring until thickened. Do not boil. Adjust the seasoning and pour over the chicken. Garnish with parsley and lemon slices. Serves 4.

Chapter One

Dawn studied the sky and found it heavy with unfallen snow. Surely, she thought, it would fall in time for a white Christmas? She couldn't decide whether to be glad or sorry. The kid in her, who still flourished at twenty-seven, insisted that it wouldn't be Christmas without snow. The veterinarian in her pointed out that her work consisted mostly of driving the countryside to visit sick farm animals, and snow would create problems. The kid won.

She got back into her ancient car and drove the few miles to Hollowdale, the village where she was the most junior member of a three-person practice. She'd arrived just before last Christmas, and had been instantly charmed by the old-world atmosphere of a place where all the time-honored traditions were kept up.

It had taken a while for her to be accepted in a country practice. Jack and Harry, the two partners, had talked about the rigors of dealing with hefty farm animals, but had finally been persuaded to give her a chance.

The farmers had been even harder to convince. A young woman with a slim, elegant frame, a mass of glossy dark hair and large brown eyes wasn't their idea of a vet for a recalcitrant bull. But Dawn was stronger than she looked and she soon proved herself capable of dealing with everything. Her dedication to the animals in her care and her willingness to turn out on freezing nights had finally won the community over to her side, and she now felt as much at home in Hollowdale as if she'd been born there.

Her route back took her past Hollowdale Grange, the huge house that for centuries had been the heart of village festivities. The carol singers always called there halfway through the evening, and sang their hearts out for Squire Davis, who gave them hot drinks to refresh them for the work still to come, and placed a generous donation in their box. And every year he'd let his home be used for a Christmas party for deprived children, just as his ancestors had done. But Squire Davis had died earlier that year apparently leaving no heir. The house had been closed and had stayed shuttered all summer and autumn.

Now, as she passed, Dawn noticed something that made her brake sharply and reverse to get a better look. Lights were on in the house. Men were carrying things in from a removal van. Dawn drove on, feeling cheered.

Harry, the younger partner, came in as she was writing up her notes. He was a pleasant-faced young man whose eyes were always warm when they rested on Dawn. She often flirted with him in a cheerful way that she never allowed to get too intense, although she knew Harry wanted more.

"Jack tells me you're going to work over Christmas," he said, sounding scandalized. "You really want to do that?"

"Somebody has to," Dawn pointed out. "Animals get sick even then, and with so many farms around here, there's every chance that someone will need a vet."

"Of course. But why should it be you again? You volunteered to be on call last year. And it was your first Christmas in Hollowdale, I remember."

"Harry, I really don't mind," Dawn assured him. "Jack's got a wife and children, and you've got your brother's family to visit. You know your little nephews and nieces count on 'Uncle Harry.' "

"Oh, I may drop in and keep you company," he said with studied casualness.

"I'm sure there's no need."

"Well, you don't think I'm going to pass up the chance to be with you, do you?" he teased.

She looked up at him, laughing, and he leaned down to kiss her lightly, vanishing before she could either encourage or reject him. Dawn sighed. It would be lovely if she could respond to Harry, a nice man if ever there was one, but one who couldn't excite her.

Only one man had ever made her heart beat strongly, and he had also broken it. That had been eight Christmases ago—long enough for any reasonable woman to recover. And she *had* recovered. It was just that she'd never fallen in love again since, and the festive season had lost some of its savor for her.

Jack, the senior partner, had just finished taking the morning surgery. He was a middle-aged, thickset man with an amiable face, and he grinned when he saw her.

"There's someone moving into the Grange today," Dawn said. "I saw the van as I passed."

Jack's grin vanished abruptly. "You don't have to tell me," he growled. "I've already had a brush with him, and come off worst."

"Why, what happened?"

"I approached him early this morning, about the children's party. I know there are only three days left, but that would still have been enough time to organize something if we worked fast.''

"You mean he said no?" she asked in dismay.

"I mean I got shown the door. 'No party. Not this year, not next year, not ever. Get out! Don't come back!' That was the message.''

"But the Grange parties are legendary. If he's a Davis, surely he knows that.''

"He isn't a Davis. The lawyers finally traced the old man's heir living on the other side of the world. All he wanted was to turn his heritage into money as fast as possible. He put it into the hands of big-city auctioneers, who know nothing about Hollowdale and its traditions, and care less. They sold it to the highest bidder.''

"Does this man have a wife? Perhaps she could talk him around?''

"He's unmarried, which has doubtless saved some poor woman from a terrible fate. His guard's impenetrable, like granite. I tried every argument—it's Christmas, the children will be heartbroken. I was still talking as he steered me to the door. This man doesn't care about children's hearts. He doesn't care about Christmas. All he cares about is being left alone. It was like talking to Scrooge. I almost expected him to wave his walking stick and say, 'Bah! Humbug!'''

Dawn gave a faint smile. "Scrooge turned out to be just an old softy at heart," she reminded.

"Anyone who thinks this man is a softy at heart is in for a nasty surprise," Jack growled. "By the way, I've had Harry on to me about letting you work over the holiday again. Did I jump at your offer too quickly? Would you rather be going home somewhere?''

"I've nowhere to go," Dawn said. "My parents are dead, and I've no close family. Don't give it another thought."

"But you're too young to be spending Christmas alone. That's for curmudgeons like 'Scrooge' at the Grange. You should be hurrying off to a lovers' tryst."

Dawn laughed. "I'm quite happy to keep trysts with sick cows and pigs."

But although she smiled, she left Jack quickly after that. She was afraid her feelings might show in her face.

Once, there really had been a Christmas of lovers' trysts and eternal vows, of blazing happiness and eager hope for the future. But it had also been the Christmas of shattered dreams, cruelty and bitter disillusion.

The man whom for a few brief, glorious weeks she'd thought of as her lover, had been the son and heir of a family of wealthy industrialists. His first name had been—Well, no matter. She'd never used it after she discovered the secret of his middle name, a secret he tried so hard to keep hidden. "Ebenezer?" she'd cried in delight. "You mean, Ebenezer as in Scrooge?"

"Yes, and *stop laughing*. And don't tell anyone, either."

She'd kept his secret, but she'd shortened Ebenezer to Ben, and thereafter that had been her name for him. *A Christmas Carol* had become their special book. They'd read it aloud to each other. Dawn had been struck by the scene where Scrooge's fiancée broke their engagement, saying she no longer believed he could love a poor girl.

But Ben had reassured her, "There's no rich or poor between us. Scrooge was a fool to let her break it off. If he'd known what I know, he'd never have let her go."

Ben had been as different from Scrooge as he could possibly be—a handsome, generous, lighthearted young man whose boyish looks had made him seem younger than his twenty seven years. But beneath his laughter he had a mature side. He took his family obligations seriously, and that was the only shadow on Dawn's happiness. For all his protestations of fidelity, in a careless moment he'd let slip that his parents were urging him to marry Elizabeth, the daughter of the firm's biggest customer.

"Hey, don't look like that," he'd urged when he saw her pale face. "I don't normally like to disappoint them, but this time I'm just going to have to—except that they won't be disappointed when they've met you."

"If they've set their hearts on Elizabeth and a profitable tie-up between your two firms, they'll be disappointed with an impoverished first-year veterinary student," she'd observed wryly.

"Not when they get to know you," he'd said, cutting off further argument by taking her into his arms.

His kisses had sent her reeling, blotting out further thought. When they could talk again Ben had slipped an engagement ring on her finger, saying, "I feel as though Christmas Past was all the Christmases I wasted not knowing you, Christmas Present is now, and Christmas Yet to Come is next year when we'll be married, and all the years after that, years we'll have together."

That moment was one Dawn still found hard to think of. It hurt too much when she recalled what had come after.

Ben had returned to his parents in the third week of December, intending to tell them everything. The plan had been that Dawn would then join them for a visit. All during Christmas she'd waited for his call, but it hadn't come. When he'd finally called, a whole week later, it had been to suggest a postponement— "Only a few days, to give them a little time. I'll be in touch."

In her heart she'd known the truth then. Ben was a good, loyal son who couldn't bear to hurt the parents who loved him. Probably he'd arrived to find Elizabeth visiting, and after that he'd fallen further and further into the trap. But she'd clung to the last shreds of hope right up to the moment he'd called her again a week later, and had said it would be better if they never saw each other again.

She didn't blame him for that, but she blamed him for what had happened next. Ben, whose love letters had once burned the pages, had written to her wishing her luck for the future, and enclosing a large check to help cover the cost of her studies. As she'd read that letter, Dawn had almost hated him. She'd given him her first love—fresh and young and wholehearted. And he'd turned out to be no more than a rich man's son, trying to buy her off.

She'd written a stinging reply, returning the check and her engagement ring, saying she could forgive him for ditching her, but not for poisoning her memories of him with an offer of money.

Then she'd gotten on with her life.

The years that followed had their own triumphs and pleasures. She was always in the top quarter of her class, and her warm nature brought her many friends and admirers. She worked hard, and went to parties, flirted, laughed and sometimes kissed. But it seemed that she couldn't fall in love again, and the reason for that was that she no longer believed in the beauty of love. It had been destroyed for her.

She ranked high in her class and had several job offers. She'd chosen to join the Hollowdale practice as an assistant, with the chance of a partnership later. Her first December here, a year ago, had delighted her. The white fields and little cottages had a picture-book beauty. She saw the harder side of country life, too, working in cold barns and helping to dig animals out of snowdrifts. But nothing could spoil the enchantment of listening to pure, treble voices raised in carol singing on Christmas Eve, or helping to organize the children's party at the Grange.

And this year there would be no party because of the intransigence of one man, she thought grimly. Well, perhaps he could be made to think again.

That afternoon she stepped out to walk the few hundred yards to the Grange. Large white flakes were coming down thickly, making it hard to see more than a few yards ahead. As she walked, she tried to picture the man she'd come to challenge. He sounded embittered and he walked with a stick, so he was probably older; but however old he was, he'd been a child at some time. Perhaps, in that way, she could reach him.

The Grange stood at the top of a slight hill, dominating the village. By the time she reached it the ground was already covered with a white carpet. Glad to see lights on in the house, she hurried the last few yards up the long drive, then climbed the steps and rang the bell. She had to ring three times before the door was opened by a grim-faced woman who looked at her without welcome. "Yes?"

"I've come to see—I'm sorry, I don't know his name."

"He ain't expecting you, then?"

"No, but—"

"If he ain't expecting you he won't want to see you. Appointment only. That's his rule."

"But if you could just ask him—"

"Well, I couldn't. I did that once before and got the sharp side of his tongue. He ain't a man to fool with, I'm telling you." The granite features softened, just a fraction. "It ain't my fault. I'm just the housekeeper. I do what I'm told. Is it about that party?"

"Yes."

"I swear he'll throw something at the next person who asks him. Do yourself a favor and be off." She began to retreat back into the house, closing the door until only her face was showing. "I say," she called through the crack.

"Yes?" Dawn looked back hopefully.

"If any of your friends are going caroling, warn them not to come here." The housekeeper shut the door firmly.

So that was that, Dawn thought. She began to walk away from the house, pulling her thick jacket about her. Then she stopped in her tracks as her spirit rebelled against tamely going home. Impulsively she turned and made her way around the house. It was worth a try.

The far side of the house looked out over extensive grounds that fell away down the slope. A man stood there with his back to her, looking out over the country-side in the fast-fading light. In his right hand he grasped a walking stick that he half leaned on. This must be the man she'd come to see, the man who seemed to hate the rest of the world. If she couldn't persuade him, she could at least give the old curmudgeon a piece of her mind. Ducking her head against the wind that blew snow into her face, she began to make her way determinedly toward him.

She got to within a few yards before a twig cracked beneath her feet and gave her away. The man turned, scowling. "Get off this property or you'll be sorry," he growled. "I won't have trespassers, d'ye hear?"

Something about his voice sent a frisson through her. It had a faint half-remembered quality that brought an onrush of pain. Through the driving snow she could make out very little—only that he was tall, and younger than she had expected, and that his face was faintly scarred.

She dismissed the thought that had flashed on her. It was impossible. "I didn't mean to trespass," she said, "but it seems to be the only way to get to see you."

He limped a step forward. "I gave orders that no one should see me. Don't you understand plain language?"

The snow swirled about her, creating strange, half-perceived shapes, making the impossible possible. In the dim light she could sense that he'd grown as still as herself, as though incredulous understanding had burst on him, too. Dawn stood rooted to the spot, torn apart by joy and pain at the shattering discovery she'd just made.

"Ben," she whispered. "Oh, God, I can't believe it! *Ben.*"

She came closer but he took a step back. "Get away," he snapped.

"But it's me—Dawn. Don't you know me?"

The wind dropped slightly, and although the flakes continued to fall between them they could discern each other's faces. Now Dawn wondered how she'd ever recognized him. He'd aged more than eight years and his eyes were sunken. She pushed back her hood to give him a better view of her own face, and saw him flinch. Then his expression hardened. "No, I don't know you," he growled. "And I'm telling you for the last time, get off my property and don't ever come back."

"Ben, wait, please—"

She went forward, hands outstretched, but he took a step back, one arm held up as if to ward her off, and the next moment he'd lost his balance and was sprawling on the ground. Dawn hurried to help him but found her way barred by his stick, which he was holding out, pointed at her. "Get away," he grated.

"Let me help you—"

"I said, get away!" he shouted. "Don't touch me, do you hear? *Get out of here!*"

Dawn could bear no more. Choking back the sob of pity that would have burst from her, she turned and fled.

She went to bed early that evening, and lay trying to blot out the sound of carol singers tramping merrily through the village. Her heart was in turmoil. Her love for Ben was over. Nothing was more certain than that. Yet it had hurt her badly to see him reduced to a shadow of his former self. Old emotions and sensations, incredibly painful, came flooding back to invade her, destroying her peace.

For eight years she'd thought of him married to Elizabeth, fulfilled, running the family business, a contented husband and probably a father. When she'd put a face to that image, it had been like the face she'd last seen—young, handsome, full of hope.

But the face she'd seen just now was marked and withered with despair. It was the face of a solitary man, a man not merely unmarried, but profoundly alone within himself.

She thought of the stick that he used as both a support and a weapon against the world, and wondered what had happened to turn a vigorous, athletic young man into a limping recluse. And when had it happened? Could this be the answer to the mystery that had tormented her for eight years?

At last she got quietly out of bed. What she was about to do might not be very wise, but she couldn't rest until she'd seen Ben again. She got dressed and slipped out into the night. The snow had stopped falling and lay in a thick, white, moonlit carpet all the way up the high street.

The gates to the Grange had a lock that hadn't worked for years, and Squire Davis, a convivial man, hadn't troubled to mend it. But tonight someone had secured the gates by twisting wire around the bars. It took all the strength in her fingers to untwist the wire, and she finished with some nasty scratches, but finally managed it. She pushed one of the gates quietly open and slipped through. The house was almost in darkness, except for a light coming from an upstairs window. Now she realized how late it was and her heart almost failed her. It was no use appealing to the grumpy housekeeper. She must find another way. She began to walk around the house.

At last she came to the library at the rear where the old squire had often sat in the evening with a brandy and a cigar. Her heartbeat quickened as she saw a faint light coming from within. Softly she crept up to the French doors. To her relief, the curtains were still drawn back and she was able to look inside.

A fire burned in the iron grate, making shadows dance on the walls and giving the room its only light. Beside it Ben was slumped on the sofa. Praying hard, Dawn tried the handle of the French doors, and to her relief it yielded. She stepped inside and closed the door silently behind her. Ben gave no sign of knowing she was there. His head rested against the high side of the leather sofa, and his eyes were closed.

Dawn moved closer to him, then stopped, unable to decide what to do next. While she thought about it she pulled up a chair and sat down opposite him. From this angle she had a better view of him. Sleep had smoothed away his anger, leaving a face more like the one she remembered. It was younger, though still too old for a man of thirty-five. But it was grief and suffering that had aged him, not years. She clasped her hands tightly over her breast, as though by that means she could silence the anguish that seized her.

He stirred, and she held her breath. He didn't awake, but a sheet of paper slipped from his hand and fell into the grate. Dawn picked it up quickly before it could burn. Then she grew very still as she realized she was holding her own letter, written to him in dreadful bitterness of spirit, eight years ago. The cruel words seemed to leap out at her—*"despicable... unforgivable..."*

She'd written those words to a healthy, hearty young man who'd callously tried to buy her off; but the man who read and brooded on them tonight was ill and oddly defenseless. Against all reason she felt guilty, as if she'd struck him a brutal blow.

He'd denied her that afternoon, but he'd come straight back and reread her letter—a letter that he'd obviously kept so close by him that even in the turmoil of moving he'd known where to find it.

He stirred again, and this time he opened his eyes so that he was looking directly at her. For a moment he didn't seem to react, but finally a gleam of life appeared. "Who are you?" he asked in a voice that barely rose above a whisper.

She'd wondered what she would say to him, and it was only now that the right words came to her.

"I'm the Ghost of Christmas Past," she told him.

Chapter Two

"The Ghost of Christmas Past," he echoed, and memory seemed to return to him. With an effort he asked, "Long past?"

"No," she said sadly. "Our past."

After a moment he nodded. "I didn't imagine you this afternoon, did I? You came out of the snow and you went back into the snow, and you might have been a dream. I prayed that you were nothing but that, that you wouldn't return—"

"Was that why you secured the gates?" she asked.

"I suppose it was. Yet you were always bound to come back to haunt me." He sat up straight, rubbing his eyes, then poured himself a whiskey from a decanter on a low table near him, and drained it quickly. "Do you drink much of that stuff?" Dawn asked gently.

"What I do is my own business," he growled.

"Once, you never touched it," she reminded him.

He shrugged. "Once! Once a lot of things were true that aren't true any longer." But he didn't pour another glass. "You shouldn't have come," he said wearily. "Things were better as they were."

"Of course I had to come. I had to find out what happened. This afternoon I got the biggest shock of my life. I could hardly believe it was you. You look so different."

"Yes, I wasn't a crock the last time you saw me, was I?" he said with a grim smile.

"The last time I saw you was the evening you left to visit your parents. We said goodbye...." She fell silent, remembering that goodbye, the suffocating kisses, the pain of being apart even for a few days, the promises of eternal love. Looking up, she saw the same memory in his eyes. He looked away quickly.

"Yes, we said goodbye," he agreed gruffly. "We didn't know it was a final goodbye, but that's how things worked out."

She stared at him, reluctant to believe what she was hearing. "Can you really dismiss it so easily, Ben?"

He shrugged. "It was eight years ago. We're both different people. We didn't even recognize each other today."

"Only for a moment—because of the snow. But I knew you soon enough, as you did me." When he didn't answer she said angrily, "I won't just be brushed aside, Ben. There are things you *must* tell me, things you should have told me eight years ago."

"I imagine you've guessed quite a bit," he said wearily.

"Perhaps. I'd like to know when this happened." She indicated the stick.

"Eight years ago, minus one week," he replied simply.

"What happened? I want to know everything. I *have* to know."

"I got to within two miles of my parents' home...." His eyes seemed to focus on the distance as if he were reliving the moment. "I was thinking of you—of us—of how you'd kissed me at the last moment. Suddenly I was skidding. The road was icy. I went down a bank, and woke up in hospital with scarcely an unbroken bone left in my body."

"Oh, God," she said softly.

Ben went on in a dispassionate voice. "I heard afterward that it took them three hours to cut me out of the car, but I knew nothing about that."

"But why didn't you send for me?" she asked passionately.

"For a week I was floating in and out of consciousness. I didn't know where I was, or recognize any of my family. When I finally came 'round I was paralyzed from the waist down, and I thought I was going to be that way all my life. When I called you I was flat on my back, with someone holding the phone up for me."

As she thought again of the eager, bright faced young man she'd loved, tears filled her eyes and began to slide down her cheeks. She tried to brush them away unobtrusively, but she wasn't quick enough.

"What are you doing that for?" he demanded irritably. "It's all over now."

"Yes," she agreed huskily. "It's all over."

"If you think about it reasonably you'll see I did you a favor. I wasn't a pretty spectacle, I can tell you. And my temper was vile. Nurses came and went. None of them could stand me."

"But you didn't stay paralyzed."

"No. It took more operations than I can remember, but I got there. I've been out of a wheelchair for two years now."

Dawn clenched her hands as she thought of the lonely, painful struggle he'd chosen to endure without her. She could have loved him for better or worse, but he'd brushed her out of his life at the first crisis.

She wiped away the last of her tears and straightened her shoulders, managing to give a wry little laugh. "To think that all this time I've pictured you married to Elizabeth," she said.

"Elizabeth married a stockbroker. They have five children. Things have worked out for the best, all the way around."

"*All* the way around?" Dawn said with a touch of anger. "Do you really think things have worked out for the best for us?"

"I didn't choose the hand I was dealt. I simply played it in the way that seemed best. What should I have done? Called you and asked you to tie yourself to a cripple?"

"I *loved* you, Ben. I thought we were so close—and now I wonder if you even knew what love meant. If we'd been as close as I thought, you'd have sent for me."

"And what then?" he demanded harshly. "When the first shock had passed and you were left contemplating a man with no body to speak of—*what then?*"

"I'd have loved you no matter what. You should have trusted my love. You should have trusted *me.*"

"You don't understand," he said angrily. "In the state I was in, I didn't want your love. I didn't want anything except to crawl away and hide. I don't know if I did the right thing for me, but I do know I did the right thing for you."

"You know nothing of the kind."

"Whatever your life has been, it's been better than what you'd have had with me. You're young and beautiful. I'd have turned you into a gray-haired old woman by now. I was strong for both of us. Be glad of it."

"Oh, Ben," she said helplessly. "You don't understand. It's not just that you sent me away when you needed me most, but you lied to me about the reason. When you sent me money I thought—"

"Yes, you made it very clear what you thought," he interrupted. "It was a very plainspoken letter. You have a pretty turn of phrase when you're angry."

"I wish I'd cut my arm off before I wrote you such words when you were ill. But your letter was so short and curt—"

"It was short because writing was agony. I wasn't trying to buy you off, Dawn. I just wanted to help. I know studying to be a vet takes a lot of money, and you didn't have any. Did you ever make it?"

"Yes. I'm with a practice in Hollowdale now."

"Good. Then life has worked out well for you."

She thought of the ache of loneliness that had never left her, night or day, since she'd lost him. She thought of her own barren heart that had never flowered for anyone but him. "Yes," she said bleakly. "Life has worked out well for me."

"How long have you been here?"

"Just over a year."

"But you're already a part of the place, I'll bet. I remember your gift for empathy. It was one of the things I—one of the things likely to make you a good vet."

"Yes, I've become a part of Hollowdale. I love the people here. They're kind and sincere, and they believe in values that other people seem to have forgotten. Jack says it's as though Hollowdale was caught in a kind of time warp so that the world could have a living reminder of how things ought to be."

"Who's Jack?"

"Jack Stanning, he's my boss."

"Stanning? I've heard that name."

"You met him this morning. He came to ask if we could have the children's party here, and you showed him the door."

"I remember. So he's your boss."

"One of them. The other one is Harry. He's the younger partner."

"Are you married yet?" Ben demanded abruptly.

"No, I'm not married."

"You should be. You were born to be married."

"I was nearly married once," she reminded him. "I fell in love with a man—fell so completely in love that nothing else in the world existed. I thought he felt the same, but I was wrong. When trouble came he didn't want my help. I guess there was no help I could give him."

She jumped as Ben slammed the point of his stick on the floor, hard. His face was harsh with anger as he got to his feet and began to pace about the room. "That's just sentimentality," he said. "Nothing lasts forever. Relationships die and you just—form other relationships."

"Did you?" she challenged.

"My attention has been taken up with other things," he said ironically. "The world doesn't look the same to me anymore." He gave a short bark of laughter. "We used to joke that I was Scrooge. Maybe it's not such a joke now."

"I don't believe it," she said urgently. "I can't believe that the man I loved has become so different. You were gentle and sensitive—and loving—" Her voice wavered perilously.

"And I used to laugh a lot," he reminded her. "Don't forget that, Dawn. I've forgotten how to laugh, just as I've forgotten how to love."

"Don't say that," she pleaded. "Perhaps you can't love me—that doesn't matter. But you must love someone."

He stared at her bleakly. "Why must I? I live very well without it."

"Hiding away from people? Hating the whole world?"

He shrugged. "I don't hate the world."

"No. It's worse than that. You're indifferent to the world. You want to drive it away."

"I want to be left alone."

"People shouldn't be alone. It isn't natural."

"It suits me."

"I don't believe it really suits you. It's just what you've settled for."

He shrugged. "Well, everyone settles for the best terms they can get."

"But do you really call it living?"

"It's better than what I had two years ago."

"But it can't ever be enough," she argued.

"It'll do!" he shouted suddenly. "What do you expect of me? That I'm going to open my arms and say let's turn back the clock? The clock never goes backward, however much we—" He took a shuddering breath. "What's done is done. For God's sake, let's put an end to this. It achieves nothing. It's a pity we met again. It opens up old wounds that were healed." He caught her looking at him and said roughly, "Let's face the truth. Neither of us gave a thought to the other until our chance meeting this afternoon."

"Did you really forget me?" she whispered.

"Completely," he said with a blank firmness.

She sat, stunned, knowing she should get up and go, yet unable to move. Whatever she'd expected, it hadn't been this brutal rejection. At last she pulled herself together and got to her feet, and as she did so, the letter she'd picked up when she first came in slipped to the floor. She retrieved it hastily.

"Where did you get that?" Ben demanded.

"You were reading it when you feel asleep," she said. "It fell out of your hand."

He snatched it away from her. The movement brought him close and Dawn looked into his eyes, seeing there everything he'd tried to hide. He'd been lying when he said he'd forgotten her, and the letter proved it. The revelation stripped him defenseless.

"All right," he grated. "I was reading your letter tonight. Seeing you this afternoon reminded me of a lot of things, and I reread your letter. Make what you will of that."

"It's not that you read it," she breathed, "but that you kept it by you all these years."

"It's been useful," he snapped. "It was always there to remind me how much I'd made you hate me, and how completely everything was over between us. Yes, I needed reminding. Is that what you wanted to hear? Yes, I went on loving you for a long time, telling myself I was a fool for it, but unable to stop. I was desperate, crazy with longing to have you to hold me and comfort me. Sometimes I was so close to calling you and begging you to come to me. . . ."

"But you didn't," she breathed. "Oh, you should have called me. Don't you think I'd have come if I'd known you needed me?"

"Yes, you'd have come," he agreed wearily. "But for what? To tie yourself to a man with nothing to give you but his need and helplessness?"

"I wouldn't have asked for anything better than to be needed by you," she said.

"I know that. I once saw you taking care of a sick dog, remember? Caring for helpless creatures is your special talent, but it's put to better use as a vet. Thank God I had too much self-respect to let you use it on me."

"Self-respect?" she echoed. "Or stupid, stubborn pride?"

"Well, perhaps a bit of both. When stupid, stubborn pride is all you have to cling to, it can become dreadfully important. I wouldn't let the wreck of my life become the wreck of yours. I loved you too much for that. Don't blame me for the decision I made. Remember what I saved you from. Now, I think you'd better go."

"Can't we talk some more? There's so much I want to understand."

"What is there to understand? We loved each other, but life didn't work out for us. It was nobody's fault. It just happened. Now it's over."

"Over," she repeated softly, as if trying to understand the word's meaning. "No, Ben, that's not true. It'll never be over as long as we're both alive. It'll never be over as long as you keep my letter by you, and as long as I—" She clasped her hands to her breast, feeling an ache there that almost overwhelmed her.

He watched her face, transfixed by its mixture of sadness and joy. There was a pain in his breast that had been threatening ever since they'd met that afternoon, a pain he'd fought not to feel. But now it overwhelmed him, half agony, half joy at being with her again. He reached out and took a step toward her, but he didn't notice a table in his path. He stumbled, lost his balance and flung out an arm. She caught him just in time, holding on to him tightly. To his chagrin he felt himself clinging to her. She helped him back to the sofa, and sat down beside him.

"You see?" he said wearily.

"Anyone can stumble over a table," she argued desperately.

"I stumble all the time," he told her with a bitterness in his voice that tore at her heart. "And then I have to get my strength back for another effort. And even then I can only walk with a stick, and not very far. I finish the day aching all over and often with a blinding headache. But that's not the worst. I can't even begin to tell you about the dark times—great black, gaping holes of depression that come without warning and swallow me up for days on end. By the time I've struggled through to the end, I'm hardly human. I'm not fit for anyone to live with. I can't bear sympathy, I can't bear pity, and I'm not even sure I could bear love. Don't you understand, Dawn? *I don't want you for my nursemaid.*"

The last words were a shout of agony, and after he'd uttered them he dropped his head into his hands. He was shaking violently as she'd sometimes seen animals shake under stress. The strong protective instincts that governed her whole life made her react at once. Without thinking what she was doing she put her arms about him, enfolding him in a comforting embrace, laying her cheek against his head and caressing him tenderly. "There, my love," she whispered. "I'm here. Hold on to me."

His hand came from somewhere and seized hers in a fierce grip. She winced with pain but made no sound, holding him tightly and rocking gently back and forth. Tears streamed from her eyes when she thought of the wasted years when she hadn't been there to do this for him. He'd chosen to fight alone, rejecting her comfort, but the battle had devastated him, and he couldn't reject it now.

At last he stirred, and seemed to realize what was happening. Dawn felt him grow tense and draw away from her slightly, and she remembered his words, "I don't want you for my nursemaid."

"I'm all right now," he said stiffly. "It's very good of you to—I assure you there's no need—Dawn—"

The last word was a whisper, uttered just before she took his face between her hands and laid her lips on his. It was the gentlest kiss she'd ever given him. There was no pressure, no intensity, no passion. It was as though he were an injured animal lashing out at the world, who must be calmed before she could help him. When she'd finished she realized that some of her own tears must have brushed off on him, for his face was wet.

Ben spoke with a great effort. "It's a myth that suffering ennobles. It hasn't ennobled me. It's made me an ill-tempered swine. It's good of you to be so friendly still, after the way I've behaved to you."

She managed a smile. "I was always your best friend. I still am. I always will be."

"Thank you." He sighed. "But I think you'd better go now."

Dawn realized with despair that she hadn't made the breakthrough she'd hoped. There was nothing to do but accept her dismissal. She turned toward the French doors through which she'd entered, but Ben said, "Not that way. I'll show you out through the front door. I still have a few manners left."

She allowed him to escort her through the house. As they reached the hall Mrs. Stanley appeared, looking worried. "Oh, sir, I wonder if I should call the police. There's a man hanging about the front gate, and he looks ever-so-suspicious."

Ben grunted and pulled open the front door to look at the man who was still standing there. He turned at the sound of the door and came toward the light. "Why, it's Harry," Dawn said, surprised.

"Is that you, Dawn?" he called from the path.

"Come here," Ben growled, "and stop acting as though you were 'loitering with intent.'"

The young man came closer to where they could both see his good-natured face. "My only intent is to make sure Dawn gets home safely," he said. He addressed her directly. "I saw you come in here and— Well, it's dark and the roads are getting slippery."

"How very chivalrous," Ben said with grim irony. "Miss Fletcher is just leaving. Good night."

Dawn bade him good-night, then went out to where Harry was waiting for her. She gave a last glance back at Ben but he'd already closed the front door.

"You didn't mind my hanging about, did you?" Harry asked anxiously. "I just got a bit worried about you after what Jack said about him."

"That was nice of you," she replied, trying to sound cheerful and not succeeding.

"Hey, what's the matter? You're not crying, are you? Yes, you are."

"No, I'm not," she insisted in a muffled voice.

"Is he that much of an ogre? Damn him for making you cry." He slipped an arm around her shoulder as they walked down the drive to the gate, and hugged her. "Come on, darling. Let's get out of the cold, and you'll feel better."

He hugged her again and drew her out into the road. They didn't look back, so they didn't see the curtain drawn aside a crack until they were out of sight.

Chapter Three

"Harry tells me you went to beard the lion in his den last night," Jack said, keeping his eyes on the snow-covered road ahead. They were making farm calls together.

"I— What was that?" Dawn took her attention from the white fields and tried to concentrate.

"I hear you went to see the new occupant of the Grange. Harry says you were upset when you left, so I suppose you didn't manage to persuade him about the party."

With a sense of shock Dawn realized she hadn't tried to change Ben's mind about the party. She'd been completely shattered by meeting him again and discovering what had happened to him; everything else had simply gone out of her head.

She'd spent a sleepless, desperate night. All the old pain of thinking he'd abandoned her was as nothing to the new pain of discovering what had really happened. Their love had meant everything to her, but he'd prized it so little that when tragedy struck, he'd simply set it aside. From whichever angle she looked at it, that was the brutal truth.

It was useless to reason that it made no difference now that her love for Ben was in the past. It was true that the intense feeling that had made her take him in her arms and kiss him last night had been little different from what she would have felt for any hurt creature. But the echo of love persisted, along with the memory of high hopes and blissful happiness when the world had been young and full of promise. That glorious time had finally died last night, and the knowledge was tearing her in two.

"No," she said now to Jack. "I didn't persuade him." She forced herself to concentrate on the present. There was work to do. "We'll be going near Haynes's farm," she observed. "I'd like to call in and look at Trixie, just to be on the safe side."

"There's no need," Jack said. He added wryly, "If there was even a hint of anything wrong with that spaniel, Fred would have been on the phone in a panic. I've never seen a man set so much store by a dog."

"I'd still like to have a look. She's getting close to her time."

Jack grinned. "Admit it. The truth is, you just feel sorry for the old boy."

"I suppose I do. He always seems so alone—just those pictures of his family, and his memories."

"I know. It's sad. Mind you, it's his own fault he's alone. He could have his children around him now if he hadn't quarreled with them both."

"Why?"

"Chiefly because he's as stubborn as a mule. Everything has to be done his way. His children had to think his way. They couldn't take the pressure, they escaped. Now all he's left with is Trixie, and she's his ideal companion because she never answers back."

"And he's terrified in case he loses her," Dawn observed.

"There's no reason for him to lose her. She may not be in her first youth, but she's as fit as a fiddle. If you like, though, I'll drop you off there while I'm on my way to see Carney's bull, and collect you on my way back."

She saw Trixie as soon as she went in through Fred Haynes's gate. The spaniel was waddling through the snow, swaying from side to side. Dawn greeted Fred with a smile and received only a grunt in return. But he immediately put the kettle on to offer her a cup of tea.

"Not long now," she said as she knelt by the fire, gently feeling Trixie's stomach and fondling her ears. "Soon after Christmas, I'd say."

"And she's gonna be all right?" he demanded in a belligerent manner that Dawn knew masked fear.

"She should be. I know you're taking excellent care of her, and she's perfectly healthy."

The old man grunted. "Reckon I shoulda put a stop to it when I found out," he growled. "Dunno what got inta me."

But Dawn knew. Trixie had apparently mated with a stray she'd encountered on the moor, and Fred had known nothing about the pregnancy until it was well advanced. To have terminated it then would have involved some risk to the spaniel, and he hadn't wanted to chance it. Now that the birth was almost due he was regretting his decision. Dawn reassured him as much as possible, and sipped her tea, looking around at the old-fashioned room, with its photographs of his children.

"That's my son, Tony," Fred told her, following her gaze. "He went to Australia. Got married."

"He looks very young," Dawn said, studying the picture.

"That was taken before he went."

"Don't you have anything more recent, showing him with his wife?" she asked, curious.

Fred shrugged. "He's got his life and I've got mine. He did send me a picture years back, just after his young 'uns were born. Twins, they were. But we've never seen eye-to-eye. I don't hear from him now. Don't want to, either."

Trixie made a grumbling sound and he bent down to pat her. The harshness left his voice as he murmured to the animal with a tenderness Dawn guessed he'd found hard to show to his children. She watched them, feeling sad for the old man in his self-imposed loneliness that he no longer knew how to end.

She heard the sound of a car horn in the yard. "That's Jack," she said. "Goodbye, Fred. There's nothing to worry about, but give me a call, night or day, if you feel she needs it."

He grunted. "Don't forget to send me your bill for this visit."

She smiled and shook her head. "What visit? I just dropped in to have a cup of tea."

He grunted again, but she thought she saw a flicker of pleasure on his face.

"It's so sad," she told Jack on the way home. "Even if Trixie comes through this all right, dogs don't live forever, and she isn't young. What will he do when the time comes?"

"Hey, you're a vet, not a social worker," he reminded her gently.

"But people's animals don't exist in isolation. They're a part of the rest of their lives."

"I know. I'm merely saying that you can't shoulder everyone's burdens for them. In the end, we're all alone."

"Yes," she said after a moment. "I know that."

Harry had just finished the morning surgery when they got back. "There's a visitor for you," he told Dawn. "It's the fellow you went to see last night."

"Good heavens! Not 'Scrooge'?" Jack demanded with a grin.

"I wish you wouldn't call him that," Dawn said, more sharply than she intended to.

"Sorry," Jack said hastily. "Perhaps this is a good sign. Maybe your charm worked on him, and he relented."

"What actually did he say when you asked him about the party?" Harry inquired.

"Well I— That is— Where is he?"

"In the waiting room."

She found that her heart was beating hard as she opened the waiting-room door. Ben glanced up as she entered. He looked terrible, as though he too had spent a sleepless night. There were black circles under his eyes and tension about his mouth. He rose awkwardly as she entered. "Ben, what's the matter?" she asked urgently. "What's wrong?"

"There's nothing wrong. I came to see you because—" He hesitated. "I understand you've been out visiting farms this morning. Am I taking up your lunch hour?"

"That's all right," she said dismissively.

"No, it isn't. You need all your strength for this work. You'd better come and have some lunch with me. Then I'll have nothing to reproach myself with."

She was about to say he had nothing to feel badly about, anyway, but she stopped herself. There was something unnatural about Ben's manner, as though he was forcing himself to appear casual against enormous odds. If she could get him away from here, perhaps he'd be more at ease. "All right," she said. "Thank you."

They went to the little café where she often ate. There were still some empty places. "We have to get our food from the counter first," Dawn said.

"Would you mind getting it?" he asked quickly. "I'll find us a spot." He thrust some money in her hand and turned away in search of a table, keeping his face averted. Dawn hastily collected some lunch and brought it across to the table he'd found by the window. She almost wished they hadn't come, because the harsh daylight gave her a clear view of his face. It was more battered than she'd realized in the dim light the night before. The scars showed, although they hadn't pulled his face out of shape. In that he'd been lucky. He was still handsome, still recognizable as the man she'd once loved so passionately. But she realized that he didn't know this, that he was morbidly self-conscious about his face. He was deliberately turning away from the room, but then some passersby looked in through the window, and he turned back again.

"Ben, it's not so bad," she said, trying to reassure him.

"Isn't it? I don't know anymore. I remember what it was like at first, and I can't get that picture out of my head." Some other customers gave him a passing glance and he averted his face again. "I shouldn't have come here. I should have invited you to the house."

"Why didn't you?"

"I was afraid you wouldn't come."

She smiled. "I'd have come."

"Even after the way I behaved last night?"

"You're entitled to be a bit niggly after what you've been through."

"Don't," he said with a soft violence that startled her.

"What?"

"Don't make allowances for me, Dawn. Don't make excuses. It makes me feel pathetic."

She cursed herself for tactlessness. "I'm sorry, Ben."

"And don't apologize when I'm in the wrong," he snapped.

She opened her mouth and closed it again, stumped for an answer. He gave a faint grin. "You see what you escaped?"

It was in her heart to say that he wouldn't be like this if he'd turned to her, for her comfort would have enveloped him and eased his pain. Then she remembered that he'd said he hadn't wanted her love. "All right," she said. "Just tell me what you want."

"It's just that I realized I'd forgotten my manners yesterday. I never asked why you came to see me. I don't mean in the evening, but earlier—when we first met. You didn't know it would be me, did you?"

"I had no idea. I just came to see the new owner of the Grange."

"Why?"

"I wanted to try to persuade you to agree to the children's party."

"Oh, I see."

"Jack told me you wouldn't even consider it."

"I've only just moved in and you want me to let the place be disrupted."

"Is that the real reason, Ben? Or is it just another way of shutting out the world?"

"Does it matter?"

"It matters to the children who'll lose their treat. They aren't ordinary children. They come from institutions. Most of them are too old to be adopted and the ones that aren't—well, they have other problems." He was silent and she went on, "You used to enjoy children, Ben. You'd pick babies up and press your face against them. It was one of the things I loved most about you. I don't believe you've really changed that much."

"I've had to change. When you see people flinching away from you, you can't inflict yourself on them. You don't understand, Dawn. I've seen the way children look at me, and I can't bear it."

Dawn was silent, wondering if she dared play her next card. At last she decided to risk it. "Well," she said, apparently casually, "you were never the most consistent of men. That's one thing in which you haven't changed."

"What the devil do you mean?"

"You want to deny these children one of the few treats they have because of your feelings, because you're morbidly conscious of being damaged. And you expect me to be understanding about that. But it was only five minutes ago you told me not to make allowances for you. You said it made you feel pathetic." She took a deep breath. "You're right. Your attitude is pretty pathetic."

He scowled at her, but after a moment his expression changed to a reluctant grin. "Caught with my own argument. You always knew how to give it straight from the shoulder."

"So, straight from the shoulder—are you going to forget about yourself and think of these deprived children?"

He hesitated. "If I say yes, who will be doing all the organizing?"

"We will. You won't have to do a thing."

"But who is 'we'? If it means you, that's all right. I just don't want to find myself in the hands of total strangers."

"So if I promise to be responsible for everything—you'll agree?"

After a long, painful pause he said, "I guess I will."

Ben held his breath at the look that swept over her face. It was a look of total joy, and it seemed to bring her back to him as she had been eight years ago. He gripped the edge of the table. "After all," he said after a moment, "I don't actually have to be around during the party, do I?"

"Not if you don't want to. But I hope you'll want to."

"We'll see. When is this party to take place?"

"December twenty-third."

"That's going to give you a tight schedule. Wouldn't it be better to put it off until Christmas is over?"

"It's always December twenty-third. That's a Hollowdale tradition, and absolutely sacred."

He gave her a wry smile. "It's just as well I gave in, then, isn't it?"

She finished eating and tucked away the remains of a roll in a paper towel. "If you're not going to finish that sandwich I'll have it," she said.

He gave it to her. "Are you really that stuck for food?"

"It's not for me, silly. I give it to the ducks on the pond. They have a hard time right now. I've just got time before I have to get back to work."

He went to the pond with her. Suddenly he'd found himself relaxing. The casually fond way she'd said, "silly," just as she'd sometimes done in the old days, had seemed to strip away the years. She looked little older than the girl she'd been then, he thought, watching her standing by the water's edge and clucking to the ducks. They came slithering over the ice to her to snatch the bread from her outstretched hand.

That was how she was, he realized—always with hands outstretched. In their eight years apart, that was the picture of her that had lived in his mind; the way she'd reached out to him with love. At every meeting she'd run to him with her arms open. At every parting she'd reached out for one final caress. At their last ever parting she'd backed away from him slowly, holding on to his hands until the last moment, unable to tear her eyes from him. He'd never forgotten her look, so full of intense, passionate love. It had haunted him so persistently that it had been almost like a living presence. And last night the Ghost of Christmas Past had finally come to challenge him, reviving memories he'd tried to bury because that was the only way he could stay sane. In a few moments she'd undone the work of years, and when she'd laid her lips on his it had taken all his self-control not to embrace her and beg her to come back to him.

He'd lain awake all night, trying to banish her and failing. Only at dawn had a measure of peace come to him with the realization that they hadn't discussed the reason for her first visit, and that consequently he had an excuse to seek her out. They would talk, he would see her by daylight and perhaps exorcise the ghost. But it hadn't worked out like that. In the short time they'd spent in the café he'd been reminded of everything he'd loved most about her—her warmth and tender compassion for suffering that never became sentimental because it was tempered by humor and robust common sense. Strange that common sense should seem an enchanted quality, but it was a part of *her*.

He watched her laughing as she fed the ducks. He was mad to agree to this party, but if he'd refused she would have thought badly of him. That alone would have been enough to take him back eight years, when he'd often curbed his young, male thoughtlessness out of a longing for her good opinion. Did anything really change? he wondered. Ever?

He followed her down to the edge of the pond. "I'll have that sandwich back," he said. "Let's see if they'll take it from me."

Laughing, she held it out to him but something caught his attention. He seized her hands and examined three long, ugly scratches. "How did you get those?" he demanded.

"Last night, undoing the wire on your gate." She tried to lighten the atmosphere by adding, "I'd forgotten to bring my housebreaking tools, so I had to use my hands."

But his face was full of horror. "I never meant to hurt you," he groaned. "I could never willingly do anything to hurt you. Tell me that you know that."

"Ben, of course I know. It was an accident. I guess it's just hard to slam a door on the world without jamming somebody's fingers."

He was swept by fierce emotion. In another moment he would have kissed the scratches. He was saved from it by the furious quacking of the ducks, and hastened to toss the bread to them. The realization that he'd nearly made a fool of himself caused him to go hot and cold. He moved hastily away from her, and rummaged in his pocket. "Here's my spare front-door key," he said, giving it to her. "It'll get you into the house if Mrs. Stanley happens to be out when you arrive to set up things for the party."

"But won't you be there to let me in?"

"No, I shall have to be out all day. I've just remembered that I have a thousand things to do."

"But Ben..."

"You don't need me, Dawn. Just treat the house as your own. Do whatever you want. Have a good party. Now I really must be going."

While she was still trying to think of a way to protest that she wanted him at the party, he limped away and soon vanished from sight.

Chapter Four

On the day before Christmas Eve, Ben had an early breakfast before getting out his car. He drove off, deliberately choosing a direction that wouldn't lead him past the veterinary surgery. He told himself he'd done everything Dawn could possibly expect, and now he wanted nothing more to do with the whole business. It was time he inspected his new property, which included several small farms whose tenants he had yet to meet.

He started with Martin Craddock. He knew nothing about Craddock except what the books had told him—that he was often late with his rent. In fact most of the tenants were. All the rents had struck Ben as being on the high side for small acreage, but there might be some compensating factor, like land of exceptional quality.

But nothing he saw on Craddock's farm encouraged this view. If anything, the land was stony and looked difficult to work. The house was empty when he arrived so he began to look around the other buildings. Everything was in a poor state of repair, possibly because the estate had been in limbo for several months. While he was inspecting the cow shed he saw a battered car lurch into the yard and stop. An apparently endless supply of children poured out and into the house, creating a merry riot and dragging their parents with them. Ben saw a middle-aged man, laughing with his children, then suddenly stop laughing as he noticed Ben's car. Ben stepped out into the open and the man began to hurry toward him.

His face struck Ben as pleasant and well-meaning, but indecisive. Right now it also looked nervous. "I'm sorry not to have been here when you called," Craddock said quickly when he saw his landlord.

"Don't apologize," Ben told him. "It's my fault for coming without warning you."

If anything, Craddock looked even more worried. "Perhaps you'd like to come into the warm," he suggested.

The inside of the house was spotlessly clean but very shabby. There was a multitude of homemade paper chains attached to the walls and ceiling, and a tree in the corner, hung with baubles that might have glittered once but now had the tarnish of age.

"Of course, the farm doesn't look its best at this time of year," Craddock said defensively. "If I'd known you were coming I'd have tidied up a bit."

Ben spoke without thinking. "Don't worry. I prefer to see things as they really are."

It was meant as reassurance, but the whole family stopped and looked at him, each face wearing the same fearful expression. What on earth had he said to make anyone look like that? he wondered.

"I see you've been Christmas shopping," he observed with an attempt at heartiness. He didn't know that his forced manner made the words come out sounding like a threat. He only wondered why the family seemed to draw together against him. Mrs. Craddock contrived to shift her bulk so that it covered a bag bearing the name of a toy shop.

"Just a few things for the children," Craddock said hastily. "They don't get many treats, and they're ever so good about it—but at Christmas—you see—"

"Of course." Ben cut the man short out of pity for his stammering nervousness. "I expect you want to get on with your preparations. I won't stay. We can discuss everything in January when I've got the books at hand. Your lease is up for renewal soon, isn't it?"

"Yes but—I mean, perhaps you'd let me show you the place properly—when I've had a chance to—"

Ben realized that the youngest child was staring at his face with frank curiosity. He repelled them. That was it. That was why they drew together and made him feel like an alien. Suddenly he couldn't wait to get out. "No, thanks," he said curtly. "I've seen all I need to. Good day."

He left the house quickly, almost slamming the door in his haste. He didn't begin to relax until he'd driven several miles. His hands were tense on the steering wheel and his body was aching with strain.

He thought of the mean little place and the excessive rent that Squire Davis had been happy to collect year after year, while giving back as little as possible. The Squire might have been an apple-cheeked old man who kept the picturesque Christmas traditions in his home, but he'd been a tightfisted landlord, indifferent to his tenants' hardship. He wondered if Dawn knew that.

He'd have to make changes on the farms, starting with a reduction in rent, and probably interest-free loans to the tenants to help them get new farm machinery. Or perhaps he could buy the best machinery himself, and rent it to them cheaply when they needed it. Absorbed in these thoughts he got lost in the unfamiliar territory, and after he'd driven around for an hour and found his way again, he discovered he'd returned to Hollowdale. He hadn't meant to come back, but his own house was just ahead and it seemed pointless to drive away again. Besides, he ought to look in to see what sort of a bear garden they were making of the place; and if it meant talking to Dawn, was that his fault?

He turned into the drive and immediately found his way partly blocked by a large, battered car, from which someone was lifting boxes and carrying them inside. Ben recognized the young man who'd come to collect Dawn the other night. The newcomer gave him a cheery wave and went on with his work. By the time Ben had limped up the stairs and into the front hall he had finished his task. "We haven't met properly," Ben said politely. "You can hardly call the other night a meeting."

"I'm Harry," the young man explained. "I'm a vet, in the same practice with Dawn. She asked me to start bringing stuff over for the party. She said it was all right with you."

"Perfectly all right," Ben replied. He studied Harry and found him slightly displeasing. He wasn't quite sure why. Harry's face was handsome and good-humored, his manner cheerful and courteous. But he worked with Dawn. He saw her every day and was happy to run her errands. He followed her so that he could see her home through the snow. There was a coziness about the relationship that Ben didn't like. Not that it was any concern of his. Eight years ago he'd released Dawn just so that she might one day find someone like this. But now that he'd met Harry, he didn't like him. "You'll have to excuse me," he said. "I know nothing about the arrangements. I've left everything in Miss Fletcher's hands."

"Fine. Fine. We'll get on. But first—" Harry checked himself. He seemed embarrassed. "I want to apologize for the other night," he said. "Heaven knows what you must have thought of me, hanging around your house like that, and I wasn't very polite to you."

"More polite than I was to you," Ben observed with accuracy.

"It's just that I was worried about Dawn—"

"Vanishing into the house of the village ogre," Ben said with grim irony.

Harry went red. "I guess I overdid it. I can't help worrying about her, you see—"

"Perfectly natural." It must have been a desire to torment himself that made Ben add, "You're very much in love with her, aren't you?"

Harry gave an awkward laugh. "I suppose it's obvious. I just can't help it. I mean, no one could know Dawn—I mean, really know her—and not love her."

"Indeed?"

"Of course you don't know what she's like, but when you do you'll discover what a wonderful person she is."

"I doubt I'll be getting to know Miss Fletcher any better," Ben told him coolly. "She's achieved her object in getting me to allow this party."

"She's very persuasive, isn't she?" Harry asked eagerly. "When she sets her heart on something she puts everything she's got into it."

"Quite," Ben said coldly.

"Everything means so much to her, and that's how she convinces other people that—"

"You must excuse me," Ben interrupted him. "I have work to do."

He limped away quickly, already passionately regretting that he'd agreed to this. But before he'd quite left the entrance hall he heard a light footstep behind him and turned to see Dawn hurrying through the front door. He stayed back in the shadows, hoping she wouldn't notice him, and saw how her face lit up when she saw Harry. But that was nothing to how Harry's face lit up at the sight of her.

"Harry, bless you for being so prompt," she said, smiling at him. "I'm afraid it's going to be a long job."

"Your knight in shining armor awaits, my lady," he replied. "Give me any task. No challenge is too great in return for one of your smiles."

"Fool," she said fondly. "But here's a challenge for you. Go and collect the cakes from Mrs. Turnbull."

"I said a challenge, not an impossibility. Dawn, please, have mercy. She's a terrible woman."

"She's never done you any harm."

"Never done me any—? She calls me 'young man' in a voice that wouldn't disgrace a sergeant major. And she makes me stand and listen while she tells endless stories about how her cakes always win prizes at the fete, and—"

"She's old and lonely," Dawn said. "Be nice to her."

"For you, anything." He kissed her lightly and vanished. Dawn stood looking after his departing form with a tender smile on her face. Ben remained absolutely still in the shadows, not moving until Dawn had picked up a box and taken it into the next room. Then he limped away into the library and closed the door behind him.

But he couldn't shut out the sound. There was a non-stop stream of cars arriving, doors slamming, cheerful voices raised. He tried to concentrate on studying account books, but Dawn's face kept getting between him and the page. He saw again the tender smile she'd given Harry. There was no passion in that look, he reassured himself. Just friendly affection. But perhaps she was ready to settle for friendly affection. Passion had only broken her heart.

He remembered the light, gentle kiss she'd given him the other night: the kiss of a friend, full of compassion and sorrow. And pity? God forbid! But had all love and desire been destroyed in her? He hadn't meant that, when he'd shut her out. He'd thought of her as forgetting him, marrying, having children, finding fulfillment. Instead, he'd taught her a brutal lesson about the uselessness of love.

Suddenly she seemed to be there with him, her younger self reincarnated, smothering him with wild kisses that tasted of honey. He groaned, trying to shut out the torturing vision, but she wouldn't be shut out. Her lips were on his and her arms were about his neck, reminding him what he'd once possessed and thrown away through pride. He groaned and let his head fall into his hands.

A knock on the door made him sit up sharply. "Yes?" he called in a ragged voice.

"May I come in?" It was Dawn.

At that moment he would rather have faced anyone in the world but her, but he controlled himself enough to say, "Yes, come in."

"I came to ask for the key to the double doors," she said, approaching him. "If we open those we can throw the two big rooms together."

"Mrs. Stanley has the key," he told her curtly.

"She says you have it." She smiled and spoke gently. "I'm sorry to trouble you."

He found the key and gave it to her, resenting her bitterly. Why didn't she go away and smile at Harry who was in love with her, who could marry her?

"Oh, by the way, I had to leave this number at the surgery. Jack's on duty, but if he's called out, people need to know where they can contact Harry or me. Is that all right?"

"Of course it is."

"I'm glad you managed to come back," she said warmly. "It'll be wonderful to have you at the party."

"I'm not going to be at the party," he growled. "I told you, I want nothing to do with it. Now, if you don't mind, I'm very busy."

She was silent a moment, and he wondered if she would come forward and put her arms around him, as she'd done the other evening. But the silence lengthened, and when he looked behind him she'd left the room.

Just as well, he thought. The less they saw of each other, the better. But against his will he found himself listening for the sound of her voice in the din of noise coming from beyond the door.

At last the noise died away to a low murmur, which lasted for half an hour. Then came a sound that made him flinch—vans crunching along the drive and disgorging children who streamed into the house chattering excitedly. He took down the estate accounts and got to work on them, scowling with concentration as he tried to shut out all consciousness of the party.

He managed to work for an hour, but finally reached the point where he couldn't proceed without a book he knew he'd left upstairs. There was nothing to do but fetch it. As he opened the door he almost collided with

Harry, who had a bundle tucked under his arm and seemed almost furtive.

"Sorry," he said quickly to Ben. "I've been roped into playing Father Christmas and I'm looking for somewhere to put this on." He indicated the bundle.

"You can use the library," Ben said, standing back to let him pass. He limped away quickly to avoid Harry's thanks, and headed for the stairs. On the way he passed the double doors that led to the big front room. They were standing open, and through them he could see a long table, loaded with food and packed with children wearing paper hats. He hurried past in case someone saw him.

When he returned a few minutes later he could see "Father Christmas" making his way around the two long tables, pulling crackers that the children held out to him. Dawn was there, acting as a waitress, making sure there were second helpings of jelly for any who wanted it. She looked happy and absorbed. Ben watched her for a moment, feeling a curious aching sensation, before moving quietly away.

The door of the library was open. He was about to close it behind him when he realized there was someone else in the room. A little girl was perched on the library steps, turning the pages of a book. Annoyed that his privacy had been invaded, he spoke sharply. "You shouldn't be in here. Didn't anyone tell you this room is private?"

She seemed to flinch, and when she looked up Ben was shocked and angry with himself. She looked about ten, and had the round face of Down's syndrome. In the same moment he became aware of the caliper splint leaning against the wall. "It's all right," he said quickly.

"I didn't mean to snap at you. You can stay here if you want to."

She looked anxious. "Is it really all right? I'm always in trouble for being where I shouldn't."

"You're not in trouble now," he said firmly. "You just took me by surprise."

He'd heard that Down's-syndrome children were notable for their gentle, affectionate natures, and perhaps it was true, for the smile she gave him was the sweetest he'd ever seen. He found himself smiling back. "Was it hard to get up those steps?" he asked with a glance at the caliper.

She shook her head. "I just held on to the shelves. It's quite easy, really. I'm good at holding on to things."

She spoke quite unself-consciously and it made him answer her equally naturally. "I wish I was good at holding on to things, but I hate people to know that I *need* to hold on."

"Is that your stick over there?"

"Yes."

"Have you always had it?"

"No, just a few years. What about you?"

"Since I was little," she said, unconcerned. "People are funny, aren't they? I mean, if you've got a stick they don't know what to say to you."

"The ones that think they do know are the worst," Ben reflected gloomily.

"They always seem to get it wrong," she said wisely.

They looked at each other in fellow feeling.

"My name's Carly," she offered.

"Mine's—" He hesitated, then gave her the name that only Dawn had ever used. "Mine's Ben."

They shook hands with solemn courtesy.

"Is this your house?" she asked.

"That's right."

"Then why aren't you at the party? Don't you like parties?"

"Not really," he confessed.

She looked anxious. "Don't you like people?"

"I—I don't feel easy with them."

"But why ever not? I think people are lovely."

"Even the ones who say the wrong things?"

"They mean to be kind," Carly said simply.

"I've rather got out of the habit of being with people," he said. "I'm always afraid they're going to look at my face."

She looked at him, puzzled. "But there's nothing wrong with your face."

He was about to say, "Nonsense," in his usual impatient way, when he realized that to her his fears would seem crazy. Her own troubles were so much greater, and she bore them so lightly that suddenly he felt ashamed. "Isn't there, really?" he asked, speaking more naturally than he had to a stranger for a long time.

She studied him more closely. The steps put her almost at his level. "You only have a few lines," she said reassuringly. "And everyone has lines when they get old, don't they?"

"I'm not that old," he said, startled.

Carly gave a little choke of laughter. She was irresistible, and before he knew it he was laughing with her. Absorbed, he didn't notice Dawn come to the door, stand watching them for a moment, then vanish quickly.

"I guess I am that old after all," he said with a grin.

"A hundred?" Carly asked mischievously.

"Less. Not much less, but a bit less. Now let's forget my age. Why don't you tell me what you're doing here? Weren't you enjoying the party?"

"Oh, yes, it's a super party. I'd never been to a Grange party before, although I'd heard all about them. Everyone said there wouldn't be one this year, but I hoped and hoped and hoped. And if you hope that much, it always comes true."

There was a sudden pricking against his eyelids at the courage with which she fended off despair. Despite the blows fate had dealt her she'd somehow clung to the belief that life was good, and it was he who'd nearly destroyed that belief. "Of course it does," he said. "But if you like the party so much, why are you here?"

"We were told not to go anywhere else in the house—" She looked at him, as if trying to decide whether to say the next bit.

He saved her the trouble. "So you just had to go exploring. I know the feeling. I was just like that at your age. Telling me not to do something was like a red rag to a bull. Do you want to see the rest of the house?"

The impish look was back in her eyes. "Thank you, but there's no point now."

"No—? Oh, I see. I spoiled it by saying yes. Then why not go back to the party? You're missing Father Christmas."

"Are you coming?"

"No, I—" He stopped. Her eyes were on him.

"It would be lovely if you came, too," she said earnestly.

"In that case—yes."

He helped her down and handed her the caliper. "Are you bringing your stick?" she asked.

He shook his head. "Suddenly I don't feel as if I need it."

They left the library hand in hand and made their way to the party. As they entered, the noise suddenly died and heads turned in their direction. For a terrible moment the old self-consciousness assailed him. Then he felt the little girl's hand tighten on his in a wordless message of comfort.

"This is Ben," she told everyone happily. "He's my friend."

Chapter Five

For a moment he couldn't take everything in. The meal was over and the tables had been cleared away, leaving a space where children were sitting and standing. Glittering tinsel decorations hung in giant festoons from the ceiling, and around the walls. At the far end of the long room rose a giant Christmas tree whose base was almost totally obscured by presents, and in front of it sat Father Christmas. But for the moment no one was looking at him. Ben's arrival had riveted everyone's attention.

As his mind cleared he realized that most of the children here were disabled in some way. Some had crutches, three were in wheelchairs, and many had Down's syndrome. Their round, smiling faces beamed at him in welcome, and they stretched out their hands to draw him into the circle, as if he were only another child who, like them, looked different from other children.

Under the tree Harry boomed, "Ho-ho-ho!" And when he had everyone's attention he cried, "Is everybody ready to play games?"

He was answered by an excited cheer. The youngsters crowded around him. A touch on Ben's arm made him look down. A little girl was standing there with a piece of Christmas cake on a plate. "You didn't have any," she said anxiously, holding it up to him.

He thanked her gravely and took the cake. She continued to watch him until he'd taken a bite and pronounced it delicious. Then she smiled and seemed to relax.

He'd had so many nurses—paid professionals who'd done their duty and departed when he became unbearable. The child's gentle concern for him pierced his heart. He'd forgotten that such care could be had freely—except for one person.

Dawn and the other helpers were putting chairs in a circle, asking everyone to sit down. Following the urgings of his new friends, Ben found himself sitting between Carly and a little boy in a wheelchair. He had no idea what was going to happen until Santa produced a huge parcel, which he handed to the nearest child. Someone began to play the piano, and the child promptly passed the parcel to his neighbor, who gave it to *his* neighbor. Suddenly the music stopped and the little boy who had the parcel began to tear off the shiny red paper, revealing shiny blue paper underneath. Before he could go further, the music restarted and it was time for the parcel to move on again.

Good heavens, Ben thought. He'd played this as a child, but not thought of it for years. The parcel came to him and he passed it on quickly. At last it stopped again and the child who had it began tearing at the wrapping. He got another layer off before the music started.

The next time the music stopped the parcel was in Ben's hands. He was embarrassed, not wanting to win the prize, but the packing was still thick, and he made a show of removing some while the children cheered. It was a relief when he could send it on its way. He could see Dawn, doubled up with laughter. He mouthed, "What's so funny?" and she mouthed back, "You."

And it *was* funny. Suddenly he could see that. Why had he stayed away from the party when there was so much fun to be had?

Reflecting thus, he almost got caught with the parcel again, but managed, at the last moment, to thrust it into the hands of the boy in the wheelchair. The child tried to pick at the wrapping but one arm was weak and he had difficulty until Ben came to the rescue, holding everything steady so that the boy removed quite a lot of wrapping. But there was still some there when the music restarted.

Round and round the parcel went, getting smaller while the cheers got louder. With one layer to go, it reached Ben again. This time he worked frantically, so that just before the music started he could thrust the gift into the hands of the little boy, with only a tiny scrap of wrapping left. As the child removed the final wisp of paper, Ben was leading the cheers.

The boy opened the box, revealing an adventure book. From his expression he'd clearly never won anything before in the whole of his short life. Ben was euphoric with triumph and exhilaration. He groped around in his mind for the last time he'd felt like this, but he had to go back a long way to come up with the answer.

It had been eight years ago, when a young woman with dark eyes and soft lips had told him she would love him forever. It had been a glorious victory, achieved after desperate efforts to fend off other men attracted by her beauty and her sweet nature. She could have had anyone she wanted, but she'd chosen him, and he'd felt akin to the gods. Nothing was going to part them. *For better or worse,* they'd promised each other, echoing the words of the marriage service they were planning.

Through thick and thin. Until death. But he'd betrayed that promise by not allowing her to keep it.

A malaise gripped him. The afternoon that had been so happy a moment ago was dimmed. He looked at Dawn, standing with a small child in her arms, and to his eyes all warmth and light, all joy and harmony streamed from her. If only he'd had more faith in her, they could have had their own children by now. She could have been standing there as his wife. The Ghost of Christmas Present had visited him, and it was a merry ghost, dancing and singing, with children clutching its hand and the hem of its flowing robes. But it was a melancholy ghost, too, reminding him that this might have been *his* present, and he'd blindly thrown it away.

After several more games the party moved on to the serious business of presents. Father Christmas sat under the tree, booming, "Ho-ho-ho!" taking the gifts Dawn handed to him, and reading the names out. Every child had a gift individually labeled and, as far as possible, chosen to fit. As yet another child whooped, "I really wanted this!" Ben made his way quietly around to where Dawn was selecting parcels to hand to Santa.

"How did you know what everyone wanted?" he murmured.

She smiled at him. "Some nifty liaison work with the people who look after them," she said, talking and working at the same time. "Most of them live in homes and hospitals. Their caregivers are wonderful, but even so, individuals tend to get submerged in the crowd. This is our chance to make up for that."

She was like a perfect bell, he thought. Strike where you would, the sound was always clear, sweet and true. It might all have been his own, but now she was smiling at Harry as she handed him the next gift, and Harry was smiling back with the unmistakable glow of a man in love. Quietly Ben moved away, choosing a moment when she wouldn't notice.

He retreated to the library and closed the door firmly, shutting out the sounds of the party, and settled down to wait for it all to finish.

But it was no good. His spirit was still out there with them, watching her jealously. He, who had no right to be jealous!

He endured it for half an hour, but then the low hum that still reached him through the thick oak door died to almost nothing, and the quiet was the worst thing of all. He went to the door and opened it a fraction. The party was still going on, but it had reached the cocoa stage. In the big room he could just see children sitting around drinking out of mugs. Some of the younger ones were beginning to nod off.

As Ben watched, Father Christmas came creeping out into the hall. He was looking around him as though afraid to be seen. When he was sure he was alone he slipped a hand into his robe, and drew it out clutching a sprig of mistletoe, which he lodged in the top of a picture frame in a dark corner of the hall. Then he went down the passage in the direction of the kitchen and when he returned, he was leading Dawn by the hand.

Ben gritted his teeth. He was enraged but helpless. A man could hardly attack Father Christmas, and nothing else would stop the inevitable. Except Dawn herself, perhaps? She might push him away.

But Santa was cunning. Holding her tenderly he inquired, ''Have I done everything you wanted?''

''Everything,'' she assured him. ''You've been absolutely wonderful.''

"In that case—" Santa pointed up to the mistletoe "—it's time for my reward."

Dawn allowed herself to be drawn closer into his arms to receive his kiss. Her manner wasn't loverlike. She even giggled and said his beard tickled, but Ben's frantically searching eyes couldn't detect any sign of her pushing him away. He retreated and closed the door again, wishing he'd never opened it.

A short while later there was a knock on the door and he opened it to find Carly. "The bus is here," she said with a shy smile. "I didn't want to go without saying goodbye to you."

"It was a pleasure talking to you," he said sincerely. "I hope we meet again."

"Perhaps we'll meet at next year's Christmas party?"

"Yes, perhaps," he agreed.

He watched as she and a small group of others were shepherded through the front door to their waiting bus. At the last moment Carly turned and waved vigorously, and he waved back. Dawn came and stood beside him, also waving. "I'm so glad you two got on well," she said. "It's such a pity that they have to go so early, but they've got quite a distance to travel."

"The party's still going, then?" he asked.

"Another hour, I should think. Is that all right?"

"Perfectly. I told you, I leave everything in your hands." Somebody called her and she turned away to chat with a child. Ben's jealous eyes searched the surroundings and finally located Harry in the big party room, munching Christmas cake. He saw him glance up at Dawn, catch her eye and blow her a kiss from behind his beard. She didn't blow a kiss back, but she waved to him cheerfully.

The phone in the library rang. Ben answered it and found himself talking to a strange woman who introduced herself as Mrs. Calloway. "I need a vet," she explained. "Mr. Stanning's been called out but I was told I could find the other two at this number."

"That's right. I'll fetch someone for you now."

He could see Dawn only a few feet away. Logic might have dictated that he summon her, but something made him walk right past her to Harry. "I'm afraid you're wanted," he said. "You can use the phone in the library."

He followed Harry back through the hall, noticing almost subconsciously that Dawn was walking away in the direction of the kitchen, and couldn't see them. Harry's conversation was brief. Ben heard him say, "Fine. I'll be there in half an hour." As he hung up he was already pulling off the Father Christmas costume. "I've got to dash," he said. "Hang this beard! It was murder to put on and it's murder to take off." He gave a grin of happy reminiscence. "And there was one part of the evening when it was very inconvenient."

"Really?" Ben said, fighting an impulse to do violence to poor Harry's well-meaning person.

Harry was still tugging at the snowy whiskers. "Can you give me a hand?"

"Delighted." Ben took hold of the beard and removed it with one wrench.

"Ouch!" Harry rubbed his chin. "No need to take my chin off, as well."

"Sorry," Ben said untruthfully. "Is there anything else I can do for you?"

"Yes. Shove the costume back in the box, and tell Dawn I had to dash away, would you?"

"You can leave everything to me."

The hall was empty as he saw Harry to the door. He watched him drive away and stood for a moment, reflecting on what he'd just done. It wasn't exactly dishonest, he reasoned. Harry was the senior vet and many customers would have considered him preferable. But the truth was Ben had seized on the chance to get rid of him.

He heard Dawn's voice coming from the kitchen. She seemed to be talking to one of the children. "Don't worry, Gary. You can talk to Father Christmas now and explain, and I'm sure he'll be able to—"

Ben felt a cold hand clutch his stomach. He'd thought no further ahead than removing Harry, but now the full enormity of his action burst upon him. *He'd sent Father Christmas away.*

Now Gary—whoever he was—would be disappointed, and Dawn would reproach him for not fetching her instead. This was disaster.

Moving faster than he'd done in years he crossed the hall, vanished into the library and shut the door. For extra safety he locked it. He was only just in time. The next moment he heard Dawn's voice directly outside. "Does anybody know where Father Christmas is?"

Desperate situations called for desperate measures. Ben surveyed the red-and-white costume, relieved that he was about the same size as Harry. It took him a moment to toss aside his jacket and pull on the garment. Luckily it was the old-fashioned kind—a massive flowing robe that came down to the ground and concealed almost everything. The real trouble lay with the beard. Having been wrenched unceremoniously off, it declined to take any further part in the proceedings, and lay there, torn and useless. The glue Harry had used had dried, and Ben couldn't find any more in the box. But he did manage to find another beard. This one didn't need glue, but hooked on over the ears. He fixed it as firmly as he could, pulled the big hood over his head, checked in the mirror over the mantel-piece to be sure he was unrecognizable, and unlocked the door.

Dawn was outside, alone. "Thank heavens," she said, smiling and seizing his hand. Ben's heart burned within him. Her smile and her touch were both for Harry, damn him! He inclined his head in a questioning manner, but didn't dare risk speaking.

"We've got a crisis," Dawn explained. "It's Gary Briggs. He's a last-minute addition. His father's dead and he lives alone with his mother, but she had to go into hospital so he's temporarily in care. Nobody knew he was coming until the last moment, so there wasn't time to get him a proper gift. I put in one from the reserve we keep for emergencies, but Gary's eleven and when he opened the gift it was a child's toy and much too babyish for him. We've got to do something, quickly. There he is. Gary, I've just been explaining to Father Christmas, and he's going to put everything right."

For a dreadful moment Ben's mind went completely blank. He pulled himself together and coughed, playing for time. When he spoke his voice was as gruff as he could make it. "Let me see—Gary Briggs." His mind groped frantically around the facts Dawn had given him and seized on one. "Your mother's in hospital, isn't she? Have you seen her?"

"I saw her yesterday."

"Is she feeling any better?"

"The doctor said she'd be out in a month."

"That's good. But it's a sad thing to happen at Christmas. Misfortunes always seem worse at Christmas. I wonder why."

Gary nodded and looked at Ben confidingly, as if he'd touched a nerve. "It's because you make so many plans," he said. "You keep remembering the things you were supposed to be doing instead of what you are doing."

"Yes, that's right. You do. And the distance between them hurts." He said the last words almost to himself, but the sight of Gary's trustful eyes on him brought him back to reality. "I expect you miss her very much," he said. "What do you miss about her most?" He was playing madly for time, seeking the essential clue that would tell him what to do next.

Unexpectedly Gary gave it to him. "Doing jigsaws," he said.

"You do jigsaw puzzles?"

"Mum and me do them together. Really hard ones. She's ever so good."

It had happened, the miracle he'd prayed for. "Tell me, Gary, have you and your mother ever done a jigsaw of eight thousand pieces?"

The boy's eyes opened wide and he shook his head.

"Suppose I give you one, and then you can see how much you can manage by yourself, and when your mother comes home you can finish it together."

Gary nodded. He was smiling and seemed beyond speech. "It isn't exactly new," Ben added hastily. "Because I've always loved jigsaws too, and I used to do this one myself when I was a young—a young Father Christmas."

"But how can you be a young Father Christmas?" Gary wanted to know.

"It's a mystery, but take it from me that you can. I've been saving this jigsaw to give to someone who was ex-

ceptionally good at them. I want you to wait here with
Dawn.''

His mind was racing with plans for getting upstairs
without actually climbing the main stairway, which
would reveal his identity. If he went through the library
and out the French doors he could slip back into the
house at the side and dash up the back stairs. Preoccu-
pied, he failed to notice Dawn staring at him as though
she'd seen a ghost.

As he hurried through the library he realized what a
task he'd taken on. Most of his possessions were still
packed up, and he had only the vaguest idea where the
jigsaw puzzle was. But his luck held and he found what
he was looking for in five minutes. He'd spoken the truth
about his lifelong fascination with difficult jigsaws—a
hobby that had become almost an obsession in his years
of illness. It was still in excellent condition, with no un-
sightly tears or scruffy patches on the lid, with its bril-
liantly colored picture of racing cars speeding toward the
checkered flag amid cheering crowds. He picked it up
and hastened back the way he'd come.

He returned downstairs to find that more children
were putting on hats and coats and being shepherded
outside to waiting buses. Ben took a moment to stand on
the step and wave them goodbye, then hurried back to
Gary. He found him sitting under the Christmas tree,
looking slightly forlorn in the rapidly emptying room.
Ben stopped at the doorway to switch off the chandelier, leaving only the Christmas-tree lights and a few
around the walls. There was enough light to give his gift,
but no dangerous brilliance to reveal his identity.

He went and sat beside Gary, holding out the jigsaw.
The boy gasped and seized it, regarding the picture with

wonder. "It's fabulous," he breathed. "And a smashing picture. Not a soppy one."

"That's why I always liked it," Ben agreed, "because it had a decent picture, not a soppy one. Also, because it's very difficult. It'll take you ages." For a moment he forgot his character and spoke as himself: "But I promise all the pieces are there. I always threw them away if any pieces were missing."

"Threw them away?" Gary echoed, aghast. "Just for one piece?"

"There didn't seem any point once they weren't perfect any more," Ben explained. Something in the boy's eyes made him add more gently, "You don't feel that way about your jigsaws?"

"They're all special—like friends," Gary explained earnestly. "I couldn't throw them away just 'cause they were a bit different. I mean, you don't get fed up with people just cuz of that, do you?"

How little he knew of the world if he believed that, Ben thought. The years would teach him differently. But with luck he would cling to his beliefs and would probably make fewer bad decisions than most men.

A middle-aged couple had come quietly into the room. They were Gary's temporary foster parents, ready to take him away. Ben got hastily back into character. They were the last guests to leave and he said booming goodbyes to them and conducted them to the front door. Gary was clutching the jigsaw as though it was the most precious thing in the world. He waved out the window until the car was out of sight, and Ben waved back.

Chapter Six

As he closed the front door Ben realized how quiet the house had become now the party was over. It was as if he were completely alone.

Then he realized that someone was still there—a figure standing in the shadows of the corner where the mistletoe was still lodged over the picture. She stepped out into better light and he saw that it was Dawn. She came close to him. "Father Christmas, you were brilliant," she said. "It meant so much to Gary." She smiled up at him, expecting a response, but Ben didn't dare speak.

Dawn glanced at the mistletoe. "Come here."

His heart sank. He'd wondered how she felt about Harry's kiss, and this was his answer. She wanted more. She was enticing him, putting her hands into his and drawing him into the shadows—or rather, drawing Harry into the shadows. Terrible temptation assailed him. What he was contemplating was monstrous, unforgivable.

"Dawn—" he said in agony.

"Hush," she told him. "We don't need words. We never did. Only this matters." She was putting her arms about his neck, drawing his head down to hers. He must tell her the truth immediately. It was dishonest to accept the love she meant for another man. But her lips were on his and she was in his arms, pressing close to him, and it was impossible to do anything but hold her tightly, and surrender to her.

His heart burned within him. This was different from the kiss she'd given him the other night. That had been gentle and friendly, a gesture of reassurance such as she might have given to any wounded creature. Now there was desire and urgency in her mouth. The lips that moved purposefully against his were full of sweet promise and infinite delight, as they had been before, long ago; as he had never thought to find them again.

He'd fought his longing for her through the bitter, lonely years, and had thought he'd won. If he couldn't murder his feelings, at least he could master them. That was what he'd told himself. Now that victory was revealed as a sham, a thing of gossamer that could be destroyed by her touch, by the memory of her eager, self-forgetting passion. He'd survived by denying love in order to forget its beauty. But love was invading him, forcing him to recognize beauty and to want it again with a blazing force that shook his battered body like a storm.

"It's true, isn't it?" she murmured against his mouth. "Only this matters."

"Yes," he said hoarsely. "It's true. It's always been true."

The battle was over. He yielded. He was hers again as completely as if there'd been no break. His arms encircled her, drawing her tighter still until she was pressed against the whole length of him. Strength flowed back into limbs that hadn't been strong for years. The body that had seemed half dead was awakening, rediscovering desire and delight.

"My love," she whispered. "Oh, my dear love..."

He murmured her name between kisses, saying the word as a kind of charm to ward off evil, and she answered, "Yes...yes..."

"Tell me that you love me," he pleaded.

"I love you," she responded instantly. "Night and day, every moment...always...until the end of my life..."

For a mad moment he was on the verge of breaking down completely, telling her how he'd always loved her, begging her to forgive him and come back. In another instant the words would have been spoken.

But there was the click of a door opening, a murmur from the kitchen. Before he could understand what was happening, Dawn had quickly freed herself. "Someone's coming," she murmured.

"Dawn," he pleaded.

"Hush," she said urgently.

Her hand brushed across his lips, then she was gone. The arms that had held her only a moment ago were empty again—as empty as if he had embraced a ghost.

The crib glowed in the soft light. The rest of the church was in darkness. Softly the choir began to sing and as their voices swelled, the congregation joined in. It was Christmas Eve, and most of the villagers were in the little church that had stood there for nearly a thousand years.

Ben had slipped in quietly a few minutes earlier, while the lights were still on, and stood by the door, trying to pick Dawn out in the congregation, but there was no sign of her.

Thirty hours had passed since the party had ended with Dawn in his arms—thirty hours during which he'd soared to dizzy hope and sunk to despair again. At some

moments it was clear that she'd known who he was all
the time, that it was himself she'd kissed with such passion and longing. At other moments it was so obvious
that she'd thought it was Harry that he castigated himself for a self-deceiving fool. Sometimes he remembered that whatever she might have guessed later, it was
Harry she'd meant to entice under the mistletoe. And
sometimes he just felt he was going crazy.

Everything depended on their next meeting, when he
could look into her eyes and read the truth there. All
Christmas Eve he'd waited for her to call at the Grange,
perhaps on some pretext about the party. But though an
army had descended on the Grange to clear up, there had
been no sign of Dawn. Nor had she called him.

He recalled that his doctors had advised plenty of exercise, and prescribed himself a walk, which might, or
might not, take him past her surgery. By an odd coincidence, that was exactly where it took him, and he was
rewarded by the sight of Dawn's car vanishing into the
distance. Presumably she was attending a farm, but
when she returned and was less busy, she would call him.
Comforted, he returned home, abandoning his exercise
after a few hundred yards.

The day had stretched on endlessly, with no call from
Dawn. The house seemed unbearably lonely after the
riotous happiness of yesterday. Carly stood out in his
mind, her sweet round face showing no bitterness at the
bad hand life had dealt her. Gary was there too, with his
strange childish wisdom about clinging to what you
loved, even when it had become imperfect. Ben didn't
want to examine Gary's words too closely. They opened
up an avenue of thought that dismayed him.

Once his life had been perfect, and had looked set to
go on being perfect. He'd been a young, strong, hand-

some man, with an innocent pride in his virility and his power to thrill the woman he loved. But the perfection had gone. The superb body and looks had been smashed, and with them his pride. So he'd thrown it all away. He'd told himself he was acting for her benefit. But now a child's chance remark had shown him a less noble motive. Had he been too proud to go to her imperfect—as a damaged man who had to cast himself on the generosity of a woman's love?

If he'd destroyed her happiness for such a reason, perhaps he deserved his punishment now. But that made it no easier to bear. As the lamps in the church dimmed he decided it was time to go, but something held him there, listening to the sweet voices raised in joy—and something more than joy. They were celebrating a human companionship that was alien to him. He'd lost it long ago, on the day he'd decided to bear his burdens alone. Standing there in the darkness, his heart aching with loneliness, he understood all over again what he'd done.

At last he slipped out the door. As he limped across the snow the sound pursued him, growing fainter as he reached his own house.

Mrs. Stanley was still up. He tensed, hoping she'd say Dawn had called while he was out, and was waiting for him, but she only observed that she'd laid out the whiskey decanter in the library. He nodded and bade her good-night.

In the library he settled by the fire and poured himself a glass. But he stopped with it halfway to his lips. *She* wouldn't like it. And she would come. Of course she would, he realized with sudden inspiration. She would be here at midnight. This was why she hadn't called him earlier. The Ghost of Christmas Yet to Come was waiting for the right moment. What a fool he'd been!

There were still ten minutes to go. He got up and checked the French doors to make sure they were unlocked, then he drew back the curtains so that she could see him, and returned to his chair by the fire.

As the last few seconds ticked away to midnight he closed his eyes, straining to hear her. There was nothing. No matter. When he opened his eyes she would be there.

But she wasn't there—not the first time he tried it, nor the second, nor the third. As one o'clock approached he reminded himself that the spirits had come to Scrooge not at midnight, but at one o'clock, and hope revived in him. But one o'clock came and went, and his heart grew cold with despair.

He'd been deluding himself. She'd sweetened him up for the children's party, and once her object was gained she no longer cared. She was probably somewhere with Harry right this minute. He should be sensible and go to bed.

But to leave this room would have been an admission that it was all over, and he couldn't make his limbs move. So he stayed as he was until he fell asleep.

When he awoke the fire was out, and the clock said it was six o'clock on Christmas morning. He cursed himself for a fool, sitting there for hours, waiting for a woman who'd forgotten him. He didn't fancy going to bed now, so he went out to the garage and started up the car. A drive around would clear his head. It was quiet in the sleeping village as he passed through and continued out into the countryside.

As he drove he was making bitter plans. He'd sell and leave here. There was no way he could stay in Hollowdale now. Better to go before he'd properly settled in. But even as he planned, he knew he wasn't going to do any of it. The meeting with the Craddocks had revealed that he had obligations he'd never suspected, and it wasn't his way to shirk his obligations.

He was so absorbed in these thoughts that he was taken by surprise when his headlamps showed a woman straight ahead, trying to wave him to stop. He took a second too long to react. At the last moment he saw Dawn's face in front of him, the eyes wide, the arms stretched out to ward him off. Then she'd vanished.

He braked sharply. Everything in him was screaming in protest as he jumped out into the snow and limped back down the road. "Dawn," he yelled in terror. *"Dawn!"*

"Here," came a faint voice from the ditch.

In his urgency he'd come without his stick. Now he flung himself into the ditch without thinking. Later he was to recall that the movement had jarred him less than he'd expected. At the time he didn't even notice it in his awful dread for her. "Where are you?" he cried frantically.

"I'm just here." Her voice was close and the next moment he had hold of her.

"Are you badly hurt? Oh, dear God! Dawn—"

"I'm fine, honest. I jumped clear in time and landed in the snow. Honestly, Ben, I'm not hurt."

He held her tightly against him. "Thank God!" he breathed. "What on earth were you doing?"

He felt her arms go around him, and her head was against his chest. "I had to make you stop. Something terrible has happened. My car's stuck in the ditch, and I've simply got to get to the Haynes farm."

"We'll go in my car. It's sturdier than yours."

They helped each other up, and Ben brought his car closer to hers so that she could use his headlamps to see what she was doing. Her vehicle was trapped, nose down in the ditch, and she had to fight to get a door open for her bag, but at last she managed it, and scrambled in beside Ben.

"You're an answer to prayer," she said gratefully.

"What are you doing out here at Christmas?"

"Someone has to be on call. Animals get sick, or give birth."

"I thought lambing was in springtime."

"This is a dog. Fred Haynes has a spaniel who's just about to whelp. He was terrified when he called me to say she'd started early. He adores Trixie. She's all he's got in the world."

After a moment he said, "How long have you been on duty?"

"Since yesterday afternoon. Really, it just means staying at the practice, in case of an emergency. There's a bed there, and I got plenty of sleep before he called."

Her voice was neutrally cordial, but now that the first agitation was over, Ben knew that something was wrong. After her first spontaneous reaction to him a shadow had fallen on her. Even as she spoke she was looking out the window rather than turning in her seat to watch him. He tried to believe he was imagining things, but when she suddenly said, "The road forks in about half a mile—we go to the left," her voice was undeniably distant.

They were climbing higher. Once, when the road turned, he could look down and see Hollowdale, where a few lights had come on. The moon came out from behind the clouds, flooding the snowy countryside with silver light. It was like traveling in a lunar landscape, and he shivered when he thought of her driving up here alone.

At last she said, "That's Fred's farm, just up ahead."

As they came to a bumpy halt the front door opened and light streamed across the snow. The next moment Fred was running toward them. "Quick," he cried hoarsely. "She's having a bad time."

Dawn hurried into the house, leaving Ben to follow her. When he arrived she was already kneeling on the floor beside a spaniel. The bitch was gasping heavily as if in pain, but she was looking up at Dawn with trusting eyes. As Ben watched, Dawn listened to the animal's heart with an intent expression.

"Don't panic, Fred," she said at last. "It's happened a bit sooner than it should have done, but that sometimes happens. It doesn't necessarily mean anything."

"But what are you going to do?" the old man cried. There was a suspicion of a break in his voice.

"I'm going to turn out most of the lights, and then we're all going to keep back."

"But that's not doing anything," he said in outrage. "She needs help—proper help."

"She needs peace and quiet," Dawn said firmly. "She hates these bright lights and people staring at her. Did she try to get away?"

The old man nodded. "She dashed outside and dug herself into the snow. I'd got it all nice for her in here and she ran off."

Dawn squeezed his hand and said gently, "She was looking for a quiet place to give birth. That's all. It wasn't a rejection, Fred."

She switched on a small reading lamp, then turned out the main lights, so that the corner where the basket stood was cast into deep shadow. At once the bitch seemed to relax. Dawn got down onto the floor beside her and stroked her gently, offering the comfort of her presence, but otherwise not intruding. After a few minutes she looked up at Fred who was regarding her with an expression of pure misery.

"If she hasn't produced the first pup in two hours I'll give her an injection," Dawn said. "But she will." She smiled reassuringly at the old man. "Why don't you put the kettle on, Fred?"

He seemed to pull himself together and went out into the kitchen. Ben occupied himself looking around the room. It was a solidly prosperous place, with furniture that was plain but well made. The television set in the corner looked new and expensive. But what struck Ben most was the complete absence of Christmas decorations. There was no tree, no paper chains, no cards lovingly propped on the mantelpiece, no sign of a family that remembered or cared. Nothing. He remembered the home of the Craddock family, full of cheerfulness despite their poverty. "Is the old boy really alone?" he asked Dawn. "There's no one else in this house?"

"No one. Of course he's got employees, but they're not friends. I don't think he has any friends at all. He barks at everyone until they run away. I actually like him, but he works hard at making it difficult."

She said all this still sitting on the floor, never taking her eyes off the spaniel. Her manner appeared normal but Ben had a strange sense that she was using the dog as an excuse not to look at him. It seemed impossible that only the day before yesterday he'd held her in his arms, feeling her passionate kiss on his mouth, her body warm and soft against his. But it hadn't been himself she was kissing. It had been Harry.

The truth was that she'd suspected nothing. Harry was her love now. After the party they'd compared notes and she'd discovered the deception. Now she was angry with Ben, and embarrassed to be with him.

Fred returned with the tea and some sandwiches. Dawn never left Trixie's side, sitting on the floor, watching her, but unobtrusively. Gradually the quiet atmosphere seemed to affect the dog, and she dozed for a few minutes. Then she was awake again, panting harder and straining. And suddenly there was a pup in the basket.

"Look at that!" Fred exclaimed in delight. His face beamed with love.

"They'll come more easily now she's borne the first one," Dawn observed, and in twenty minutes there was another pup. Dawn felt Trixie's abdomen very gently. "That's it," she said. "Just those two."

Trixie was contentedly licking her babies. Dawn steered Fred firmly away. He was over the moon. "Did you see them?" he kept asking. "Aren't they beautiful?"

"They look a bit like sausages," Ben observed.

"Beautiful sausages," Dawn corrected him firmly. "The most beautiful sausages I ever delivered. What are you going to do with them, Fred?"

"Keep them," he said at once. "They're Trixie's. I couldn't give them away. And I'll have them when . . ." His voice grew husky and he cleared his throat suddenly.

"That's a good idea," Dawn said. "You ought to give them Christmas names, Fred."

"Nay, that'll sound daft," he declared, belligerent in his relief.

"Call them Holly and Cracker," Ben said unexpectedly. "That won't sound daft."

"That's it!" Fred agreed, beaming more than ever. "Holly and Cracker! I'll get some more tea."

Chapter Seven

When he'd gone Dawn threw herself into a chair with her eyes closed. She looked worn-out. After a moment she opened her eyes again and looked at Ben. She smiled at him, but only briefly. The excitement of the moment was over, and once again there was constraint in her manner. Ben had a sensation of floundering, trying to get to her, but being unable to pass a barrier she'd set up. A terrible depression dragged at him. How naively he'd let himself be lured on by the bright dreams that had seemed to dance around him in the last few days. Why, he'd even imagined—

Unable to stop himself, he sat down and buried his face in his hands. The descent back into despair after the rebirth of hope was cruel.

"Ben, whatever's the matter?" She was there beside him, kneeling on the floor, reaching up to him. He pulled himself together.

"It's all right, Dawn. I should have known better."

"About what?"

"About us. When you appeared in my library the other night—it felt as if you'd come out of my dreams. Stupid, eh? All the things I said to you that night were sensible. They're still sensible. It's just that I—" He forced himself to stop. He'd been about to say, "I don't believe them anymore," forgetting that it wasn't the same with her.

"Just that you what?" Dawn asked in a tense voice.

"They're still sensible. That's how things stand. I just hoped that we could put the bitterness behind us and find a way to be friendly."

"Friendly," she echoed in a blank voice.

He was too absorbed in his own inner struggle to heed her tone. "But ever since the party, you've changed. And I know why."

"Do you?"

"Well, it's obvious, isn't it? You got what you wanted, and I'm glad. You were right all along about that party. Those children deserved a treat, and I'm glad you talked me into it. But I hadn't expected you to change toward me quite so soon. You *have* changed, haven't you?"

She hesitated before saying cautiously, "I don't feel exactly as I did two days ago."

"Of course not. You don't need me anymore."

"That's a wicked thing to say," she told him hotly.

"Why is it? You've just admitted that you have changed."

"Only because *you* have. When I found out what you'd done to the Craddocks, I couldn't believe it. The man I used to love would never have been so mean and hard—"

"Whoa, wait a minute! What am I supposed to have done to the Craddocks?"

"Oh, Ben, please don't pretend," she begged. "I saw them yesterday and they told me all about it. They're devastated. How could you throw them out of the place their family has farmed for so long, and at Christmas?"

"What are you talking about? I haven't thrown them out."

"But you're going to. Mrs. Craddock told me everything—how you went looking around when they weren't

there to defend themselves, and implied that they'd been
wasting money on the children when it should have gone
to the farm, and when Mr. Craddock tried to explain,
you cut him short by saying his lease would be up soon.
How could you do anything so cruel? How could *you* be
so cruel? It's as though I've never really known you.''

"It seems you didn't know me if you thought I could
behave like that," he said indignantly. "Of course, I'm
not going to throw them out. Mrs. Craddock seems to
have got hold of the wrong end of every possible stick. I
didn't go snooping behind their backs—at least, I didn't
mean to. I happened to drop in when they weren't there,
and I just looked around to pass the time until they came
back. And I never implied that they were wasting money
on the children. I remember seeing her trying to hide a
bag from a toy shop, but she didn't have to."

"But you said—"

"I was only making small talk about Christmas
shopping. I didn't know what she was reading into it."

"And that remark about their lease. Was that small
talk?"

"No. I have plans for that farm, but the plans include the Craddocks. Dawn, listen to me. In the few days
I've been here I've heard nothing but praise for what a
grand old gentleman Squire Davis was, and how he loved
to keep Christmas with his neighbors. Tell me, do you
know what this 'grand old gentleman' was charging the
Craddocks in rent?"

"No."

He told her.

"That much?" she gasped. "But the farm can't be
worth a quarter of that."

"I agree. That's why they're so poor and the place is
going to wrack and ruin. Davis doesn't seem to have

cared about that as long as he extracted the last penny from them. I plan to rewrite the lease, cutting the rent. Then I'll make them an interest-free loan, plus I have a few other ideas that will help get the place back into good condition. I'd no idea how they'd take an innocent remark.''

Her face was full of joy. "You never meant to force them out?''

"Of course not. You should have known that.''

Dawn's eyes softened. "Yes, I should. It's not a bit like you as I remember you, but you're so different now, that anything seemed possible.''

"A man doesn't change that much," he said gently. "Not inside. Maybe on the surface.''

His voice was full of meaning and he saw a light come into her eyes as though she'd understood him. He wanted to say so much more. It was hard to find the courage he needed, but if she would help him—

A clatter announced that Fred was ready to serve breakfast. Ben rose reluctantly, but his heart was lighter.

They ate in the room where Trixie lay in her basket. Every few minutes Fred would rise from the table and go to caress her ears, murmuring words of love. "She really does need to be left alone, Fred," Dawn chided him gently. "Let her get to know her babies in her own way.'' After that he stayed at the table, but his glance went constantly to the basket. Ben glanced at Dawn, but she was looking at the old man, her eyes filled with infinite pity.

"It's getting light," he said tentatively. "Perhaps—''

"Have some more coffee," Fred suggested quickly. "I was going to make some fresh.''

"Just one cup, then," Dawn said gently. "Oh dear,'' she whispered when Fred had returned to the kitchen. "I hate leaving him when he's so lonely, and on Christmas Day, but we must go soon.''

"How come he's all alone? Doesn't he have any family?''

"Oh, yes. He has a son and daughter but he's managed to drive them both away. That's their photos on the sideboard. There's a new one since I was last here. That picture of the two toddlers. He told me his son had sent him that years ago, but he didn't have it on display before. Perhaps Christmas has softened him a bit.''

Ben rose and picked up a picture of a young woman just as Fred returned with the coffeepot. "That's my daughter, Linda," he said. "She was a good lass in her way.''

"Was? You means she's dead?'' Ben asked.

"As good as dead for all I see of her," Fred declared heavily. "I blame that chap she married. He set her against me. We got on all right, me and Linda, before he came along." He stomped back into the kitchen and Ben asked in a low voice, "Did they really?''

"Not according to Jack. I think she married the first man who asked, just to get away." She spoke softly as Fred was coming back.

"I told her she'd regret it if she married him," he said. "And she did. He ran off and left her with two kids. I said she could come back here. I'm still her father even if she did treat me bad. But was she grateful? Not her.''

"Perhaps you used the wrong approach," Dawn suggested gently. "Maybe if you'd told her you missed her and really wanted her, she might be more willing to come back.''

Fred sighed. "Maybe. Maybe not. I've never been a man for fine words. She knows she can come back if she wants to.''

"A man can lose a lot from not being willing to give an inch," Ben said reflectively. "He may even lose the thing he wants most in the world."

Fred grunted. "Oh, aye!" It was clear that he considered this remark in the category of "fine words" and not to be paid serious attention.

Watching him, Ben was appalled. The old man's empty, loveless life seemed like some ghastly parody of his own. *But it was different,* he argued. *He was no Fred Haynes living in bleak isolation in a windswept farm on the moor.*

But the argument wouldn't do. In his heart he knew that his comfortable, rich man's house meant nothing. His true isolation was as bleak as Fred's could ever be, and for the same reason. Instead of seeking human warmth he'd driven it away. He'd been certain, eight years ago, that he'd made the right decision, for Dawn as well as himself; so certain that he'd imposed that decision on her, without reference to her wishes. And now the Ghost of Christmas Yet to Come had raised a curtain, revealing the full horror of his own future.

But was that future set in stone, immovable, unrelenting? Was there no hope?

"Men's courses will foreshadow certain ends...but if the courses be departed from, the ends will change."

"What's that?"

Startled, Ben found Fred's eyes on him. He hadn't realized he'd spoken aloud. "Nothing," he said hastily. "It's just a quote from a book I once read."

"Oh." Fred shrugged. "Books."

Ben realized Dawn was watching him. She'd recognized the words they'd once read together beside a roaring fire, but he couldn't interpret the message in her eyes.

He gazed at her frantically, trying to understand, until Fred's blunt voice broke the spell.

"The other picture's Tony," Fred grunted. "He got himself tangled up with a young woman from Australia."

"Fred," Dawn protested, "when you say, 'got himself tangled up,' do you mean he fell in love with her?"

"Call it what you like. I told him she weren't the right lass for him, but would he listen? Not him. Stubborn. Always was."

"I wonder where he got that from," Dawn murmured.

"His mother," Fred declared at once. "She'd never listen either."

"How did it work out for Tony and this woman?" Ben asked.

"He went off to live with her in Australia."

"You told me they had twins," Dawn remembered. "That's their picture, isn't it?"

Fred grunted. "I just came across it," he said. "I can't think why I bothered to put it there."

But they knew. The old man's pride was all that kept him going, but his lonely heart was breaking from the results of his stubbornness. Despite the warmth of the room, Ben shivered.

"It's time we were going," Dawn said.

"Not yet," Fred protested. "Have another coffee."

"We really must go. I'll call back in a few days and see how Trixie is."

He followed them out to the car and stood watching as they drove away. Dawn glanced in the mirror and saw him still standing there, a lonely figure against the sky, growing smaller and smaller.

"Oh, heavens!" she said. "How terribly sad."

"But it's true, surely, that men can change their fate by 'departing from their courses'?" he asked cautiously.

"It would be true if they could do it. But how many people can?"

"Very few, probably," Ben agreed. "But that's because not many people see what they've done clearly enough to understand what they *must* do. But if a man gets that insight—somehow—and if fate gives him a second chance—"

"But that's it. I think in his heart Fred suspects the truth, but I don't think he's going to get that second chance."

"Oh, yes," he said, deflated. "Fred."

"Well, we were talking about Fred, weren't we?"

"Yes, of course we were."

He drove in silence for a few more miles, until Dawn said, "Ben, you've been absolutely wonderful tonight and I— Well, I don't know how to say this—"

"Yes?" he said eagerly.

"I've put you to so much trouble already, but if you could bear to turn off at that fork up ahead, and go on to the Craddock farm—then you could tell them they didn't need to worry."

Disappointment made him irritable. "It's miles out of the way, Dawn. I'll write them a note."

"But they won't get it until after Christmas and— Oh well, never mind. You're right. I'm really grateful for what you've done tonight."

The sun was up, casting a brilliant light over the white fields so that the glow almost blinded him. He blinked, wondering if he was imagining things or if there really were two figures by the roadside, trying to hail him.

As he drew nearer, the figures took more definite shape as a young man and woman. Ben pulled off and leaned out the window. "Is your car stuck?" he called.

"No, the car's fine, thanks," the woman answered cheerfully. "We just need some directions. Is this the way to the Haynes farm?"

"Right up ahead," Dawn answered. "You've got about five miles to go. But—" An unfamiliar accent in their voices had struck her, and their faces were curiously alike. "Who are you?" she asked with rising excitement.

"I'm Fred Haynes, and this is my sister Jenny," the man said. "We're visiting from Australia and we thought we'd look up our grandfather. We should have arrived yesterday, but we got lost."

Dawn got out of the car and went closer to them. They were attractive youngsters, tall and strong, with open, cheerful faces, who looked as if they lived active lives. "You're Fred's grandchildren from Australia?" she cried. "Oh, that's wonderful!"

"You know him?" Jenny asked eagerly.

"We've just left him," Dawn told her. "I'm a vet. I've been caring for his dog while she had her pups."

"Do you think he'll be glad to see us?" Jenny asked practically. "Dad's always told us he's a bit of a grump. Will he want strangers bursting in on him at Christmas?"

"He wants you," Dawn assured her. "But he might pretend otherwise because he finds it hard to show his feelings."

The two young Australians grinned at each other and spoke with one voice. *"Just like Dad."*

"Did you say your name was Fred?" Dawn asked the young man.

"That's right. Dad named me after his own father."

"I reckon old Fred will be thrilled about that," Ben said. He'd left the car and come to talk to them.

Jenny looked around at the whiteness. "I think this is all just wonderful. We've never even seen snow before. Dad's always talking about this place, how beautiful it is, and we just had to see it for ourselves."

"You'd best hurry on," Dawn said, smiling. "Straight ahead. You can't miss it."

"Thanks." They headed for their car and got in. Just before they drove away they waved out the windows, calling, "Merry Christmas!"

"Merry Christmas!" Ben and Dawn called back together.

Dawn gave a crow of delight and jumped up and down in the snow. "That's *wonderful*. Now old Fred really will have a merry Christmas."

Ben grinned. "Not merry," he said. "Happy, I hope, but all the clowns in the universe couldn't make that man merry."

"You're right. He'll grumble like mad, but he'll be happy underneath and that's what matters. And those two won't be upset by his manner because they're used to it in their father and they know how to cope with it. He's been given another chance, and that's the best part of all."

He looked at her, finding himself suddenly misty-eyed. "Other people's happiness really means that much to you, doesn't it?" he asked tenderly.

"Well, you can't be happy all on your own, can you?" she asked poignantly.

"I guess not. Are you happy now, Dawn? Do you have the things you want?"

"Not all of them," she reflected. "But some." Her eyes met his. "And I have hopes of the others."

"Come on." He seized her hand and began to pull her in the direction of the car. "Get in."

"Where are we going?" she asked as she settled into the passenger seat.

"The Craddock farm, of course. Where else?" He was turning the car as he spoke, and soon they were traveling back up the road to the fork.

They arrived just as the Craddock family was pouring out of the house, buttoned up in warm clothes. From the alarmed looks they cast him Ben realized that Dawn had been right. "We were just off to church," Mr. Craddock said. "If—I mean, if you've come to—"

"I've only come for a moment to wish you a happy Christmas, Mr. Craddock," Ben said quickly, anxious to dispel their wretchedness. "Miss Fletcher told me that I'd worried you with my remarks the other day, and I just want you to know that there's no question of you having to leave. When we talk in the New Year you can tell me what you need, and when we've arranged a lower rent for you, I'm sure you won't find it so hard to make ends meet."

It took a moment for them to understand. The Craddocks looked at him, then at each other, then back at him. At last the reality sank in and joyous smiles broke over their faces. Suddenly everything was pandemonium. The children cheered and threw snowballs at each other and everyone else, while their parents threw themselves into each other's arms. That sight brought home to Ben the reality of the fear he'd accidentally created. The memory of how he nearly hadn't come here today made him feel badly.

Dawn squeezed his hand. "Thank you," she whispered.

Mr. Craddock pumped his hand vigorously before yelling, "Come on, you kids! Into the car and get to that church. We've got something to sing carols about, now."

Ben smiled with pleasure as he watched them. "A Merry Christmas!" he called as they all squeezed into the car, and they shouted the words back to him joyfully.

"Merry Christmas, Ben," Dawn said when they were alone.

Now was the time to voice the feelings in his heart. But his courage failed him. He couldn't risk breaking the spell. "Merry Christmas," he told her, and wondered if he imagined a fleeting look of disappointment on her face.

Chapter Eight

A little farther along they came across her car stranded in the ditch. "Leave it," Ben said. "I'll send someone to haul it out as soon as Christmas is over. If you get called out again, I'll take you."

"But that'll spoil your Christmas."

"I don't feel as if Christmas is being ruined, Dawn. I feel as if it's the first Christmas I've truly celebrated since—well, since—" He left the sentence hanging in the air.

After a moment she said, "That's how I feel, too."

They could see the village now, slightly below them. Already church bells were ringing out across the snow, and villagers were streaming toward the ancient stone building. Dismay seized Ben as he realized that they were almost there and he hadn't said any of the things he wanted to. But then, he wasn't sure exactly what it was he wanted to say, or whether she wanted to hear any of it.

Now they were entering the village. "Dawn—" he said desperately.

"Could you drop me at the surgery, please?"

It was over. She didn't want him. What was the point of him "departing from his course" if she wouldn't depart from hers? Her "end" was foreshadowed. She would become Harry's wife.

Yet although he said the words inwardly, somehow he couldn't believe them. The ghost that had come to him out of the past was a benign ghost, sent for his redemption. There was only one way it could end. He clung to the thought.

Near the surgery they met Jack walking to church with his family. Dawn explained about the car and gave a brief account of Trixie, then Jack said, "You've done your share. Harry's taking over. Be off and enjoy yourself. Merry Christmas."

When they were alone Dawn said, "I think I'd like to go to church now."

There was an appeal in her voice and Ben immediately responded, "I'll come with you."

Together they made their way along the snow-covered street. He'd left his stick in the car, yet strangely he was no longer troubled by the thought of stumbling. An arm about her shoulder was all he needed—all he would ever need. Gradually they fell into step with their neighbors, all heading for the little church where the bells were ringing out their joyous message. People were looking at him—not staring, but giving him smiles of welcome. Someone called, "That was a grand party!"

He called back, "Wait until next year. Then you'll really see a party!" There were smiles and cheers, and he wondered why he'd never realized there was such good fellowship in the world.

The road to the church lay beneath a clump of oak trees, stripped bare now. Before they reached the door he slowed and began to draw her aside. He didn't stop until they were both hidden behind the huge trunk of one of the oaks. "Dawn, before we go into church together, I have to know."

"Yes?"

"The other night, at the party, when you kissed Father Christmas the second time—did you know who—?"

He never finished the question. Dawn's arms were around him, her hands drawing his head down until she could lay her lips on his. "Do you think I could kiss you and not know it?" she asked. "Even after eight years?"

Joy flooded through him, almost too great to bear. "When did you realize I wasn't Harry?" he asked hoarsely.

"When you were talking to Gary. I suddenly remembered about your passion for jigsaw puzzles. I was in your apartment once, and you kept the door of the living room locked. You said you had a puzzle with eight thousand pieces spread out on the floor. When you told Gary about an eight-thousand-piece jigsaw I was pretty sure. While you were getting it I looked outside and saw that Harry's car was gone."

He was breathless with hope. "So when you lured me under the mistletoe—?"

"I knew exactly who I was luring. I wanted to kiss you, and I guessed the only way was to let you think you were fooling me."

"I've been so jealous. I thought you loved Harry."

"I do. But only as a dear friend. We had a long talk after the party. He's accepted the truth now. He'll be all right. Half the young women for miles around are in love with him, and he's too warmhearted to stay alone for long."

Looking into her eyes he saw happiness waiting for him. But not yet. First there was one more thing he must say.

"I was wrong," he told her. "All those years ago I was wrong to send you away. In my heart I think I've always known it, but I wouldn't admit it. It was too terrible to face. Can you forgive me?''

"There's nothing to forgive," she said simply. "But we must make the years ahead splendid, because of the ones we lost."

"You kissed me the night you came back to me. And you kissed me again the other night. Will you promise to kiss me every Christmas for the rest of our lives? Otherwise there'll be no hope for me."

"I promise, Ben. It's all I want."

She drew his head down and kissed him again, and they held each other very close in a wordless vow for the future.

High above them the Christmas bells were pealing out across the snow, calling everyone to celebrate the miracle of rebirth. Ben's heart overflowed with joy and thanks too deep for words. Silently he took her hand and they went into the old church together, as now they would always be.

*   *   *   *   *

A Note from Lucy Gordon

Being married to an Italian from Venice, I've had the chance to spend Christmas in that romantic old city, and it was an enchanting experience. Most people think of Venice as it is in summer—bathed in glorious sunshine and crowded with visitors. But in winter, when everything is under heavy snow, it's like wandering through a magical, haunted place. There are no cars in Venice, only boats, and sometimes the only sounds are the soft distant cries of the boatmen.

When the tourists are gone you see the Venetians, the real Venetians who live there all the year, in good times and bad, and who become themselves only when their city is returned to them in winter. They move silently, like ghosts, their footfalls muffled by the snow.

But once you're off the street, in the bars and the homes, this is no ghost city. There the fun is lively as they clink glasses and wish each other *Buon Natale*. Christmas in Italy means *panatone*, a huge sponge cake made with raisins and tasting of chocolate.

I remember lights blazing over St. Mark's Square in the evening, and the midnight service in St. Mark's Church, with the sound of singing drifting over the snow and out across the lagoon. They are enchanted memories that I'll always carry with me.

But, being English, I'm also in love with Christmas in my own country, the home of Charles Dickens, whose books did so much to shape the way we think of that time of year. Nothing summed it up better than *A Christmas Carol*, and when I came to write my modern tribute to that book I tried to include in it all the traditional things, not just snow and Yule logs, children's parties and Santa Claus, but also love, which is always timely, but never more so than at Christmas: love half-forgotten but called back to life, and regeneration through love—not just the romantic kind, but the kind of love that turns a man's (or woman's) heart outward to his fellow creatures and makes him bless them—every one.

Lucy Gordon

FOUR FABULOUS AUTHORS—
WHAT'S NEXT ON THE THEIR AGENDA?

Four magnificent stories...each filled with love, laughter and, of course, romance!

Lisa Jackson — *Silhouette Special Edition*, February 1994
HE'S MY SOLDIER BOY (Mavericks)

Army life may have toughened Ben Powell's resolve, but it hadn't erased the memory of his youthful love for Carrie Surrett. So returning home to find Carrie back in town soon had this Maverick's will power crumbling....

Emilie Richards — *Silhouette Special Edition*, March 1994
THE TROUBLE WITH JOE

Joe *loved* children. But when a child showed up on his and his wife Samantha's doorstep, all hell broke loose. Finding the parents would be difficult, especially when his heart didn't want to....

Joan Hohl — *Silhouette Desire*, July 1994
WOLFE WATCHING

What does detective Eric Wolfe *really* think divorcée Tina Kranas is guilty of? Find out in *Wolfe Watching*, Book Two of Joan Hohl's sexy Big Bad Wolfe series.

Lucy Gordon — *Silhouette Desire*, June 1994
UNCAGED

Megan Anderson had spent three years in prison for a crime she didn't commit, thanks to police officer Daniel Kelly's diligence. *Now* he was out to prove her innocence.

Only from

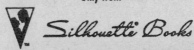

Also available by popular author

EMILIE RICHARDS

Silhouette Intimate Moments®

#07337	RUNAWAY	$2.95	☐
#07357	FUGITIVE	$2.95	☐
#07401	DESERT SHADOWS	$3.29	☐
#07409	TWILIGHT SHADOWS	$3.29	☐
#07456	FROM A DISTANCE	$3.39	☐
#07498	SOMEWHERE OUT THERE	$3.39	☐
#07511	DRAGONSLAYER	$3.50	☐

Silhouette Special Edition®

#09684	ALL THOSE YEARS AGO	$3.25	☐
#09750	ONE PERFECT ROSE	$3.39	☐
	(limited quantities available on certain titles)		

TOTAL AMOUNT	$
POSTAGE & HANDLING	$
($1.00 for one book, 50¢ for each additional)	
APPLICABLE TAXES*	$————
TOTAL PAYABLE	$————
(check or money order—please do not send cash)	

To order, complete this form and send it, along with a check or money order for the total above, payable to Silhouette Books, to: *In the U.S.*: 3010 Walden Avenue, P.O. Box 9077, Buffalo, NY 14269-9077; *In Canada*: P.O. Box 636, Fort Erie, Ontario, L2A 5X3.

Name: —————————————————————

Address: ————————————— City: ——————

State/Prov.: ———————— Zip/Postal Code: ——————

*New York residents remit applicable sales taxes.
  Canadian residents remit applicable GST and provincial taxes.

ERBACK1

Silhouette

Relive the romance...
Harlequin and Silhouette
are proud to present

A program of collections of three complete novels by the most-requested
authors with the most-requested themes. Be sure to look for one volume each
month with three complete novels by top-name authors.

In September: **BAD BOYS**   Dixie Browning
                                                Ann Major
                                                Ginna Gray
No heart is safe when these hot-blooded hunks are in town!

In October: **DREAMSCAPE**   Jayne Ann Krentz
                                                Anne Stuart
                                                Bobby Hutchinson
Something's happening! But is it love or magic?

In December: **SOLUTION: MARRIAGE**   Debbie Macomber
                                                Annette Broadrick
                                                Heather Graham Pozzessere
Marriages in name only have a way of leading to love....

Available at your favorite retail outlet.

REQ-G2

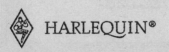 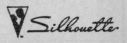

Silhouette Books
is proud to present
our best authors,
their best books...
and the best in
your reading pleasure!

Throughout 1993, look for exciting
books by these top names in
contemporary romance:

DIANA PALMER—
The Australian in October

FERN MICHAELS—
Sea Gypsy in October

ELIZABETH LOWELL—
Chain Lightning in November

CATHERINE COULTER—
The Aristocrat in December

JOAN HOHL—
Texas Gold in December

LINDA HOWARD—
Tears of the Renegade in January '94

When it comes to passion,
we wrote the book.

BOBT3

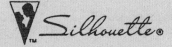

MEN MADE IN AMERICA

Fifty red-blooded, white-hot, true-blue hunks
from every State in the Union!

Look for MEN MADE IN AMERICA! Written by some
of our most poplar authors, these stories feature fifty of
the strongest, sexiest men, each from a different state in
the union!

Two titles available every other month at your favorite
retail outlet.

In November, look for:

STRAIGHT FROM THE HEART by Barbara Delinsky
(Connecticut)
AUTHOR'S CHOICE by Elizabeth August (Delaware)

In January, look for:

DREAM COME TRUE by Ann Major (Florida)
WAY OF THE WILLOW by Linda Shaw (Georgia)

You won't be able to resist MEN MADE IN AMERICA!

When the only time you have for yourself is...

Christmas is such a busy time—with shopping, decorating, writing cards, trimming trees, wrapping gifts....

When you do have a few *stolen moments* to call your own, treat yourself to a brand-new *short* novel. Relax with one of our Stocking Stuffers— or with all six!

Each STOLEN MOMENTS title
is a complete and original contemporary romance that's the perfect length for the busy woman of the nineties! Especially at Christmas...

And they make perfect **stocking stuffers**, too! (For your mother, grandmother, daughters, friends, co-workers, neighbors, aunts, cousins—all the other women in your life!)

Look for the STOLEN MOMENTS display in December

STOCKING STUFFERS:

HIS MISTRESS Carrie Alexander
DANIEL'S DECEPTION Marie DeWitt
SNOW ANGEL Isolde Evans
THE FAMILY MAN Danielle Kelly
THE LONE WOLF Ellen Rogers
MONTANA CHRISTMAS Lynn Russell

HSM2

Christmas Classics

Share in the joys of finding happiness and exchanging the
ultimate gift—love—in full-length classic holiday
treasures by two bestselling authors

JOAN HOHL
EMILIE RICHARDS

Available in December at
your favorite retail outlet.

Only from  *Silhouette®* where passion lives.